Too Close To The Sun

Jess **Foley** was born in Wiltshire but moved to London to study at the Chelsea School of Art, then subsequently worked as a painter and actor before taking up writing. Now living in Blackheath, south-east London, Jess's first novel, *So Long At The Fair*, was published in 2001.

Praise for *So Long At The Fair*

'Jess has really captured the sense of a family united against great odds. The heroine, Abbie, is strong but flawed as all good heroines should be and as we follow her triumphs and trials we see her change from a girl to a woman in the most dramatic and satisfying of ways' Iris Gower

'A jolly good read . . . Abbie is a great character, buffeted by fate but a powerful woman of her time' Susan Sallis

D0635536

Also by Jess Foley

So Long At The Fair

TOO CLOSE
TO THE SUN

Jess Foley

ARROW

Published by Century in 2002

3 5 7 9 10 8 6 4

First published in the United Kingdom in 2002 by Century

Random House Group Limited
20 Vauxhall Bridge Road, London SW1V 2SA

Random House Australia (Pty) Limited
20 Alfred Street, Milsons Point, Sydney,
New South Wales 2061, Australia

Random House New Zealand Limited
18 Poland Road, Glenfield
Auckland 10, New Zealand

Random House (Pty) Limited
Endulini, 5a Jubilee Road, Parktown 2193, South Africa

Random House Group Limited Reg. No. 954009

www.randomhouse.co.uk

A CIP catalogue record for this book is available
from the British Library

Papers used by Random House
are natural, recyclable products made from wood grown in
sustainable forests. The manufacturing processes conform to
the environmental regulations of the country of origin

ISBN 0 7126 6996 5

Typeset by SX Composing DTP, Rayleigh, Essex
Printed and bound in Great Britain by
Bookmarque Ltd, Croydon, Surrey

For Victoria

PART ONE

Chapter One

On the day that was to see the course of Grace's life change they had found a spent rocket in the hedgerow by the stile. Billy saw it and hooted with excitement. Moving to the hedge he stretched up his hand, then with a little moan sank back.

'It's too high. I can't get to it.'

Giving a sigh as if she were indulging him, Grace stepped to the hedge, reached up and caught the rocket by its stem.

'Here you are. Though what you want it for I can't imagine.'

The rocket was just one of many fireworks that had been set off last month in celebration of Queen Victoria's Golden Jubilee. The whole village had had a party on the green, and the bonfire and fireworks that had followed in the evening had provided a spectacle such as Billy had never seen in all his eight years.

'Will it go again?' he asked, and Grace said, 'No, unfortunately it won't. It's all used up. You might as well throw it back where it was.'

'You sure it won't go again?'

'Absolutely sure.'

Billy looked at the rocket for moment longer, then, with a shrug, moved and threw it into the hedgerow. That done, he resumed the conversation that had been interrupted by his sight of the rocket.

'Will you be going away, Grace?'

At his words Grace turned and glanced down at the top

of his head as he limped along at her side. His thick brown hair had been touched by the sun and in its highlights shone a dull auburn. When she remained silent, he lifted his freckled face and looked up. 'Will you?' These days he seemed to be full of insecurities and questions.

'I've told you already,' she said, 'it depends how things work out. I must wait and see what happens.'

'Pappy said when you get married you'll be leaving us anyway.'

'*Get married*,' she said. 'If that's going to happen I'd be glad if somebody would let *me* in on the secret.' Grace was just twenty. A slim girl of just above middle height, she had the beauty that youth itself possesses and also that inherited from her mother. She had dark eyes, and hair of a rich chestnut that could shine tawny gold in the sun. Now, her wide, pink mouth was compressed in impatience. 'Seems like I'm the last to know some things,' she said.

Billy looked up at her. 'And your Mr Stephen – would he be the last to know as well?'

Grace nodded at the look, and smiled. 'You think you're so clever, don't you? Just make sure you're not too clever for your own good.'

Having taken short cuts to avoid the roads, they were following a narrow footpath traversing a meadow. Up ahead was a stile, then just one more meadow and they'd be close to their destination. After the recent rains the green of the grass was rich and lush. Birds skimmed the air in their foraging for food, and butterflies danced over the hedgerows.

It was Saturday, almost 10.30. They had set off from Green Shipton almost an hour before, the two of them, carrying two framed pictures, oil paint on canvas. The frames, made and fitted by their father, had been fashioned of elm, and carved and polished with the greatest care. Prior to Grace and Billy setting out, their father had wrapped each frame in a protective covering of burlap, then tied each with string, in such a way as to form a little handle for carrying. The canvases were fragile, and it would not do for any damaging pressure to be put on them. Grace carried one picture, and Billy the other.

On the right of the path a few yards ahead lay a pond, where sometimes the cattle came to drink. Fringed by trees and shrubbery, it seemed a mysterious little spot in the middle of the green expanse of the meadow.

'I don't like this pond,' Billy said as they drew nearer to it.

'Why not?'

'I just don't.'

In its shadows vaguely threatening, it lay only four or five yards from the edge of the footpath. Not that one could see much of the water itself, overhung as it was by the foliage that crowded its banks.

'Is it really so deep?' Billy said.

'I've no idea how deep it is.'

'Some boys – they said a whole cow drowned in it.'

'Oh? And when was this supposed to have happened?'

'They didn't say.'

'Well, not in my lifetime; I'd have heard of it.'

'That's what they said anyway.'

'Perhaps they made it up. Or perhaps it's an old legend.'

'What's a legend?'

'Well, it – it's a story that's been kind of – handed down – and perhaps nobody knows after so long whether it's true or not.' She paused, glancing down at him again. 'Did they say anything else, the boys?'

'What d'you mean?'

'Well –' she wondered how best to put it, 'were they – being unkind to you?'

'No,' he said at once. 'No, they were fine.'

'Oh – that's all right, then.'

There had been a few occasions in the past when some

5

lout or other had taken the opportunity to have some fun at Billy's expense, once or twice reducing him to tears. And at such times, Grace would never forget, their mother's protective wrath had been formidable. Small and slim, Mrs Harper had never given a thought to her lack of physical power, but had approached the victimizer as if having all the strength in the world. And like a tigress defending her cub, she had known no fear. Grace had seen her on one occasion when she had confronted a boy from a neighbouring village, a boy who had picked on Billy as an easy victim for his ridicule, focusing on his ungainly gait. But the boy had reckoned without Mrs Harper. She had run from the house with hair and apron flying, dashing at the boy and at the same time unleashing a torrent of reprimand that had him rooted to the spot. She had not used any physical violence, had not attempted to strike the boy; Grace had never known her to strike anyone, though where Billy was concerned, Grace was fairly sure that she might not have held back in particular circumstances if moved enough.

As they walked, Grace looked down at him with a smile. He was not tall for his eight years, added to which he was slight and fine-boned – like Grace herself, taking after their mother's side of the family, though Grace was taller than her mother had been. 'You'll look after Billy, won't you?' her mother had said several times during those final days. He had been in her thoughts right up to the last, in ways that Grace herself never could have been. But Grace had not quite the needs of Billy. Should it come to it, Grace thought, she could manage on her own. Billy, though, was a different matter.

As they reached the last stile Billy came to a stop with a little groan. Grace halted beside him. 'What's up?' she said. 'Is it getting too much for you?'

'Oh, it's such a hot day,' he said. 'I need a rest.'

'Come on, then, let's sit down for a minute.'

With Grace leading they moved a few yards alongside the hedgerow, and there in the shade of a small hawthorn tree Grace set down the wrapped picture, very carefully leaning it against the tree's trunk. With admonitions to be careful, Billy did likewise with his package.

As Billy sat down beside her, Grace pushed her straw hat to the back of her head. Running her hands over her hair, her palm came away damp with perspiration. 'Oh,' she sighed, 'it's not the day for doing anything.' Taking her hat off, she sank back until she was lying full length in the grass. 'Sometimes,' she said, 'it would be so nice to have no responsibilities, to have nothing to do.'

'That wouldn't suit you at all,' he said. 'You like to be busy.'

'Not always.' She opened her eyes and turned her head towards him. He sat plucking blades of grass and tossing them aside. 'Sometimes it's good to just relax or have fun,' she said.

After lying there for several more minutes she sat up and replaced her hat, then got up and brushed down her dress. 'Come on, young William, let's be off.'

And they set off again, over the stile and into the lane and so on to the road. And after a while there ahead of them was the old low stone wall that marked the front boundary of Asterleigh House. Minutes later they were starting up the drive.

Asterleigh House, situated a mile from the village of Berron Wick, stood back from the road on the top of a low ridge, surrounded by elms and oaks and the green rolling fields of Wiltshire. To the northeast lay the city of Redbury, and beyond that the railway town of Swindon. Directly to the east was the market town of Corster. To the south lay Salisbury and the Wiltshire plains. The house, with its façade of white stone, was large, comprising over thirty rooms, and stood hemmed by well-laid herbaceous borders and green lawns. Begun in the 1850s, it was said that the house had never been finished. But finished or not, to outsiders it was impressive; few people in the surrounding villages knew any other dwelling as fine.

Grace and Billy had never been inside any similar house in their lives, and nor had they been that close to any. Not that they had been very *deep* inside Asterleigh; they had only been into the kitchen; but even entry into the kitchen of such a place was worthy of remark.

And now they were approaching the kitchen again, moving across the cobbled yard from the side gate. A maid was in the yard, beating a carpet, a colourful, oriental piece, that for convenience's sake hung on a line. As they went to move past her towards the rear door, she let her hands fall at her sides, as if having let go a huge weight, and gave the deepest sigh. 'Yes, can I 'elp you?' she said. She was plain in appearance, with frizzy reddish hair and a mass of freckles over her pale pink face.

'We've brought something for Mr Spencer,' Grace said.

As she finished speaking, another maid, this one wearing a neat white apron and cap, opened the back door.

'It's all right, Annie,' she said, then, looking at Grace and Billy she raised her eyebrows and said, 'Yes, miss?'

With Billy following, Grace crossed to the door. 'We've brought something for Mr Spencer,' she said again.

'The master's not in right now,' the girl said. 'Can you tell me what you've got?'

'Two of Mrs Spencer's pictures.'

'If you'd care to wait a moment, I'll let the missis know. Who shall I say it is?'

'Miss Grace Harper.'

'Right.' As the maid began to close the door behind her she added, 'I'd better shut this and keep out the dust.'

The door closed behind the maid as she went back into the house. In the yard the red-haired maid resumed beating

8

the carpet, pounding out little puffs of dust that floated away on the warm air. As Grace watched, her eyes met the other girl's. The latter relaxed her beating for a moment and smiled. 'You want a nice job, miss? This ent the day for beatin' carpets, I can tell you.'

A minute later and the maid was back. 'You'd better come in,' she said. 'The missis'd like to see you.'

'Mrs Spencer?' Grace said, a little awed.

'Yes. You must come indoors.'

As the maid stood aside, Billy held out the wrapped picture to Grace and murmured, 'You go on, Grace, I'll stay here.'

'Of course not,' Grace replied. 'You must come with me.'

The maid was waiting, and after a moment Grace and Billy – after carefully wiping their shoes on the doormat – moved past her into a rear passageway, on the left of which was a washhouse and, on the right, the kitchen in which a cook and a maid were at work. The parlour maid closed the door behind them and said, 'If you'd like to follow me, miss . . .'

She opened the door in front of them and they passed through into the spacious main hall. The floor, laid in circles and rectangles of marble in pink, white and grey, seemed to stretch to a vast distance, enclosed by a staircase that curved elegantly down from the upper floor in a sweeping, graceful arc. Grace and Billy looked around them. They had never been in this part of the house before. Now, seeing the lavish interior, it was like being in another world. On the walls hung tall paintings of men and women in clothes from the past; there were long velvet drapes at the tall windows. The whole room seemed so enormous; its great fireplace – all laid with logs even in this day of July – and its sofa and fine chairs seeming to take up so little space in the vast room.

And, looking up, there were even more wonders to see,

for the great height of the circular hall went to the very top of the house, ending in a great cupola glazed with coloured glass that let through shafts of light of different hues that touched the walls and stairs; and touched too a gallery that ran almost all around the hall on its top floor, a gallery with statues standing in niches in the wall.

There was no time to stand and gape, though, for the maid was speaking to them, a trifle impatiently. 'Please,' she said over her shoulder, 'come this way.'

Grace had never had any thought of being invited into the house proper – and even less so of being summoned in to meet Mrs Spencer. Had the possibility occurred to her, she would have taken more trouble with her appearance. As it was, she was wearing her oldest summer dress, a cotton affair with pink and blue flowers on a white back-ground. When new, it had been very attractive, and had suited her well. Now, however, its best days were past: the blue had run in the wash and it had been darned at the right shoulder and elbow. Grace wore it nowadays – as on this day – only for unimportant errands – and errands when she did not expect to encounter anyone of importance. Very conscious of her dress having seen better times – as had her plain hat and dusty boots – Grace, with Billy reluctantly following, went after the maid along a deeply carpeted passage.

Some way along, the maid came to a halt, knocked on a door, pushed it open and bent into the room. Grace heard her murmur something and then the girl was turning back to them. 'The mistress says if you please to come in.'

Grace had no idea what to expect. *Mr* Spencer she had seen on two or three occasions during his visits to her father's workshop, but Mrs Spencer was something of a mystery. The story went that, although born in the area, she had lived most of her life in Swindon, only returning following her marriage – a marriage that had come comparatively late in her life. However, although resident in the general area once more, she was very rarely seen in the nearest village, Berron Wick. Going by what Grace had heard, about the only place she was ever glimpsed was in the local church on occasions such as Easter, Christmas, and Harvest Festivals. And even then she was barely in evidence, always sitting right at the front in the reserved pew, and swathed in her hats and veils.

But now Grace and Billy were being ushered into the room, and, supposedly, into the woman's presence.

The door clicked closed behind them and with the sound Grace realized that the maid had departed. She and Billy stood side by side, Billy so close he was almost touching her. Here in this room it was so much cooler. It faced north, so the light – today unclouded and bright – was subtle, steady and unchanging. It was not a large room, but it gave a feeling of spaciousness due to the lack of any great amount of furniture in the place. What was there was comprised in the main of a couple of rather distressed chests of drawers and a bureau. Also a gate-legged table – once a handsome, highly polished piece, now scratched and paint-stained. The walls were hung with paintings, some framed, some on unadorned canvas stretchers. They consisted of landscapes, still lifes and a few animal studies. They were, Grace observed, in a similar style to those which she and Billy now held in their hands. For the rest of the furnishing, there were several rows of shelves also, bearing what looked like stretched canvases and various jars and pots, some of which held artists' brushes. In the air hung a smell of linseed oil and turpentine – smells that Grace recognized from her father's workshop. Over the carpet was spread what looked to be old dustsheets and hessian – obviously to protect the carpet from paint stains, of which not a few marked the make-do covering. The greater part of the paint stains lay around an area a few feet from the window on which stood an artist's easel with a canvas on it. Before it, sitting on a chair and leaning forward with paintbrush in hand, sat Mrs Spencer.

Seeming almost to be unaware of them – though of course that could not be – she continued with her work. Sitting almost with her back to the newcomers, she was working on a painting of a still-life composition that lay before her on a table: white roses in a vase, with lemons and pears, the whole arrangement placed on a chequered cloth. Another table, not far from the woman's right hand, bore a paint-smeared palette, a jar holding paintbrushes, small bottles of liquid and a scattering of tubes of paint.

Grace observed as Mrs Spencer sat back in her chair, paintbrush in hand, and looked judiciously and doubtfully at the canvas before her. She appeared a tallish, slender woman. She was not young, Grace could see; she must be well into her fifties. She wore a large hat, resting low on her forehead, which did not completely cover her grey hair, cotton gloves – once white, now stained with a hundred different paint colours – and an artist's smock, its own whiteness also marked with paint stains of different hues. At her throat was a dark crimson bow. The whole effect reminded Grace of portraits of famous artists she had seen in picture books over the years.

'So,' the woman said, 'I understand you've brought my pictures.' She spoke with a soft tone, looking at the unfinished canvas with her head a little on one side. She lifted the brush as if she would use it on the palette to mix more colours, but then, just as quickly, she seemed to decide that she would go no further for the time being, and put it down on the painting table.

'Enough, enough,' she said, endorsing her action. 'I'm not getting anywhere, so what's the use?' Still without turning to them, she raised her gloved hand and crooked her index finger. 'Come. Come closer. Both of you.'

12

Grace stepped forward and Billy followed and came to a halt at her side. Only then did the woman turn towards them.

'So,' she said, ' – my pictures. My husband had intended them to be a surprise for me, but he won't mind if his little surprise is rather spoiled. I never could rest on anticipation.' She held out her gloved hands and Grace took a step forward and placed the burlap-wrapped package into them. Fumbling with the strings, Mrs Spencer said, 'Mr Harper made the frames and set the paintings in them, is that so?'

Grace raised her head and nodded. 'Yes, ma'am.'

'And you're his daughter, is that correct?'

'Yes, ma'am.'

Getting nowhere with the strings, Mrs Spencer impatiently thrust the package back towards Grace. 'Here – your fingers are more nimble than mine.'

Grace took the package from the woman. In moments she had the strings untied and was taking from its wrapping the framed canvas. Measuring about fourteen by ten, it was a landscape: green fields fading away to a high horizon beneath a rather stormy sky. Grace held it out and Mrs Spencer took it, held it before her and looked at it long and hard. As she did so, Grace took the painting held by Billy, and unwrapped it. Mrs Spencer put the landscape down, leaning it against the side of the easel, then took the second painting from Grace. After looking at it for several seconds in silence, she murmured with irony, 'Well, it's certainly a lovely frame. He does fine work, your father.'

'Yes, ma'am,' said Grace.

'We have a bureau that he made, and an excellent little footstool. My husband has spoken of having your father make us some other items. We thought perhaps some more shelves for the library, and maybe a chessboard. And, of course, there's the cabinet your father's now working on.' A brief pause, then, tilting her head slightly, she said, 'And what is your name?'

'Grace.'

'Grace?'

'Grace Helen Harper.'

'I see, and what do you do, Miss Grace Helen Harper?'

'Do, ma'am?'

'For a living? I assume you do something.'

'Well, yes – for the time being I'm teaching. I'm a governess.'

'A governess. Does that mean you have a brain?'

'I hope so, ma'am.'

'And do you live with your employers?'

'No, I'm daily, visiting.'

'I see. And whom do you visit?'

'The sons of Mr Marren. He's a businessman who lives not far from where we live in Green Shipton.'

'How many sons?'

'Two. They're twins. Nine years old.'

'Do you enjoy it? Teaching them?'

'Most of the time, ma'am, yes.'

The woman's mouth moved in a slight smile. 'Most of the time?'

Grace shrugged. 'Well – sometimes they can be – testing.'

'I'm sure they can.' Silence. Then Mrs Spencer spoke again. 'What did you mean just now when you said you're teaching *for the time being*?'

'Oh – well – my employment with the Marren boys is coming to an end.'

'And why's that?'

'They're due to go away to boarding school.'

'So you've become redundant.'

'In a manner of speaking, yes.'

'Oh, dear. So what will you do? Look for a new position?'

'Soon, yes. I have just three more days teaching the boys, then I must think about my future.'

'I should think you'd have given it some thought already.'

'Yes – of course.' Grace felt at a disadvantage, and increasingly somewhat like a child who has caused displeasure. 'I do have certain responsibilities at home,' she said. 'Apart from teaching I help out at home, helping to look after the family.'

'And how did you come to be a teacher?'

'I was taught by my mother.'

'Was your mother a teacher? – a governess?'

'No, she – she wasn't anything. I mean, she didn't have any particular position. She was the daughter of a vicar, the Rev. Cleeson of Coller Down.'

'Cleeson. I'm not familiar with the name.' Mrs Spencer shook her head, then said, 'I understand that your mother died not so long ago.'

'Yes, that's correct. She died just this past spring.'

Mrs Spencer nodded, then turned in the direction of Billy. 'And this young man is, I imagine, a member of your family?' The cadence of the woman's voice clearly directed a question at him, but Grace responded.

'Yes, ma'am. Billy's my brother.'

'And do you have other brothers? Sisters?'

'No, ma'am, there's just Billy and me.'

'Just the two of you? There is a great difference in your ages.'

'Yes, ma'am. My mother always spoke of my brother as her "late blessing".'

'I see. And have you had the burden of caring for him and your father?'

'Oh, it's not a burden. Besides, we have a lady who comes in just three or four times during the week to help out. Mrs Tanner – she lives in the village – she's been a great help over – over difficult times.'

'I'm glad to hear it. And when your pupils have gone away to school, what will you do? Find another position, I suppose. There's no shortage of boys and girls who need tuition. May I ask how old you are?'

'I was twenty in April.'

The woman brushed a hand over her forehead in a melodramatic gesture. 'Twenty. Is it possible that anyone on earth is twenty.' She looked at Grace for several seconds in silence, then said, 'Well, Miss Harper, I just hope you make the most of it – being twenty. Because it'll never come again. As you'll learn. Have you got a young man?'

Grace found herself colouring slightly at the question, and was at a loss as to how to answer. 'I have – I have a – an acquaintance,' she said after a moment.

'Well, that's something,' Mrs Spencer smiled. 'At twenty it's time you were thinking about getting settled. May I ask who this acquaintance might be?'

'His name is Stephen Cantrell. He lives in Green Shipton.'

'And how old is he?'

'Twenty-six.'

'And do you have hopes – plans – where he is concerned?'

Grace briefly lowered her gaze, uncomfortable at the line of questioning. 'No plans, ma'am,' she said, then quickly added, 'I wouldn't presume so. We haven't – spoken of such things.'

'Well, perhaps it's time,' said the woman. She continued to gaze at Grace, then lowered her eyes to the picture again, running her fingers gently over the frame. 'Yes, the frame is very well made.' Then she added, with a touch of irony in her tone, 'Though I'm not that sure about the painting.' Abruptly she turned the face of the canvas towards Grace and Billy. 'What do you think of it?' she asked, addressing the question to Grace.

The painting, which Grace had of course seen previous to

their starting out that day, was a still life, the subject comprising a bowl with apples, a small bunch of grapes and a blue china vase holding two or three lilies set off by sprays of fine maidenhair fern. The whole thing was painted in the most delicate detail, in the English artistic fashion of the day, and must, Grace was sure, have taken a considerable time to complete.

'Well?' the woman prompted. 'What do you think?'

Grace dreaded saying the wrong thing. There was no overestimating how touchy people could be when it came to things they held dear.

'I like it very much,' she said at last.

'Oh, you do?'

'Yes, very much,' Grace said.

'And you, young man.' Mrs Spencer turned her attention to Billy. 'I'm sure you can do better than your sister. What do *you* think of it?' Then before she could receive an answer, she added, 'What is your name, by the way?'

Billy just looked at her, silent, awed, and Grace said:

'Billy, ma'am. His name's —'

The woman held up a gloved hand. 'Let him speak for himself.' Then to Billy: 'Your name, little boy. Tell me your name.'

Grace willed him: *Don't stammer. Oh, Billy, don't stammer. There's nothing to be afraid of.* And Billy drew back his chin, sucking in air, as if trying to snatch and draw in courage. 'P-please, ma'am,' he said, 'it's B-B-B-Billy.'

'Billy?' Mrs Spencer said. 'Is that William?'

He nodded.

'Right.' She gave a little nod. 'So – tell me, Master William Harper, what do you think of my painting?'

Billy began to take a step back but Grace put out her right hand and laid it across his shoulder. Touching him, feeling his nervous body beneath her hand, she gently pressed his shoulder with her fingers. 'Go on,' she murmured, giving

17

him an encouraging smile. 'Tell the lady what you think.'

'Yes, do,' Mrs Spencer said to him, 'though while you're about it maybe you shouldn't be too honest.' She peered at him, fixing him with her gaze, waiting. 'So, tell me – what do you think of it?'

'Go on,' Grace prompted, 'tell Mrs Spencer how much you like it. I know you do; you told me so.' A pause. 'You did, don't you remember?'

He nodded.

'Tell the lady, then.'

Still he said nothing.

'Come on,' the woman said. 'We're waiting.'

'It's true, ma'am,' Grace said. 'He does like it. When my father was wrapping the paintings Billy said how much he liked them. He really did.'

Mrs Spencer looked at her coldly. 'I don't care to be patronized, young lady.'

Grace felt herself flushing with embarrassment. 'No, really, it's true. He said that –'

'Please,' the woman said, 'don't go on.' She turned to Billy. 'It's the boy's opinion I want. Tell me, what do you think of my painting?'

Billy flicked the swiftest glance at Grace, then, receiving an encouraging nod from her, said, 'Please, m-ma'am – I like it very much.'

'Oh, you do? How old are you, young man?'

Billy bent his head and looked down at the floor again.

'He's eight years old,' Grace said.

'Let him speak for himself,' Mrs Spencer said. 'How old are you?'

Now Billy spoke. 'E-e-eight,' he said.

'Eight years old,' Mrs Spencer said, putting the painting down beside the other one. 'And what are you learning at school?'

He remained silent.

'Do you like painting?'

'Yes,' Grace said, 'we enjoy painting, don't we? And we like looking at paintings too.'

'How fascinating,' the woman said. She nodded, then reached out and took hold of a silver-headed cane. Leaning on it, she rose to her feet and moved to the window. And as she walked, Grace and Billy's eyes became fixed upon her skirts, seeing the way she limped heavily on her right leg. At the window she raised the sash a little more, then turned and moved back to her chair. And still the two pairs of eyes focused on her limping gait.

'Well,' she said, her eyes flicking from Billy to Grace as she stood before her chair once more, 'have you seen enough?' Her voice was like ice, her eyes like steel points. 'Or would you like me to perambulate around the room again?'

Grace flushed with embarrassment, then managed to say, 'I – I think we had better be leaving, ma'am. We've taken up enough of your time.'

'Indeed so. I'll ring for the maid to show you out.'

As the woman turned to move towards the bell pull and tugged upon it, there was a sudden little flurry of movement in the room. And almost in the same moment Billy was turning, giving out a little cry of anguish. Grace saw the reason for it: a bird had flown in at the open window and was flying about the room in a panic. And even as she watched, the small, swooping creature flew against one of the closed windows, struck the glass pane and fell onto the floor. At once Billy left Grace's side and was dashing across the room.

Gently he picked up the small bird in his two hands, and peered at it through the space between his fingers. 'It's a little hedge sparrow,' he said, his cupped hands held before his chest. 'It's quite stunned.' And then after a few moments his face lit up, and he turned first to the woman and then to

19

Grace. 'It's moving. I can feel it moving in my hands. I can feel its heart beating.'

Mrs Spencer now stood with her eyes fixed on Billy.

Billy said with a breathless little laugh, 'I can feel him in my hands – he's that desperate to be free.'

Limping to the window, he thrust his cupped hands, closed like a clamshell, out into the air. And then slowly he withdrew his upper hand. The bird lay on his palm, quite still. 'Come on,' Billy whispered. And then the bird stirred and raised itself on its feet. Then, giving a little shake and opening its wings, it lifted off and took flight.

Billy watched as the bird flew away and disappeared from sight. Then he turned back, the smile still on his face, to his sister. 'He'll be all right now,' he said.

Stepping to Grace's side he seemed suddenly to become aware of the situation again, of being there in an unfamiliar room in a great house, with a disapproving woman before him. But then the maid was there, and Grace and Billy were turning and following her out of the room.

With Asterleigh House behind them Grace said to Billy, 'Shall we call in at the Pits on the way home? It'll be nice by the water.' And he said, 'Yes, all right,' and they left the road to follow a short path that led them to the old disused clay pit. It was a beautiful spot. The water sparkled under the bright July sun, while around the banks tall willows cast their shade as small fish darted in the shallows.

The venue was a favourite with the people from around the area, and many times throughout her life Grace had been there. At first alone with her mother, and then later with her brother also along. Then, over the last year, when her mother had become too ill to make the journey, Grace had herself taken Billy for the occasional excursion.

On this particular day there was no one else about, and while Grace settled down in the shade of some silver birches, Billy wandered off, Grace's exhortations to be careful lingering in his ears. While he was gone, Grace sat gazing out across the lake, listening to the birdsong and the breaking of the water's surface as the fish came up to feed. Apart from such sounds, all else was still, peaceful, with barely even a breeze to ruffle the water's calm. Soon Billy was back, flopping down on the grass at her side.

'You've been quick,' Grace said. 'I thought you were going off exploring.'

'I don't want to today.'

'You don't feel like it?'

'Not today.'

'You could go in for your swim.'

'No, not today.'

'Why not? A fine swimmer like you – to miss a fine chance like this? You'd soon dry off in this sun.'

'I don't feel like it. Perhaps another day.'

'As you like.'

She felt a sense of disappointment. She had thought that the little sojourn would have a positive effect on him, but it had not. Looking at him, she thought that he appeared dull and preoccupied, and totally uninterested in the surroundings which he had usually found so fascinating. He sat silent, his gaze unseeing over the water. Grace, twelve years his senior, could see her own features reflected in his. He had been a surprise child for their parents, a joyous surprise, born to them when neither expected to have another.

'What are you thinking about?' Grace asked him.

'Nothing much,' he said; and then: 'Imagine – Mrs Spencer limping like that, Grace.'

'Yes,' she said.

She looked at him but he sat with his gaze still over the water. After a few moments he said:

'I came here with Mam a few times.'

'Oh, I know that. We had some wonderful times.'

'No, I mean *me* – just me and Mam on our own. Nobody else, just the two of us.'

'Oh, I see.' And Grace realized how important it had been to him. 'She used to like those times, with you.'

He gave a little nod. 'Did you ever come here with her? Just the two of you?'

'Oh, yes, when I was younger.' Grace thought back, smiling faintly at the memories. She had often sat in this same spot with her mother. But they had been on so many jaunts together. Sometimes there had been errands – as with herself and Billy today – but at other times there had been no purpose to their excursions other than pleasure – the pleasure of their surroundings and at being in one another's company. She could remember so many occasions so clearly, walks in the meadows, and through cool woods where no grass grew and the birdsong had a different ring. And, of course, little sojourns here by the waterside.

'I can't imagine,' Billy said, 'what it would have been like – to be with Mam on my own – all the time, I mean.' Grace suddenly realized that he had not really had his mother's exclusive company for any sustained periods.

'Sometimes,' Billy's voice came, interrupting her thoughts, his words delivered on the back of a sigh, 'sometimes I worry.'

'Oh? What about?'

He did not answer.

'Well, whatever it is,' Grace said, 'you've no need. We'd never let anything happen. Pappy and I – we'd make sure you're all right.'

'I know.' There was no conviction in his voice.

Grace got to her feet. 'Come on,' she said, 'I suppose we'd better start back.'

*

They were now drawing very near to Green Shipton and ahead, visible beyond the trees, though still some good distance away, the tower of the village church rose up.

Grace said, 'I thought we might go by way of the churchyard.'

'But we haven't got any flowers.'

'Mam wouldn't care about that. I usually go on a Saturday anyway, you know that.'

Reaching the end of the path, they passed through the stile and there was the village and the church right before them. As they walked towards the church gates Grace glanced up at the clock on the tower and saw that it was almost one. 'We're later than I'd anticipated,' she said. 'Pappy'll be wondering where we are.'

Billy went on ahead of Grace now, stepping carefully over the manicured grass of the walkways between the graves, making his way to the newer grave that lay further to one side, near the wall. As Grace neared it, he came to a stop at the grave's foot, standing very straight, almost to attention, the manner of his stance like some mark of respect. Then, bending his head a little, he said, his tone sorrowful and a little matter-of-fact: 'I'm sorry, Mammy, but we haven't got you any flowers today.'

'She won't mind,' Grace said. 'It's enough that you're here.'

Their mother's headstone was the newest in this particular area. Of a simple white stone, it bore in neat chiselled letters, all in upper case: ANNE ELIZABETH, BELOVED WIFE OF SAMUEL DAVID HARPER – and told that she had lived forty-eight years.

'We should have brought flowers,' Billy said to Grace. 'I always do. Even if it's just three or four.'

Suddenly tears were running down his cheeks, and Grace, lifting her skirts, knelt before him on the green grass. Putting her arms around him, she drew him close and held him. It had been so little time, and he had hardly paid more than lip service to the fact of their mother's departure; in reality he had not yet taken it in that she was gone and would never return.

'Oh, Billy,' Grace said, her right hand lifting to stroke his hair. 'I know what you must be feeling.' She could feel tears pricking her own eyes. How suddenly life could change, she said to herself. Things were now so much more difficult without her mother.

'Oh, Grace,' Billy said, 'make her come back. Please make her come back.'

There were no words she could find. She held him closer still, feeling his tear-wet cheek on the side of her neck. Like Billy, she missed her so much; at times it was all she herself could do not to give way to weeping.

After a while Billy's sobbing eased to a little, dry catching sound. He sniffed once or twice then drew back. 'Mam wouldn't like to see me make such a fuss.'

'No, it's all right. Whatever you did she would approve. You were *her boy. Her young man.*'

A turned-down smile came at this, while the tears swam in his eyes. 'I was, wasn't I?' He paused. 'I could be your boy too.'

'You already are.'

'But you'll be going away.'

She raised her hands and gently placed one on either side of his face. Beneath her fingers his cheeks were warm from the afternoon's sun, warm and as smooth as silk. 'Not yet. And if I do go away I shall come back and see you very often.'

'I don't want you to go.'

'You'll have Pappy.'

'I know, but if you go away maybe I shan't see you again.'

'Oh, that'll never happen. I'd never leave you for good. In

any case, I shan't be going anywhere for a while yet.' They had been over this so many times, in various ways.

As they moved back among the graves, Billy said, 'If all these poor people are in heaven, it must be a very crowded place. How would you find anybody?'

Outside the churchyard they set off again, walking beside the green. Then, a turn around the bend in the lane and there before them was home.

They came to the gate at the front of the house, opened it and, with Grace leading, went around the side of the house to the rear. As they came to the back yard the first thing Grace noticed was a chestnut mare tethered to a stanchion by the side fence. Billy recognized the horse before Grace did. 'Oh,' he said, 'it looks like Mr Spencer's come to see Pappy.'

'Yes,' said Grace, 'so it would seem.'

Chapter Two

'What's the matter?' Billy was looking up at her.

'You go on indoors,' she said. 'I want to check on a couple of things before I go in.' So Mr Spencer had called on her father. The thought went through her mind that perhaps he had ridden over at the behest of his wife, who was angry at the behaviour of her and Billy. But they had not meant to stare, the woman would surely have known that – though her anger had certainly been there nonetheless.

'What things d'you want to check on?' Billy asked.

'What? Oh – well – that the hens are locked up safely, for one thing. The fox was mooching around last night.'

'The hens are safe. You said yesterday you'd made sure of it.'

'Please, Billy – do as I ask.' The truth was, she did not wish to see Mr Spencer. She had met him on two previous occasions when he had called on her father, and he had a way, inexplicable, of slightly unnerving her.

'All right,' Billy said.

As he stepped towards the house, Grace turned and started across the yard. She didn't get far. Almost immediately she heard a voice calling her.

'Miss Grace . . . ?'

She halted, turning to the sound, and saw Mr Spencer coming towards her. Billy passed him halfway across the yard and the man smiled at him, saying, 'Hello, young Master William. And how are you today?' And Billy shyly returned his smile and murmured polite responses. The man's glance followed Billy as he went into the house and then turned back to light upon Grace once more.

'So – Miss Grace . . .' He came to a stop before her, gave a little nod and briefly raised his hat.

Grace nodded, 'Mr Spencer,' adding a little smile of politeness. 'I was just about to go and look at the chickens.'

'This is fine timing,' he said. 'Another minute and I'd have ridden off and missed you.'

She did not know how to respond; she only wished she had been five minutes later in returning. 'We've just been to Asterleigh,' she said, 'delivering Mrs Spencer's paintings.'

'Yes, so your father's told me. I could have saved you a journey.'

'I handed the pictures to Mrs Spencer.'

'Oh, did you now?'

'She was painting in her studio.'

He nodded and smiled. 'I see.' He was wearing riding breeches and jacket, and a soft felt hat. A good-looking man, she reckoned he could not be more than thirty-seven. He was tall and broad-shouldered, still slim at the waist, and his dark hair was dense and rich in colour. His brown eyes shone as he smiled at her.

'It must have been a hot walk over to Berron Wick,' he said.

'It was rather. On the way back we stopped at the Pits. Just for a little while.'

'And very nice too. I'm sure your young brother appreciated it. Nice to have a big sister who'll do things for you, take you places . . .'

She moved to take a step away, preparing her departure. But Mr Spencer forestalled her, saying, 'Did you have a nice time by the water?'

'Yes, thank you.'

'Were there many others there?'

'I think we were the only ones. I didn't see anyone else.'

27

'You need to be careful, you know, swimming in that place. There have been a few mishaps over the years. People have drowned.'

'I know. But we didn't swim. In any case, we're always careful.'

'I'm sure you are – sensible young woman like you.'

She became aware that he was holding her glance – a little longer than was comfortable for her, and she lowered her eyes and shifted from one foot to the other. From over to the right the tethered mare lifted her nose into the air and snorted. Mr Spencer looked at her, called out soothingly, 'Don't worry, Biddie, we'll soon be on our way,' then, turning back to Grace, gave a little smile. 'She's a bit like you, Miss Grace, somewhat anxious to get going.'

'No, really,' Grace murmured, '– it's just that I was going to check on the hen-house. Make sure they're safe from the fox tonight.'

'So you said.'

There fell a little silence, which he broke, saying: 'But if you want to go and look at your chickens, don't let me hold you up.'

Relieved, she took her first step away, then he added, 'I'll come with you if I may.'

With the man beside her she walked to the other side of the yard beside the shed where stood the coop and run, both empty at present; all the chickens pecking and scratching away over the yard. They would return to the coop at dusk. At the open door to the run Grace bent and, while Mr Spencer stood in silence, went through the charade of checking that all was secure. As she had only checked it the previous day she had little doubt that all would be well.

'Everything all right?' he said as she straightened.

'Yes, everything's fine. You have to be so careful; that old fox is so wily – always trying to catch us unawares.'

'And has he ever done so?'

'Oh, we've lost quite a few chickens over the years. And as you know, the fox never kills just as much as he needs to feed his family; if he gets the chance he'll kill the whole lot.' She brushed her palms one against the other, brushing off the dust. After the morning out in the sun she felt in need of a wash and a change of clothes.

'It's a very nice spot, this,' Mr Spencer said. 'I'm sure you must love it here.'

She shrugged. 'Well – it's my home. I couldn't imagine living anywhere else.'

'Unless you got something very special offered to you.'

'I can't think what that would be.'

'No? You're telling me that if the right person came along you wouldn't be tempted to consider your situation?' He smiled. 'It happens.' He ducked his head a little, peering more closely at her, trying to read her expression. 'Is there no one? Does your silence mean there is no one?'

She looked away, avoiding his searching gaze. 'I'm kept very busy at home, Mr Spencer.'

He gave a little laugh. 'I'm sure you are.' His smile faded. 'I'm sorry. I shouldn't tease you. Forgive me.' A pause. 'You say you're kept busy at home, but your father tells me you'll probably be moving on before too long.'

'Oh, well – I shall be looking for a new post at some time or other. Just as soon as things get a bit more settled here.'

'You'll be going as a governess again.'

She shrugged. 'There's nothing else I can do.'

'I remember that in your present position you live at home, and go in on a daily basis.'

'That's the way it suits Mr and Mrs Marren. Me too for that matter. And they're situated close enough.'

'Your father said your pupils are going off to boarding school.'

'Yes, to Crewkerne – when school starts again in

29

September. But my time ends with them this week. On Wednesday they're off to Bristol to spend time with their grandparents.'

'Will you miss them?'

She sighed. 'I haven't thought about it. Though I'm sure I shall.'

'And I suppose you'd like your next post to enable you to continue living at home.'

'Certainly I'd like to be able to stay close to home for the near future.'

He nodded. 'It's only about three months since your mother's death – it's not a very long time. It can be such a dreadful blow.'

'Yes. Though thankfully I have a lot to keep me busy.'

'I'm sure you do. And you don't dwell on things.'

She wanted to say, Oh, yes – sometimes I do. Sometimes it's impossible to escape from it. But she bit back the words and simply said, 'I try not to.'

'And you cope,' he said. His face was grave, but she could see sympathy in his eyes.

'Well, yes,' she said, ' – we have to. We have no choice. Though of course some people cope with it better than others.' She sighed. 'Oh – why do things always have to change?'

'I know what you mean,' he said. 'But I'm afraid that's the nature of life – life changes. Our circumstances change.' He paused. 'Your brother. How is he managing without his mother? He must miss her too. So much.'

'Oh, indeed.'

'I've no doubt he was badly affected by his mother's death.'

'He misses her dreadfully.'

'He's a nice little fellow. It's such a terrible shame he's not – well – like other lads his age. Life can be so unfair.'

Almost sharply, she said, 'He's all right. Billy's fine.'

Mr Spencer raised a hand, palm out, briefly pleading. 'Oh, please – I was only – observing. He's a grand little chap; I didn't mean anything to the contrary.' He frowned, trying to read her expression. 'Are you angry with me? Don't be. I meant nothing by it.'

'It – it's all right.'

A brief silence fell. Grace gave a little sigh and looked towards the house. 'I really shall have to go in,' she said. She stepped forward and the man moved along at her side. Together they crossed the yard towards the rear of the house. Mr Spencer took out his watch, glanced at it, returned it to his waistcoat pocket and sighed. 'How the time passes,' he said. 'I must make my way also. Much work to do, I'm afraid.'

'Oh, there's always work to do,' she said. 'Thank heavens Mrs Tanner comes in to help out here. I don't know what we'd do without her.'

They had reached the back door of the house. 'I'll have to leave you here,' Mr Spencer said. 'I called to see how your father's getting on with my cabinet. Work is well under way, I was pleased to see. It's coming on splendidly.'

'Good,' Grace said. She could think of nothing else to say.

'Though I can't say I found your father looking too robust. I thought he looked a little tired.'

'Well – he's been working very hard . . .'

He nodded. 'What a terrible blow for him – losing your mother like that. Tragedy is no respecter of feelings. One still has to go on working, earning a living, caring for others. Anyway –' he took a step away, 'I'll let you go. I told your father I'll drop by again very soon. And perhaps the next time I come you won't be in so much of a hurry. Perhaps you'll be able to chat for longer than five minutes.'

At his words Grace's embarrassment rose up and she gave a nervous little laugh. It was not the reaction he expected, and visibly he stiffened. 'Am I amusing you?' he said. 'I hope not.'

She could feel her cheeks suddenly burning. 'No – no, of course not . . .' Her voice trailed off, then she added, 'I'm sorry, I must be going.'

He touched at his hat. 'And I'll wish you a very good day, Miss Grace.' He gave a brief nod, and turned and walked away across the yard. Grace did not watch his departure, but went into the house.

The house – where Grace had been born – was Tudor, of red brick, and stood in an acre of ground on the eastern edge of the village of Green Shipton. The building was of two storeys, with a tiled roof, having a small garden at the front and the greater part of its land at the rear. The dwelling had once been a very small farmhouse, but years before the Harpers had taken over the rental the farm had fallen into failure and, as a result, most of the land had been sold to a neighbouring farmer. What little remained was now laid to orchard, a kitchen garden, and a paddock where the pony ran and the goat grazed.

Inside the house, Grace went along the short passage to the kitchen where she found Billy drinking a mug of water.

'Where's Pappy?' she said as she took off her hat.

'In his workshop. He said he had to get on. I'm hungry, Grace.'

Grace saw that her father had eaten the cold dish she had left for him: meat, potatoes, lettuce and beetroot. 'All right,' she said to Billy, 'I'll get you something. I'm hungry too.'

When she had set the food on their plates, she and Billy sat down to eat. As they ate, Grace looked around her at the large kitchen, the room where her small family congregated – except for some Sundays when the fire was lit in the front parlour. The summer light in the room seemed to show up the room's drabness, and Grace was suddenly aware that it appeared rather shabby and the worse for its years of wear. It was evident in the worn arms of her father's armchair, the near-threadbare patch on the rag rug before the fire, the stained area of wall beside the door where the coats brushed as the family members entered. But there was another difference from how it had been in the past. Though the furniture was essentially the same – the same pictures on the walls, the same curtains at the windows, the same cushions on the windowseat – there was still a difference. And that difference, she knew, was partly due to the lack of her mother's presence. Her mother had spent so much time in this room, either cooking, mending, working on their father's accounts and letters, or helping Billy with his schoolwork. She had been the essence of the place. Sometimes it was impossible to believe that she had not merely gone outside, and in moments would return and take up her chair.

'Mr Spencer doesn't only work around Berron Wick,' Billy said. 'Pappy said that sometimes he has go to Redbury and to London. And to other countries – like Italy. Did you know that?'

'No, I didn't,' Grace said. She pushed aside her plate and got up. 'I'm going to make some tea and take some to Pappy.' She moved across to the stove where the kettle was sighing on the hob.

Billy said, 'Pappy said he heard there's a position for a governess in Harbrook. Would you fancy going there?'

'I wouldn't mind,' Grace said, 'but it's so far away. I'd like somewhere a little closer to home. At least for the time being.'

When she had made the tea she poured a mug and took it outside.

Her father's workshop stood separate from the house on its western side across the cobbled yard, a long, red brick, single storey building, with windows along one length and at one end. Here it was that he spent the greater part of each day, working on the cabinets and bureaux and whatever else he was commissioned to provide.

Inside the well-lit room she found her father busy with a plane, working on a piece of timber that was held in a vice. He acknowledged Grace's entrance with the briefest nod, but continued working with the plane for a few seconds longer. Then, setting the tool aside, he loosened the vice, took out the piece of wood and tested it with his set-square. After putting down the tool on the work-scarred bench, he turned to Grace and smiled.

'Hello, Our Gracious.'

She put the mug of tea down on his workbench. 'There you are. A drop of tea for you.'

'Thanks, I can do with that.' He picked up the mug, sipped from it. 'I thought you were coming to give me a hand.'

She laughed. 'Oh, I wish I could.'

He lifted up the piece of timber and held it up to his eye, squinting, peering along its length for variations in its surface. 'So,' he said as he laid the piece of timber down on the bench, 'there you were, going off to deliver the frames, and along comes Mr Spencer calling at the house.'

'Yes, I know. I saw him in the yard.' She paused. 'When we went to Asterleigh we saw Mrs Spencer.'

'Oh, really?'

'Yes, we gave them to her.'

'Did she look at them?'

'Oh, yes. She had them unwrapped right away.'

'Did you bring back the burlap?'

Grace clapped a hand to her forehead. 'Oh, Pappy, I forgot. Mrs Spencer said you did excellent work. She was very complimentary.'

'Well, that's nice to hear. And what's nice too is that Mr Spencer paid me.'

34

'Oh, that's good.'

'Not like Mr Copperstone when I delivered the walnut chest last week.'

'He didn't pay you? You didn't say.'

'No, well . . .'

'Oh, Pappy, this is no good at all.'

'He said he'd be sending it to me – but I wanted it paid, on the spot.'

'Of course you did.'

'And he still owes me for the footstool. That was almost two months back.'

'Well, if you don't hear before long, you'll be justified in writing to chivvy him up.'

'Maybe.' He nodded. 'At least Mr Spencer pays on time. And he's been a good customer over the past year or so.'

'Give him his due there.'

He grinned, taking in her tone. 'You make sure you don't go overboard in your praise of the man, now.'

Grace pulled a face, perplexed. 'It's just that I don't know how to take him.'

'What do you mean?'

'Well – he's so – attentive.'

He frowned. 'He hasn't made any – improper remark to you, I hope.'

'Oh, no, not at all. It's just that he's so – pleasant.'

'And you don't like pleasant?'

'Pappy, you know that's not what I'm saying.'

'I'm not sure that I do.'

'Oh, I don't know. It's just that I – I don't always know how to take him, I suppose. At times he seems so pleasant and yet . . .' She let her words trail off.

'You must tell me if he says anything – untoward. You will, won't you?'

'Yes, of course.' She shook her head, then gave a sigh

dismissing her concern. 'Oh, I'm imagining things, that's all.'

Her father was silent a moment, considering this, then said, 'So, what did you think of *Mrs* Spencer? I've never even seen the woman.'

A moment of hesitation. 'I – I'm not sure. She's older than he is, that much is clear. I should think she must be fifty-something.'

'Mrs Tanner tells me she's disabled in some way. Crippled. Is she?'

'Well,' Grace shrugged, ' – she limps on her right leg.'

He nodded. 'She came from Swindon way, I heard. I don't know much more than that.'

She smiled. 'You're not much of a one for gossip, are you, Pappy?'

He chuckled. 'Your mother had enough interest for the two of us. But I don't think a lot is known about them – the Spencers. Well, as they haven't been in the area for that long – five or six years – and pretty much mind their own business. There must be money in that family. With him having the business in Redbury. And what they've spent getting Asterleigh House up together again. Must have cost a fortune.'

'It's a huge place.'

'A beautiful place, they tell me. I'll bet Billy was impressed.'

'We both were.'

'And did you have a nice relaxing walk?'

'Oh, yes, it was fine. We stopped at the Berron Pits on the way back.'

'Your mother used to take you there when you were a girl.'

'Yes, I remember very well. They were wonderful times. And you came with us once, don't you remember? We took a picnic: you, Mama and I.'

36

'So we did.'

'One of those rare times when Mam could persuade you to leave your workbench.'

He nodded wryly. 'Things were a little easier then.'

'I'm sure.'

'Did Billy swim today? I should think the water would be very pleasant.'

'I couldn't persuade him to. He didn't feel like it.'

'How is he, d'you think? He says so little.'

Grace shook her head in a little gesture of helplessness, briefly opening her hands. 'We stopped at Mama's grave – and there were some tears. But he was all right afterwards.' She put her head a little on one side, and moved a step closer. 'Anyway, Pappy, how are *you*?'

'Me? Oh, I'm all right.' He affected an expression of surprise that she should ask such a thing. But Grace was not taken in.

'Mr Spencer said he thought you looked tired.'

'Yes, well, I'm not really that interested in Mr Spencer's observations.'

'No – well . . . Have you managed to get much work done today?'

'A good bit – when I wasn't interrupted.'

'As I'm doing now.'

'Oh, Gracie, my love, I don't mean you.'

Grace reflected that in his workshop he had been somewhat unproductive of late. Certainly compared to how it used to be. Before her mother's death he had been so industrious and productive. Since that time, however, he had seemed only to work in fits and starts. And when he did put his hand to work Grace had never believed that his heart was really in it. Today, however, she had hoped that things were changing for the better. Yesterday he had worked steadily through the day, and this morning he had expressed the intention of doing the same.

A bee hummed in at the open window, hovered about the room for a few seconds, then drifted out again. Grace looked at her father as he turned, picked up the piece of timber he had been working on and peered closely at it. He was a tall man, with a lean build and square shoulders, becoming a little stooped of late – which was surely due to his work, the constant bending over his workbench. He was two months away from his fifty-sixth birthday, and she reflected briefly that over the past year he had begun to show his age. His hair, once a thick and luxuriant dark brown, was now thinning and fading, and growing in grey at the front and over his ears. His face was strong, with a square jaw and heavy brows, the flesh of his forehead for ever marked in creases from his frowning concentration as he worked, his mouth pulled into one thin line.

Edward Spencer had spoken of him looking tired. And though she had somewhat resented the man's comment, she had to admit that perhaps he was right. Her father did look rather tired. He'd been working too hard, there was no doubt about it. Not that she could foresee any way in which he could ease off. They needed the money; it was as simple as that. And a sad thing about it was the fact that despite his hard work, so little money seemed to be coming in. This was not for any want of craftsmanship in his work. There was no lack in that. Part of the problem – it must be, Grace had to admit – was in the matter of his business acumen. Over the years, for as long as Grace could remember, it had been her mother who had handled the administrative side of his work. Taking off his hands all the bothersome business of dealing with payments from customers, of paying the bills for his timber and other materials, she had given him what he wanted – the time and opportunity to work at his carpentry unhindered. She it was who wrote to customers if there were questions concerning the design or progress of the work in hand, she who sent the customers their bills, and wrote to them again if the bills were not paid; she who managed to write the ultimately persuasive letter that eventually got results. She believed passionately in the value of her husband's work and tried to make sure that others did also. She would not allow him to work at cut rates, no matter how much he might like a certain individual. His work was their livelihood, she said, and he could not afford to give it away.

But with the coming of Mrs Harper's illness their joint way of working had gone, and with her death he had shown less and less interest in his own well-being. And Grace had not needed Mr Edward Spencer to point out to her that her father had changed. Of course he had changed. Anyone close to him could see it. Before his wife had died, he had lived as if his life was full. With her death, though, it was as if a shadow had come over him. He no longer seemed to have the same interest. And not only in his work, but in everything around him – even his children sometimes seemed to him a distraction.

'If you don't hear from Mr Copperstone, I'll write to him,' Grace said. 'You'd only have to sign the letter.'

'Well, we'll see.' He gave a sigh. 'I've no doubt it'll get sorted out in the end. We'll not worry.'

'No, Pappy,' she said, 'we won't worry.'

Chapter Three

'Oh, for heaven's sake, what a lot of fuss about a little splinter.'

Her father's voice came to Grace as she rounded the corner of the house and approached the rear door. She had spent the morning and afternoon of that Wednesday in the schoolroom of the Marren household, situated just over a mile away, teaching the couple's twin sons, Edgar and Roger. With the impending excursion to relatives only days away, they had been less than attentive throughout their English and history lessons, and Grace was relieved when the school day had finally come to an end. At 3.30, for the last time as their teacher, she had said her goodbyes to the boys.

Now as she turned in at the kitchen door from the rear yard of Bramble House she was met by the sight of her father sitting at the kitchen table with Mrs Tanner, the occasional charwoman, standing beside him, bending over his hand. Mrs Tanner turned her head and straightened as Grace made her appearance. Mr Harper said:

'Here's Our Gracious. She'll do it.'

'What's wrong?' Grace said.

'Just a bit of a splinter, that's all,' said Mr Harper. 'But all the fuss and carrying on, you'd think it was half a plank.'

Mrs Tanner looked around as Grace entered the room and said with a sigh, 'I'm glad you're here, Grace. My eyes are not what they were, I'm afraid, and I have to admit that your father's not the best patient.'

'He's a man,' Grace said with wide eyes, as if that explained it all, and Mrs Tanner straightened and let fall Mr Harper's hand. 'Of course, why didn't I think of that?'

Mr Harper lifted his large right hand and peered at the thumb. 'The dashed thing. I've tried myself, and I just can't get it out.'

'Grace'll do it,' Mrs Tanner said. 'Her eyes are good.'

'Just give me a second.' Grace went through into the hall where she took off her hat. Then, back in the kitchen, she washed her hands and moved to her father's side. Mrs Tanner, having relinquished her role of nurse, now went back to her task of wringing some cotton and linen that she had washed. Sarah Tanner was fifty-two years old, a widow from the village, mother of a married son who lived nearby, and an unwed daughter who lived at home. Mrs Tanner had been with the Harpers for eight years now, having originally come to help out shortly after the birth of Billy. The family could not afford her on a daily basis but she came in regularly three or four times a week to clean and help with the cooking and washing. She could be a little short-tempered at times, and occasionally cut corners, but she was faithful, inexpensive and reliable.

Grace checked that there was hot water in the kettle, then poured some into a bowl. 'Now let me see,' she said, and took her father's right hand in her own.

'It went in under the nail,' her father said. 'It's not much, but it stings a bit.'

'Pappy,' Grace said, 'you're not safe to be left alone, you really aren't.' Lifting his hand up to catch the best of the light she could just see the end of the splinter, embedded under the thumbnail. 'How did you come to do it?'

'Smoothing out a piece of wood – and obviously not paying as much attention as I should have been doing.'

Grace nodded. 'Well, you certainly did a good job of this.'

From her sewing basket she fetched a pair of tweezers

along with a small pair of scissors and a needle. Then, holding her father's hand once more, she carefully trimmed the thumbnail back as far as she could. She could see the end of the splinter much more clearly now. Bending close, she managed to grip the splinter with the tweezers and pull it out.

'There.' Grace laid the splinter of wood in her father's palm. 'And next time be more careful.'

'What a good girl.' Samuel Harper flicked the splinter aside and sucked at his thumb. 'That feels better.'

From one of the kitchen cupboards Grace took a little bottle containing a very small amount of iodine. Carefully she poured the remaining drops onto a tuft of cotton wool and dabbed it on the site of the injury. Her father sucked in his breath.

'I know, Pappy, it stings,' Grace observed. Removing the stained cotton, she threw it into the fire. 'We'll have a cup of tea now,' she said. 'I need one – and especially after dealing with those Marren boys all day.'

She filled the kettle and put it on the stove. When the water was boiling she made tea, and was pouring it as Mrs Tanner came back into the room after hanging out some washing. Grace asked her if she would like a cup, and the woman thanked her but declined. She had better be getting back, she said.

'Were the boys difficult?' her father asked when Mrs Tanner had departed.

'No,' Grace replied, 'just young and full of life and energy.'

'Still, you won't be bothered by them again.'

'It was never a bother,' Grace said. 'And I shall miss them. And who knows what's in store for me instead.' She took a sip from her cup, then said, 'Where's Billy?'

Her father replied that he had gone to spend the day helping a neighbouring farmer, Mr Timmins, with his work. Billy was always happy to be out on the land, and to be invited to spend the day with the farmer and his two sons was like a gift from heaven to him.

Grace sighed.

'What was that for?' her father asked.

'I was just thinking about getting another position. Now that I've finished with the Marren boys, I really shall have to find something. And if I get another post locally where I can work from home I can help out here too.'

'Well, let's hope you can. If you go off to stay, it'll be just Billy and me.' He picked up his cup, drank from it and replaced it in the saucer. 'Though of course it might be the best thing for you – to get a position away from home.'

'Why d'you say that?'

'Well, as much as I'd like you to remain, it wouldn't be a good thing for you to stay as some kind of unpaid housekeeper. I've seen it happen in other families. The girl gets stuck at home to look after her father or brothers and stays on for years, never really having a life of her own. Then over time the situation changes and she becomes redundant, or else she's out on her ear, or both.'

'Don't worry, I can't see that happening to me.'

'I'm glad to hear it. Though wherever you go you mustn't stray too far away. You'd need to be near in case a certain person comes looking for you.'

'A certain person?' She couldn't help but be amused at his lack of subtlety. 'What do you mean?' His smile was catching, and she found herself smiling back.

'You know very well what. Your Mr Stephen.'

'*My* Mr Stephen?'

'Well, whoever's.' He paused. 'Aren't you curious to know what he has to say?'

'Stephen? You mean there's a letter from him?'

'It's in the hall.'

She gave a little gasp of excitement. 'Oh, Pappy, why didn't you say?'

'I just did,' he said, but she did not hear; she was already out of her chair and starting across the room.

The letter was lying on the front hall table, and quickly she took it up, opened it and read it. Minutes later she was back in the kitchen, the letter in her hand.

'So?' her father said. 'What does he have to say?'

'Oh – he's well, very well. And sends you his best wishes.'

'That's nice of him. Where was he writing from?'

'From Kingston, Jamaica.' She looked at the date. 'He wrote it almost six weeks ago. He says his ship was just about to set out for New York with a cargo of sugar, after which he'll be returning to England.'

Mr Harper nodded. 'Well, that's good news.'

'Oh, yes. His mother will be so pleased to see him.'

'His mother? And what about you?'

'Me? Oh – well, I shall be pleased to see him as well. Of course.'

'No doubt you will. And he should be back in a fortnight or so, weather permitting.'

Up in her room, Grace sat and thought over the news that Stephen was soon to return.

They had first met in the village one Saturday afternoon of the previous summer while he was home on shore leave, and afterwards he had come to the house, asking permission of her father to take her out for a drive. The arrangement had been made and he had called at the appointed time the following day and they had driven out together in his parents' carriage that he had borrowed for the occasion. The sojourn had been so very pleasant and, as it had turned out, had been the first of several. Grace had enjoyed his company, and they had laughed together, sharing a good humour, and she had been happy in the obvious warmth of his affecton. After his departure to rejoin his ship, he and Grace had corresponded as well as they could. But the very nature of his occupation had denied any means of regular and reliable contact. Still, they had met on the occasion of each of his leaves, and with each departure she had found herself missing him more.

And now he was due back, soon she would be seeing him again.

By the time Grace was up the next morning Billy had been gone an hour, hurrying off to join Mr Timmins on his weekly visit to the Corster market. Grace was also going to Corster, but she would be travelling later, and making her own way.

Before her departure, Grace and her father stood together in his workshop. Wearing her hat and second-best dress, Grace was ready to leave.

From his pocket Samuel Harper took his purse and counted out money which he handed to Grace. 'There's enough here to buy Billy's shirt and the other odds and ends and also to pay for any refreshments you'll want during the day.'

Grace thanked him and looked at the coins in her palm. 'I don't need anything for refreshments. I've got money for that.'

'Are you sure?'

'Absolutely.'

He paused. 'I wish things could be different. But one day things'll pick up again.'

'Oh, I'm sure they will.'

'I've been wondering – perhaps we should put off Mrs Tanner. We could save a bit there.'

'Oh, but such a little bit, Pappy. And while I'm around it would be all right, but I shall be working again soon, and then who would clean and cook and wash for you? No, you need her. The little she costs we'll have to manage.'

As she put the coins into her purse her father raised his hand, looked at his thumb and briefly put it in his mouth.

'Is your thumb bothering you?' Grace said.

'It's a little sore, but that'll go away.'

'I'll bring some more iodine from town, shall I?'

Soon after, just after 8.30, Grace set out. The morning was fine and sunny, the few clouds that had gathered at dawn now disappearing beyond the horizon. Seeking the shortest route, she cut across the fields, walking along the footpaths and beside the hedgerows, and then at last, after an hour, reached Liddiston. There she emerged onto the Corster road – which was unusually busy – as befitted a Corster market day. In ten minutes she had attracted the goodwill of the driver of a pony and trap driving to market with his wife. Not missing the enquiring looks of the young woman at the roadside, he brought the cob to a halt and asked Grace if she would like a ride into Corster. Indeed she would, Grace replied, and in no time was climbing up into the trap.

Grace thought the faces of the man and woman were somewhat familiar and was not surprised to learn that they were from Coleshill, the next village to Green Shipton. Sitting on the seat behind the pair, Grace kept up a desultory conversation with them until at last they reached the town.

It was after eleven when the man pulled up outside a public house in the town centre, and Grace got down and gave her thanks and said her goodbyes.

When the man and his wife had driven on, Grace set off meandering through the streets, stopping here and there to look in shop windows. Her first project was to buy Billy's shirt, and when this was accomplished she set off for the market square.

The bustle of the streets was as nothing compared to that

of the market square. It was like a different world. There were so many people coming and going, and the noise at times was almost overwhelming. There was not only the loud hum of people's voices as they went about their shopping, but also the yelling of the stallholders as they shouted out information about their goods. For some time Grace wandered among the stalls, looking at the huge variety of goods displayed for sale. Everything was there, from pigs' trotters to silk ribbons, and she took it all in, along with the excitement that went with the bustle of the place. At one particular stall, one selling medicines and other curatives, Grace bought a small bottle of iodine.

Beyond the general market square was the cattle market, and there Grace went next, being met not only by the general sounds coming from the live animals there, the squawks and bleats and lowing from the chickens and sheep and cattle, but also the smell. There could be no mistaking where she was.

Grace stood to one side, standing well out of the way of the various livestock-holders and dealers who went back and forth through the manure- and urine-tainted straw, while Grace looked around and eventually spied Mr Timmins some yards away beside a pen over by the right near the wall. Billy was with him. Grace lifted her skirts out of the way of the dirt and picked her way through the straw.

Mr Timmins was standing beside a pen in conversation with another man. Nearby Billy leaned over the side of a pen and scratched the back of one of the two small heifers within it. He looked up as his sister drew near, and as soon as she got to his side he said to her, 'I'm stayin' here, Grace.'

'Well, of course you are,' Grace replied. 'Did you think I'd come to take you away with me? Good heavens, no. What would you want with traipsing round the shops with your sister for? You're much better off here.'

At that moment Mr Timmins's companion moved away and Mr Timmins turned and saw Grace there. He came towards her. 'Morning, Miss Grace. You've come to give me an 'and with my livestock, 'ave you?'

Grace laughed. 'Oh, I'm sure I could help you a lot, Mr Timmins, I don't think. No, I just came to say hello to Billy, and see that he's all right.'

'Oh, I should think he is. Is that right, young Bill?'

Billy nodded, smiling. 'Of course.'

Mr Timmins said to Grace, 'Are you here on your own?'

'Yes, I am.'

'How are you getting back?'

'I'll probably get the train to Liddiston and walk from there.'

'Well, we shall be leaving at four, so if you'd care to wait till then we can give you a ride. Long as you don't mind roughing it a bit among the churns and chicken coops. Though we'll make you as comfortable as we can. And I'll put down some cloths so as you don't get dirty.'

Grace thanked him but declined his kind offer, saying that she would be setting off home well before four. So, saying her goodbyes, she wandered on again, until she came upon a bookshop where she stopped to linger, shading the glass in order to peer in. She would so like to buy a book, she thought. After a few moments she pushed open the shop door and went inside.

She felt she could have spent so long browsing in the bookshop, and so much money, too. But whereas she had plenty of time, she had no great supply of money. She would have liked to buy a copy of Thomas Hardy's *The Woodlanders*, and although she stood for a moment with the book in her hand, she decided that it was an expense that she could ill afford. After all, there was no knowing when she would next have employment and be able to earn money. Carefully she laid the book back on the shelf, then went from the shop.

Outside in the street again she made her way to the Golden Hart, though on arrival she had to wait a few minutes in order to find a seat. The place was so busy; with it being a market day it was as if the world and his wife had come in to eat and drink. At last, however, she got a seat on a bench near a window where she relaxed in the hubbub. From the serving maid she ordered a slice of cold game pie, and lemonade to drink.

When she had finished eating, she set off to do the remainder of her shopping, buying from the haberdasher a length of cotton which she intended to make up into a nightdress. And at last her errands were done and it was time to go home.

She caught the train to Liddiston, and from the station there set out to walk the remaining distance to Green Shipton. She kept to the right-hand side of the road, facing the thin trickle of traffic. The sun still shone but there was a pleasant breeze coming over the hills. Of those few cart- and carriage-drivers who came up behind in the same direction on their left, Grace had hopes one would take pity and offer her a lift. But the time stretched out, and although a few vehicles came by, no offers came. The nearest to such a happening was when a cart came along with a group of farmhands on board. As it approached Grace from behind and to her left, there came a voice from the vehicle, calling out, "Ello, there, sweet'eart,' in a jovial manner, and Grace turned and looked up. A row of young male faces grinned at her over the side of the cart – which now perceptibly slowed slightly. 'Hoy-up there, Jake!' one of them called to the driver, a man just a little older, ' – passenger on the starboard side.' The cart slowed further so that for a few moments it just about kept pace with Grace's stride. 'You want a lift, my darlin'?' called

the young man. 'There's room for you up 'ere along of us.'
'Ah, that there is,' shouted another. Their words were
delivered in a good-natured tone, their laughter ringing out
in the warm early evening air.

Grace looked away and slowed her pace.

'Oh, Miss Hoity-Toity,' yelled another young man. 'Too
grand to get up 'ere are we?' 'Yeh,' yelled another, '– 'fraid
of catchin' summat, are we? Nothin' to be afraid of 'ere,
darlin'.'

'No, there certainly ain't,' said the first young man. 'And
there's plenty of room – 'specially if you sits on my lap.'

Another half minute of calls from the young men, then
the driver called over his shoulder to them, 'Looks like yer
out of luck, lads; some folks don't know a good thing when
they sees it,' and clicked his tongue and called to the horse.
In a few seconds the vehicle was picking up speed and
moving on again.

In spite of the good-natured tone of the words from the
young men, it was with relief that Grace watched the cart
move on ahead.

Three more vehicles passed her during the next ten
minutes, but then came a fourth, and Grace's fortune took a
turn.

Hearing yet another vehicle approaching behind her,
Grace turned and saw a pony and trap coming over the
brow of the hill, and in her brief glimpse made out two men
sitting in the driver's seat. She had turned back to face
ahead once more when she now heard a voice from the trap
as it drew close up behind:

'Well, I declare – it's Miss Harper, out for a walk.'

Hearing the words, Grace at once turned, and saw there
Mr Spencer sitting up holding the cob's reins, an unfamiliar
man sitting at his side. Calling out, 'Whoo-ah, Clarrie,' Mr
Spencer brought the trap to a halt beside Grace, and lifted
his hat.

'Miss Grace,' he said, 'to what do I owe such a pleasure? Have you been to the market?'

'Yes, I have,' Grace replied. Of all the people she might have wished to meet, Mr Spencer was not one of them. Nevertheless she turned and smiled at him.

'And now on your way home, I assume,' he said to her.

Then before she could answer, he added, 'I'm forgetting my manners here. Rhind, this is Miss Harper. Miss Harper, this is Mr Rhind, my groom and valet and all things good to me.'

Grace murmured a few polite words and the man nodded to her, the trace of a smile touching his mouth. 'Miss . . .' he murmured.

'And this is my cue to offer my help,' Mr Spencer said to Grace, ' – and my great pleasure. If I can offer you a ride back to Green Shipton, I shall be very happy to do so.'

'But it'll mean going out of your way,' Grace said.

'Not by so much,' Mr Spencer replied. 'And Clarrie here likes a worthwhile walk.' He smiled at her. 'So, shall it be yes?'

Without waiting for a reply, Mr Spencer was jumping down to help Grace up into the trap, as he did so saying to Rhind, 'Say, Rhind, old chap, it'd be as well if you sit in the back, all right?' and to Grace: 'And you, Miss Harper, perhaps you'd care to sit up in the front along with me. I have to say you'll be prettier company than Rhind.'

To her annoyance Grace found herself blushing slightly at his words. She watched as Rhind moved into the back and then she got up and took a seat beside Mr Spencer. Then Mr Spencer called out to the cob and the trap moved off again.

Mr Spencer did most of the talking as they drove, most of the conversation comprising questions and answers between him and Grace. He asked about her visit to

51

Corster. Throughout the ride the man Rhind said barely a single word. He sat facing the moving scenery, never acknowledging Grace's presence with more than a glance, and barely more than the odd word, and this only when he was drawn into the conversation by his employer. He was a man of less than average height, wiry in his build, and about forty-five years of age, with black, tightly wavy hair, hair which without restraint curled in spite of its Macassar dressing. The darkness of his hair was also seen in the bluish tint of his shaven chin and cheeks, and in the thick moustache and brows. His eyes, fringed with thick lashes, were almost as dark as his hair. His mouth, with narrow upper lip, and full lower, was set and unsmiling, and Grace, glancing back over her shoulder at him, could only conclude that he was resentful of her company – though why he should be, she could not imagine.

And then at last Green Shipton came in view, and they were soon entering the boundaries of the village.

Mr Spencer pulled up the trap outside Bramble House then jumped down and reached up for Grace's hand. As he did so, Rhind stood up in the back, ready to step down and resume his earlier position in the front. As his head came within a foot of Grace's, he leaned over a little closer and said, very softly:

'You might fool some people, but not me. I can see through you – like glass.'

Then, the next second, as if he had not spoken, he smiled and jumped down out of the trap.

Chapter Four

The following week, on Saturday, soon after breakfast Grace set about preparing her things to pack in her box, for the following morning she was due to leave for Remmer Ridge to stay for a week with her Aunt Edie, her father's elder sister. Grace had made the trip on several occasions over the past few years, and now that her aunt was widowed felt that her company was even more welcome. This particular sojourn had been decided upon three weeks earlier, planned to coincide with Grace's employment with the Marrens coming to an end. Grace was looking forward to the break; it would be good to have no responsibilities for a while, and though Aunt Edie could be a little exacting at times, nevertheless her heart was in the right place, and she had a fine, irreverent sense of humour. All in all, Grace's stays with her had generally proved to be fun and entertaining.

In the kitchen her father poured two mugs of water to take into his workshop, one for himself and one for Billy.

'How's Billy managing?' Grace asked.

'Oh, well enough. I've got him doing some sanding for me. It's a simple enough job. I've told him that when he's done he can go on over to the farm. He'd much rather do that. And I can't say as I blame him.'

As he moved to pick up one of the mugs Grace noticed the condition of his thumb.

'Pappy,' she said at once, 'are you all right? Your thumb doesn't look too good.'

He nodded. 'It's still a bit sore, I'm afraid. That damned splinter.'

'Come into the light – let me look at it.'

In the light close to the window she examined his thumb. It was swollen, the flesh about the nail red and angry-looking. When she gently pressed the nail he winced.

'Oh, dear,' she said, 'I think you have a little infection there.'

'Yes, I'll bathe it before I go to bed.'

As he finished speaking Mrs Tanner came into the room carrying a basket of clothes, ready for ironing. As she set the basket down, Mr Harper picked up the other mug, excused himself and went out into the yard and to his workshop.

'So,' said Mrs Tanner as she began to sort through the clothes, 'have you got everything ready for tomorrow?'

'Just two or three things to iron,' Grace replied, 'and then it'll be done.' She added, 'I bought some cotton in Corster. I might take it with me and work on it there.'

'Your father told me as how you was lucky enough to get a ride home – with Mr Spencer from Berron Wick.'

'Yes – I was very fortunate.' Grace had thought several times about the journey back from Corster in Mr Spencer's trap, her thoughts for the most part focusing on his man-servant, Rhind. And still she could hardly believe that he had said such words to her: '*You might fool some people, but not me. I can see through you – like glass.*' What had he meant? His words had been uttered so softly – so softly that only she had heard them. Now Mrs Tanner's words had brought it all back.

'Mr Spencer's manservant was with him,' Grace said. 'A man by the name of Rhind – I think that's his name. A very – dour sort of character.'

She had half-hoped that her words would prompt some recognition from Mrs Tanner, but there was none.

'Rhind? No, I never heard anything about him,' the

woman said, 'but there was a bit of talk in the past about his master.'

'Oh? And what would that be?' Grace asked.

'Well, nothing against him, as such.' Mrs Tanner took from a cupboard two smoothing irons and began to wipe their surfaces. 'But people do say as he fell on his feet, so to speak.'

'Fell on his feet? What d'you mean?'

'Well, marrying as he did. The Addison woman. She had everything – and he had nothing. Not even a name.'

This was interesting, and nothing now could have prevented Grace from saying: 'Not even a name? I don't understand.'

Mrs Tanner hesitated before answering. 'Well,' she said, 'there was a bit of talk when he was a child – not much, but I recall it happening. About his birth.'

'Tell me,' Grace said. The ironing was now forgotten.

'Well,' Mrs Tanner said again, ' – they said as he was only born the right side of the blanket by the skin of his teeth, as you might say. That was the talk, anyway. I mean – well, the fact is that his mother married when she was already well on the way with him – and on her wedding day holding her bouquet much higher than usual. The way they do. She married a much older man. There were lots of rumours about, but it was only a nine days' wonder, you understand, and without fuel gossip soon dies down. While he was still a boy he went off – to London, some said, and also to foreign parts. And then didn't come back to Berron Wick until he came back with his wife – Mrs Spencer. Miss Addison as was. So there you are –' another shrug, 'whatever the truth of it, there's no denying that he made the best of his beginnings. Certainly he's now got everything he can possibly want.'

'The house is huge,' Grace said. 'It's so grand. It's like a palace.'

Mrs Tanner nodded. 'Yes. Mr Gresham certainly left his niece well off. Nice to have an uncle so well placed, don't you reckon? And be the only beneficiary. And if you're a man, how nice to have your wife come into so much money.'

'Have you ever seen Mrs Spencer?'

'No, but there's been a bit of chatter about her too. She lived in Swindon before she married Mr Spencer. And she was no spring chicken either when they were wed.'

'I met her,' Grace said. 'The other day when Billy and I went to Asterleigh House to deliver some pictures for Father.'

'And?' Mrs Tanner looked at her curiously. 'What was she like? I hear she walks with a limp.'

'Yes, she does,' Grace replied. 'Though I don't think it's so very bad. What I did notice is that she has beautiful skin. She's very well preserved.'

Mrs Tanner laughed. 'And I'm sure she'd thank you for saying so, my dear.'

After Mrs Tanner had proceeded with the ironing for a while, Grace took over. Not only ironing her own things, but those of her father and Billy. This would give the older woman's back a rest, and allow her to start preparing vegetables for the main meal.

Grace was coming to the end of the basket of clothes to be ironed and Mrs Tanner had gone to another part of the house when Billy came in. 'You look a little warm,' Grace said as she exchanged the cooling iron for the hotter one that waited on the stove.

'I am,' he said, then added, by way of explanation, 'I've been sanding wood. It's thirsty work. Now I'm off to see Mr Timmins. Pappy told me I can go and help him. Mr Timmins says the harvest will be starting soon. He'll need all the help he can get.' These days Billy was spending so much of his time at Timmins's farm, helping out in any way he could. He loved to be active and thrived on being useful.

Moving to the wall beside the kitchen door, he stretched up, reached down his hat and put it on. 'Mr Timmins says not to forget my hat. This hot sunny weather, he says I mustn't risk sunstroke.'

'No, you certainly must not,' Grace said.

Billy was turning in the doorway now.

'When'll you be back?' Grace asked. 'Are we likely to see anything more of you today?'

'Later,' he said, 'when I've finished.'

'You be back by six, all right?'

'All right.' He turned, tapped his forehead as if prompting memory. 'I meant to tell you, I saw your Mr Stephen.'

'You what?' She asked the question but she had heard him, clearly. 'You saw Mr Stephen? Mr Stephen Cantrell?'

'I saw him yesterday. He was near the post office.'

Grace stood there with the smoothing iron raised in the air, then carefully set it down on the stove again. 'And – and what did he say?'

'He didn't say anything. He didn't see me.' He took a step away, eager to be gone.

'Where was he? Tell me.'

'I told you, near the post office. He was on his horse, riding along the street.'

'You're sure it was him?'

'Of course I'm sure.'

'How come he didn't see you?'

'He had his back to me. As I turned the corner I saw him riding away.'

'Perhaps you're mistaken. Perhaps it was somebody else.'

'No.' He frowned and shook his head as if such an error was beyond him. 'I know what he looks like.' He paused. 'I must go.'

'What? Yes, you go on, then. And have a nice time.'

'I'm going to *work*,' he said, as if work and nice times couldn't go together. And adding, 'I'll see you later on,' stepped out into the yard and was gone.

After a moment Grace left the ironing and went out into the yard. Another few steps and she was turning in at the door of her father's workshop. He looked round at her expectantly as she entered and came to a stop in the room. When she didn't speak, he said, 'Yes, Gracious? Was there something?'

'What?' She gave a little laugh. 'I don't know what I'm doing here.' She put a hand to her forehead. 'My mind is going. Too much sun.' His woodworking tools were all around, sitting on shelves, hanging on the walls, lying on the bench. Her eyes saw it all but took nothing in.

'What's the matter?' her father said.

After a moment she said, 'Billy – Billy had some foolish story that Stephen is back home. He said he saw him yesterday in the village.' She shook her head. 'Billy couldn't have seen him. It must have been someone else he saw.'

As she spoke, she heard the sound of hoofs, and turning, saw a horse and rider trot into the yard. As they passed the window she said, 'It's the Cantrells' groom. What does he want?'

With her words she passed through the open door into the yard. As she emerged, the young man, the visitor, turned the mare and got out of the saddle. Seeing Grace, he straightened and put fingers to his cap. 'Miss Harper,' he said, ' – just the one I've come to see.' He took an envelope from his pocket and held it out. 'A note for you from Mr Stephen. He says I'm to wait for an answer.'

Grace thanked the man and took the envelope from him. It was addressed to her in Stephen's familiar hand. Turning away, she came to a stop, quickly tore open the envelope and took out the letter. She read it through, then lifted her head to see her father standing in the workshop doorway just a few feet away. He was eyeing her expression keenly.

'Seeing the Cantrells' man,' he said, 'and the smile of excitement on your face, I can only assume the letter's from Stephen.'

She looked at him and nodded, then went back to the letter. 'He says he arrived back yesterday morning.' She sounded a little breathless. 'He wants to come round this evening at six o'clock – if it's convenient.'

'And is it?'

'Oh, Pappy . . .' She turned again, took a few steps towards the groom who stood beside the horse, now hitched up, and said, 'I'll just keep you a minute,' and then went quickly into the house.

Up in her bedroom she got pen and paper, and, sitting at her small writing desk, quickly wrote a reply to Stephen's letter, and sealed it in an envelope. Back down the stairs again and she was out in the yard and moving to the young groom. She thanked him again for delivering the letter and handed him her letter in reply. She watched then as he unhitched the horse, swung up into the saddle, and clattered away across the cobbles towards the lane.

She remained standing there for some seconds after he had turned out of her sight. Stephen was back in Green Shipton, back at his family home in the village, where he usually stayed during his periods of leave from the merchant ship on which he was Second Officer.

With a little sigh of pleasure she turned and moved towards the workshop.

Her father did not look around as she entered, but continued at his work, sanding a piece of timber. 'So,' he said, still without looking up, 'have you sent the young man an answer?'

'Yes. He'll be round at six.'

*

59

Somehow Grace got through the time remaining, spending most of it helping Mrs Tanner with the chores about the house. Then, when Mrs Tanner left at five, Grace went upstairs and began to prepare for her visitor. When she was ready she sat waiting.

It was 5.50 when she heard the sound of hoofs on the cobbles. Yet she would not look from the window, but remained there, on the chair. She heard the hoofs stop, and after some seconds the sound of voices, Stephen's voice and that of Billy. Two minutes later came the sound of hurrying feet on the stairs, and then a knocking on the door. She opened the door to see her brother standing there, a little breathless, his face flushed from exposure to the afternoon sun. 'Your Mr Stephen's here,' he said, thrilled to be the bearer of good tidings. 'You didn't know, did you? He's here, now, downstairs, in the parlour.'

'Thank you.'

'Are you coming down?'

'Of course I'm coming down.' It would not do to seem too eager. 'Just give me a minute.'

He turned and she called his name and he came back across the landing.

'What is it?' he said.

'Billy, when I come down – you make yourself scarce, all right?'

'Why?'

'Billy.'

He sighed. 'All right.'

'Thank you.'

After Billy had withdrawn and his footfalls had faded on the stairs, Grace remained there, looking at her reflection in the glass. Stephen was back, and here she was planning to leave the village for a fortnight. How could she? How could she be away when he was here? Hands fluttering slightly, she touched at her hair, adjusting the pins, then twitched at the sleeves of her blouse and skirt. And, dear Lord, she thought, I look so dowdy. But there was nothing to be done about it now. She leaned forward a little, closer to the glass, and pinched a little more colour into her cheeks. Then she rose, smoothed down her skirt and left the room.

Downstairs in the hall she moved towards the parlour, pushed open the door and went in.

He was standing by the fireplace, tall, slim, and dressed in a dark grey, single-breasted suit. He had turned at the sound of her approaching step, and now greeted her with a little smile. She came to a halt just inside the doorway and smiled at him in return.

'Hello, Grace,' he said.

'Hello, Stephen . . .' A brief pause. 'Welcome back.'

'Thank you.' As he spoke he lifted a hand to brush his fingers through his thick fair hair. Grace saw a touch of nervousness in the gesture, and for a moment wondered at it.

'Please, Stephen,' she said, gesturing towards an easy chair on the other side of the fireplace, 'do sit down.'

He muttered thanks and sat. She followed, sitting in the chair facing him. It had been almost four months since they had last met. Their meeting had taken place not long before her mother's death. So much of that time now was hazy in her memory, but she could remember his being there, his presence, their walking in the lane, his concern at her mother's illness.

Now as she exchanged glances with him she thought how well he looked with his tanned skin and his hair bleached a paler shade by the sun. 'You're looking well, Stephen,' she said.

'Thank you, Grace.' He looked down at his hat resting on his knee, then said, 'Oh, I was so sorry to learn about your mamma, Grace. That was so – so awful for you. For all of you.'

She nodded. 'Thank you. It was indeed. It was a dreadful thing. But I so appreciated your letter, Stephen. Your letter to Father, too. They meant a lot to both of us.'

He shrugged. 'It was nothing. How are you now? Are things a little easier?'

The sympathy in his voice was dangerous. One had to be so careful. Sympathy – it could make a break in the strongest dam, fracture the strongest resolve. 'Yes,' she said, 'things do get easier. But – well, I suppose we just take it a day at a time.'

'Yes. And how are the rest of your family – your father and your brother?'

'They're well.' A little shrug. 'We keep busy.'

'Of course. When young Billy let me in just now I thought, how he has grown.'

'Oh, yes, he grows so fast. You can't keep up.'

His glance left her own, drifted away, then lowered again, settling on his hat once more.

'You almost missed me,' Grace said after a moment. 'Tomorrow morning I'm supposed to be leaving for Remmer Ridge to stay with my aunt. I'm to stay with her for a fortnight.'

'Then it's as well I called today,' he said.

She smiled. 'It is indeed.'

A little silence fell, and to fill the space she added, 'Now that I've finished working for Mr and Mrs Marren I have a little free time, you see. So it seemed an ideal time – to visit my aunt.'

'What time are you leaving?'

'Pappy's driving me to Liddiston station at ten. I shall get a cab at the other end.'

'You've stayed with her before, haven't you?'

'Oh, yes, on several occasions over the years. She's my father's elder sister.'

'Well, I'm sure she loves your company.'

'I hope so.' This was so much small talk, she thought, chatter to fill space. 'Billy said he saw you near the post office,' she said. 'You were riding through the village.'

'Oh, I didn't see him.'

'No – you were going in the other direction.'

'Ah.' He gave a grave nod.

The conversation was not easy, Grace thought. 'How long are you home for?' she asked.

'At least seven weeks, as far as I know. There's some refitting to the ship to be done. Then we sail for Jamaica again.'

'So you have a nice long time at home.'

'It will be pass in the blink of an eye. It always does.'

Grace nodded. The period between their meetings had caused a certain shyness between them, she thought. But it was only natural, and they would get through it soon. They would have time now that he was back.

A little silence fell between them, then Grace said, 'Goodness, I don't know what I'm thinking of – I haven't offered you any tea. Would you like some?'

She began to rise from her seat, but he gave a hurried gesture for her to remain. 'No, thank you, really. I had some just before I came out.'

'It'll only take a minute.'

'No, honestly, thank you. I can't really stay that long.'

His words took her a little by surprise. 'Well,' she said, 'I'm sure you must have a lot to do, having just arrived back.'

'Yes – this and that.'

There was something wrong, Grace thought. Granted, there would be acknowledgement of the death of her mother, and the family's grief, but in spite of that there should have been a greater ease between them. But it was not there. He had not even made a step towards her. And the conversation, such as it was, was constrained, stilted. In her mind she had pictured their reunion – and it had never been like this. She was aware suddenly of the silence in the room, and in the quiet she heard the singing of a blackbird in the flowering cherry just outside the window.

'And how have you been, Stephen?' Grace asked.

'Oh – well, thank you. Very well.'

'You certainly look well. The tropical air obviously agrees with you.'

'Perhaps it does.'

The silence again. Then he said, 'I came a little earlier this evening because – well, because I had to talk to you.'

She studied his expression, noting the way his glance shifted away, as if unable to rest on hers for more than a moment. 'Couldn't it wait?' she said with a smile.

'I – I suppose not.'

Another little silence.

'Are you sure you won't have some tea?' Grace said.

'No, really, thank you.'

'Perhaps,' lifting a hand, gesturing towards the sunlit window frame, 'you'd care to go outside. It's such a lovely day – and cooped up in here on such a day, it seems a crime.' The thought flashed into her mind that she was playing for time.

'Grace,' he said quickly, 'Grace – this is very difficult for me. I don't know how to begin.'

A little silence, then Grace heard herself say, 'What is it you want to say to me, Stephen?' She was forcing herself to sound calm. 'Tell me.'

There was a long pause and then, still avoiding her eyes, he said:

'I – I'm to be married.'

His words, soft in the stillness of the room, struck her like a blow, and inwardly she flinched. She felt that she wanted to rise and run from the room, but she could do nothing except remain where she was, standing there, gazing at him, while outside in the cherry tree the blackbird filled the early evening air with his song. And then at last Stephen turned his eyes to her again – and now it was her turn to look away.

'I'm so sorry to tell you like this,' he said.

She gave an inward little shrug, and forced a smile to her mouth. 'Well, it is something of a surprise, I must admit.' In truth, she thought, it was like living in a bad dream; perhaps in a moment she would awake and reality would be there. But for the time being she must behave as if she were not moved. 'Do I know the lady?' she asked.

'No. She – Miss Shilford – Victoria – was a passenger on board the ship.'

'Ah,' Grace heard her voice say, ' – so that's how you met.' She could feel pain in the tightness of her throat. 'When is it to be?' she asked. 'The wedding.'

'Oh, well – we've not set a date yet – but some time in the spring, we think.'

'Well, let me say that I hope you'll both be very happy.'

'Thank you, Grace.' And then he was rising from his chair, was coming towards her, was reaching out. As she rose before him her hand was taken in his, suddenly cool in the warmth of his own. 'Grace – my dear friend,' he said. 'Thank you.'

'For what, Stephen?'

'For being so – understanding.'

'Oh, Stephen, please . . .' She withdrew her hand and turned away. His dear friend he had called her. Had his words been so carefully chosen – chosen in order to place their relationship on an uncomplicated footing? Dear Friend. Taking a deep breath, she spoke again, now trying to sound more brisk and casual. 'Look, I'm afraid you caught me at a difficult time. I've got a dozen things to do, and –'

'Yes, I'm sure you must have.' There was no missing the note of relief in his voice. 'And I mustn't detain you.'

Forcing herself to keep up the charade of being calm and unmoved, she gave him a smile, then turned, opened the door and led the way out into the hall. Neither spoke as they reached the front door, where, with the door open, they stood awkwardly facing one another again.

'Where is she from?' Grace said, ' – your Miss Victoria?'

'From Redbury.'

'She'll be lonely when you go back to sea.'

'Yes, well – I'm resigning my commission in the service. When I go away next it will be for my last voyage.'

'I see. And then where will you go? To Redbury?'

'Well – when we're married, Victoria and I – we'll come to live here.'

'In Green Shipton?'

'I'm to help my father in the running of his business. It's what he's always wanted.'

'I see. Yes, of course.' Grace nodded. 'You've come to some very – swift decisions.' She was aware of a sharp little note of bitterness touching the edge of her voice, and fought to dispel it. Careful of her tone, she added, 'So you and your wife will be living here in Green Shipton.'

'Yes. Oh, Grace, I know that you and Victoria will become such good friends. She really is the finest young lady you could wish to meet.'

She remained standing in the room after he had gone, standing there with one hand on the back of a chair, in the very same position she had been in when he had reached out, shaken her hand and, with a final uncertain goodbye, had gone from her sight. And still she could hear the echo of the sound of the horse's hoofs fading on the cobbles of the yard. A sound at the door, and she looked around to see Billy standing there, looking at her questioningly.

'Grace, are you all right?'

'What?' Grace gave herself a mental shake and smiled.

'Of course I'm all right.' She bent and began to rearrange some flowers in a bowl on the table. 'Why shouldn't I be?'

'He was only here a few minutes.'

'Well, yes – he has things to do. He's a busy man – having just arrived back home.' She straightened, clasped her hands before her in a businesslike manner. 'And I have things to do as well. I can't stand here all day.'

How she managed to keep any semblance of equanimity as she walked past Billy and up the stairs she did not know. But once in her bedroom, with the door closed and bolted, she sank down onto the bed and put her head in her hands. Moments later she heard over the sound of her sobbing a light tap on the door.

'Oh, Billy,' she cried out, 'I can't talk to you right now. I'm busy at the moment. Leave me for a minute, please.'

'It's not Billy,' came her father's voice, ' – it's me.'

'Oh, Pappy, can it wait a while? Please?' Try as she might, she could not keep the tears out of her voice. 'I'll be down in a minute.'

'Gracie –' his voice was soft, almost a whisper through the door, 'let me in for a moment, please.'

'Pappy –'

'Please, Grace . . .'

A pause. 'Just a second.' She sniffed, dabbed at her eyes and nose with a handkerchief, then got up from the bed. Standing before the glass she touched at her hair and smoothed her hands over her cheeks. It made no difference; there was no hiding the fact that she had been crying. At the door she slipped back the bolt, opened the door and turned away from it. She was standing by the window when she heard her father enter the room, heard the door close behind him. A moment later he was standing right behind her and she was feeling the light touch of his hand upon her arm.

At the touch she swiftly turned, and then his arms were coming around her and she was burying her face against his shoulder. 'Oh, Pappy, Pappy . . .' She sobbed out the words, her voice muffled in the fabric of his coarse shirt. She could smell the sawdust that lingered in the folds of the cotton. After a while the sounds of her sobbing grew softer, until at last it fell to a little catching of the breath. And this too faded.

Throughout her weeping her father had said nothing. Now he drew back a little, looked down into her tear-stained face and said, 'I knew something was wrong. I saw him arrive, but only a few minutes later he was riding off across the yard again. And you didn't come out to see him off. I knew something was up.'

'Pappy, he – he's to be married.' The tears that had died threatened now to rise again like a new spring, and she had to fight to keep them down. 'He's to marry a young woman he met on his ship.'

'Oh, my dear.' Her father's arms clasped her again. 'I don't know what to say to you. I wish there were something I could say that would make you feel better. But there's nothing. Nothing that you'd believe, anyway.'

Grace did not speak. After a moment she broke from his embrace and sat down on the side of the bed. Her father sat down beside her. A minute passed, during which time they remained silent, the only sound that of their breathing.

At last Grace spoke.

'I've been a complete fool,' she said.

'A fool? What makes you say that?'

'I have. This is all my fault. I brought this all on myself.'

'Why are you saying that?'

'It's true. I have to face the truth. Stephen didn't owe me anything. He made me no promises.'

'Maybe not, but –'

'No, Pappy, he promised me nothing. He called at the house, and we went out walking together on a few occasions. But that's all it was. There was no engagement.

68

He's at perfect liberty to go and marry whomever he likes.'

She gave a deep sigh and got up from the bed. Her father got up behind her.

'Well, this won't get the work done,' Grace said. 'The world has to go on.' She turned to face her father. 'That's one thing we all realized when Mamma died – that the world has to go on. It doesn't matter how unhappy you are, it doesn't matter the tragedy that you might have gone through, the world goes on. The tradesmen still insist on being paid, the livestock still demand feeding, the goat will still want milking.' Turning to look in the glass, she put up a hand and absently smoothed her hair back in place. As she looked at her father in the glass she noticed that his right thumb was now bandaged. She turned to him and reached for his hand.

'Oh,' she said, 'your poor thumb. How is it?'

'It's getting better. I put the bandage on because I've been polishing, and with an open wound it makes it sting a bit.'

'Ah, Pappy.'

'I'm all right, girl,' he said. 'It's you as needs the attention.'

'I shall be fine,' she said. 'Really I shall.'

'All right, then. I'll get back to work. Come on down if you need me.'

'I will.'

As he got to the door she said, 'The trouble is, Stephen's leaving the service soon and coming back to work in his father's business. Which means I could be running into him at any time. Or his wife.' Then, waving a dismissive hand, she added, 'But that's just something I shall have to deal with when it happens. And I'll manage.'

'Of course you will.'

'Yes.' She nodded. 'Anyway – you go on back to your work, Pappy. I shall be all right, I promise you.'

He stood there facing her, one hand on the doorknob. Grace said:

'I don't think I can go to Aunt Edie's tomorrow.'

'Why ever not?'

'I just can't.'

'But why not?'

'Not now. Not now this has happened. I shan't be good company.'

'Nonsense. It'll be the best thing for you. Get a change of scene for a while.' He opened the door, turned in the doorway and looked back at her. 'Are you sure you're going to be all right?' he said.

'Absolutely.' She forced a smile to her mouth, a fleeting expression that came and went.

She remained looking in the direction of the doorway for some moments after her father had closed the door behind him and after she had heard his footfalls die away as he descended the stairs. Then, turning from the door she sank back down onto the bed, bent her head and put her hands to her face. The tears began again, filling her eyes and running down her cheeks. Falling forward, she lay down on the bed and buried her face in the coverlet.

Chapter Five

It was after five when Grace arrived at her aunt's the following day. It had been a pleasant enough journey in her father's trap for the first part, and in the cab at the end. However, it had been warm in the closed railway carriage. Grace would have liked at least one window open, but a middle-aged matron sitting near a window had made a fuss about the smuts in the smoke, so Grace and the elderly man also present could do nothing but suffer the close air.

Eventually, however, Grace alighted from the cab outside her aunt's cottage, the cab driver had set down her little trunk at her feet and was climbing aboard again.

Seconds later Grace was being welcomed by her aunt and carrying her trunk upstairs to the little room that she would share with her aunt for the next few nights.

That evening after they had eaten, the two relaxed into conversation and Grace was able to inform her aunt of the family's comings and goings. Aunt Edie was in her late fifties, a large, jolly woman who seemed to Grace to have a great appetite for life, and who rarely allowed its vicissitudes to get her down. With her rounded figure, pink cheeks and suspiciously red hair she was a picture of good nature, a picture that was not denied in the reality.

It was not long into their conversation that Stephen came to be mentioned, and soon after that the news of his planned marriage that he had brought to Grace the previous day.

'Oh, my dear . . .' Aunt Edie reached across the space

between the chairs where they sat and pressed Grace's hand. And once again, with this touch of real sympathy, Grace could feel the tears stinging her eyes and threatening to spill over onto her cheeks. With an effort she forced them back. She had wept already for Stephen; if she could in any way help it, she would not weep for him again.

Over the following days Grace did her best not to think of Stephen. But it was not easy. Unbidden, thoughts of him would come to her at the most unexpected times. She would imagine him in the lane, walking at her side; see him astride his horse as he stopped outside the house and bent to her from the saddle. So often she told herself that she had no rights where he was concerned. It was true what she had told her father – Stephen had made her no promises. There had been no promises, declarations of love, or discussions of a shared future – from either one of them. And although he had kissed her on two or three occasions, the kisses had been chaste and proper and without passion.

Grace did her best to fill her days in Remmer Ridge. If her aunt had no proposals for other pastimes, Grace would, soon after breakfast, put on her hat, a light shawl and her pair of sturdy boots and set off alone for a walk. She did not always choose the same route; on some days she walked across the surrounding meadows, following the narrow footpaths beside the hedgerows that skirted the fields, at other times walking beside the river that ran along beside the road before cutting off across the fields on its meandering way. Perhaps in the afternoons her aunt would accompany her on a shorter walk, and sometimes in the evenings Aunt Edie would play the harmonium and Grace would join her, adding her light soprano to her aunt's rich contralto in singing romantic ballads and songs and hymns of praise. At other times the two would play parlour games, chess, draughts or bezique or sit talking over their needlework – Aunt Edie her embroidery and Grace over the nightdress she was making.

And the hours, the days went by, and although the time passed Grace found that barely an hour would be spent without her thinking of Stephen. Everything she did, she thought, was merely a diversion. Whatever she did, all it succeeded in doing was filling time, passing time. Whether she was playing chess with her aunt, quietly trying to read, working on her sewing or walking by the river, Stephen would be always there, somehow or other finding a way of looking over her shoulder. Her father had been wrong; he had thought that a change of scene was exactly the thing that was needed to help Grace over her unhappiness. But it was not. If anything, it made it worse, for she had not even the comfort about her that comes with being with familiar things.

And such was her unhappiness that at night when she got into the bed she shared with her aunt she almost remarked to herself that she had come through the day without dying from heartbreak. And throughout it all, over and over again, she told herself, Stephen would in time turn again to her.

Not that she waxed vocal about her unhappiness. Her preoccupations were of the quiet kind, so that all a stranger might observe was a certain constraint about her, a certain seriousness of mien, a lack of readiness to laugh. Her aunt, having traversed such territory herself in days gone by, understood the situation and was sympathetic. And being sympathetic she did her best to find ways and means of further diverting Grace's preoccupations, while at the same time she was old enough and wise enough to know a lost cause when she found one. In the end she let things be, and merely offered kind, sympathetic words and under- standing when she thought they were required.

And as the days passed, Grace, like a sick animal that

heads for his lair, found herself looking forward to getting back home.

As a matter of course she had written to her father immediately on arrival at Remmer Ridge – just to say that she had got there safely – and four days later she wrote again to confirm the day and time of her return. It had been arranged that her father would meet her in the trap at Liddiston station, and now as the time for her departure approached, she felt she could not get back soon enough.

And at last the time came when the cab – booked on her outward journey – stood waiting at the gate and she was saying goodbye to her aunt.

Her journey back was uneventful, and Grace found comfort and a degree of pleasure in the very knowledge that she was heading back home, and even more in the knowledge that when she reached Liddiston she would find her father waiting for her.

And there he was as she came out of the station, sitting up there with Robin, the young gelding pony, between the trap's shafts.

As a young porter carried her trunk to place it in the back of the trap, her father jumped down and hurried forward to embrace her. She saw at once that his left thumb was still bandaged.

'Welcome back, Gracious,' he beamed as he put his arms around her and drew her close. Gladly she let herself be held, for a moment giving herself up to the warmth of his touch, the comfort in the smell and familiar strength of his body.

But there was something wrong. As she drew back a little and reached to take his hands he flinched, sucking in his breath slightly and drawing a little away.

'Pappy, what is it?' she said, concern sounding in her voice.

'Ah, the thumb's been playing me up a bit,' he said. 'But we'll be better now that I've got my nurse back.'

She took his left hand and looked at it closely in the bright afternoon light. 'How does it feel?' she said.

'Well,' he said, 'it's throbbing like billy-o and I've a lump under my arm the size of an egg.'

She could see that the thumb was shockingly swollen, and there was a dark reddish line moving from his knuckles up under the cuff of his coarse shirt. She reached up and laid the back of her hand against his forehead. 'You've got a temperature,' she said. 'Pappy, you've got a fever. Come on, let's go on home.' She pulled herself up into the trap then watched as her father climbed up beside her. 'Would you like me to drive?' she asked.

'No, dear,' he replied. 'That's all right. And you know how fussy Robin is when it comes to who has the reins.'

She allowed herself a smile at this. 'Oh, I do indeed.' She hooked her right arm through his left one, careful not to touch anywhere near his hand. 'I should never have gone away,' she said with a shake of her head. 'All I've been doing is thinking of myself.'

Grace would always remember the ride home. After initial conversation about her stay with her aunt, and how her aunt was, and what the two had done, her father lapsed into silence, and Grace surmised, correctly, that he was not in the mood to talk. And as they progressed, her concern for him began to change to feelings of alarm. It was quite clear that he was in great discomfort from his injured thumb, made even clearer when the carriage rode over a deep, jarring rut in the road and he winced and gave a little gasp.

'Pappy,' she said, 'we've got to get you home and look at that hand. You shouldn't have come out. You should be at home, resting, waiting for the doctor to call.'

'Doctor,' he said. 'You know how I feel about doctors.'

'Nevertheless, there are times when they're needed. And it's no good complaining about the cost. There are such things as false economy.'

By the time they reached Bramble House just after 5.30 Samuel Harper was shivering. Grace was regarding him with alarm; she had never seen him in such a state before. And why should he be shivering so, when the day was warm? 'You go on indoors, Pappy,' she said to him. 'I'll unhitch Robin, and give him his feed. You go on into the house and sit down. I'll be in in just two or three minutes.'

He would not have it, though. 'No, I can manage,' he said. At that moment Billy came from the house, and Grace, after only the briefest word of greeting to him, said, 'Billy, come and give Pappy a hand with Robin.'

Leaving the two to deal with the pony, she went into the house and before doing anything else filled the kettle and put it on to boil. She had just taken off her hat and cape when her father and Billy came into the kitchen. She watched anxiously as her father, giving a slight groan, lowered himself into his chair.

On questioning her father, Grace learned that the shivering fit had started earlier that day. And also, she discovered from him, three abscesses had formed on his body, one behind his knee, another under his arm, and another, he indicated, on his lower belly.

Grace gently removed the bandage and looked closely at his thumb. It was huge, swollen to nearly twice its size. The nail, partly lifted away from the flesh beneath, rose up an unnatural bluish-black. The skin surrounding, strangely discoloured, looked distended to the point of bursting.

Grace turned to her brother. 'Billy, you must go immediately and fetch Doctor Harrison.' At once Billy reached for his hat, and she turned and followed him to the door. Outside in the yard she said, lowering her voice to an urgent whisper: 'Tell him it's urgent, and tell him what the trouble is – that Father's got a poisoned hand, and that he's shivering all the time.'

'What if the doctor's not there?' Billy said.

'Well, if he's not there, then leave a message for him to come as soon as possible. Now be as quick as you can.'

Without hesitating another moment Billy turned and was hurrying across the yard.

Grace, her eyes reluctantly leaving their focus on her father, got up and moved to the kettle. She made tea for him and poured him a mug. Then, going upstairs to his bedroom, she brought down a heavy blanket and wrapped it around his shoulders. But still he kept shivering.

'Oh, Pappy,' she said, 'I don't know what to do for the best.'

The minutes slowly passed by, their passage marked by the solemn ticking of the grandfather clock that stood beside the chimney breast. Grace found her eyes returning to it again and again. Billy and the doctor should have been back before this time; Dr Harrison lived not far away, just on the other side of the village. It would only take Billy fifteen minutes at the most to get there.

And then at last there was the sound of horse's hoofs and carriage wheels in the yard, and Grace got up from her seat and hurried to the door. She reached it and opened it as Dr Harrison, with Billy following, came across the cobbles towards her.

The doctor took off his hat as he approached and gave Grace a curt nod of acknowledgement: 'Miss Harper . . .' He was in his forties, a slimly built man of medium height with reddish side whiskers and moustache and thinning hair. Grace greeted him, thanked him for coming, and led the way into the kitchen.

The doctor went straight to Samuel Harper where he reclined in his chair. The latter made as if to get to his feet, but the other quickly waved a hand, instructing him to remain seated. Drawing up a chair, Harrison opened his black bag, took out a thermometer and put it into the man's mouth. After taking his temperature he set about taking his blood pressure, holding the man's right wrist and at the same time turning his gaze to the clock face. As the doctor counted the seconds Grace turned to Billy who stood beside the table, and gently indicated that he should leave the room. Silently the boy crept out of the room and into the hall. A second later Grace heard the creak of the treads as he went upstairs.

Left alone with his daughter and the doctor, Samuel Harper told of how the splinter had gone in under the thumbnail, and of how an infection had taken hold, and of how, now, several days later, abscesses had begun to develop at various sites on his body. Hearing this last, Dr Harrison frowned and looked grave, and glancing round at Grace murmured, 'I think it might be better if you leave us for a minute or two.' At his words Grace rose and, like Billy before her, silently departed.

She did not go upstairs but remained in the hall, ready in case she should be needed. And, standing there while the sun shone on the climbing rose beside the window, she became aware of the silence of the place. It was a silence that seemed to point up the little sounds coming from the kitchen, the murmur of the voices of her father and the doctor, the brief creaking of her father's chair, the faint rustle of his clothing.

And then, after some time, the door opened and the doctor was there. Grace started forward as if to go into the room, but he put up a hand urging her to remain. A moment later he had come through into the little hall and was closing the door behind him.

He stood looking at her for a moment, eyebrows raised and mouth set in an expression of consternation. Then he gave a little shake of his head and let fall a deep sigh. At once Grace felt her heart begin to thud in her breast.

Keeping his voice very low, the doctor said, 'Well, I'm very sorry to have to tell you that the situation is very serious. Very serious indeed.'

Grace's hand flew to her mouth while her eyes searched the man's expression, trying to read there some evidence of hope. But he remained grave, his brow furrowed in perplexity.

'I'm afraid we have a very serious case of pyaemia. Blood poisoning.' He spoke in a whisper, hurriedly, as if anxious to get the information over. 'It's madness, letting a thing like that go on. You get an infection, and it seems like a small, unimportant thing. But in no time at all it can take hold, and once it does, it can be the devil's own job to banish it.' He shook his head again. 'And he's got those abscesses now – and they're a very bad sign. He's got them behind his knee, under his arm, and a very severe one in his groin. They're an unmistakable sign that the poison is spreading. The abscesses erupt when the arteries get blocked by the poison and the blood can't get through. So what happens –' he spread his hands, 'is that the poison has to find an outlet. Hence the abscesses. Left without treatment they'll just increase in number.'

He half-turned towards the door to the kitchen, then, turning back to Grace, went on: 'Well, he'll need very careful nursing. You might want to make up a bed for him downstairs – it'll make it easier to nurse him if you do. But he must keep up his strength with some good, nourishing food. He might not have much of an appetite but that's by the by. Get him some concentrated soups, and beef tea and milk and so on. Good food in fluid form. He must keep his strength.' He gestured off, in no particular direction, and added, 'Your young brother gave me an idea of what was wrong so I've brought two or three things with me.' He turned back to the door, reaching out for the handle. 'Now, let's go in and see him. And we'll start off by doing something about that thumb.'

In the kitchen again the doctor gave Samuel Harper a little opium to relieve his anticipated pain, and then got Grace to prepare a bowl of water with a quantity of salt. As Grace did this he took from his bag a couple of instruments. After rinsing them in the boiling water that Grace poured from the kettle, he had Samuel Harper sit at the kitchen table near the window with his left hand resting on the table on a folded linen cloth. While Grace nervously looked on, the doctor took a scalpel and, holding Samuel's thumb steady in his left hand, cut deeply through the nail from the bottom to the top. The injured man gritted his teeth and drew in his breath at the shock and the sharp, stabbing pain. And as he did so the yellow pus rose up and oozed out over the severed halves of the nail and ran down the sides of the grotesquely swollen thumb. After the doctor had squeezed the thumb, releasing a greater quantity of pus, he placed the poisoned hand in the bowl of salt water. Throughout it all Samuel Harper made no complaint.

The doctor left some forty minutes later, having given his patient a dose of medication in the form of a saline powder. This was necessary, he said, to help relieve the power of the poison at its source. To help diminish the fever, he gave Grace a bottle of quinine, of which she was to give her father small doses at six hourly intervals. The doctor also left dressings for the hand, with instructions to Grace as to how to use them. He would, he said, call again the following day.

When the doctor had gone and Billy had come back into the room, Grace suggested she and her brother bring out from the workshop where it had been stored for so many years an old truckle bed. They could set it against the wall beneath the window. Her father would have none of it, however, saying that he would prefer his chair in the kitchen by day, and the privacy of his bedroom at night. The only change to be effected was that Billy would no longer be able to share his bed, but would have to sleep downstairs on the settle.

That night Grace lay in her bed overlooking the small front garden. She had seen her father fed with a good meat broth, then had seen him up to his bed with his medicine taken, his hand dressed, and a little of a sleeping draught to help him to relax and deaden the pain. He had begun to perspire heavily during the later evening, but the doctor had prepared Grace for the eventuality so she was not surprised by it. Back downstairs she had got Billy's bed made up.

Now, turning in her bed, she found it almost impossible to relax, though she did know a certain relief in the fact that the doctor had been sent for and that her father was therefore in good hands. Beyond that, however, she could find little cause for comfort. It was a long time before she eventually drifted off into sleep.

The following morning just after eleven, Dr Harrison returned.

Grace greeted him hopefully with the news that her father's shivering had ceased and that he seemed much better. She expected the doctor to look pleased with the information, but he merely gave a nod, as if her words were confirmation of his thoughts.

'That's the pattern such an illness takes,' he said. 'I'm sorry to say it, but I think there's no doubt that the shivering will return in time.'

Before leaving, he examined Samuel's thumb again and gave him a little more opium.

That evening her father's shivering returned, and this time more violently than before. This was followed once again by a bout of sweating. His fever was running high, and as the hours dragged on he began to take on a sallow look and to appear dull and heavy. Touching his wrist, Grace could feel his pulse fluttering beneath her fingers; his tongue looked brown and dry and his lips parched.

Through bouts of shivering and sweating Samuel Harper passed through one day to another, now never moving from his bed, and Grace, observing him, began to fear for his life. When Dr Harrison called on one of the later mornings she asked him for his thoughts and his prognosis. He stood before her in the kitchen and after a moment of consideration said:

'Are there other close members of your family?'

'He has a sister – my aunt in Remmer Ridge.'

'Could she get here without too much trouble?'

The doctor's words caused Grace's heart to lurch, for there was no escaping the meaning behind them. 'Oh,' she said, and again, 'Oh.' And then, miserably, 'Yes, she can get here in a relatively short time.'

He reached out and briefly, gently touched a hand to her upper arm. 'Then if I were you, I would write to her at once.' He paused and added, 'At once.'

The next morning at just after twelve o'clock Aunt Edie, with her little fox terrier Tippy under her arm, was boarding a train for Liddiston. She had been at work in the kitchen earlier that morning when Grace's letter had been delivered. It had been marked urgent. Once Mrs Edie Winslow had read the letter, however, she quickly organized her departure, and within an hour she had left the house.

She arrived at Bramble House later that afternoon, travelling by cab from Liddiston station, and was met by Grace as she hurried across the yard.

Grace was in tears, and seeing the tears, her aunt could see at once that she was too late.

Chapter Six

Rain showers fell on several of the days preceding the funeral, but on the day of the burial itself the sun shone brightly again, shining on the bleached stones of the church graveyard and shimmering on the leaves of the rowan tree that stood in their midst. As custom forbade women's attendance at funerals Grace and her aunt – and Billy with them – remained at Bramble House while the coffin holding Samuel Harper's body was carried to its last resting place.

Afterwards the few neighbours and friends who had attended the service and the burial came to the house where Grace and her aunt, helped by Mrs Tanner, served tea, parsnip wine, ale, sandwiches and cakes.

Once or twice Grace had found herself wondering whether Stephen might appear. After all, he had written a letter of condolence to her on hearing of her father's death. But no, he had not attended the funeral. Not, Grace told herself, that she had expected him to. Such an appearance could only have made matters worse where he and Grace were concerned.

The tears of Grace and Billy had dried now. They had wept over the days past, unable to believe that such a catastrophe had taken place; how could it? How could so much have hinged upon one minute incident? – an incident that for all its seeming trivialness had destroyed the rest of their happiness and their peace of mind.

*

When the last of the mourners had left the house, the women cleared away the remains of the food and drink and washed the dishes. Afterwards, when Mrs Tanner had left, and Billy had gone upstairs to change back into his everyday clothes, Grace and Aunt Edie sat in the parlour with further cups of tea. It had been agreed that her aunt would remain at the house for two more days at which time Grace would drive her to the station.

Sitting in Samuel's favourite chair, Aunt Edie, still wearing her little feathered hat perched on her red hair, stirred her tea and took a sip, then, looking down at her little dog, which sat looking up expectantly, she patted her ample lap, and said indulgently, 'Come on, then, Tippy, there's a good boy. I can't bend. Come on up with Mamma.'

She patted her lap again and the little dog managed, after one unsuccessful attempt, to leap up. Aunt Edie held her cup and saucer up out of the way as he turned in a circle and settled into his familiar, comfortable nest.

'So, Gracie,' Aunt Edie said, now giving her attention to her niece, 'what are you going to do now? Have you given any thought to the future?'

Grace would have been happy to give a satisfactory answer, but she had no such thing to give. She had had several days now to think on her situation, and that of her brother. Her father had left the simplest will leaving whatever he owned to be shared between his surviving children – the share of Billy to come to him at the age of eighteen. But how much there would be, Grace was sure, would only be very little. And certainly not enough to free them from uncertainty and concern.

'I really don't know, Aunt,' Grace said.

'You'll be looking for another position, of course.'

'Yes, of course. I intended to do so before this – and would have if Father had not been taken sick. Then everything happened so fast; there was no time for anything.'

84

'Well, you'll need to move fast, won't you?'

'I shall indeed.' Grace didn't need reminding of the precariousness of the situation. 'But I'm hoping to get a little more time.'

'What do you mean?'

'In the house. The lease is up for renewal in less than three weeks. We're paid up till then. I hope to be able to go and see the landlord next week. I've written to ask for a meeting about the lease. Pappy rarely spoke about him, but he seems a decent enough man. I had a very nice letter of condolence from him the other day. I don't think he'd see us out on the street.'

'What do you hope he'll do for you?'

'Well, I'm hoping he'll give us a while longer in the house to enable us to get things sorted out. As things are, there won't be enough time, not with the auction and everything. I just hope I can get a position soon, and then find a place where we can live.'

'And what if you can't?' Aunt Edie said. 'What will you do then? And even with a new position you won't be able to get very much in the way of lodgings – not for the two of you, anyway. A governess's wages won't stretch very far.'

A brief silence fell and then Grace said, 'Billy'll be down in a minute, Aunt; we mustn't speak of this in front of him. He'll only worry.'

Billy was the factor that was uppermost in Grace's mind. She had to make sure that he was cared for, and he had to have his schooling too. She could find employment again, she was sure, but at the same time she had to provide a home for her brother.

Footfalls sounded on the stairs, and Grace looked to her aunt. 'Here he is now. We'll talk about something else.'

The next morning Grace, Billy and Aunt Edie made their way to the churchyard and there stood at the graveside where their father now lay with his wife. The flowers were wilting under the August sun. Later, Grace decided, she would arrange for an inscription for her father to be added to the stone.

As they stood there they heard the sound of a horse's hoofs and, turning, saw Mr Edward Spencer pulling up his mare at the lych gate. After tethering his horse he came into the churchyard, taking off his hat as he came, his tall figure stepping out on the neatly trimmed grass between the graves. Reaching Grace's side, he gave a sombre little smile and put out his hand to her: 'Miss Grace,' then shook the hand of Billy.

Grace introduced him to Aunt Edie, and after they had shaken hands she thanked him for the letter of condolence that had come from him and Mrs Spencer.

'I would have come to the funeral,' he said, 'but I was away. So I thought I'd come over today and pay my respects.'

Grace thanked him again, then said, 'Your little bureau, Mr Spencer – I'm very glad to be able to tell you that Father was able to complete it before he – died. Some time in the next few days Billy and I will bring it over in the trap.'

He was grateful, he said, but it would be as easy for him to call and collect it, and Grace said, 'Whatever is most convenient for you.'

'Yes, I'll come and collect it,' he said. 'I'm sure that you'll have enough to think about over the coming days without bothering yourself about such a minor thing.'

Grace was pleased, and particularly glad to see that he had shown her father this last token of respect.

'Well, I'll leave you now,' he said and bowed to the ladies before putting his hat back on. Then he turned and stepped away, heading towards the lych gate and his horse. Seconds later Grace saw him astride his horse and riding away.

*

On the Friday morning Grace helped Aunt Edie up into the trap. It was not an easy operation and the whole contrivance shook a little as the woman hoisted her bulk on board. Grace then handed up Tippy to her, who was at once settled to rest on the floor at his mistress's feet. 'Oh, dear,' Aunt Edie cackled as she shifted in her seat, making the trap jiggle on its axle, 'Tippy, you're overweight. We'll have to cut down on your dinners, my lad, I can see that.'

It was Grace's intention to drive her aunt to Liddiston station for her train. Billy had asked if he might go along with them for the ride, but Grace had demurred at his request; with the weight of the trap and herself, she had hinted, in addition to the considerable weight of Aunt Edie, she feared it might be too much for Robin to deal with.

After checking that all belongings were safely aboard, they were all set. And Grace, clicking her tongue, said to the pony, almost with a note of pleading in her voice: 'All right, let's be off, Robin. And please – don't give me any difficulties today. I have enough already. I know you'd far rather that Pappy were here holding the reins – and so would we. But for the time being you'll have to be like the rest of us and make the best of what there is.'

On returning home after leaving her aunt at the station, Grace unhitched and stabled the horse and went into the house. The first thing she saw when she entered the kitchen was a note in Billy's round hand saying: GONE TO SEE MR TIMMINS TO HELP OUT. HOPE THAT'S ALL RIGHT. BACK LATER. She didn't blame the boy. He was lost and needed diversions like anybody else. Slowly she took off her hat. Now she was alone in the house – and how silent it all seemed. The ticking of the clock seemed unnaturally loud, and she became aware also of the creak of the house's timbers. She had been alone in the house before, but never like this. In the past there had always been the promise of movement and sound. Not today; never again would she look around and see her father's tall figure come stooping in at the kitchen door. Never again could she go over the yard to his workshop and find him labouring over his carpentry. And soon after her father's death the house had become busy with the comings and goings of its occupants. And they had been welcome distractions, distractions that had prevented her from dwelling on the realities. Now the distractions were gone, and she was forced to face up to the situation. 'Oh, Pappy . . .' she breathed. She felt so close to tears, and it was all she could do not to give in and give herself up to weeping. Not only was it the grief for her father, but the desperate circumstances in which she and Billy found themselves. She could only hope and pray that at least her coming meeting with Mr Grennell, the landlord, would ease the severity of their plight.

On writing to Mr Grennell, Grace had arranged an appointment to see him at his small office in Corster on Monday at two in the afternoon.

On the appointed day Grace waited outside the Golden Scythe public house for an omnibus that would take her into Liddiston, from where she would catch the train to Corster.

On arrival in the town she was in plenty of time for her interview; a good deal too early, in fact, and to kill a little time she bought a newspaper. Then, taking a seat in the main square, in the shade of a chestnut tree, she studied the classified advertisements in search of what might be a suitable position.

When it was close to the appointed time she rose and set off for the street wherein Mr Grennell conducted his business.

Grace had never been to the landlord's offices before, and indeed had only seen the man himself from a distance when once out walking in the area with her father. Now, arriving at the address, she discovered that half of the ground floor of the small house was occupied by another businessman, an accountant. Both Mr Grennell and his tenant – for that was what the other man was – had signs posted outside, and Grace, touching at her hat, and smoothing down her dress, entered beneath the sign over the arched entrance way. A moment later she was knocking at the landlord's door.

The door was opened by Mr Grennell himself, smiling at her from a height not that much above her own, and then extending his hand in greeting.

'Miss Harper,' he said, beaming. 'You're very prompt. Well done. Do please come in and sit down.'

While he opened the door wider and moved aside to allow her to pass through, Grace stepped into his office. There were two chairs placed before his desk and Grace moved to the one he indicated. He watched as she settled in the chair and then moved around behind his desk and sat facing her.

He was a man of sixty or so, Grace guessed. Wearing a grey striped suit and stiff collar, he had a smooth complexion, silver-grey hair, and blue eyes framed by wire-rim spectacles. His smile was warm and affable, and Grace at once felt a sense of hopeful anticipation.

It was apparent from the look of the office that the man worked alone there. And was kept occupied too; his desk was littered with papers, some spread out on the desk's surface, others in wire trays. Behind him were shelves bearing a number of box files and books. Clearly Bramble House was not the only property of which he was landlord.

Now the man clasped his hands before him on the desktop and gave Grace a smile, a smile touched with an air of compassion.

'Let me say at once, Miss Harper,' he said, 'how very sorry I was to hear of the death of your father.'

Grace thanked him, and thanked him also for his letter of condolence.

'Not at all,' he said, brushing aside her thanks. 'I'm sure it must have been a dreadful blow to you. Indeed, I've no doubt it still is.'

Grace thanked him again, adding, 'It is difficult, of course, but –' here she shrugged, 'one has to get on with things.'

'Indeed one does – and one is helped by such a sensible attitude. Pragmatism is at times the only course, I'm sure you'll find.'

Grace nodded.

Mr Grennell went on, 'Your father and I did not have occasion to meet on any regular basis – he usually paid my agent – but when we did meet I always found him to be the most upright and ethical of men. I was saying as much to Mrs Grennell just yesterday when I mentioned that you were coming in to see me. Still,' he added with a sympathetic smile, 'I'm quite sure you don't need to be reminded of his qualities.' He gave a little nod. 'So let us, without further ado, get to the business of your visit here today.' He smiled again. 'Tell me, please, what can we do for you?'

Grace took a breath. 'Mr Grennell,' she said, 'I've come to see you as I'm in something of a precarious situation.'

He said nothing, but waited for her to go on.

'I believe, Mr Grennell,' Grace continued, 'that going by what my father said, and from looking through his papers, our rent is paid up for the next two weeks – a little less than two weeks – and then the lease is up for renewal.'

Without the need to consult any document he gave a brief, decisive little nod and said, 'On the tenth, precisely.'

'At which time,' Grace said, 'the new lease and the next six months' rent will be due.'

She came to a stop, almost as if waiting for him to confirm the situation, but he said nothing, keeping silent as if any confirmation of her words was unnecessary.

'It is,' Grace said, more hesitantly than she intended, 'a large sum, and –'

He broke in here, saying: 'A large sum, I wouldn't say such.'

'No, I mean – well – relatively speaking, if you see what I mean.'

He waited.

'What I want to say,' Grace said, 'is that I am not in a position to renew the lease.'

'But?' he said. 'Can I hear a little "but" hovering there somewhere?'

'The fact is,' she said, 'we can't possibly afford to keep it on. So – I was wondering if you might consent to let me rent it from you for a much shorter term.'

There, it was said, and he was still smiling.

'For precisely how long did you have in mind?' he said.

'A – a month. That should be long enough to see us settled.'

'I see,' he said. 'And what do you hope to achieve in that month?'

'Well, I hope by that time to have found perhaps a couple of rooms somewhere. Somewhere where my brother and I can live until we get everything sorted out.'

'What is your present situation?'

'I've been earning my living as a governess, and – well, I'm not in employment at the moment, but I'm applying for several positions – not only around the area of Green Shipton but also in places further afield. I need a position which is on a daily, visiting basis. A post as live-in governess would not suit, as I wouldn't be able to take my young brother with me.'

'How old is he?'

'He's eight, coming up to nine.'

'And you, of course, are now responsible for him.'

'He has no one else. We just have one another.'

He nodded, sighing. 'It's a difficult situation. You say you've been earning your living as a governess . . .'

'Until just a month ago. I left because my two pupils no longer have need of a governess; they're going off to boarding school.' She added quickly, 'I have excellent references from my post.'

'I've no doubt you have.' He fell silent for a moment while he simply looked at her. 'And have you no other prospects on the horizon?'

'Prospects? No, all I have is my work. I'm sorry to say that my father left very little.'

'No, I mean – prospects in other ways. I wondered whether perhaps there might be something else – perhaps a marriage in the offing.'

'– No. Nothing like that.'

He smiled. 'No engagement imminent? No handsome young suitor knocking on your door? A pretty girl like you, I can't believe it.'

Grace felt herself colouring slightly, and could not meet the man's twinkling eyes. 'No,' she said, 'there's no one.'

'Oh, well,' he said, nodding his head sagely, 'just give it time. Give it time.'

Trying to get the conversation back onto the rails, Grace said, 'A month really ought to see us all right, Mr Grennell. Just a month. I've already been in touch with the auctioneers. All our possessions are to go under the hammer in three weeks. We shall be left with the very barest essentials for living. But it doesn't have to be for long.'

'Oh, dear,' he said, shaking his head, 'that sounds most distressing for you.'

She shrugged. 'I hate the thought of it, but what else are

we to do? The house has been my home all my life, and inside it is everything I grew up with. All those things that belonged to my mother and my father. But what else is to be done? We can't take the things with us.'

'Of course not.'

'So you see, a month would enable me to sell off all the things from the house and also find work and somewhere decent for my brother and me to stay.'

'And do you have funds for that extra month's rent?' he asked.

'I was hoping to let you have it once our effects have been sold.'

'I see – you don't plan to pay me in advance, then?'

Grace was silent at this.

'It is the usual procedure,' he said.

'I know,' Grace said again. 'But really, Mr Grennell, I'll get the money to you just as soon as I can.'

He smiled at this. 'That is how we live, we property owners. You don't think I'm being mercenary, I hope. But everyone has to live. I own a number of properties over the area, and if you only knew the number of times tenants come asking for favours. And I suppose they all mean well; they all mean it when they say they'll pay. And of course one would like to help. But at the same time of course one is not running a benevolent society.' He sighed, gave a little shrug. 'There is an old Chinese proverb which I've found to have a certain measure of truth in it: *He who does a good deed will assuredly be made to pay the price.*'

Grace could feel herself colouring again. 'We shall have the money,' she said. 'The auction will bring in more than enough. For one thing, Father has certain carpentry tools – and of excellent quality – and they'll fetch something. If you can help us I can faithfully promise that I'll pay you. I wouldn't have that debt hanging over my head. For one thing, I've got too much pride.'

She could hear herself almost begging him, and felt her humiliation like a cloak, heavy and all encompassing, and the shame stung at her eyes and brought a lump to her throat. In moments Mr Grennell was getting up from his chair and standing behind his desk.

'Ah – Miss Harper,' he said, catching a brief glimpse of the tears threatening in her eyes, 'I don't see any reason for you to be upset. I'm just speaking generally – having had so many – disappointing experiences over the years. Please – don't be upset.'

'I meant it,' Grace said, pulling herself up, ' – when I said you would be paid – I meant it.' She paused then added, 'I'm my father's daughter and he was an honest and honourable man.'

'I'm sure.'

'So,' Grace said after a moment, 'Mr Grennell – can you help me?'

He stood there a second longer, one hand raised to touch his pink chin, then moved around the desk and stepped towards the empty chair at Grace's side. Sitting down in it, he clasped his hands before him and leaned slightly towards her.

'That's better,' he said, '– get rid of that barrier of the desk – and now let's talk and see if we can't sort something out between us.'

Grace waited, her little bag clutched before her on her knees. She could see a warmth in his smile, and her hopes rose.

'How would it be if I also reduced the rent a little for this period of a month?' Mr Grennell said. 'That would help you, wouldn't it?'

She could scarcely believe what she was hearing. Was he quite serious? Briefly she frowned, studying his expression. But no, his eyes were touched by his smile, and his smile looked sympathetic.

'I'd like you to understand that I do understand your particular circumstances – and I am not unsympathetic. Far from it. I'd like to do what I can to help you and your brother. God knows, no one would wish to see the two of you out on the street.'

Grace felt the greatest relief at his words. 'Then you will help us?' she said.

'Indeed, yes. A month isn't so very long, and if it will enable you and your brother to get settled, then I'll be more than happy to help.' He paused. 'And as for the financial amount, I think we could see our way to reducing it by a third.'

'Oh – thank you so much.'

In her great sense of relief, Grace reached out and took his hand. He grasped her hand and shook it. 'There,' he said. 'We've made a pact; we've shaken hands on it.'

'Thank you. Oh, thank you.'

And he still held her hand, and now he leaned across the space between, closer, and through the thin cotton of her gloves she could feel the warmth of his skin.

'You appear to me to be a most kind, considerate, and deserving young lady,' he said. 'And I'm sure you were a credit to your late father. Indeed, I should think that any man would be glad to have you for a daughter.' Then without warning, his right hand moved up to her face, touching at the softness of her cheek. Gently he brushed his fingertips over her skin. 'Any man,' he said.

Grace drew back a little, stiffening in the chair, but he still held her hand.

'And if you needed to stay on in the house for longer,' he went on, 'I can't see any reason you should not. And I'll be happy to call in and make sure that you're – comfortable.'

Before Grace could make a move to stop him, his hand had moved to the back of her neck and pulled her head forward. In the same moment he leaned closer and planted

95

a wide, moist kiss on her mouth. His breath smelled of parma violets and tobacco. Quickly, without hesitating for a moment, she leapt to her feet, brushing his hands aside. Breathing heavily, she wiped the back of her gloved hand across her mouth. At the same time tears of shame sprang to her eyes.

'Mr Grennell . . .' Again she wiped her mouth with her hand. 'Mr Grennell, you've made a great mistake.'

He had looked a little taken aback by her violent response, but now he affected a rather casual air. 'Well,' he said, getting to his feet, 'I wouldn't go so far as to say a *great* mistake. If indeed I've made a mistake at all.'

'Well, you've made a mistake in *me*,' Grace said. Her hat had gone slightly askew in the movement of the kiss, and she put up a hand and adjusted it. 'I don't know where you might have got the notion, but I'm not the kind of person who can be bought for a month's rent.'

'Calm down, calm down,' he said, looking not greatly moved as Grace stood there with her breast heaving, glowering at him. 'You said earlier that you have pride.' He nodded. 'Well, yes, I can see that. But I do think it's a bit misplaced.' Raising one eyebrow, he added a little sardonically, 'For one thing, I'm wondering if you can *afford* such pride. I always bear in mind that every man has his price – and that goes for every woman too.'

Grace opened her mouth to speak in protest, but no words would come. In another moment she was turning and moving towards the door. Grennell remained where he was, his expression showing no measure of distress as she opened the door.

'Don't forget, then,' Mr Grennell said, 'be ready with the house keys. I'll expect to receive them from you when I call round.'

Grace, about to close the door, turned on the spot and looked at him.

'But you said – you said I could stay on for a further month.'

'I don't recall saying any such thing,' he said.

'But – we shook hands on it.'

'My dear young lady,' he said, 'you have a powerful imagination. You must be careful with it, lest it get you into trouble.'

Grace stood staring at him. 'Mr Grennell, how can you do this? How can you be so unkind?'

'Unkind, my dear?' he said, gazing back at her with wide eyes. 'Kindness doesn't come into this. I've no time for sentiment; I'm a businessman.' He moved around to stand behind his desk. 'Now,' he said, 'I'm also a busy man, so if there's nothing else for the present . . .?' He gestured towards her with a little motion of his hand. 'And please be careful not to slam the door when you close it.'

The sun was shining brightly out of a sky that was clear apart from odd wisps of cloud on the horizon as Grace alighted from the train at Liddiston. She could see that the walk in front of her to Green Shipton was to be a warm affair. Nevertheless it had to be done. She could not give in to her desires and hire a cab. There simply was not the money. If she had learned to be frugal in the recent past, she must make even greater efforts now.

Less than two weeks, she said to herself, as she walked. Less than two weeks. The phrase went through her brain. She could scarcely believe it. She had set out to see the landlord with such strong feelings of hope, and she had thought the meeting was going well. But then suddenly everything had fallen apart. How could I have been so naïve? she asked herself. She was not a child. Should she not have seen it coming? But she had allowed herself to be swept along, believing in the man's good nature. Less than two weeks – and she and Billy would have to be out of the house.

But what was she going to do? There would not now be time for the goods to be auctioned off. Therefore she would have to find some other way of disposing of everything. Which would probably mean getting in touch with a house clearer. Losing the sale of their possessions through auction would mean that she would lose so much of their value, for a dealer would take everything, lock, stock and barrel, regardless of the value of individual items. And she needed to get as much money as possible. All she had was her wages from Mr Marren and the little that her father had left in cash. All told, it amounted to not very much – certainly not enough to keep her and Billy in food and clothes and shelter for very long.

Even so, she and Billy would very quickly have to search around and find lodgings somewhere. She had expected to have to do such a thing in any case, but now there was very little time. She had been casting her eyes about, and asking questions of neighbours, in the hope of learning about available rooms for rent, somewhere, but there were so few available. One thing she had come to realize was that she and Billy would probably have to move to Corster or some other town.

At last Grace reached Green Shipton and headed along the lane towards Bramble House. As she reached the house and turned into the yard she saw a pony and trap standing there. It took her just a few seconds to recognize that it belonged to Mr Spencer.

As she stopped beside it she heard the scrape of footsteps on the cobbles, and turned to see Edward Spencer coming round the side of the house. He smiled broadly when he saw her. 'Ah, Miss Grace, you're here.'

Grace smiled in reply. 'Hello, Mr Spencer.'

'I've just seen young Billy,' he said, gesturing towards the house. 'He said you'd gone off out on business.'

'Yes,' she said, 'I've been into Corster.'

She did not say more on the subject, and after a moment's pause he said, 'I came round for the bureau.'

'The bureau – oh, yes, of course.' She had forgotten about the Spencers' bureau. The payment for it could not have come at a better time.

'I didn't want to come round immediately after the funeral,' he said. 'Perhaps I should have written first – to see whether it's convenient.'

'It's fine,' she said. 'It's fine.'

Turning, she stepped away across the yard. 'It's in my father's workshop. He left it all ready to be transported. He would have delivered it to you if he hadn't fallen sick.'

The man followed her. 'I've no doubt he would,' he said.

It was the first time she had been inside the workshop since her father had taken to his bed. Now, without his presence, and without the knowledge that his presence would soon again be there, the place had a forlorn air. The tools and everything else were just as he had left them, everything neatly in its place, the piece, unfinished, that he had been working on still lying on the bench.

The bureau, wrapped in pieces of cloth for protection, was standing to one side. Grace carefully pulled aside some of the covering and exposed the polished cabinet beneath.

'It looks beautiful,' Mr Spencer said. 'Just beautiful. Mrs Spencer will love it.'

When the bureau had been stowed safely in the trap he took out his purse and took money from it. Then into her hand he counted out coins.

Grace looked at the money in her palm and said, 'You've given me too much by a shilling.'

'No matter,' he said. 'I'm well pleased with the bargain.'

'No, please,' she said, 'you struck the deal with my father, and a deal's a deal. I know how much it was for; he wrote everything down.'

'No, honestly –'

He began to protest again, but Grace cut in, holding out the coin. 'Mr Spencer, please take it. We must stick to what is right, what was agreed.'

'Very well, if you insist.' He took the shilling from her and put it back in his purse.

'I'll write you out a receipt.' She turned, about to move to the workshop again, but he waved a hand to halt her.

'That's not necessary.'

'Very well.' She dropped the coins he had given her into her bag. She expected him then to climb up into the trap and be away, but he remained there, for a moment silent, then he said:

'How are you now? Are things getting a little easier?'

'Well – there's certainly a good deal to do. Though perhaps in some ways that's all to the good. It takes one's mind off things. There's not much time for dwelling on unhappiness.'

'I'm sure there isn't.' He paused. 'You do seem rather – preoccupied at the moment. Though it's hardly to be wondered at.'

She nodded. 'I suppose I am. I haven't had the most successful morning.'

'Is it anything that I could help with?'

'No – but thank you, anyway.'

'Would you care to tell me what it is?' Then he smiled. 'Or do tell me to mind my own affairs, if you wish.'

She shrugged. 'Well, there's no harm in telling you. I've been to see the landlord in Corster – to ask if he could let us stay on for a further month. I'm afraid he ended up refusing.' She would say nothing of the events that had led to his reneging on their agreement; it would serve no purpose, added to which it was an embarrassment she wanted to put behind her.

'Well, that's an unfriendly thing to do, I must say,' Mr Spencer said. 'Surely he can't have someone already waiting to move in. It'll take him a while to let the place anyway, I should think. Who is this man, by the way?'

'His name is Grennell.'

'I think I've heard of him.' Mr Spencer nodded. 'Did he give any reason for his refusal?'

'Oh, Mr Spencer,' Grace said, 'I'd really rather not talk about it, truly. I need to put my mind to dealing with the situation we're in. We have to be out of here by the tenth of next month.'

He looked at her a little more closely at this, and she, feeling his eyes upon her, felt as if he could read her thoughts, read the shame she felt at the experience at Grennell's hands.

'Well, it certainly doesn't give you much time, that's for sure,' he said, stroking his chin. 'What do you plan to do with all your possessions?'

'I wish I had the answer to that. I had planned to bring in the auctioneers, but now there won't be time. It looks as if I shall have to find a dealer who will just take everything off my hands. I can't see any other course.'

'I think that might be the only thing. I do know one or two dealers. If you like, I could get in touch with them and see what their situation is. Would you like me to do that?'

The offer was so welcome. How could she refuse? 'Well,' she said, 'I have to say that I think that is most kind of you. I honestly don't quite know where to begin.'

And all at once the events of the past weeks, her father's illness and death, and then that morning's encounter with Mr Grennell and all that it entailed, seemed to push her beyond the edge of her control. Like a cup being overfilled, she was suddenly incapable of containing herself, and tears welled into her eyes and threatened to spill over.

She spoke no word, but just stood on the cobbles, one hand clenched at her mouth, fighting to keep the tears at bay.

'Oh, Grace – Miss Grace.' Mr Spencer started to reach out to her, but then drew back his hand. 'Please – I can't stand to see you cry. Tell me what it is. I'm sure it can all be sorted out.'

When she said nothing, he gestured towards the house behind her. 'Shall we go inside? I think you should sit down. We'll have some tea and perhaps you'll tell me what it is. Please?'

She took a breath and brought herself more nearly under control. 'Billy's indoors,' she said. 'I don't want him to see me upset. His world's all topsy turvy as it is.'

She stepped away, moving across the yard, purposeless, directionless, coming to a halt beside the well. Mr Spencer hesitated a moment then moved to stand facing her again.

'So you have to be out of here in less than a fortnight?' he said.

'According to Mr Grennell, yes.' She shrugged. 'Of course, he's acting perfectly within the law, so I can't challenge him in any way. I've just got to find somewhere else to live, and that's that. And find a place soon.'

'D'you have anything in mind?'

'I shall go out tomorrow and start looking. I bought a copy of the local paper when I was in Corster this morning, so perhaps there'll be something advertised in it. I have to find a new post too. It's not enough just to find a place to live, I also have to find some means of paying for it.'

He stood in silence for a few moments, then said, 'I'll make some enquiries in the area. Perhaps someone will know of some available, suitable rooms. Do you mind where you go? Within reason?'

'No, I don't mind. So long as it's not the ends of the earth. I just need to find a decent place for the two of us – and where Billy can go to school. Perhaps I should find a position first – wherever it might be – and then concentrate on finding somewhere to live. The trouble is, there's so little time.'

He nodded. 'Well, let's see what we can do. In the meantime, don't worry about finding a dealer to take your things. I'll go and see one now and try to arrange for him to come and see you.'

'Oh, that would be so kind of you,' she said.

'Well, you won't get a lot for it, one never does in that kind of transaction, but at least it will be off your hands and you'll have a little something.'

He drew some water for the pony, and watched as it drank its fill. Then he said goodbye and climbed up into the driver's seat of the trap.

Grace watched as the vehicle turned out of the yard and into the lane, then she went round the rear of the yard and into the house. There was no time to dwell on her problems. She must try to get them sorted out. In the meantime Billy would be wanting his dinner.

That evening, Billy said his goodnights to Grace preparatory to going up to the little room in which he now slept alone. 'Are you coming up to see me?' he asked as he took up the lighted candle, and Grace replied, 'Of course. When do I not?' Their mother had always gone up to see him safe in bed, and since her death it had fallen upon Grace or their father to give this particular little comfort. Now with their father gone, it was down to Grace alone.

She continued with her mending for five more minutes, then put it aside and went up the stairs. A tap on Billy's door, followed by a called 'Come in,' and she opened the door and went inside.

In the light of the bedside candle Billy lay with his eyes open, the sheet drawn up to his chin. As she moved to the bed he slid over under the covers to allow her space to sit. She patted his knees. 'Are you all right?' she said as she sat down.

'Yes.'

'Did you have a good day today at the farm?'

'Yes.'

'Is it all going well? – Mr Timmins's harvest?'

'Yes. I heard Mr Timmins say they'll start with the barley tomorrow.'

'And will you be going back there to help?'

'Yes, if it's all right.' There was a slightly anxious note in his voice, as if he feared being forbidden.

'Of course it's all right. Just so long as you're wanted there, and that you don't get given too much to do.'

'No, I can do it.'

'I'm sure you can.'

His hand came out from under the covers and briefly brushed at her wrist. 'Do we still have to leave, Grace?'

'I'm afraid so. And there's something I haven't told you. We have to leave earlier than I'd anticipated. We have to be gone from here in less than two weeks.'

In the dim light she could see the look of consternation that flashed into his eyes and settled. 'But the harvest won't be in by that time.'

Grace shrugged. 'Well – I'm sorry about that. But we don't have any choice.'

'Everything's changing again,' he said.

'I know. I'm sorry.'

A little silence fell in the room. In the quiet Grace could here the singing of the blackbird in the cherry tree beyond the window. Then Billy said:

'Grace . . .?'

'Yes? What is it?'

'Pappy used to look after us, Grace, didn't he?'

'Yes, he did, and very well too.'

'Yes.'

'Yes, indeed.'

'Who's going to do it now? Who's going to look after us now?'

'I am,' Grace said. 'I am.'

Chapter Seven

'No, I agree it isn't a large room,' the woman said in response to Grace's comment, 'but it's a pleasant room. And the outlook is very nice.'

Mrs Packerman was in her late forties, with greying hair, a large chin, and a heavy bosom. She wore an apron and a little heart-shaped lace cap, and, right now, an expression of jolliness and good humour. She was the landlady of a lodging house situated just off one of the main streets in Corster, and Grace was there because she had seen in the window the sign saying Rooms to Rent.

Grace stood in the middle of the room – or as close to the middle as it was possible to get, what with the bed, the wardrobe, a chest of drawers and a washstand and sundry other items taking up so much space.

'Really,' Grace said, 'I was hoping to find a larger room – with two beds in it. To have a bed for my little brother . . .'

'Well, that could come expensive, dear,' Mrs Packerman said. 'How old's your brother, anyway?'

'He's eight.'

The woman gave the hint of a snort and a little chuckle. 'Eight – and expects a bed of his own? Whatever next. Oh, he sounds a very grand young man. Perhaps he'll be too grand for the likes of us.'

'It's not that,' Grace said. 'But I'm a restless sleeper lately, and he needs to get his rest.'

'Well, if you're set on it, I could get the truckle out for him. He'd be comfortable enough on that. Mind you, it'd cost extra – what with all fresh bedding to be supplied. It's all extra work, my dear.'

Grace said nothing, and Mrs Packerman waited; she could not but be aware of Grace's lack of enthusiasm. 'Well, it's up to you, dear,' she said. 'I'm sure you won't find anything similar at a better price.'

Grace nodded. She was aware of this. And she could not continue as she was. She had come into Corster that morning with the express purpose of finding somewhere for Billy and herself to stay. Time was passing all too swiftly, and if she didn't find a place soon, the two of them would find themselves on the street. She had chosen to look in Corster as, being a town, it was certain to offer more opportunities. And also, once she was living there she would surely find it a more convenient place from which to seek out work.

This lodging house was the fifth one that Grace had visited, and with all its drawbacks, it nevertheless looked to be the most promising. Two of the others had just been far too expensive, a third had refused to have Billy there – 'Sorry, miss, but no children,' – and a fourth had been situated next to an abattoir, and the smells had so permeated the offered room that Grace had felt almost sick.

So this one was the best that she had seen. And, she reminded herself, it didn't have to be perfect; it wasn't for ever, only until she got settled with a position. Then, once she was earning some money, she and Billy could look around and find something much nicer. Also, he could go back to school again, something he would want to do.

And she had to decide on a room without delay. Now there was only a week to go before Bramble House had to be given back to Mr Grennell. She had thought briefly of going to see him again and pleading for a little more time, perhaps appealing to his better nature. But she could not. She had her pride and it would not allow her to stoop so low. She would manage. She and Billy would manage. Taking it a day at a time, all their obstacles would be overcome.

'Yes,' she said to Mrs Packerman, 'I'll take the room.'

'And will you want the truckle, dear?'

'No. We'll manage without it, thank you.'

Mrs Packerman gave a broad smile. 'That's fine, then, dear. And I'm sure you won't regret it. When will you want it from?'

'A week today, if that's all right.'

'Yes, that's all right, dear. Though I shall need a deposit – the first week's rent.'

'Yes. Yes, of course.' Grace opened her purse and began to count out coins.

'And once you move in I shall want the remainder of a month's rent in advance.'

'A month's rent?' A month's rent would be such a large sum, and would make a great dent in her finances. 'Does it have to be a month?' she said.

'Oh, I'm afraid it does, dear. I've nothing against you personally, of course, as I don't know you. But if you were aware of the number who try to do a moonlight flit the day before the rent is due, you'd understand. Sorry, my dear. Take it or leave it, that's the way it is.'

'All right.' There was nothing else for it. Grace sighed. 'I'll have the money ready.'

After leaving Mrs Packerman's house Grace headed at once for home. There was no time to waste, for she had made an appointment for a dealer from Corster to visit Bramble House and look over the contents. The day before, she had been visited by one from Harbrook – a Mr Clemmer of Clemmer and Sons – the visit arranged by Mr Spencer who had gone to call on the man on Grace's behalf. The dealer, a house-clearer by trade, had not spent long at the house; he

108

hadn't needed to; from long experience he had cannily, with a practised eye, taken in the contents of the house and Samuel Harper's workshop.

Grace stood by waiting while he walked around. At least the livestock had already been sold, she reminded herself. Mr Timmins from the nearby farm had called the day before, and after some deliberation had made Grace an offer for the creatures. She had accepted it, and later that day he had come with one of his farmhands and taken the animals away. The chickens, the goat, the pig, all had gone. Most affecting of all, though, was the loss of the Robin, the pony. Grace and Billy had wept when saying their goodbyes to him, and the two of them had turned away as he had been hitched up to the trap and driven out of the yard for the last time. They would never see him again.

Now Mr Clemmer, having looked over the effects of the house and workshop, made Grace his offer. But the sum he had offered was so small, a pittance it seemed, and Grace had made a gentle protest.

Yes, he had said, it was true that there were two or three good pieces, but there was also a great deal that he would never sell. She could, if she wished, go to an antiques dealer who would come and do his cherry-picking and pay her for three or four items – but what about the rest of it? 'Do you want to be left with a house half full of worthless furniture and odds and ends?' he said. 'No dealer would go for that. Yet that's all you'd be left with.'

Then, seeing the dismay in her face, he had added, 'Well, you think about it and make up your mind. Let me know in the next day or two.'

And he had gone. And right away Grace had made enquiries about bringing another dealer to the house.

And now, the arrangements made, the man was due at 4.30.

By way of walking part of the way and taking a cab for

part of the way, Grace reached Bramble House just on four. And fifteen minutes later the clearer's wagon was pullling up in the yard and the man was climbing down.

The visit was over in no time at all; he was there an even shorter time than the previous dealer. Grace took him on a tour of the house, pointing out various items of furniture etc. that she thought would be of special interest, and at intervals he gave little non-committal nods and turned down the corners of his mouth, as if careful not to show a trace of enthusiasm. And Grace found herself becoming increasingly dismayed. How could he not look at the lovely pieces that her father had made for her mother and not be impressed? The trouble was, there were so few of them. And her spirits sank further when she showed the man into her father's workshop. He looked at Samuel's treasured carpentry tools and seemed to sum up their value in seconds. Outside in the yard he stood in silence for a moment or two, eyes screwed up and cast heavenwards, and then made Grace his offer. It was even smaller than that given by the previous dealer.

Was that the best he could do? she asked. Surely it was worth more than that.

'I'm sorry, miss, but it is,' the man said. 'And I doubt you'll get a better offer. Specially seeing as you've such little time left.'

And that was part of the problem, Grace said to herself. Knowing that she had so little time before she had to vacate the house, any dealer would know that she was in the very weakest position. No matter how much she might have wished to, she could not hold out for a good price; there simply wasn't time.

When the man had gone, with Grace having told him that she would think about his offer – 'Well, don't be too long about it,' he had said – she went back into the house and sat down at her little desk and immediately wrote to Mr

Clemmer, the first dealer, and informed him that she would accept his offer. She would expect him, she added, on Friday the 9th of August which was the penultimate day of tenancy at the house. When the letter was finished, she signed and sealed it in an envelope. She would take it to the post office first thing in the morning.

Also, in the morning she would send off further applications for positions. She had seen two more advertised in the papers, and she must look into them. So far she had had no luck. She had applied for four situations but for various reasons they had not worked out. One of them had offered insultingly low wages while at the same time demanding a great deal of work – the task of teaching five children under eleven was, in Grace's eyes, a little more than she would wish to take on. Not only that but it was requested that on regular occasions she would have to sleep over at the house. A second advertised position turned out to be for that of a resident governess, and since Grace had the responsibility of caring for Billy, the post was of course out of the question. A third situation would have been suitable, except that the prospective employer didn't want the position filled for another two months, and Grace had to find something long before that time. The fourth situation she applied for turned out to have been filled by the time she turned up for her interview. She would persevere, however. In time she was bound to find something suitable. The trouble was, time was not on her side.

Grace busied herself about the house, and a little later Billy came in, having spent the day at Timmins's farm, helping with the harvest and generally giving a hand where he could. At the kitchen sink he washed his hands and face as Grace stood watching him. He would be so sorry to leave this place, she knew. And to go and live in the town would be an added cause for disappointment. All through the summer holiday he had spent as much time as he could at the farm, not only enjoying his labours and the feeling of being useful, but also earning a few pence for his efforts. Soon it must all come to an end, though: in just a week they would be leaving Bramble House – and who could say what the future would hold?

Billy was hungry as usual, so as he sat down at the kitchen table Grace began to prepare some little refreshment for him, cutting a slice of bread and spreading it with strawberry jam. He was just about to begin eating when there was the sound of a horse's hoofs in the yard, and looking through the open door they saw a horse and rider walk by. At once Billy got up from his chair and went to the door, turning back to Grace a moment later to say, 'It's a man. I don't know who. I've never seen him before.'

'Come back and sit down,' Grace told him, then smoothed her hair and walked to the open door.

As she reached it and looked out the man was hitching up the horse to the stanchion, and as he turned Grace recognized him. It was Mr Rhind, Mr Spencer's man.

She remained standing in the doorway as he walked towards her across the yard, touching his hat as he came.

'Miss Harper,' he said as he came to a stop before her, 'I've come to bring a message from the missis at Asterleigh House.' He spoke rather quickly. There was no charm about the man, no graciousness in his manner of speech to her. He stood as if uncomfortable in the situation, as if reluctant to be there and anxious to get the meeting over with.

'Yes?' Grace said. 'Mr Rhind, isn't it?'

He nodded. As she faced him she thought again of the words he had spoken to her as she had got down from the trap on her return from Corster following her visit to the town. And thinking of them again she had to ask herself whether she had heard aright.

112

Without wasting time, he said, 'Mrs Spencer – she'd like you to come to the house tomorrow.' He looked past her, his eyes taking in Billy as he stood beside the table. 'And your young brother too,' he added. 'You're to take him along with you.'

'Did she say what for?' Grace asked. 'What is the reason?'

'It's not for me to know Mrs Spencer's mind,' he said. 'She doesn't confide in me. She merely instructed me to pass on the message – that you go and see her tomorrow, you and your brother. If you're able to, then I'm to bring the trap for you at ten o'clock.'

Grace turned in the doorway and looked at Billy who stood there listening, open-mouthed. 'Did you hear that, Billy? No time at the farm for you tomorrow. We're going to Asterleigh House.'

Billy nodded in reply, and Grace turned back to the man.

'Thank you,' she said. 'Please tell Mrs Spencer we'll be ready to leave when you come for us tomorrow morning.'

Grace and Billy were up early as usual the following morning, and when Rhind came in the trap they had been ready and waiting for some twenty minutes.

He helped Grace up into the trap without managing to look directly at her, though to Billy he spoke not unkindly, saying, 'Up you get, young man,' as he handed him up through the door. And then they were off.

He spoke hardly at all on the journey, and, slightly intimidated by his presence, Grace and Billy sat silent as they faced one another in the back of the trap.

And at last they arrived at Asterleigh House.

Without speaking, Rhind pulled up the mare in the back yard, got down and stepped smartly around to the rear where he opened the door and held out a hand to help Grace down. Ignoring his hand, she supported herself without his help, and on stepping down onto the flags, turned as Billy jumped down behind her. Rhind then moved to the back door of the house, pushed open the kitchen door and called out to one of the maids: 'Visitors are here.' Then, his duty done, he moved back to the horse and trap and, taking the cob by the bridle, led it away across the yard.

Grace watched the man go, then turned as she heard a voice calling to her from the rear doorway. It was the housekeeper, Mrs Sandiston, who led them into the main part of the house. And once again they found themselves in the spacious hall, walking on the marble tiles and glancing about them at the tapestries and paintings that adorned the walls.

Moving to a door, Mrs Sandiston came to a halt outside it. 'If you'd like to wait here a moment,' she said, 'I'll tell Mrs Spencer you're here.'

She tapped on the door, opened it and went in. Grace heard a murmur of voices from inside and then the woman re-emerged from the room.

'If you'd like to go in, miss,' she said, then added, gesturing to Billy, 'The young man is to wait here for a minute.' She turned, gesturing to a chair a few feet away beneath a tapestry showing a scene of the hunt. 'Why don't you sit down there, my dear?'

His hat in his hands, Billy moved to the chair and sat down. Grace gave him a smile, then moved to the door and went in.

She found herself in what she assumed was the drawing room, a large room with windows reaching almost to the ceiling. Paintings and tapestries hung on the walls. Near the wide fireplace, the grate almost hidden behind a huge vase of roses, sat Mrs Spencer on a sofa of dark green velvet. She wore a loose-fitting gown of deep rose with cream and yellow roses on it, a small lace cap with her hair parted in the centre and tied at the back of her neck with a narrow black velvet ribbon. As Grace entered the room she said, 'Ah, there you are,' in a tone that was surprisingly warm.

At the woman's bidding, Grace closed the door behind her, and Mrs Spencer beckoned to her, and gestured to a chair facing the sofa on which she sat. 'Please – sit down.'

Grace took the seat and waited. Mrs Spencer gazed at her for a moment in silence then went on:

'I asked you to come and see me today as my husband told me that you were looking for a situation. And what I have to say might be of interest to you.' She paused. 'Also, I understand, you are being forced to move from your home.'

Grace nodded. 'Yes, ma'am, that's correct. I knew we would have to leave when the lease was up, but I had hoped to delay it for a little while. Hopefully until I managed to find a home, and a position as a daily, visiting governess.'

'And how have your searches gone? Have you found anything?'

'I've found somewhere to live for us for the time being.'

Mrs Spencer was looking at her expectantly and with curiosity, so Grace added, 'At a lodging house in Corster. With a Mrs Packerman. We move there in a week.'

'And does it look promising? Obviously it does, or you wouldn't be planning to go there.'

'Well,' Grace gave a little shrug, 'the landlady seems pleasant enough. It's only one room, but I'm afraid we can't afford to be too particular. Besides, it doesn't have to be for ever, and we'll move to somewhere better when things start to improve.'

'What about work? Have you not yet found anything suitable?'

'Not yet – though it's not for want of trying. I'm quite sure, however, that I'll find something soon. I've made other applications I'm waiting to hear about.'

'You don't have long, do you?'

'No, but once Billy and I are settled in our new lodgings I shall be able to devote more time to finding something.'

'Have you any other prospects?'

'Other prospects? No – nothing.'

'What I mean is – I'm referring to a certain young man. You spoke of him when you were here visiting before. Your acquaintance. Is he in a position to be of assistance to you?'

'No,' Grace said shortly. 'We don't meet. We shan't be meeting again.'

Mrs Spencer gazed at her at this, as if waiting for elaboration, but Grace volunteered nothing further on the matter.

'And how,' Mrs Spencer said, 'is your young brother coping through all the upheaval?'

'He's taking it very well. He's not happy about it, but he's taking it well. He doesn't complain.'

'And with a sister like you to stand up for him, he'll never be alone.' A pause, then Mrs Spencer continued: 'You know, I was a teacher once. So we have some things in common. For a few years I taught at a school on the outskirts of Swindon.' She turned and glanced about her, her gaze moving out of the window. Taking in the sight, she said, 'It's a pleasant view, isn't it? I have to say that much.'

'It's beautiful.'

'It is. And I do appreciate it.' She gave a little sigh. 'I'm not so accustomed to living in the country. I was accustomed to living in a town. I only came here as my husband was set on it. And I was a stranger to the place. My uncle left me the property as his only relative, but I only ever saw it once in my life before it was bequeathed to me.' The glance she cast around the room seemed to take in the whole house. 'But it is an impressive house, there's no denying. And if you think it's large, think how it must have appeared to me as a girl. The place looked absolutely enormous. I thought the stairs and the rooms would go on for ever.'

Grace wondered where all this might be leading, but she had no choice other than to be patient.

'I've lost track of what I was saying,' Mrs Spencer said, putting a finger to her chin. 'Oh, yes,' and she nodded, ' – so as I say, I was never used to living in the country. And I find now, after living here upwards of five years, that it doesn't get easier.' She paused, looking at Grace appraisingly, as if finally making up her mind, then added, 'As I said, my husband has told me of your situation following the sad death of your father. And this is the reason I've asked you to come here and see me today. Do you paint and draw, by any chance?'

'Always, ever since I was a child. My brother too. Billy is a better draughtsman than I. He has so much talent. I haven't painted much of late. There just hasn't been the time. Also, to be honest, oil paints cost money, and there isn't always money to spare for such things.'

Mrs Spencer gave a nod of understanding. 'My painting is very important to me, as you might have gathered. And I would like to get out more and paint in the open air. Oh, I arrange my still lifes from fruit and vegetables and flowers and pots and such in my little studio, but sometimes I would love to just drive out with my easel and my paints and find a nice spot with some lovely view that's just asking to be painted. I go out into the grounds of the house sometimes with my materials, but I'd like at times to go further afield. Unfortunately, though, I can't. Or rather I wouldn't feel comfortable going on my own. My husband is far too busy with his business to think of keeping me company on such an excursion – and indeed I would never dream of asking him to. He'd be bored to distraction within five minutes and be desperate to get going again. And it wouldn't be any good just having a maid along. No, what I need is a companion for such excursions. And ideally a companion who would share some of my enthusiasm and enjoy sharing the experience. And for exhibitions too. I would love at times to go to the museums and look at the works of art on display, but one needs company at such times. One needs to have someone to talk to about the works. Do you see what I mean?'

'Oh, I do indeed,' Grace said. 'A visit to an art gallery is always so much better when it's shared.'

'Quite.' Mrs Spencer nodded and sat looking at her with a slightly quizzical expression on her face. 'Do you play chess?' she asked.

'Yes. My father and I used to play quite frequently.' Grace smiled. 'I think we were quite evenly matched.'

'So –' said Mrs Spencer, and then came to a halt. After a second or two she gave a little nod and said, 'Well, what I'm coming to is to ask you – I wonder if you would care to come here to Asterleigh in the capacity of companion to me – and general assistant. Apart from coming with me when I go off on outdoor painting jaunts and such, I need a person who can generally give me a helping hand. I have no doubt that you could be that person.'

Grace looked at the woman, hardly able to believe what she had just heard. For all her wondering as to the purpose of the invitation, nothing had prepared her for such an offer.

'Of course,' Mrs Spencer said, 'we would work out precisely what your responsibilities would be. And apart from your wages you would have your room and board.'

Grace said, 'But I have to think of my brother, ma'am. I have to think of him first.'

'Indeed, and of course I understand that. And I haven't forgotten him. I've given thought to that matter also.' She gave a little sigh here, and for a moment cast her eyes down. Then, looking back at Grace, she said, 'I fear I was a

118

little hard on you both when you were here before. I've tended to become rather isolated. And I've discovered something – that the less one's ways get challenged the more one tends to get set in one's ways. Perhaps also I don't spend enough time in the company of young people. Anyway, to the matter of your young brother. Billy, isn't it?'

'Billy, yes.'

'Billy. Well, we have so many rooms in this house, and so many of them are unused and shut up. It will be the easiest matter to find a small room for him. And there is, I'm given to understand, a fine little school in Culvercombe. Also, if he wanted to make himself useful, Mrs Sandiston or Mr Johnson could no doubt find him some odd jobs to do. Either in the kitchen or about the house or in the stables. Or Mr Clutter could probably do with some help in the gardens.' She came briefly to a stop, and here smiled for the first time, showing her small teeth, a smile that transformed her face. 'But think about it,' she said. 'I don't want an answer right this minute. What I would like to do, however, is talk to your brother.' She paused. 'When you go out, please ask him to come in and see me, will you?' She got up from the sofa, moved to the bell pull beside the fireplace and gave it a tug. 'In the meantime, perhaps you'd like to see something of the house. Would you like to see the conservatory? There are wonderful plants there. I'll get someone to show you into it. You'll find it interesting, I have no doubt. I'll send your brother to find you when we're through talking.'

Grace went out of the room then, and spoke to Billy, and a moment later he was knocking at the door and being invited in. Grace, watching him go, saw his nervousness, his uncertainty.

Left alone on the landing, Grace stood thinking over what Mrs Spencer had said to her. A place was being offered to Billy too. It was almost unbelievable. And why should she not accept it . . .? It was a position that she was eminently capable of filling, and it could be the answer to their present plight.

She had no more time to think upon it then for the housemaid appeared, knocked on the door and went into the room. A moment or two later she was back out and saying to Grace, 'The mistress says I'm to show you to the conservatory, miss. Will you come this way . . .?'

Grace followed the maid through a long hallway along the rear of the house with doors opening off at intervals, and one side, the south side, looking out over the landscaped gardens with their colourful lawns and flowerbeds, and green paddocks on the flanks. And then they were entering a large, glass-walled conservatory full of lush and exotic plants and flowers. Towards the centre of the rear wall a little arbour had been created in the midst of the foliage, and here were placed wicker chairs and a table.

'If you'd care to sit down, miss,' the maid said, 'I'm to offer you some tea or other refreshments – if you'd like.'

'Thank you,' Grace said, 'but we shall be leaving soon.'

When the maid had gone, Grace looked around her. It was warm in the great glass room, and the light seemed odd, coming through the panes and being filtered by the leaves and blossoms of the great number of plants. And the plants themselves looked very curious; she was sure she had never seen any of them before in her life. And it was not only their appearance, but the smell of them also; strong and pervasive, it seemed to hang in the room like a curtain. There was also the sound of birds chirping, and leaning forward and looking to her left she saw there was a birdcage amid the greenery, with three small exotic-looking birds inside it.

Getting up from her chair, Grace moved to the birdcage and looked inside. The birds were tiny, with vividly coloured wings. The creatures were obviously not from Britain's shores.

'So, what do you think of them?'

The voice came from behind her, and she knew the owner of it before she turned and saw him standing there.

'Oh – hello, Mr Spencer.'

'Miss Grace.' He nodded, smiling a greeting, then gestured to the birdcage. 'They're from Africa. Lovely, aren't they? Such pretty little creatures.'

'Well – y-e-s.'

He smiled, frowning. 'You don't sound too sure.'

'Well, they are pretty, no doubt. But I also think they're rather sad.'

'Sad? But they're so bright, so colourful.'

'I know. But I can't help thinking of how they would be in some tropical forest. They should have so much space to fly in. A whole world of space, not just one small cage.'

'Yes,' he said, 'you're right, of course. They were a present to my wife from someone coming back from Africa. What can you do?' He shrugged. 'You can't let them loose into the wild. In our climate they'd die of cold on the first chilly day.'

'I suppose they would, poor things.'

'Anyway,' he said, 'I think they're as comfortable as is possible, considering the circumstances.' He raised a hand, taking in the rest of the conservatory. 'Have you looked around? Seen some of the various plants and flowers?'

'They're wonderful. I never knew so many different kinds existed.'

'They're my wife's. She's had them brought from so many far-flung places – all round the world. One of her passions. And I've picked up a little of it from her.' He reached out, his hand briefly touching a broad, fleshy leaf, then said, 'Have you travelled at all?'

'To other countries, you mean? No. I've never been outside England. You have, I should imagine?'

'To several places – Brazil, the West Indies, America, Europe.'

'And you came back to settle in Berron Wick.'

An ironic smile. 'Oh, there's no place like home.' A thought occurred to him, and he added, 'Where's your brother? My wife said he was coming with you.'

'He's with Mrs Spencer now. She wanted to see him alone.'

'I told her about your situation – as you will have gathered.'

'Yes, so I understand.'

'Yes, I told her and between us we came up with an answer. And let's hope it's the right answer.'

Grace did not know how to respond. She was grateful for the offer Mrs Spencer had made, and it sounded excellent – but she needed time to think about it.

Mr Spencer was looking at her closely in the strange light, his head tipped a little to one side. 'I think perhaps,' he said, 'this is all happening a little too quickly for you, is that so?'

'Everything is happening too quickly right now,' Grace said. 'I can't keep up with the changes. Billy and I, we don't know where we are.'

'Have there been any further developments in your situation regarding the house?'

'I've accepted the offer from the house-clearance dealer you sent.'

'Though it probably wasn't much, right?'

'No, it wasn't very much. But it's the best I can expect – under the circumstances. And I thank you for it, for your help.'

'Please – it was nothing.'

'I'm very grateful.'

A little pause, then Mr Spencer said, 'Come, let me show you some more of the sights we have in here.'

He turned, and Grace stepped beside him and they began to walk through the conservatory. As they went, he pointed out plants of special interest, some because of their appearance, some for their smell, and others for the particular ways in which they functioned. A few of them, as he remarked, were carnivorous, while others carried deadly poisons, either in their seeds or in the sap from their leaves and stems. One in particular, he pointed out, had seeds that were especially deadly, and Grace stood and looked at the tall plant with awe. At another plant she stooped to take in the scent of a flower like a large pale yellow lily, but quickly Mr Spencer stepped forward and put a hand on her arm. 'Don't go too close,' he said. 'It bites.'

'Bites?' Grace said as she straightened.

'Not literally, but if you allow the leaves to touch your skin it can leave a very nasty sore weal behind – and one that will drive you crazy with itching.'

'Why do you have such plants here?' Grace asked, taking a step away.

He paused and smiled, shrugged. 'That is an excellent question, indeed. I suppose part of it is the challenge. It's no small feat, surely, to be able to grow in an English house a plant that by rights should only be growing in the middle of a jungle.'

They were standing so close, facing one another, and Grace was aware of the lingering feel of the brief touch of his hand upon her arm.

'I do hope you'll accept my wife's offer,' he said. 'I'm sure you could be happy here. Certainly we'd do our best to make sure that you were. That goes for your brother too, of course.'

'I'm so grateful for the kind offer,' Grace said. And she asked herself why she did not at once say, 'Yes, I will accept it', and realized that it had to do with Mr Spencer himself. It was not any specific thing he had said; he just seemed too

– fond, too solicitous. When he had touched her his hands stayed a fraction of a second too long, and when their eyes met she always had to look away first. Perhaps she was being foolish and oversensitive, but these things – as lacking in substance as they were – whispered to her of some possible danger.

'Billy and I, we must talk it over,' she said. 'And I'm settled for now with a place for us to stay. But as I say, I must think about it. Please don't think me ungrateful, will you?'

'I would never think of you as ungrateful.'

They had reached the end of the conservatory.

'I think you've seen enough of this for today,' he said. 'Let's get out of here. Some of the scents can get a bit overpowering. Would you like to see something else of the house?'

'I'd like to,' Grace said politely, 'but right now I have to wait for Billy. Mrs Spencer's sending him here.'

'We can't have him getting lost, then.' He turned and side by side they walked back towards the main entrance. As they reached it Billy came into the room, saw Mr Spencer and came to a stop.

'Hello, young William,' Mr Spencer said, and Billy gave a grave nod and murmured, 'Sir.'

'So,' Mr Spencer said to Billy, 'did you have an interesting conversation with Mrs Spencer?'

Billy hesitated, then nodded. 'Y-yes, sir.'

'And what did you have to talk about?'

A pause. 'Oh – l-lots of things. She asked me if I liked d-drawing.'

'And what did you say?'

'I said yes.'

'Good.' The man looked from one to the other for a moment, then said, 'Well, I'll leave you now. Rhind will see you safely back home.'

Grace thanked him. He held out his hand and Grace put out her own hand. He took it, briefly pressed it and wished her goodbye. A moment later he was walking away through the door and into the passage.

When Mr Spencer had gone from their sight, Grace said to Billy, 'How did you find your way here?'

'The maid showed me the way. And Mrs Spencer wants to see you again before we go. She told me to tell you.'

Together they moved out of the conservatory and back towards the main hall, where they stopped beside the drawing room door and Grace knocked upon it. A moment later, hearing Mrs Spencer's voice from inside, she pushed open the door and went in.

Mrs Spencer was standing at the window, looking down onto the lawn and flowerbeds at the side. Grace came to a halt some feet away from her.

'My brother said you wanted to see me, ma'am.'

'Yes, just for a moment.' Mrs Spencer turned and looked at the ornate clock on the mantel. 'Then you must be getting back. Did you get time for some tea in the conservatory?'

'I didn't want any, ma'am, thank you.'

'Very well. I just wanted to say that your brother and I have had a little talk. I sounded him out about living here, and he seems – not averse to the notion. But there, perhaps he was just being polite. However, be that as it may. What about you? Have you had time to think about the offer?'

Grace did not know how to respond. 'I haven't, ma'am, I'm sorry.'

'No, well, that's all right. I shouldn't expect you to make a decision quite so quickly. But I'll keep it open for, say, ten days, and you let me know within that time whether you wish to take it up. And let's hope I haven't changed my own mind during that time. It's been known to happen.'

Still at a loss, Grace stood there, trying to think of the right words. Then Mrs Spencer said, 'I asked your young brother how his leg came to be like that. He told me he was injured in a fall. He said he fell from a stile.'

'Yes, that's right.'

'How sad. And such an injury from a little incident like that. But he doesn't appear to allow it to get him down.'

'No, ma'am.'

Mrs Spencer gave a thoughtful little nod, then glanced again at the clock, and said:

'Anyway, you go on out into the yard and Mr Rhind will drive you back home. I've already sent a message to him. He'll be waiting for you.'

Grace took her leave of the woman and, promising to let her know her decision very soon, left the room.

Billy was sitting in the chair beside the door, and he got up and together he and Grace moved through the hall towards the rear of the house.

Outside in the yard they found Rhind waiting beside the pony and trap, and without a word and without making eye contact he helped them up into the vehicle. He spoke briefly, just saying, 'Back to Green Shipton, yes?' and Grace said, 'Yes, thank you,' and he swung himself up into the driver's seat and the next moment they were moving away.

Grace and Billy barely spoke on the journey back home – their silence due mostly to the intimidating presence of the driver of the trap. He ignored them totally.

Then at last, after what seemed an age, the trap was pulling to a halt outside Bramble House and Rhind was turning in his seat and saying to Grace, only meeting her eyes for the briefest moment, 'Will this do you, miss?'

'Yes, it's fine, thank you.'

With the man making no move to help her down, Grace gathered up her skirts and climbed down onto the road, Billy following. She turned then to Rhind, making one last effort: 'Thank you – very much.' And he gave a nod, with the faintest semblance of a smile touching his mouth. 'Miss,' he murmured, then looked ahead, touched his hat and flapped at the reins. A second later he was driving away.

'Do you like that man?' Billy asked as he and Grace stepped into the yard.

Grace, avoiding answering the question, said, 'Well, we don't really know him, do we?'

'No, but – only he never speaks in a friendly way.'

'No, he doesn't,' Grace agreed. 'But maybe that's just how he is.'

They reached the rear door and went through into the kitchen where Grace filled the kettle and put it on to boil. 'You're probably hungry, are you?' she said to Billy, and he agreed that he was.

Grace began to busy herself getting food for their midday dinner. As she washed lettuce in a bowl she said to Billy, 'Tell me, what did Mrs Spencer have to say to you? You were with her some time. What did you talk about?'

He had just washed his hands and was now drying them on an old towel. 'She asked me lots of questions,' he said. 'Questions about school and that kind of thing. She asked what lessons I liked best. She asked me how I hurt my leg. And she asked me if I was sad at having to leave here, and I said yes. Then she asked me if I'd like to live at her house.'

'Oh, she did. And what did you say?'

'I said to her, "Yes, ma'am." And she said, "Well, we'd have to see about it."' He paused. 'Are we going there, Grace? Are we going there to live?'

Grace did not answer him at once. She would have to come to a decision at some time. And there was little time left. She thought again of the house. It was such an enormous place. What must it be like to live in such a house? And to have no more financial cares, to be able to

127

spend one's day without stress? And what would her work consist of? – accompanying Mrs Spencer on her painting expeditions and to museums – and being a general companion and helper where she could. There was no doubt that Mrs Spencer now seemed so much more approachable. After all the stress and pressures of the last months, Grace thought, such a move could bring so much relief.

But she could not at the same time put out of her mind her reservations, her fears. And for the most part they concerned Mr Spencer. And she thought of him again, and his hand upon her arm, upon her own hand, the lingering glance as his eyes fell upon hers.

'I don't think so, Billy,' she said. 'But we'll be all right. I'll find a good job soon, and we'll be comfortable at Mrs Packerman's until we find a better and more permanent place to stay.'

All the previous day the bonfire had been burning, but now, early on Friday morning, the flames were out, and not even a thread of smoke rose up from the pile of ash. Grace stood before the bonfire's remains. So much had been consumed. She and Billy had fed it for hours, throwing onto it all the things that they would no longer need, and which were not to be bought by Mr Clemmer the house-clearer. So old shoes, old clothes, papers, useless bits of her father's timber, it had all gone to feed the flames. Now, in the house, in the hall, stood a box, a small trunk and a suitcase – all the effects that Grace and Billy would keep, and which would be travelling with them to Mrs Packerman's lodging house. All the rest of the house and workshop's effects were waiting to be collected and loaded onto a wagon by Mr Clemmer. The day before, Grace had said her goodbyes to Mrs Tanner. The woman had gone off in tears, and Grace herself had wept again.

Moving from room to room, after they had filtered out

the things for burning, Grace had again felt tears on her cheek. The reality of the change was coming through to her: soon she and Billy would be gone, would have left the house for ever. It hardly seemed like their home any more. In the bedrooms on the beds the bolsters and the mattresses had been rolled up, the sheets and blankets neatly folded. In the parlour the ornaments and pictures were neatly stacked, and in the kitchen the pots and pans and china and cutlery had been laid upon the bare table, ready to be packed away by Mr Clemmer and his helpers.

Some things had remained the same, however. Grace had still got nowhere in her search for a position. Two days earlier she had had the second of two interviews following responses to advertisements in the newspaper columns. The first was with the mother of two small boys of seven and eight, and it would have been promising had the family not been living in the village of Collerway, which proved to be so difficult to get to that Grace was sure that she would be spending all of her wages on cab fares. The second had been in Harbrook, but the house into which she had been invited had had such a filthy appearance, and the two girls for whom the teacher was required had been so loud and coarse that Grace knew that it would never work. Which left her exactly back where she had started – and she must begin looking all over again.

Now, standing before the bonfire's grey ashes, she knew that only minutes remained before Mr Clemmer would be there. And even as the thought went through her head she heard the sound of a wagon and horses pulling into the yard and then Billy was there, running to her, telling her that the man had arrived.

Mr Clemmer appeared, driving a wagon pulled by two hefty mares, and accompanied by two of his sons, both freckled, powerful-looking young men, who were leaping down from the wagon even before it came to a halt.

It was three o'clock before Clemmer and his helpers had finished. And during the hours they had sorted and packed, piling everything from the small house and the workshop onto the wagon until in the end both house and workshop were bare and every square inch of the wagon was packed. Throughout the whole process Grace and Billy had sat on one side on the old bench in the yard, watching as the men moved back and forth. And then at last Mr Clemmer had come to her and, taking out his purse, counted out coins into her palm, the amount agreed between them. She put the money into her own purse alongside that given to her by Mr Timmins and Mr Spencer. As small as the total sum was, she had never had so much money in her life before. Not that it was all hers; an equal part belonged to Billy, and in time he must have his share.

And then she and Billy were standing side by side on the cobbles watching as the effects of the only home they had known in their lives was borne away.

When the wagon had turned the corner out of sight, Grace gave a deep sigh and, with some trepidation, entered the cottage. She was fearful of seeing it without all those things that had given it meaning. And followed by Billy she went from room to room. Everything was bare. The floors were bare, the walls were bare, and in the rooms their hushed voices echoed, and their footsteps rang in the hollow spaces. A few minutes and it was enough. The place was not their home any more.

'Billy,' she said, turning to her brother who stood beside her looking around with a tearful, wide-eyed, bewildered expression, 'let's go and get the fly and leave.'

Leaving their belongings in the hall, Grace and Billy left the cottage to walk to the far side of the village – only a short distance away – to the stables of the fly proprietor, Mr Hammond. He was out on a call when they arrived, but his wife said that he was expected back very soon. So the two waited together until, after some fifteen minutes, the cab came into the yard. Two minutes later, Grace and Billy were on board and being driven back to Bramble House.

On arrival Mr Hammond helped load on board the pair's trunk, suitcase and box, and then, with the doors of the house securely locked behind them, Grace climbed up into the fly beside her brother.

On the way through the village Grace had the fly stop for five minutes at the churchyard while she and Billy went inside. There, standing beside the graves of their mother and father, the two said their goodbyes, Grace bending low over the earth to whisper, 'We don't know, Pappy, when we'll ever be round this way again.'

And then they were climbing back into the cab once more, and the cab was setting off. It was no good looking back, Grace said to herself as they left the village; that part of her life was over.

In Corster the fly waited outside Mr Grennell's office while Grace knocked and went in. Grennell was, as before, sitting behind his desk, and Grace noticed that he could hardly bring himself to meet her eyes as she opened her bag and took out the keys to the house. She placed them on the desk before him. 'I would like a receipt, please,' she said, and he nodded, and said at once, 'Ah, yes, of course.' And straight away he took up a sheet of paper and began to write out a receipt for the keys. As he blotted the ink he said, looking up at her, a solicitous note in his voice:

'Will you be all right?'

'Will I be all right?' Grace frowned. 'I'm afraid I don't understand what you mean.'

He held out the receipt and Grace took it from him. 'You have somewhere to go, have you?' he said.

A small ironic smile touched her mouth. 'Whether I have or have not, Mr Grennell,' she folded the receipt and placed it carefully in her bag, '– I can't see that it can matter at all to you.'

He flushed, the colour rising in his pink face. 'Well, I – I would not wish to see you turned out onto the street . . .'

'The thought didn't bother you before, sir,' Grace said, 'and I don't see why you should concern yourself with it now.' She turned and moved to the door. In the doorway she turned. 'I shall not starve, Mr Grennell. And neither will my brother. And neither will we go without a roof over our heads. Rest assured on that. And as we shall not meet again you may also rest assured that I shall never again make the mistake of asking you for anything.' With her words she turned and stepped out again into the sunshine.

Back in the fly she gave the driver the address of Mrs Packerman's lodging house and they set off once more.

They were hot and perspiring when they finally sat down in the room at the lodging house, and they were grateful and relieved to see the last of travelling for a while. It seemed to Grace that they had constantly, since that morning, been on the move. But now Mrs Packerman's handyman had brought up their box, trunk and suitcase, wheezing asthmatically as he did so, and after lingering in the room for a gratuity when the job was done, had left her and Billy alone.

'Well,' Grace said, falling into a rickety chair by the window, 'we're here at last.'

She looked at Billy as he sat on the bed. There appeared to be no relief or gladness in his face. Getting up, she went over to him and sat beside him.

'It'll be all right,' she said. She bent her head, trying to look into his lowered eyes.

'Yes.' He nodded.

'It will be all right,' she said. 'Truly it will.'

'I just wish we could go home.'

She was silent at this. They could never go home again. There was no longer any home to go to. But he would accept this in time. Together they would make a new life, and they would be happy.

There came a knock on the door, and the next moment Mrs Packerman was pushing open the door and stepping over the threshold. She had merely, she said, wished to check that they were comfortable and had what they needed. Grace assured her that they were fine, and were, thankfully, now starting to relax.

'There is just one other thing,' Mrs Packerman said, ' – the matter of the rest of the month's rent. As I told you, if you remember, payment's due a month in advance.'

Grace had not forgotten, and from her purse she carefully counted out the sum and placed it in the woman's hand.

'Thank you, my dear,' Mrs Packerman said, 'it's as well to get these things out of the way. When I go downstairs I'll write you out a receipt.' She paused, smiling a wide smile with lips closed. 'And another thing to mention is that I don't allow food up in the rooms.' She shook her head. 'Can't afford to do it, dear. Start that and you run the risk of attracting the rats, and I like to keep a clean house, as you'll appreciate.' She looked from one to the other. 'Though that doesn't mean you've got to starve, does it? So what about something to eat, my dears? It's after six o'clock. Have you eaten today?'

Billy had eaten a pie bought from a shop in the town earlier on, but Grace had eaten nothing since breakfast. Well, they would certainly be needing to eat something before too long, Grace said. Mrs Packerman then suggested that she provide them with supper, which she could have ready for them in an hour, for very little extra payment.

So it was that just after seven o'clock Grace and Billy found themselves sitting side by side at a long table in Mrs Packerman's dining room, eating a meat stew and vegetables. The meat was stringy and Mrs Packerman hadn't spared the gristle, but the vegetables were acceptable, and Grace and Billy managed to eat their fill.

Later, in their room, Billy lay back on the bed, fully dressed, while Grace sat at his side on the bedside chair.

In the light that filtered in from the lowering sun Grace looked at her brother's face. He lay with his eyes closed, saying nothing.

'I know this isn't what we want,' Grace said. 'But we don't have to stay here for ever. It'll only be for a few weeks. And we'll get used to it too.' She looked around her at the humble furnishings, her glance taking in the bruised, scratched furniture, the cracked jug and wash basin on the washstand, the thinness of the blankets, the dullness of the white ticking on the bolster. That they had come to this, she said to herself. But she must not be despondent. She must keep a positive attitude, if only for Billy's sake.

'We'll feel better in the morning,' she said. 'And tomorrow I must write to Aunt Edie and tell her where we are. Yes, and also I'll buy the newspapers and see what advertisements there are for positions. I'll soon find something, you'll see. And I don't have to be a teacher; there are all kinds of jobs that I can do. And when I do get something we'll find a much nicer room.'

'We could have gone to stay with Aunt Edie,' Billy said. 'She would have looked after us.'

'No, Billy,' Grace said, 'I'm afraid we couldn't ask that of her. Her cottage is so small, as you know, with only the two rooms. There wouldn't be room for us, and besides, she suffers so from her arthritis. We can't ask anything of her.

134

Poor woman, it's as much as she can do to provide for herself and Tippy.'

She looked down at his face now, and saw his lower lip quiver. He looked full of tears. Oh, Billy, don't cry, she said silently. She herself felt so emotional that she knew that with his first tear her own defences would go.

Grace lay on the bed, Billy beside her. She could tell by the sound of his breathing that he was not asleep. She knew that, like herself, he was unable to relax.

From below came the sounds of voices, of people going past the house at the end of the day. From further off came the striking of a church clock telling the hour of eleven. The cotton on the pillow beneath Grace's head was coarse, and the pillow itself smelled slightly of singed feathers.

'Grace . . .' Billy's voice, whispering.

'Yes, what is it?' Grace whispering too.

'I can't sleep.'

'Come cuddle up a little. And just try to relax.'

He snuggled up to her for a moment, and kissed her on the chin. Then, turning away, he lay curled into her body, spoon fashion, her arm around him. In moments he had drifted off to sleep.

The night was so warm and Grace had awakened. Surfacing from sleep in the warm night, she scratched a particularly aggressive little itch about her midriff. Beside her in the bed, Billy had moved a little away from her, unconsciously, in his sleep, putting space between the heat of their bodies. He slept restlessly, tossing a little, his head moving on the pillow, hands rubbing at his body beneath the thin sheet. It was the heat, Grace thought, making him restless.

She lay there thinking of the day past, of all that had taken place. She had seen the last of her home in Green Shipton, something undreamed of a month ago. And now here she was, sleeping in a strange bed in some cheap lodging house with her brother, trying to make ends meet and think up a future for the two of them. She reached down and, through her nightdress, scratched at her upper thigh, and then, drawing up her leg a little, at a spot behind her knee. She supposed she would get used to the bed in time, though it was nothing like as comfortable as the ones that Mr Clemmer had carted away that afternoon.

Opening her eyes she looked around the room, all shadows and recesses in the pale light that crept in between the thin curtains. The place would not do for them to live in for very long. It was not just a matter of it being strange, she realized; it was so different from the home they had known that she was sure they would never get used to it. She scratched again, at an area just below her breast, and noticed that Billy, in his sleep, was scratching too.

And then Grace was lying staring up into the dark, eyes wide, and feeling sure that she could feel something moving on her body. Quickly her frantic fingers were pulling up her nightdress and touching her skin, and then she was feeling the tiny, firm shape – no bigger than the head of a hatpin – that had leeched onto her flesh and was gorging on her blood. She caught it between her trembling finger and thumb, squeezed it, and felt it burst between her fingertips like a tiny ripe fruit.

In a moment she was moving, climbing over Billy's stirring form to get out of bed and stand on the threadbare piece of carpet that served as a bedside mat. Hands shaking feverishly, she felt for the matches and candle, and lit a match and set it to the candle's wick. Then, lifting the skirt of her nightdress she looked at her bare right leg in the pale light. She could see small red blotches up her calf, and when she pulled up her sleeve she could see more bites on her arms. She had been bitten all over.

And then from behind her came Billy's voice, waking,

bewildered, irritable: 'Gracie, I'm itching. Everywhere I'm itching.'

And letting her nightdress fall she turned to him and saw him sitting up in bed, scratching at his belly and his thigh.

'Get up, get up.' Grace pulled the covers away from his body, and as he moved aside she took up the candle and held it over the sheet where they had been lying. And she could see them, the bedbugs, running from the scene, little dark, round, swarming creatures, all running for cover from the light and the cooler air. In just three or four seconds there was not a single one to be seen.

Dawn came and found Grace and Billy sitting on the only two chairs in the room, both fully dressed. Having drawn back the curtains they had been there for hours, speaking barely a word, sitting side by side, waiting for the first faint glimmer of sunrise to touch the horizon. When it did, Grace reached out and took Billy's hand. He looked at her, acknowledging her look of relief. 'Yes,' she whispered, pressing his hand, 'soon we can leave.'

And they continued to sit there while the shadows grew paler and the ugliness of the room became once more exposed. When the church clock struck eight, Grace nodded and got up.

'I'll go and get a cab,' she said, 'and bring it back. Then we shall be out of here for good.'

On finding a cab Grace brought it back to the lodging house. She had had no wish to confront Mrs Packerman, but at the same time she was reluctant to lose all the rent she had paid in advance. So there was nothing for it but to speak to the woman. Not that Mrs Packerman had been hiding away. On the contrary, she was very much in evidence when Grace got the porter to carry their luggage downstairs.

137

'Does this mean what I think it means?' Mrs Packerman said to Grace, standing in the hall watching as the trunk was carried out to the waiting cab. 'Are you leaving us so soon?'

'We are indeed, Mrs Packerman,' Grace replied, drawing herself up, while her heart was thumping. 'And I should be greatly obliged to you if you could refund part of the rent we paid you in advance.'

Ignoring this last request, the landlady said, her voice concerned, almost solicitous, 'May I ask why you see fit to leave so soon after arriving? Wusn't you comfortable? How come you're in such a hurry?'

'Yes, we are in a hurry,' Grace countered. 'And we're leaving not a moment too soon if we are not to be bitten to death.'

'Not to be –' Now Mrs Packerman looked outraged. 'What exactly are you suggesting, miss?'

At this Grace turned to Billy and said, 'You go and wait in the cab, Billy, and I'll join you in a second.' When, reluctantly, he had gone, casting uncertain glances from the woman to his sister, Grace turned back to the woman.

'I'm not suggesting anything, Mrs Packerman. I'm stating a fact. We're leaving because we cannot stay. The mattress we slept on – or tried to sleep on – last night was crawling. It was *alive*. Perhaps your other houseguests might be prepared to put up with it, but we are not. We are accustomed to something better, and although times are a little hard we are not so desperate as you obviously imagine.'

Mrs Packerman's mouth now fell open in a kind of theatrical outrage, falling open and then stretching wide, wider in supposed amazed horror. 'Are you suggesting that I keep a dirty house, miss? Are you suggesting that there are bugs in my beds?'

Grace's heart hammered in her breast. 'Go and see for

yourself,' she said. 'Or better yet, try sleeping in that bed. Though maybe you're so used to it that you wouldn't notice anything amiss.'

'Get out!' Mrs Packerman cried. 'Get out! Get out!' And then launched herself, arms flailing, at Grace.

But though she flinched initially, Grace stood her ground, hands clenched at her sides. Mrs Packerman came to a stop.

'Well,' she blustered, 'if you think you're getting any repayment of your week's rent in advance, you can think again.'

'It was a month altogether,' Grace said. 'I paid you the remaining three weeks just yesterday, when we arrived.'

'You must show me your receipt, then. You're bound to have a receipt.'

'I haven't got one. You said you'd bring one to me – but you never did.'

Mrs Packerman sniffed. 'You're wasting my time, miss. I don't recall any extra three weeks rent. And I'd be grateful if you'd get off my property – this very minute.'

And so Grace did. She had no choice. It was obvious to her that she would never get her money back. Angry and humiliated, she turned and marched out to the waiting cab, beside which the driver waited, having listened to every word of the exchange.

So too, Grace found, when she got inside, had Billy. And having heard the angry voices, the woman's hostility directed at Grace, he was in tears.

'It's all right, it's all right,' Grace said, putting her arms around him. 'No harm's done.' She held him closer as he sniffed and wiped at his eyes. 'But in any case, we're leaving now, and we'll never have to see this place again.'

An hour and a half later they were being let down in the rear yard at Asterleigh House, and Grace was asking the driver to wait while she went inside. She just prayed that Mrs Spencer was at home.

She was, and within minutes Grace was being shown into her studio where she was at work at her easel. In a few words Grace told her what had happened, ending by saying that if the offer was still open, she and Billy would be pleased to accept it. Very soon afterwards the cab driver had been paid and sent on his way, and Grace and Billy's luggage was being brought into the house.

PART TWO

Chapter Eight

'Are you all set?' Grace asked. She and Billy were in his room that looked out over the yard. Thirty minutes earlier the two of them had breakfasted together, and now Grace had come to see that he was ready for school. She entered his room to find him making up his bed. It was Thursday, 5th April. Billy had now been going to the Culvercombe National school for five months.

Five months, Grace said to herself as she observed him tidying up his bed. They had been there five months. The time had flown so fast, yet their first day in the house was as clear in her mind as if it had been yesterday.

Fresh from their horrifying night at the lodging house and her humiliating encounter with Mrs Packerman, Grace had stood in trepidation at the door of Asterleigh House waiting to know whether Mrs Spencer would see her. And soon afterwards she was standing before Mrs Spencer, telling her what had happened at the lodging house, and asking if the offer to live and work at Asterleigh House was still open.

'Why should it not be?' Mrs Spencer had replied. 'You had a perfect right to see if you could find something that suited you better, something in your chosen profession.' And after a brief pause she had given a nod of the head and added, 'And I doubt I'm wrong in saying that it's not thoughts for yourself alone that have brought you here now. No, when you have responsibility for another, you cannot always do exactly as you would choose.'

Grace and Billy had moved in that same day.

In the intervening time they had settled well into the house and into their new lives. Within days of their moving in, Grace had taken Billy to the nearest National school, some three miles distant. And from Monday to Friday he made his way back and forth on foot. There had been times in the past, at Green Shipton, when he had been reluctant to go to school in the mornings, particularly following the death of their mother. So far, however, he had shown no such great reluctance at his new school. Grace was so relieved, so pleased. Even so, she must keep ever vigilant. She knew well that with his disability there was always the chance of some bully picking on him. She must be on the lookout for any signs, for if it should happen she would not allow it to continue.

But he seemed happy. She had wondered if he would miss his work on Timmins's farm, but he seemed not to; his whole life had changed and there was so much that was new for him to get accustomed to: new school, new surroundings, new people in his life. And he was not one to complain. His concerns, when they came, were practical. 'How shall we get to the Green Shipton churchyard to see Mama and Pappy's grave?' he had once asked. 'How can we when we're so far away?'

'We'll get there,' Grace had replied. 'Not as often as before, but we'll find the time to go.'

'And what about the flowers? Now we haven't got any of our own.'

'Perhaps the gardener will give us a few from the garden. But don't worry, everything will be fine.'

For herself Grace felt she had done equally well. It had taken a little time to get used to the unaccustomed luxury around her in the large house, but now she was getting used to it, and as far as she could, she enjoyed her time there. And the hours she spent with Mrs Spencer were interesting and generally enjoyable. The two of them would paint or sketch together, sometimes in Mrs Spencer's studio or in the conservatory – Billy occasionally joining them when he could. At other times Grace and her mistress would play chess or bezique; Grace would accompany her on little excursions to places of interest, museums, historic buildings. And now with spring in the air there was talk from Mrs Spencer of driving out to sketch out of doors.

One particular interest of Mrs Spencer's was in a portrait she had begun of Grace. It was on a large canvas, larger than any usually used by Mrs Spencer. She had Grace in her second-best dress of coffee and white, sitting in an old upright chair, and looking towards the window. After a time Mrs Spencer got a mirror and placed it carefully so that Grace could watch in it the progress of the painting. Grace was fascinated to see the picture grow beneath the older woman's hands.

Billy, now giving a last smooth to the bedcover, said, 'I saw Mrs Spencer yesterday.'

'To talk to?' As he kept more or less to the servants' part of the house – not only at Grace's suggestion, but also by his own wish – he rarely crossed the path of his benefactress.

'Yes.' He straightened. 'I was sitting on the back step, cleaning Mrs Sandiston's boots, when Mrs Spencer came by from the stable. She asked me how I was, and how I was enjoying school, and I told her that I liked it all very well. Then she asked me –' He came to a stop here, and Grace prompted him. 'And then what? What else did she ask you?'

'– She asked me about my leg again. How I came to fall.'

A little pause, then Grace said, 'What did you tell her?'

'I just told her that I fell . . .' He picked up his books. 'Then she gave me a penny,' he added.

'That was kind of her.'

'That's the third time she's given me money.'

'Very kind.' Grace turned and glanced towards the window. 'It's going to be another lovely day. What lessons will you be having?'

He tapped his English primer. 'First, English – and then we shall have arithmetic and English history. In history we're learning about William the Conqueror and the Norman invasion.'

'That'll be interesting. Have you got your tuck?'

'Mrs Sandiston gave me some bread and butter, a little ham, and an apple. Two apples.'

'So you won't starve. Since when could you eat two apples?'

'I shall give one to Roland.'

'Roland? Who is Roland?'

'He's my friend. He's in my class. He lives in Culvercombe.' He moved to the door. 'Are you painting today?'

'No, I'm going into Corster to get some things for Mrs Spencer – and maybe some items for Cook too. There's to be a dinner party on Saturday.'

'A party?'

'A dinner party.'

'Shall we be invited?'

She laughed. 'No, of course not. The guest is a friend of Mr and Mrs Spencer. What would we be doing there?'

She bent, gave him a peck on the cheek and then he was gone, the sound of his feet echoing slightly on the back stairs.

Moving to the window, she stood looking down into the yard and a few moments later saw him emerge from the house. Halfway across the yard he looked up at the window and gave a wave. She waved back and watched till he had gone out of her sight.

Soon she must leave for the town to do the shopping for Mrs Spencer. She looked across the stable roof and the tall elms to the morning sky. The day was so far bright, though a few clouds were drifting on the breeze from the west.

Her thoughts again returning to the time before she and Billy had moved to Asterleigh, she suddenly thought of Stephen, picturing him there in Bramble House, his body stiff and awkward as he had told her of his engagement to the young woman on the ship. She had heard nothing more of him since. He might well be married by now, she thought, though she had heard no murmur that he was. Would she ever see him again? she wondered. But no, it was unlikely that they would ever again meet. He was building a new life, a life in which she had no part; and as for her, she was building a new life too.

Turning, she looked around her at the room, taking it in. It had been Billy's room since the day they had arrived at Asterleigh House with their few belongings. And he had really made the room his own, she thought. But there, a room of his very own was a luxury he had never known in his life before. She looked at his neatly made bed, his towel hanging on the washstand. She could see his pride in it all. And being given the room it had not taken long for him to put his stamp upon it. When Mrs Sandiston, following directions from Mrs Spencer, had shown them into it, saying: 'And this, young William, is to be your room,' he had hardly been able to believe his ears or his eyes. The room had been somewhat bare at that time, just holding a bed with a small dresser beside it and a taller one in which to hang his few clothes. Now, with permission, he had hung a number of pictures. One of them was a watercolour by Grace herself, a study of primroses growing on the heath that she had executed one spring. Two others were framed prints given to him by Mrs Spencer, one of a schooner under full sail, artist unknown, and the second of a Venetian canal scene, seemingly by Canaletto. On the small chest of drawers stood a little model sailing ship that he had made from balsa wood and paper, its sails and figurehead painted in the most surprising detail. Also there was a large seashell, a present from Mr Spencer. It was a wonderful item, a thing of strange colours that gave the sound of the sea when held to the ear.

Grace picked up from the dresser a little sketchbook that she had bought for him some time ago, and flicked through its pages. All the pages were full, some with several smaller sketches to a page, others with a single page bearing one large, detailed drawing. Although she had seen the drawings before, nevertheless his artistry never ceased to amaze her. It was evident on every page. There were sketches of buildings, the house, the village church, a small cluster of cottages in Berron Wick; there were studies of flowers and plants, dog roses in the hedgerows; and there were living creatures, birds, rabbits, three or four of the horses in the stables; and there were people: there was Mrs Sandiston, the cook-housekeeper, and Annie, the kitchen maid. The latter were not posed portraits such as might have been produced had the subject sat for the likeness, but quick sketches, made from life, of the person moving about, caught in the act of living. And although they were drawings made by a boy of nine years old, all the budding talent was there, all the promise of a great ability to come. And Grace could only wonder at what he might achieve in time. She herself had a certain ability in draughtsmanship, but it paled into insignificance next to Billy's.

And seeing his talent once again, becoming aware of it all over again, Grace was so glad. For she knew that it could be the saving of him. Several times since starting school he had spoken of drawing pictures for his class-mates. His ability had set him apart, she could see. He might not be able to play football and cricket like the others, but he had a gift of his own, and they appreciated it, acknowledged it and admired it. His great talent it was,

Grace surmised, that brought him acceptance among his peers.

Grace let herself out of Billy's room and moved along the landing to the door of her own room. There she went inside, closing the door behind her.

Like Billy's room, and those of the house servants, the room was in the west wing on the second floor. Grace's room was considerably larger than Billy's, and although in no way could it be termed luxurious, it was not quite so simply furnished as his. She rather had the feeling that Mrs Spencer had chosen it and its furnishings: the wardrobe, chiffonier, the decorative Japanese screen, to her eyes they had been put there with some thought; and at least once a week the maid put flowers in her room.

Grace sat and did some mending for half an hour or so, then put her sewing basket away, put on her coat and hat and picked up her purse. Then, after looking out at the sky – were those clouds a little more threatening? – decided to take her umbrella. As she turned to leave the room the clock on the mantelpiece over the small fireplace showed the time to be just after 8.30. By arrangement made the previous day she went down to the breakfast room. She knocked on the door, and Mrs Spencer's voice was heard, calling to her to enter, and she went inside.

Mrs Spencer sat at a small table near the window in the morning sun, eating her breakfast. She wore a lilac peignoir over her white nightdress, and a little cap on her braided hair.

Grace wished her good morning, then said, 'I've come for your list, Mrs Spencer. I shall be leaving soon.'

Mrs Spencer nodded, took a swallow of coffee, put down her cup and picked up a small sheet of paper from the tablecloth beside her. As she handed it to Grace she said, 'There are some silks – in the colours listed – to get from the haberdashers, and also a few tubes of oil paint from Mr

Lowmarsh. You'd best also get a small bottle of linseed oil as well. I think we're almost out of it.'

As Grace went to put the paper into her purse Mrs Spencer added: 'I tell you what, Grace, perhaps you could also get me a little drawing book. Nothing too large.' She held up her hands, palms apart, to describe the required size. 'Something so big . . .'

'The kind you usually have, ma'am?'

'Yes, but this is not for me.'

Grace nodded.

'And,' went on Mrs Spencer, 'I'd like you to get an ounce of tobacco. Get it from Mr Hill, the tobacconist. Tell him it's for my husband and he'll know which brand. And also perhaps a little bottle of hair oil. Carman's. Mr Spencer says he'll have no truck with such things, but it won't hurt him to pamper himself occasionally, don't you agree?'

Grace nodded her head. 'Oh, indeed, ma'am.' Taking a small stub of pencil from her bag, she wrote on the list the additional items.

'Here, this should be enough . . .' Mrs Spencer held out some coins and Grace took them and dropped them into her change purse.

'Oh, yes,' Mrs Spencer went on, 'perhaps you'd better have a word with Mrs Sandiston and see if there's anything she needs. The deliveries will be made of course, but she might have forgotten something.'

'Yes, I will.'

Mrs Spencer gave a little shake of her head, as if in wonder at events and said, 'It's so long since we had a guest for dinner. This guest is an old friend of Mr Spencer, so we're looking forward to the meeting. He's recently come down from London with his little girl, and they're staying in Corster while he looks for a house. He's an architect. It'll be a quiet evening, just the three of us. I don't think Mr Fairman is the type to go in for lavish, noisy, social soirées.' She gave a faint smile. 'Mr Spencer is more fond than I of entertaining. I believe that before our time here there were fine dinner parties at the house. Guests would come for the weekend. The men coming for the shooting, the way they do. The women for the gossip. And all those maids and valets, all that coming and going. Not now, of course. We live without fuss here – which is the way it suits me. I'm sure my husband must sometimes find it very dull being married to such an unadventurous spirit.' She sighed and smiled. 'But we're the way we are, and there's no changing it. So of course Mr Spencer's pleased that you're staying here. At least it gets me out of the house. Our little excursions, our little jaunts. And it is better – and very different from the way it used to be, when I stayed indoors most of the day. I'm afraid the days go by and before you realize it another season, another year has passed. And you tell yourself, next year, next spring, next summer I'll seize the day, and do something with my time – get out, see something. But then you find the time has flown by again, and you've done nothing.' She smiled. 'But now you're here – and you'll be good for me.'

'Oh, I hope so, ma'am. If there's anything at all that I can do, you only have to say . . .'

'Yes, thank you.' Mrs Spencer was silent in thought for a moment, then said, 'So, it will be interesting – and pleasant, I hope – to have a guest for dinner. I shall have to think of what I shall wear.' She put a hand up to her head. 'And if you don't mind, Grace, I'll get you to do my hair for me. You always do it so well.'

'Of course, ma'am.' Grace had taken to dressing Mrs Spencer's hair over the past weeks, albeit taking the job away from Jane, the parlour maid. Since the change, Grace thought perhaps she could sometimes detect a slight coolness in the maid's manner towards her. Or could it be her imagination? Still, she told herself, real or not, it was up to Mrs Spencer to have things done as she wished.

Now Mrs Spencer took up her coffee cup again, took a sip and said, 'Young Billy's gone off to school, I suppose.'

'Yes, he went just after eight.'

'How d'you think he's settled in? Has he? Settled in?'

'Oh, yes, ma'am. And I think he's liking his school. I would have heard otherwise. And I think he's made a friend – going by what he said. So that's a very good sign.'

'I should think so. I spoke to him yesterday. He was doing Mrs Sandiston's boots, out on the step, after he got back from school. He's a very willing young lad, and makes himself useful in a variety of ways, I hear. Mrs Sandiston said so. He's done the boots and shoes, and helped the maid with the knives.' She smiled. 'We shan't need to employ an odd job boy if he continues like it.' She paused briefly as if debating whether to continue, then said, 'I asked him again about his leg. He's sensitive about it. Understandably, of course. He didn't want to talk about it.'

'No, he doesn't,' Grace said.

'Anyway,' Mrs Spencer added, 'you want to get off into the town, and I mustn't keep you. How are you getting there?'

Grace shrugged; there was only one way. 'I'll walk to Berron Wick and get the train in.'

'And coming back? You'll have things to carry.'

'Oh – nothing of any great weight.'

'Well, you must get the station fly from Berron Wick on the way back. And you must certainly get Mr Johnson or Mr Rhind to drive you in. You'll probably find Rhind around the stables or helping my husband. Mr Spencer got back from London last night.' She paused. 'Anyway, it's up to you.'

'Thank you, ma'am, but I think I'd prefer to walk to Berron Wick.'

'As you wish.'

Grace had left her employer's room and was moving

through the hall towards the rear of the house when a door from the conservatory opened and Mr Spencer appeared. He was in riding breeches and a cord Norfolk jacket and carried his hat in his hand. It had been almost two weeks since she had seen him. He was away from the house so much, she had learned, either travelling to London or Birmingham on business, or at the paper mill in Redbury or at the soap factory in Milan, Italy. In the pursuance of his business he believed in keeping a close eye on things.

'Good morning, sir,' Grace greeted him.

'Good morning to you, Miss Grace.'

'You've been away, sir. We haven't seen you around in some days.'

'Yes, I got back from London last night.' He brushed a palm across the thigh of his riding breeches. 'I've just been out now for a very nice morning ride – blowing the cobwebs away. And you're off out, are you?'

'I'm going into Corster. Mrs Spencer needs a few art materials, and some silks for her petit point. I have to see Cook before I go, also, in case she needs anything for Saturday when your guest arrives.'

'How are you getting into town?'

'I just told Mrs Spencer I shall walk to the station then catch the train. Either that or I'll take the omnibus.'

'Why don't you get Mr Johnson to take you in?'

'He's busy, sir, and I can manage perfectly well.'

'Well, if Johnson's busy, then get Mr Rhind. He's free, I know that.'

'No,' she said, a little too quickly, 'really, sir, but I think I'd prefer to make my own way.'

'Really? He'll have the time right now. Why walk when you don't need to?'

'No, truly, I wouldn't want to bother him, and it's not far.'

'It won't be any bother.' He made as if to turn and step away. 'Let's go and find him.'

'No, really, please.'

He stopped, turned back to her. 'Why are you so reluctant to use Rhind's services?' he said. 'Do you have a particular reason?'

Grace was at a loss as to what to say, and remained silent a moment too long.

'You *do*,' Mr Spencer said. 'You do have a particular reason.'

'Well –' Grace got out the one word then fell silent again.

'Tell me.'

'I think that for some reason or other he doesn't like me.' And even as she finished speaking she thought how pathetic her words sounded. But the words had been said.

'Has he been rude to you?'

And could she tell him of those words that Rhind had spoken to her in the trap back in the summer of the previous year when he had been with Mr Spencer and Grace had been given a ride to Green Shipton? Now, at this remove, she was not even certain that she had heard the man aright. Perhaps she had imagined it. After all, there had been nothing on his face, no expression, no hint of any kind to indicate that he had said anything amiss.

'If he has,' Mr Spencer said, 'then you must tell me. All right?'

'Yes.'

'He's been a most faithful helper over the years,' he said. 'I don't know what I would have done without him.'

'He's been with you a long time, has he?'

'Oh, many years. And no one more loyal. But tell me, why do you suppose he doesn't like you?'

'Please – Mr Spencer, forget I said anything.'

'No, we can't forget it. You must have a reason.'

'No, really, it was just – just perhaps a feeling I got.'

He thought about this for a moment, then said, 'Very well, I won't press you any more. But if there is anything you must let me know.'

'Yes.'

'Remember that now. All right?'

She nodded.

'I do know that he can get rather – possessive at times. But he means nothing by it. And I have the greatest loyalty from him. It's a rare thing. Anyway,' he smiled, 'be that as it may.' And then in a different tone: 'How are you? Are you well?'

As he spoke he took a small step closer to her, and it was all she could do not to take a step away.

'Yes, I'm very well, thank you,' she said.

'And your brother? Young Billy?'

'He's in excellent health. He's off at school right now.'

'Yes. My wife's been telling me that you and she have had a fine old week. She says you got the train into Redbury and looked at the town's museum.'

'Oh, yes, it was so enjoyable. We took our sketchbooks.'

'And did you produce some good work?'

'Well, Mrs Spencer did. Speaking for myself, I can't say. It was certainly interesting, though. We had a very pleasant time.'

'That's good. I'm delighted to hear that Mrs Spencer is getting out a little. She's been staying in far too much. She got out of the habit of leaving the house. So let's hope there'll be plenty more opportunities.'

'I'm sure there will be, sir. We've talked about driving out somewhere and taking our drawing materials.' And now she had the chance to step away. 'And which I have to buy some more of today for Mrs Spencer.'

He nodded. 'So you're off into Corster, are you?'

'Yes, sir. Is there anything you need from the shops while I'm there?'

'Thank you, but I can't think of anything. No doubt I shall remember something the moment you've left the house.'

*

The only thing Mrs Sandiston needed was a small quantity of angelica, and with the item added to her list, Grace set off, heading for Berron Wick and the railway station.

She had been walking for just a few minutes when a horse-drawn carriage came along beside her. Looking up, she saw that the driver was Rhind. She came to a stop and he pulled up the horse beside her.

'Mr Spencer sent me after you,' he said. 'If you want, I'm to drive you to Berron Wick station, or if you'd prefer it, I'm to take you into Corster, and wait while you do your shopping.'

'Thank you, but it's not necessary,' she said. 'I told Mr Spencer I could make my own way.'

'I don't know anything about that, miss,' Rhind said. 'All I know is what Mr Spencer told me.' He managed to say all of this without meeting her eyes.

Grace realized it would be foolish to keep refusing, so she gave a nod to Rhind and said, 'Very well. You may take me as far as the station. And thank you.'

'There's nothing to thank me for, miss,' he said, then leapt down from the driver's seat and offered her his arm to help her up. 'I'm only obeying the master's orders.'

When Grace was seated he swung up into the driver's seat, and with a little jolt the carriage started forward.

Grace felt awkward and self-conscious sitting there with Rhind so silent and so close, and the only sound the sound of the horse's hoofs and the carriage wheels. It was a ridiculous situation, she thought. They were both employees of Mr Spencer and there was no reason for Rhind to behave as if she were some kind of rival. She was no threat to him in his loyal relationship with Mr Spencer, and he had no call to be so rude, suspicious and cold in his manner towards her.

They rode on in their own silence for a while. The sun shone down, though the breeze was cold. The green of the fields was rich and lush, and new spring lambs skipped in the meadows. Taking a breath, Grace said: 'Mr Rhind?'

The man made no sign that he had heard, though she could not but doubt that he had. She spoke again, this time more loudly.

'I say, Mr Rhind . . .?'

And now he half-turned on the seat. 'Yes, miss,' he said over his shoulder, throwing the words out into the breeze.

Now that she had his attention she was uncertain as to how to go on. Then, taking a breath, she said, feeling foolish as she did so, 'Do you think the weather is likely to stay fine?'

'I've no idea, miss,' he said. 'I'm not much of a judge when it comes to the weather.' He turned back to face the road.

'Well,' she said, 'let's hope the rain keeps off – at least for a while.'

He said nothing to this, and she felt she could hear the echo of her words hanging in the air.

'Mr Spencer was saying,' she said after a moment, 'that you've been with him a very long time.'

He kept silent.

'Is that so, Mr Rhind?' she said.

A pause, then he said, 'Is this of interest to you, miss?'

She felt herself flushing. 'I wouldn't have asked if it were not.'

He said nothing.

'Mr Rhind,' she said, 'I would like us to be friends. And if we can't be friends, at least we can be polite to one another.'

'I have no wish to be impolite to you, miss,' he said.

She wished she could see his face as he spoke, but he kept looking ahead. She could make nothing of his tone. And then after a few moments he said, without so much as a half-turn in her direction, 'Yes, I've been with Mr Spencer for some time, miss. He's been very good to me. I owe him a lot.'

Grace leaned a little closer to catch his words, for he spoke without raising his voice and it was not easy to hear him over the sound of the wheels and the horse's hoofs.

'I've been with him throughout his travels,' Rhind went on. 'I was with him in America and I was with him in Brazil. Pretty well wherever he goes I've gone too. And shall do, in the future.'

'What did you do,' Grace asked, 'before you met Mr Spencer, and came into his employ?'

'What did I do? It's not important. It doesn't matter.' He half-turned on the seat and threw back a cold glance. 'The only thing that counts is my time with him.'

His look lingered on her for a second, as if he was waiting for her to make some remark, some comment. As if he was somehow challenging her. Grace said nothing, and after a moment he looked away to face the road ahead again. From that time on he did not speak again until they had drawn into Berron Wick.

As Rhind pulled up the carriage outside the railway station, Grace said, making conversation and gesturing to the Leaping Hare public house that stood nearby, 'Will you be having some refreshment here, Mr Rhind? I should think you could do with a little ale after that dusty road.' With his help she climbed down out of the carriage.

'I don't drink ale,' he said, '– or any alcohol for that matter.'

'Well, whatever you do, Mr Rhind,' she said stiffly, 'I'm sure you'll please yourself.' Turning, she started away.

'Miss?' he said. 'Miss Harper?'

She stopped and turned. 'Yes?'

'Do you know what train you'll be getting back? If so I'm to come and meet you.'

She looked at him for a moment in silence then said, 'I

have no idea. So please don't bother to try to meet me. I shall walk or take the station fly. Whatever you do, don't trouble yourself about me.'

She turned and started away again, but in moments he had hurried forward and overtaken her. Stopping in front of her and so bringing her to a halt before him, he said:

'I didn't mean to be rude, miss.'

'Didn't you?'

'No, really. I get a bit – het up at times. I didn't mean to take it out on you.'

Was this something near to an apology? Grace wondered. She said nothing. She could detect no note of contrition in his voice.

'I'm sorry, miss,' he said. But still he did not meet her eyes.

And now Grace did not care any more. She wanted nothing of him. She did not believe in his apology for one moment; it had only been offered, she guessed, for the sake of his relationship with his master.

'Excuse me,' she said. She went to step around him, but he moved to the side, blocking her way again, and now met her eyes with his.

'Miss, please. I'm sorry I was rude. It was uncalled for, completely.'

She had determined to have no more truck with him, but his apology was disarming. She remained silent, not knowing what to say.

'Will you accept my apology?' he said. 'We're both employed by Mr Spencer. There's no reason why we shouldn't get on.'

'That's been my view all along, Mr Rhind. It's you who's chosen to think otherwise.'

'I'm sorry.'

Grace gave a sigh. She had no wish to prolong this distance, this unpleasantness. 'I just want to get on with people,' she said. 'I have nothing against you, Mr Rhind. Let's just forget the whole thing.'

'Thank you.' To her surprise his mouth was moved by the touch of a faint smile. 'So,' he said, 'what time shall you want to go back to the house? I'm at your disposal.'

'It's not necessary,' she said. 'As I told you, I shall walk or take the station fly. I've no idea what train I'll be getting back.'

As she finished speaking she moved past him and went through the station entrance.

Corster market square was packed with stalls, the aisles filled with busy shoppers, and the air filled with the sounds of voices, loudest of all those of the stallholders crying advertisements for their wares.

Grace decided that she would look around the stalls later, but would first make sure of getting the things that Mrs Spencer required. She went to the haberdasher's initially, in a little shop just off the main street, to buy the little skeins of silk for Mrs Spencer's embroidery, and that done set off for the small shop where art materials were sold. There, after consulting her pencilled list, she bought the tubes of oil paint, the bottle of linseed oil and the small sketchbook. There were certain art materials that she would have liked for herself, but for the time being she would have to do without.

She went to a grocer's next and bought the angelica for Mrs Sandiston, and after that bought a daily newspaper and went into the Harp and Stars to sit down and have a little refreshment.

Over a cup of tea she looked at that day's edition of the *Morning Post*. Then, rested and refreshed, she left the pub and set off for the tobacconist's shop to buy Mr Spencer's tobacco.

Arriving at the shop, she spoke to the young man behind

the counter, asking for an ounce of tobacco for Mr Spencer at Asterleigh House. The young man turned and called into the rear of the shop, 'Tobacco for Mr Spencer at Asterleigh House, Dad. What'll it be?'

In response an elderly man came through from the back and on looking enquiringly at his son was told, 'This young lady here.'

'Ah, miss, yes. You want tobacco for Mr Spencer at Asterleigh?'

Grace said she did. 'I'm to get an ounce, but I don't know which brand. Mrs Spencer said you would know.'

'Yes, indeed, miss. Mr Spencer uses Franklyn's Fine Shagg. An ounce, you say, miss?'

When the tobacco had been weighed and wrapped, Grace paid the man and took the small package and put it in her bag next to her purse. Then, thanking the man, she turned away. The door opened as she stopped before it, opened by a tall man who held it for her to pass through. But in the same moment the shop proprietor called out, 'Miss, you didn't pick up your change.' About to pass through the doorway, Grace abruptly turned away from it and, without an apology, left the tall man standing there, holding the door open. As she picked up her change from the counter she heard the man behind her give a little sigh of exasperation and say with a chuckle, 'It's perfectly all right, miss, I have nothing better to do in my life than stand here as lackey to the passing trade.'

'I'm sorry,' Grace said, stung, turning back to him, 'I didn't mean to make you wait there.' With her words she swept past him out into the street, and without looking back stalked away.

Looking up at the clock face on the town hall, she saw that it was 12.45. She had only the hair tonic to buy for Mr Spencer and then her shopping was finished. She knew from past visits to the market that there was a stall selling hair oils and tonics and such things, so she headed for it now.

People came from miles around to do their weekly shopping, and at times the aisles between the market stalls were congested. And not only with those out to buy, but sellers, too, men, women and children who moved through the aisles with trays on their breasts, selling ribbons and bootlaces, cotton thread and all kinds of knick-knacks and other items that were fairly portable and didn't take up too much space. And not only were all the early risers still busy about the place, but all the latecomers had now arrived to swell their numbers.

Looking around for the stall offering the hair tonic, Grace was drawn to a stall where the holder was selling handmade lace. She stopped at the stall and carefully picked up a short length of the lace, looking at the fine work. There was no denying that it was very beautiful. Machine-made lace was widely used now, making the handmade kind so much more expensive.

As she held the lace up to the light under the approving eye of the stallholder she heard a voice say, 'Beautiful, ain't it, miss,' and saw that the words had come from one of two young lads of thirteen or fourteen who stood side by side grinning at her. She smiled back at them. 'Yes, it's very pretty.'

'Like you, miss,' the shorter of the two boys said, and Grace gave an ironic little bow and thanked him, and the two boys good-naturedly punched one another on the upper arms and laughed loudly at their own impertinence.

After several moments' deliberation, Grace decided to buy half a yard of the lace. She would send it to Aunt Edie as a little present with her next letter. It would look so pretty dressing up a plain nightgown.

Grace paid for the lace, and as she put it safely in her bag with her other purchases the older of the two boys said with a wide grin and an arched eyebrow, 'You gettin' married, miss? That'll look right grand on yer weddin' gown.'

'No, I'm *not* getting married,' she said, laughing, to which the youth replied, 'Oh, that's good to 'ear! So d'yer reckon there's a chance for me?' And then hooting raucously into the air, he and his companion turned and were off through the crowd.

Grace also moved on, and after another minute was standing at a stall where she could see on display the hair tonic that she was to buy for Mr Spencer. When she had bought a bottle of it, she put it in her basket. On the slip of paper that was her shopping list she wrote with her pencil the cost of the hair tonic, adding it to the prices of the other items she had bought for Mrs Spencer. That done, she moved on, stopping at a nearby stall where she found herself attracted by a show of colourful prints of classical artworks, by artists including Raphael, Murillo and Constable, as well as more modern artists such as Millais and Burne-Jones. She found particularly attractive a print of a painting by the Spanish artist Murillo, showing peasant boys eating fruit. The print was simply but attractively framed, and she stood gazing at the picture wishing she could afford it.

And then suddenly her attention was taken by the sound of an altercation close behind her, and turning she saw a flurry of movement among the people and then realized that a tall man had taken hold of a boy by the arm and the scruff of the neck and was trying to drag him away. She recognized the boy as one of the pair who had spoken to her a few minutes before. Still holding the picture, Grace, along with many others stood and watched the little drama. And Grace realized that she knew the man's face also; he was the one who had held open the tobacconist's door for her. Now she watched as the boy lashed out with his boot, catching the man on the right shin. The man responded by giving a yell of pain, and releasing the boy just long enough to give him a clout on the side of the face.

This was enough for Grace. Putting down the picture, she picked up her basket that she had placed between her feet and stepped forward.

'Sir,' she cried, 'how dare you strike that boy!' As she finished speaking she became aware of the many pairs of eyes now taking her in as a part of the increasingly dramatic scene.

The man said nothing, but concentrated on holding the struggling boy.

'What has he done to you,' Grace said, 'that you should treat him in this way!'

'The answer to that, miss,' the man said, 'is nothing at all.'

'Then I suggest you release him at once.'

The man ignored her. With the boy struggling and squirming in his grasp, he was trying to hold him at arm's length and so avoid his swinging fists and feet.

'Did you hear me?' Grace said. 'Let him go.' While she spoke she could not escape the feeling that by interfering she had somehow committed herself to the situation and could not now turn and fade into the background – which might have been the best course if she was to keep her dignity intact. To add to her discomfiture, the man seemed to treat her with little less than contempt. Over the flailing limbs and the sound of the boy's protests he looked at Grace and gave a kind of groan.

'Dear God, save me from the morally righteous,' he said, briefly casting his eyes up heavenward. Then looking directly at Grace again, he added with a sardonic smile, 'Our second meeting in an hour, miss. We mustn't make a habit of it or people will begin to talk.'

'Release that boy at once,' she said angrily. 'At once, I tell you.'

As if taking his cue from Grace, the boy gave a violent

squirm and twist in the man's grasp, and opening his mouth, closed his teeth over the man's wrist and bit down. The man yelled and let go at once, and in less than a second the boy was away, slipping through the crowd.

After seeing the boy vanish, Grace turned to the man who now had his wrist up to his mouth, soothing the bruised flesh. But unable to think of anything further to say – and thinking that perhaps she had already said more than enough – she merely gave him a contemptuous glare and turned away. As she stepped smartly between the stalls, head held unnaturally high, she was aware of the eyes of the crowd upon her, and could feel herself blushing under their scrutiny. Intent now only on making her retreat she walked briskly away. Behind her she heard the man's voice as he called out, 'Wait a minute, miss. Don't be in such a hurry,' but she ignored his words and hurried on.

'Miss! I say, miss, will you wait a minute . . .?'

Half-turning, glancing back over her shoulder, she saw that the tall man was coming in pursuit of her. She quickened her pace, though knowing that with his stride she couldn't possibly hope to outpace him for long. And then, moments later, he was striding along beside her.

'Miss – will you hold up there a second?'

Pointedly ignoring him, she walked on. The attention she had provoked from the bystanders had made her feel uncomfortable and now she wanted to leave the scene as soon as she could – not to mention the one who had been the cause of it all.

'I've got longer legs than you, miss,' the man said now, matching her stride with his own. 'And you'll get tired before I do. It's only a matter of time.'

'Sir.' Grace spoke through gritted teeth, keeping her eyes full ahead. 'I have nothing to say to you, and I'd be obliged if you'd not bother me.'

'Oh, I'm bothering you, am I?'

Hearing his challenging tone, she dared flick a glance at him and saw that he was smiling at her. The smile, however, was as sardonic as his tone. In her brief glance she also took in the fact that he was tall and youngish, and was wearing a brown Norfolk jacket with a muffler about his neck. He, catching her eye, put up his hand and briefly raised his hat. Grace looked ahead again.

'Please, sir,' she said, 'I would be grateful if you would kindly leave me alone.'

'Oh, I understand,' he said, 'you think I'm some masher who's out to make a score, is that it?'

'I don't think of you as anything,' she said. 'I know nothing about you.' Coming to an abrupt stop, she turned to him as he came to a halt beside her.

'Look' she said, 'what I *can* tell you is that I'm in rather a hurry, and that I'd be grateful if you would please leave me alone and stop pestering me.'

'Well, I'd like you to tell me one thing,' he said.

'Oh? And what's that?' She thought his eyes seemed to be mocking her. And why was she listening to him? She shouldn't even be standing there long enough to give him as much as the time of day. 'I must go,' she said.

'Just tell me one thing,' he said. He reached out to her as he spoke, and it seemed for a moment that he would put his hand upon her arm. But he did not, and let his hand fall back to his side. 'Just tell me – where did you put your purse?'

'What?' she said. 'You embarrass me in front of everybody in the market and then –'

'*I* embarrassed *you*?' he cut in.

Rather than prolong the encounter she decided to let this pass and not split hairs. 'Well, whatever,' she said, and then: 'Why on earth do you want to know about my purse?'

He sighed. 'Please – I promise I'm neither madman nor masher. Just tell me, please. Make sure it's safe.'

And there was something in his face, some expression. Something that captured her attention and said that he was not, indeed, an escapee from the local asylum. Echoing his own sigh, she shook her head, as it were to a recalcitrant child who must be favoured, and said, 'Well, just to indulge you for a second . . .' and turned away, as if hiding from his view the contents of her bag while she delved into it. A moment or two later she turned back to him.

'My purse is gone.'

He nodded, lips compressed. 'That's what I've been trying to tell you.'

'You – you knew? But then –'

With a flourish which, in the circumstances she forgave him, he put his right hand inside his jacket and the next moment whipped out her purse. 'Yours, I think, miss, if I'm not mistaken,' he said.

Her mouth open, Grace took the purse from his out-stretched hand. 'My purse,' she said vacantly. 'But how did you –' And then realization dawned. 'The boy. Those two boys who were fooling about and being so friendly . . .'

'Exactly. And now you know why I collared one of them.'

Grace had put her hand to her mouth, and now slowly lowered it. 'Oh,' she said lamely, 'sir, I don't know what to say.'

He smiled. 'You don't need to say anything, miss. All's well that ends well.' And with a slightly mocking inclination of his head he turned and walked away.

Chapter Nine

Grace was sewing, mending one of Billy's shirts, and sitting close to the window in order to catch the last of the fading light. Although the rain had stopped falling, it still dripped from the leaves of the elm tree beside the stable. And undeterred by the damp a blackbird sang among the wet branches. In the late April evening his song was the most beautiful sound, incredibly varied and almost unbearably sweet, sometimes delicately fragile and at others rich and full-throated. At times his singing was so arresting that Grace found herself pausing in her stitching just to concentrate on his song, briefly holding her breath lest some exquisite phrase be missed.

The small clock on the mantel showed the time at almost 9.30. Billy would be asleep by now, she thought. Earlier, around seven, she had been sitting with him in his room, listening to him read, when in through the open window had drifted the sound of a horse and carriage moving into the stable yard below. It was, Grace had known, the carriage that had brought the Spencers' dinner guest.

Billy had gone to the window and looked down into the yard.

'You can't see anything,' Grace had said from her armchair. 'I don't know why you bother.'

'Yes, I can,' he had said. 'It's a pony and trap. Though nothing grand. Mr Spencer's groom's just getting down. I suppose the visitor will have got out already at the front door. I can't see any sign of him.'

'Of course he will. You don't expect him to come round to the back, do you?'

Billy then had come from the window and sat on the bed. He had been out in the garden for much of the day, helping Mr Clutter on the herbaceous borders. And later he had spent time in his room trying to model a steam engine from cardboard, a design that he had drawn, painted and cut out. The half-finished model now sat on the top of the old bureau, scissors and pieces of cardboard around it. He was making the model for Mrs Spencer, who had the previous day given him the sketchbook that Grace had brought from Corster.

'I'll leave you to get on with your model,' Grace had said at last and, closing the book, had put it on the side and got up from the chair. At the same time Billy had taken up the train model, judiciously held it up to the light and then picked up the scissors.

'But don't work too late,' Grace had said.

'I won't.'

Now, back in her own room, Grace squinted at the sewing in her fingers and then put it aside. The daylight was growing too dim for her to continue, and she did not want to light the lamp just yet as it attracted the moths.

Her sewing forgotten for the moment, she leaned back in her chair, rested her head against the faded velvet and looked out at the rain that dripped from the ivy just outside the window. Yesterday, Friday, had begun with the weather unusually warm for the time of year and Mrs Spencer had considered having Johnson drive them out so that they could do some painting outdoors. It was the first time she had proposed such a thing. But then rain clouds had begun to gather on the horizon, and while the two women waited, hoping that the clouds would pass, the skies had got darker still, and the rain had begun to fall. So the two had contented themselves with setting up a still life in Mrs Spencer's studio and sitting over their watercolours while outside the rain lashed down. Grace's painting, the result of her efforts, now stood on her bureau, propped up against the wall. She was relatively happy with the picture, though she knew she would never be as good as Mrs Spencer or Billy.

Her thoughts were distracted by the sound of light footsteps on the landing, and moments later there came a tap on her door. She got up at once and opened it. The maid, Jane, stood there.

'Please, miss,' Jane said, unsmiling, 'but the missis has asked if you could go downstairs in a little while.'

'Go downstairs? They have a guest there for dinner, haven't they?'

'Yes, miss. They're just about to have the pudding. Mrs Spencer asks if you could go down to the drawing room in about twenty minutes or so to join them for coffee.' A pause. 'Shall I tell her yes?'

'Oh, but, Jane – I'm not properly dressed. And my hair . . .'

'It's not for twenty minutes, miss. You got a little while.'

'Well –' Grace gave a sigh, 'it'll take me all of that.' She turned and glanced at the clock, registering the time. 'All right, Jane, will you tell Mrs Spencer that I'll be there.'

'I will, miss.' The maid turned and stepped away.

After closing the door behind the departing footsteps of the maid Grace stood still for a moment. She couldn't imagine why her presence was required with the visitor there. She looked at herself in the oval mirror and frowned: her hair was coming loose and there was no way she could go downstairs wearing the old worn dress that she had on. Still, it was no time to stand around.

Twenty-two minutes later, with her hair brushed and put in place again, and having changed into a dress that looked a little less casual and altogether more suitable, she left her room and went along the landing to the main stairs and started down.

At the foot of the stairs she crossed the wide hall towards the drawing room. As she did so she heard from beyond the door leading to the dining room a faint murmur of a male voice. She continued on, tapped on the drawing room door, opened it and stepped inside.

The evening had turned much cooler and a welcoming fire burned in the wide grate. Mrs Spencer was sitting on the sofa before a low table with a laden silver coffee tray on it, in her hands a cup and saucer. She was wearing a dress that Grace had not seen before. In pale lavender brocaded silk, trimmed with fine lace, its simple lines complemented the general air of elegance that always seemed be a part of her appearance.

'Jane said you wanted to see me, Mrs Spencer.'

Mrs Spencer smiled at her. 'Ah, Grace, yes. Thank you for coming down at such short notice.' She held out a hand, palm up, and gestured for Grace to sit beside her.

Grace sat down on the sofa, wondering what was the purpose of the impromptu summons.

'The reason I asked you to come down,' Mrs Spencer said, 'is because I think you are in a position to do a great service – if you would be kind enough to do it. And at the same time find something a little more interesting to do with your time.'

Grace waited.

'I thought this would be a good opportunity,' Mrs Spencer went on. 'We were at dinner, talking, and it suddenly came to me. *Grace*, I said to myself – she's the answer to this. So I thought, while the men enjoy their brandy and smokes I'll have a quiet word with you, and see how you feel – then they can join us for coffee.' She paused, adjusted the shawl about her shoulders, then went on: 'Our guest, Mr Fairman,' here she gestured vaguely in the

171

direction of the dining room, 'is an old friend of Mr Spencer's – I hadn't met him myself before tonight, actually. He used to live in London – but has now come to this part of the world. He's taken rooms in Corster while he looks for a suitable house. He has a small daughter, did I tell you? They've been here just a couple of months or so.'

Realizing that she had been sent for in order to join the Spencers and their guest over coffee, Grace became more conscious of her appearance. Had she taken enough trouble with her hair? And her dress . . . should she have worn the mauve poplin? It was all too late now; she must just sit and go through with it.

Mrs Spencer was continuing: 'It's his little girl I wanted to have a word with you about. Mr Fairman is a widower. His wife died a few years ago, leaving him with his daughter to bring up alone. She – Sophie – is now seven years old. And, so he tells us, is in need of a teacher. She's had one in London for two years, but now of course he wants to find one for her here. He says ideally he's looking for a *temporary* governess for her – just for two or three months, until he gets settled in his new home and is able to make more permanent arrangements.'

'And you think I would be suitable . . .'

'Oh, indeed yes. Absolutely. As I say, it wouldn't be permanent. Once he's found a suitable house I don't doubt he'll want a full-time, permanent governess for his daughter or will send her to school. But at least, if you're there in the meantime he won't have to hurry into anything, you understand?'

'Yes.'

Mrs Spencer sat in silence for a few moments, her eyes trying to read Grace's expression. 'So,' she said at last, smiling at her, 'what do you think about it?' And adding before Grace had a chance to reply: 'And I do think it would be good for you also.'

'Good for me?'

'My dear, you were never brought up to be a companion, were you? And I have to tell you that there have been so many occasions when I've wondered what you are doing with your time. Oh, I know we draw together and paint together, and there are times when you help me with my hair, and we go shopping together, and visit the museums and galleries. But I often have the feeling it's not enough for you. You were trained by your mother as a teacher, and I'm sure you have a lot to offer a child. Don't you get bored sometimes here, with so little to do, and so little call on your intellect? I'm sure you do.'

Grace was not sure how to answer this question. There were indeed times when she was less occupied than she would have wished. Though perhaps it would not be politic to admit it at present. She kept silent.

Mrs Spencer went on: 'I have felt for a good while now that you need more to occupy your time, Grace – and this seems to me an ideal opportunity. It will give you a little more variety in your life – heaven knows there isn't much in it right now. And we shall still have time for our painting and our little excursions.' She gave an ironic smile. 'And if the weather today is a portent of what's to come it'll be a long time before we're able to get outside – and you'll have more time on your hands than ever. So . . .' She came to a halt, waiting. 'Well, Grace? What do you think about it?'

Grace had already decided that she would accept. For one thing she did not see how she could possibly refuse. Mrs Spencer had already acknowledged the fact that Grace's time was not fully utilized, and in doing so was not telling Grace anything that she did not already know. Besides, Grace could not forget the great kindness that Mrs Spencer had shown in taking her and Billy in in the first place.

'I – I think it would be very interesting – and very

enjoyable,' Grace said. Not only did she want to please Mrs Spencer, but she truly did feel that it would be something she could enjoy. 'I think I'd like to do it very much,' she added.

'Good. That's splendid. I thought that would be your reaction. And you'll also have the satisfaction of knowing that you'll be helping out Mr Spencer's friend. It's all in a good cause.' As Mrs Spencer finished speaking she got up and moved to the bell pull beside the fireplace. Soon after she had sat down again there came a tap at the door and the maid entered.

'Oh, Jane,' Mrs Spencer said, 'would you bring the coffee, please, and also be so kind as to tell Mr Spencer and Mr Fairman that you're about to serve it?'

'Yes, ma'am.'

As the door closed behind the girl, Grace said, 'But what about Mr Fairman? Are you sure this is all right with him? He hasn't seen me yet. I might not be quite what he has in mind.'

'Oh, believe me, you will be,' Mrs Spencer said. 'And you're being presented to him on our recommendation –' she smiled here, 'so he wouldn't dare cast aspersions in that respect, would he? And as for your liking him as an employer, I'm sure you will. Anyway, you'll be meeting each other in a minute, so then there'll be no further need to wonder.'

Soon afterwards the maid was back, bringing in the coffee and setting it down on the low table before Mrs Spencer. A minute after the maid had left the door opened again and Mr Spencer and their guest came into the room.

To her great astonishment, Grace recognized him at once.

And as the necessary introductions were made, so it was that Grace found her hand being taken by the man who only two days earlier had intervened to save her purse.

The visitor was in his early to mid-thirties, Grace

guessed. His hair was very dark, and against the fashion of the time for moustaches and sidewhiskers he was clean-shaven. Like Mr Spencer he was in formal day wear, sporting a winged collar and double-breasted frock coat. As he took Grace's hand he bowed slightly over it, and she felt a little frisson at the strangeness of encountering him again so soon and in such surprising circumstances.

Invited to sit beside Mrs Spencer, Grace sat down on the sofa. Pressed by her employer she said yes, she would like a little coffee. As she sat there while the coffee was poured she felt very much at a disadvantage. The man, Mr Fairman, had given no sign of recognition either by word or action, and for a moment she found herself wondering whether he remembered her from their encounter. And then, turning slightly, glancing in his direction, she found his dark eyes upon her and knew without doubt that he did. There was that same look – what was it? – sardonic and slightly mocking perhaps? If it was, then bearing in mind her humiliating memory of the scene in the market square, she could hardly wonder at it. She shifted her glance at once and turned to Mrs Spencer who was pouring out the coffee.

Directing her words to the visitor, Mrs Spencer said, setting down the coffee pot, 'I've spoken to Miss Harper about your little girl, Mr Fairman. She seems to find the idea quite agreeable. Isn't that so, Grace?'

Grace was having second thoughts now, but did not think she could very well express them at this moment. However, she was saved from finding an answer as Mr Fairman spoke up.

'I wonder if perhaps we're not moving a little too fast for Miss Harper,' he said. His voice was deep, somewhat flat in tone – as if its owner was careful to give nothing away. 'Perhaps she would like to think about it for a while before she commits herself.'

Mr Spencer spoke then, saying with a smile, 'Well, what do you think, Miss Harper? As you can see, he looks fairly normal. And I can recommend him, I promise you. My only criticism is that he's kept out of our way for the past few years.'

'In that case,' Mrs Spencer said to him, briefly pausing to hand Grace her coffee, 'let's hope you find a suitable house soon, so you'll want to stay. I'm sure London must be a wonderful place, but I can't help but think that a country town might be a better spot in which to bring up a child.'

'Oh, I have no doubt you're right,' Mr Fairman said.

'The things one reads in the papers,' Mr Spencer said, '– the amount of crime that goes on in the cities. London in particular, I'm sure. It isn't a spot where I'd care to raise a child.'

'Well, the newspapers do tend to exaggerate the scale of the problem,' Mr Fairman said. 'And criminal misdeeds aren't confined to the metropolis. You have your rogues here – not nearly so many, of course – your share of thieves and pickpockets.'

Without looking at him, Grace could feel the man's eyes upon her now; and she was glad of the coffee cup and saucer, otherwise she would not have known what to do with her hands.

'Anyway,' Mr Spencer went on, 'now that you're here, old chap, maybe you'll stay and put down some roots. And as for young Sophie, I'm sure Miss Harper will be only too glad to do what she can for her.'

'I do hope so,' said Mrs Spencer, turning to Grace, and added, 'I haven't had the pleasure of meeting Mr Fairman's daughter – though my husband has – but I've no doubt she's a very sweet child.'

Mr Spencer said, 'Oh, by the way, Miss Harper, it was my idea to speak to you about this, so if it doesn't suit, then I'm the one you have to blame.'

A brief silence fell, and Grace was aware of the three pairs of eyes upon her. She did not know what to say. To form a working relationship with the visitor was not something she relished – but how could she refuse? She was employed by the Spencers, and clearly they wanted her to provide her services to the man.

'Well,' she said, 'if I can help at all, then I'll be only too happy to,' she heard herself say. Then she added, 'Though I should mention that I've never worked with girls. I've only ever been governess to boys.'

'Oh, I'm sure that won't matter,' Mrs Spencer said. 'I've no doubt that Mr Fairman's daughter is a well behaved child.'

As the coffee was drunk and the conversation continued, it was suggested by Mrs Spencer that Grace go the next day to Mr Fairman's rooms in Corster, and there meet his small daughter and make arrangements for her tuition.

And so it was left. Twenty minutes later, with Grace still feeling somewhat manipulated and less than happy about it – but at the same time doing her best to hide her feelings – she got up to take her leave of the small assembly. As she said goodnight to Mr Fairman he briefly caught her eye, and quickly she lowered her gaze. Another minute and she was out in the hall and heading for the stairs and her room.

As was their wont, the following morning Grace and Billy went to church, the local church of St Matthews in Berron Wick, braving the discomfort of the April rain. But come the afternoon the weather had cleared and the sun was out, making a little less miserable the prospect of Grace's visit to Mr Fairman's lodgings.

Before she went, however, she sat down at her little table and began a letter to Aunt Edie, bringing up the surprising possibility of teaching the small daughter of one of Mr Spencer's friends. And without going into the details of her initial encounter with Mr Fairman she spoke of having previously met him, and at the same time of not being overly impressed. She would that afternoon, however, be going to see the child. She wrote:

This is one chore I do not look forward to, for I can't see a wonderfully happy teacher/pupil relationship developing. But anyway, the job being tendered is not something I shall be forced to take, notwithstanding that I might feel some obligation to Mrs Spencer. You can be sure that I shall do what I can to resist Mr Fairman's offer.

There was no time to write more; for soon she would have to leave for her appointment in Corster.

To Grace's relief it was Johnson the groom who was given the task of driving her to Berron Wick station that afternoon. Alighting from the train in Corster, Grace took a fly to the address she had been given. The driver pulled up his horse before a house which was situated on the western side of the town between the river and the railway station. The house was Georgian and rather nondescript in appearance, with red brick walls and a plain façade. As the coachman drove off, Grace rang the bell. It was answered by a maid who when Grace enquired for Mr Fairman, said, 'I'll show you up, miss,' and led her up the stairs to the first floor. There she rapped on the door of a room off the landing. The door was opened by Mr Fairman who thanked the girl and invited Grace inside. Turning back to the maid, he said, 'Julia, d'you think you could provide some tea and cakes for my visitor and me?' He smiled. 'And not forgetting Sophie, of course. She'll be returning any moment. I think perhaps a glass of milk for her.'

'Of course, sir.' The maid smiled at him and bobbed, then turned and headed back for the stairs.

The man closed the door and then turned to Grace. He

was dressed casually, wearing a woollen smoking jacket and a soft-collared shirt and tie, and held an open book in his right hand. He set down the book on a bureau and took Grace's cape and laid it over the back of a chair. He thanked her for coming, then added with a smiling sigh, 'We have a nurse and a maid, but I'm afraid both of them are out right now. Still, we shall manage all right.' They were standing in a small vestibule and he gestured towards the room in front of them. 'Please, come this way.'

Grace stepped into a wide room, with windows over-looking the narrow street where the carriages trundled by. Briefly, passing a looking glass, she caught a glimpse of her reflection and saw herself, a tall girl wearing a dress of russet brown with a velvet bodice and draperies of lace. Her hand moved for a moment as if she would touch her chignon, but she did not, and took the seat that the man was gesturing to.

She sat down on the sofa. He stood for a second looking down at her – he seemed enormously tall from this vantage point – then took a seat in a chair at right angles to her. 'Mrs Simkin's maid will bring our tea soon,' he said.

Grace nodded and gave a half-smile. She could think of nothing to say.

'Did you have a good journey over?' he asked.

'Oh, yes, thank you.'

'And you had no difficulty finding the place?'

'No, none at all.'

She avoided his eyes when they fell upon her – though she could somehow sense that he himself was not totally at ease. She felt that he was making conversation just to fill the silence. She felt increasingly disconcerted, and wished fervently that she had not been placed in such a situation. There was no changing it, however, at least not for the moment.

After staying silent for a few seconds, Mr Fairman said,

'You don't have to go through with this, Miss Harper. Really you don't.'

She did not look at him as he spoke, but even so she could feel that his eyes were not directed at her, but were looking elsewhere in the room. His words, so bluntly delivered, took her by surprise.

'Do you mean,' she said, 'my being asked to –'

'Precisely. I mean your being asked to come here – to be sent as governess to my daughter. I'm quite sure it's the last thing you want. And I can't say I blame you. I have no doubt that Mr and Mrs Spencer meant well, but I'm not sure that I myself would exactly welcome being thrust into such an unwelcome situation.'

And now Grace spoke, lifting her face to him as he was looking at her. 'Mr Fairman,' she said, 'I know we got off on the wrong foot – and I know also that it was as much due to me as it was to you, and I –'

He frowned at this. 'As much due to *you*?' he said. 'Miss Harper, it was *all* due to you. I did nothing to you. I merely saved your purse from a casual thief – a young gypsy who had charmed you into thinking that he was merely an innocent young lad, and as such could do no wrong.' He pulled back the sleeve of his jacket and the cuff of his shirt and lifted his arm, exposing the discoloured bruise on his wrist. 'And if you want evidence of his goodwill, you have only to look here,' he said.

'Mr Fairman, I don't know why you have bring all that up,' Grace said. 'If I caused you embarrassment then I –'

'No more than you brought upon yourself,' he broke in.

'– As I was saying,' she said evenly, 'if I caused you embarrassment, then I regret it. But having said that, I'd as soon leave the matter forgotten and in the past, if it's all the same to you. Of course, if you wish to dwell upon it, then I'm sure I can't stop you.'

'Miss Harper, I'm sorry.' He leaned forward slightly in

his chair, his voice rising a little in its pitch. 'Forgive me. I shouldn't have said that. I suppose neither one of us came out of that incident with any credit,' and here, seeing her inhale, seeing her expression of displeasure, he quickly raised a hand, ' – and if I'm presuming too much in saying that, then forgive that too. I mean no offence, believe me.'

Grace held her breath for a moment, let it out in a sigh, then said, 'Sir – I would be so glad if we might simply – well – call a halt to this. Do you think we could?'

'A truce?' he said, his mouth moving in a smile. 'I would be glad.'

'Oh, yes,' she said with relief. 'And I think, I must admit, that perhaps I came out of it better. After all, I came out of it with my purse, whereas you had a painful bite.'

'True.' He nodded, and looked ruefully again at his wrist. 'But it's mending.'

'I'm glad to hear it.'

They smiled, relaxing a little, then he got up and moved to the window. Looking down onto the street, he said, 'Sophie should be back any minute now.' He turned to Grace. 'I think she's quite looking forward to meeting you.'

'Well,' Grace smiled, 'and I'm looking forward to meeting *her*. Is she enjoying being in Corster?'

'Oh, I believe so. Though I think she misses her little friends. Still, she'll make new ones before too long. Of course everything is so new to her here. And being so close to all the fields and woodland and rolling downs – well, it's quite wonderful. We've driven out to look at the surrounding countryside on two occasions and I think to her it's like finding a different world. She's only known London, of course. And then only one part of it.'

'I've never been to London, though I can imagine that everything is so very different.'

'Indeed, yes. We didn't live in the centre, the West End, mind you – which is the part that all visitors see, of course.

We lived in a residential area, in the borough of Kensington – which is less built up and much more attractive. It's very pleasant with all its parks and squares and beautiful trees. And we were particularly fortunate in that our house backed on to private gardens where Sophie and her friends could play.'

'You make it sound very attractive. I'd love to visit there. See some of the fine buildings, the great stores and the theatres and museums. There's so much to see there, so much to do. I should think you and Sophie must find Corster a very unadventurous spot in comparison.'

He gave a smile, slightly rueful. 'Sometimes unadventurous is what is required.'

'Well,' she said, 'let's hope you and Sophie don't get bored with the scene here.'

'We shan't do that, never fear.' He turned his head, gazing off along the street below again. 'We're going to build a new life, Sophie and I. I owe her that. Of course at the moment we only have these rented rooms, but I think I've found a more permanent place for us. A very nice house I've been looking at in Upper Callow. I think it'll be just fine – will suit us very well. You know the village, do you?'

'It's a most attractive place.'

'The house I've looked at is close to the river. It's really very nice. And if it doesn't work out there will be other pleasant places. I've been looking at properties since we arrived. It hasn't been easy to find something.'

'What made you come to Corster when you left London? You could have gone anywhere you chose.'

'Yes, we could. It's because I visited here when I was young. It was the first place I ever saw outside of London. I came with my father when he travelled down on business one year.' He gave a little shrug. 'I suppose it made an impression on me. I mean, there's nothing exceptional about it, but that's what people do – they tend to go to the places they have some familiarity with – no matter how slight.'

'Is this where you and Mr Spencer met and became friends?'

'No, we met on the way to Italy. I and my wife and daughter were going out to Naples. He was travelling on business also. Oh, that was years ago. It was just a chance meeting but we became friends – the way it happens. The common factor was his coming from this area, and my having visited it. So, as I say, we became friends.' He smiled at the thought. 'Later we lost touch with one another – as happens. But then, coming down to Corster, I ran into him here in the town and found that he's living nearby, not that far from where he was born.' He gave a little nod. 'It's a small world indeed.'

'What about your work? Mrs Spencer tells me you're an architect.'

'Yes, I am. And I love my work.'

'Of course you'll be able to do your work here just as well as in London, won't you?'

'Yes. As soon as I get a place where I can start work I can get organized.'

As he finished speaking there came a sound from the outer door beyond the vestibule.

'Ah,' he said, turning towards the sound, 'it's Sophie and Nancy.'

He moved towards the door and as he did so the far door opened and Grace saw coming towards her a small figure, a little girl in a burgundy coat and straw hat. Behind her came a young woman in her early twenties wearing a dark brown cape. The child came to a halt a few feet away, looked up at Grace and said, 'Are you Miss Harper?'

'I am indeed,' Grace said. 'And obviously you are Sophie.'

'Yes, I'm Sophie,' the girl said. She was slightly built, with her father's dark hair and dark eyes, eyes that looked up at Grace with warmth and spirit. Then, turning to the girl beside her, she added, 'And this is Nancy. We've been to the river, feeding the ducks.'

With Grace introduced to the nursemaid, the young woman took off Sophie's coat and left the room. Seconds later there came a knock at the door and the maid entered bearing a tray.

'Ah, good,' said Mr Fairman, 'here comes our tea.'

By the time tea was finished Grace had learned a great many things about her putative young pupil; not least among them that the child had a quick and alert mind and an obvious eagerness to learn. Over the tea and sandwiches and cakes they spoke of the different ways of London and the country market town that was Corster; and it was a conversation during which Grace felt she gained as much as she gave. It was also clear that notwithstanding the fact that the child had had no formal education, her father had not neglected her learning. When the subject of reading was brought up Sophie immediately – with permission from her father – got down from the table and fetched one of her books. Then, back in her seat she took pride in demonstrating her reading abilities. What was clear also was the affection between Sophie and her father. Grace lost count of the number of times the child made reference to him: 'Papa says . . . Papa says . . .' and also noted the father's pride in his daughter's achievements.

When tea was done Mr Fairman suggested that Sophie take her afternoon nap and allow him a little more time to talk to the visitor.

'I hope you'll teach me,' Sophie said after wishing Grace good afternoon. 'Do you think you will?'

Mr Fairman broke in here: 'We mustn't put Miss Harper

184

under pressure, Sophie. She has to make her decision when she's on her own and away from charming influences like you.'

Sophie left them then to go to her room where the nurse awaited her, and Grace said she had better think about getting her train.

In the vestibule Mr Fairman helped her on with her cape. 'Let me say how much I've enjoyed your visit,' he said. 'And I know that Sophie has also. She's not had a happy time of late, and it's good to see her take to someone so.' As Grace stood before the glass he looked past her head at her reflection. 'So – now that you've met her,' he added, 'perhaps you'd give some thought to helping her with her lessons. I know she would like it – and I would be so glad.'

Grace nodded, but did not meet his eyes in the glass.

'But please bear in mind what I said earlier,' he said. 'I meant it, truly. If you don't want to go through with it, then you must say so. I shall perfectly well understand, and I shan't hold it against you. After all, I do realize that you've been somewhat – edged into the situation – without anyone meaning to do it, I hasten to add. But if you decide you don't want to do it I shan't mention it to Mrs Spencer. I'll give her some other excuse. You won't come off badly, I promise you.'

'Oh, but Mr Fairman –' she began, but before she could speak further he interrupted her.

'Don't give me your answer right now,' he said. 'Think about it first. That way I'll be more certain it's the true one.' He smiled and stepped to the door. 'Come – I'll walk with you to the corner and we'll find you a cab.'

Back at Asterleigh, upstairs in her room, she looked at the letter she had started to her aunt. She read its contents through and eventually came to the part where she had spoken of her possible employment as governess to Mr

Fairman's daughter: *You can be sure that I shall do what I can to resist Mr Fairman's offer*.

But she knew now that she would not.

Carefully she tore the page across and again, until she was left holding only fragments.

Chapter Ten

'I'm so pleased you're going to teach her.'

Mrs Spencer was in the library on the first floor, directing her words to Grace who stood by the window. The woman had suggested that Grace use the room as a schoolroom for the time being. 'We'll make sure there's a fire lit,' Mrs Spencer said. 'But if the room's not suitable, let me know and we'll find something else. But as I said, I doubt the teaching's going to last that long, anyway. For as soon as Mr Fairman has settled his house, Sophie will be studying at home with a permanent governess or going off to school.' She looked around her. 'D'you think this will be all right? Will you have everything you need?'

'Oh, it's a wonderful room to teach in,' Grace said. 'And we shan't need much. We have all the books we could possibly want – not to mention space and comfort. And Sophie will be bringing her own slate and chalks, she tells me.' She looked at some spare sheets of paper that had been placed on one corner of the desk. 'And Mr Spencer's given us paper for writing and drawing. Oh, we shall be very well provided for.'

'Good. I'm glad you're pleased. And if Mr Spencer should wish to be busy in here, why then you could always use my sewing room.' She moved over to where a card table had been folded and leaned against the side of a bookcase. 'You could use this,' she said. She pulled out the table, unfolded it and moved it into place, adjusting its position. 'There – what do you think? Sophie will have her own little table.'

'It's ideal.'

'What time is your pupil due to arrive?'

Grace looked at the clock over the fireplace. It showed the hands at 9.40.

'At ten o'clock.'

'And what time is she leaving?'

'I thought – two o'clock. That'll give us a little break for some refreshment at midday. It'll be a long enough day to start with. After all, she's only seven – we can't go on too long.'

'Of course not. What are the precise arrangements you've made as to the teaching hours?'

'Well, I suggested that I teach Sophie Mondays to Fridays from ten until two – except on those days when you would like me to work with you or accompany you out somewhere. And I thought that if something should come up unexpectedly – such as a decision to visit a gallery or something – we could send a note over the day before. Mr Fairman understands that I have my duties concerning my employment with you.'

'What about lunch? Have you arranged things with Mrs Sandiston?'

'Yes. She's going to send up a tray for us. I hope that's all right.'

'Absolutely.' She cast her eyes around the room. 'I'm afraid it doesn't look much like a classroom, does it? It would be so nice if we had a little blackboard, don't you think?'

Grace nodded enthusiastically. 'Yes, but it's really not necessary. We shall manage perfectly well.' She pointed to the globe on its stand. 'We've even got a globe for our geography.'

Mrs Spencer smiled. 'I shall be fascinated to hear how it all goes. You say she's due to go at two – well, in that case come and have some dinner with me this evening, and tell me how it all went. It'll be a very simple meal with Mr Spencer away from the house. And don't get all dressed up. You know I don't stand on ceremony – particularly when I'm here on my own. Come down at 7.15. I shall look forward to hearing all about your time with the child.' She paused for a moment. 'Just think – children in the house. We already have Billy here, and now there's this little child. I never thought to see such a thing in my time.'

Sophie arrived ten minutes early. Grace had expected her to be brought by hired cab, but she appeared with her father who came no further into the house than the hall. He and Grace hardly exchanged more than a few polite words of greeting, and then he was saying that he had appointments to keep and would be back for his daughter at two.

'Now,' he said to Grace, taking her to one side and keeping his voice low, 'you're absolutely certain about doing this?'

'The teaching? Oh, of course.'

'Good. I can't tell you how pleased I was to receive your note telling me you'd be willing to give Sophie some lessons.' He smiled, showing his even white teeth. 'I mean, I know you were somewhat pressed to it.'

Grace shook her head. 'Please, Mr Fairman, I'm more than happy to do it. I'm looking forward to it.' She turned and looked over at Sophie where she sat on the stairs, head back, looking up at the circular rail, the figures in the niches and the cupola high above. 'I hope Sophie is too. So don't worry about it. We have our lessons to get on with, and you have your appointments to keep.'

'Thank you. I shall be for ever grateful to you.' He gave a little inclination of his head to her and moved across to his daughter. She got up as he approached and reached to him as he bent to her. 'You'll be my good girl, won't you?'

'I will, Papa.'

He kissed her on the cheek, gave her another embrace, straightened and then moved to Grace's side. Bending a little to her, he said, 'We haven't spoken about your fee, Miss Harper. We have to make some arrangement for that.'

'No, really, sir,' Grace said. 'It isn't a subject I wish to say much about, but let me just say that I already receive wages from Mrs Spencer, so no other fee is due to me.'

He stood in silence for a second. 'Are you sure about that?' he said.

'Absolutely, sir. And if I may say so, I would prefer it to be left at that.'

'Very well.' He nodded, twice, then waved his hand in a salute to Sophie, turned and left the house.

'Well,' Grace said, turning to the child, 'now it's just you and me, Sophie.'

Sophie nodded her head, her shoulders nodding also. 'Yes,' she said absently, still looking upwards. Then before Grace could say anything further she added, 'I've never been in a house so big.'

'It is large, isn't it?'

Still concentrating on the sights around her, Sophie said, 'Is this where you live, miss?'

'Yes – for the time being.'

'Won't you live here always?'

'Well – no. At some time my brother and I – we'll have to move on and find another home for ourselves.'

'If it were my house I'd want to live in it for ever.'

The girl continued to look in awe about her for a moment or two longer then turned and looked at Grace. 'We must begin our lessons, mustn't we?'

'We must indeed. Come – let me show you upstairs to the library.'

A minute or two after they had entered the library and Sophie had taken off her hat and cape, Mrs Spencer came and tapped on the slightly open door and stepped inside the room. 'I just came,' she said, 'to welcome our guest and see that everything is all right.'

Grace made the introductions and the child gave a little curtsey while looking up at the woman and shyly biting her lower lip. A few moments of light chatter and Mrs Spencer said she would leave them to get on with the lesson, and made her departure.

On their own again, Grace and Sophie talked together. Grace already knew that the girl was bright and alert, and the further conversation between them only served to endorse such a view. Sophie had brought two of her own storybooks with her, and after she had read aloud from some of the familiar pages, Grace got that day's copy of the *Morning Post*. Choosing an anodyne item from it, she had the child read it to her. At the end of the exercise she gave a nod of satisfaction: teaching the little girl was going to be an enjoyable business.

After the pair had spent upwards of an hour with reading and vocabulary, Grace turned the subject to English history. In this also the girl continued to prove herself a willing and earnest pupil. Grace decided that she must make a visit to a Corster bookshop at the first opportunity and find some suitable primers for the child.

Sophie did a little drawing towards the end of the morning, using her pencils and crayons to make a picture of the baby Moses in his little nest of bullrushes. And then, at noon, they put on their capes and hats and walked out into the gardens at the rear of the house, first through the part where the gardens were neat and carefully tended and then on into the park, a wider area which had been allowed to grow wild, and nature had control. There was a small copse in one part and as they wandered through it Grace took pleasure in pointing out some of the many items of interest, the different plants and the great variety of wildlife. To

Sophie, who had known only London's gardens and public parks, it was like walking in a new world. Back in the house they found that a tray had been left for them in the library, and soon they were eating soup followed by bread and ham with pickles and glasses of milk.

As they sat eating, facing one another across the card table, Grace said, 'Well, Miss Sophie Fairman, and what do you think of it all so far?'

The girl looked at Grace over the rim of her milk glass. 'Do you mean my lessons, miss?'

'Yes, your lessons and – well, everything. Everything is new to you today, isn't it?'

The child's upper lip was lightly glazed with milk, and she put down her glass and dabbed at her mouth with her napkin. Giving a nod of agreement she gazed around the room. 'Everything.'

'And do you think you'll want to come back for more lessons?'

'Oh, yes.' A vigorous nod here, and for a moment a fleeting look of uncertainty as if the thought had suddenly occurred that the lessons might end, and end too soon. 'Oh, yes, indeed I shall. And please, you must tell Papa that I do.'

Grace could see that it was important to the child, and found herself wondering at the girl's life; after all, here she was, living in an unfamiliar place, far away from her old friends, while her father, her only relative, was preoccupied with the business of trying to forge a new life for them. And what, Grace found herself silently asking, could be the reason for a man to uproot himself and his child and come to live in a strange place?

'Well,' Grace said, 'if your father asks me, I shall tell him that you've worked very hard at your lessons today. And I shall tell him that you produced really excellent work.'

'Will you?'

'I will.'

'And I shall give him the picture I drew for him of the little baby Moses.'

'I'm sure he'll love it.'

A little silence. Sophie ate some of her bread and cheese, took a sip from her milk glass, then gave a sigh. 'I hope the other days are just like this,' she said.

Grace was touched by the child's sentiment. 'Do you mean with your lessons?' she asked.

'Yes.'

'Well, there's no reason they shouldn't be. But we're only just starting. We must try to make them even better.'

'Miss Lewin used to hear me read at times.'

'Miss Lewin? Who is Miss Lewin?'

'She's a friend of Papa's. We knew her in London. She used to come to the house sometimes. She's very nice. And very pretty.'

'And she used to listen to you read?'

'Yes. Only my storybooks, though. We didn't read newspapers together. Papa says she's coming down to see us soon. He had a letter from her. She'll get the train, as we did. Miss Lewin has the most beautiful little dog – he's a King Charles spaniel. I don't know whether he'll be travelling down to Corster with her. I hope so, but – we'll have to see. I asked Papa if we could have a dog, but he said the time wasn't right.' She gave a little sigh. 'Perhaps someday it will be. Miss Lewin said to Papa that one has to be very careful when choosing a dog as a pet, for she said with some breeds the dog's hair comes out and gets over all the furniture and one's clothes. She has the nicest clothes, Miss Lewin does. Some of her dresses have all this lace, all these ribbons. She looks so beautiful. I shall have nice clothes when I'm grown up.' She sighed again. 'I wonder how long it takes.'

'How long what takes?' Grace asked.

'To be grown up.'

'Oh, believe me, Sophie, you'll get there in good enough time.' Grace smiled. 'And that will be very nice for you if Miss Lewin comes down to Corster to visit, won't it?'

'Yes. But I wish I could see some of my old friends also. Susannah, Georgie, Abigail. I miss them.'

'Ah.' Grace's tone was sympathetic. 'I'm sure you do. But you'll make new friends here. Just give it time.'

'Well, we've been here a month and I haven't met anyone. And Papa's so busy most of the day, I don't see so much of him either. I spend so much time with Nancy, my nurse. Oh, she's very nice, but sometimes I'd like to meet other people, talk to other people. And that's one reason it's so nice to come here today.' She looked around her at the room. 'I like it here in this house.'

'Well, soon you'll be moving into a nice house of your own.'

'Yes, that's right. Papa says he thinks he's found something that's really very nice. A house just outside of the town – a house with a nice garden. That's where he's gone this afternoon. Oh, I do hope he can buy it. I don't care to keep living in furnished rooms. I like our own furniture, our own rooms. It's not the same.'

'Did your nurse, Nancy, come down with you from London?'

'Yes. She's been with me for over a year now. I'm glad she could come with us. If not, I wouldn't have known anyone. My governess, Miss Cheadle, couldn't come.' She paused, concentrated on her food for a few moments, then said, 'When we've eaten we'll get on with our lessons, shall we? I want Papa to know that I've worked well.'

Grace and Sophie spent the last hour studying geography in a rather informal way. With the help of the globe, they traced out where Sophie's father had been on his travels: to

France and Italy. And then they tracked Mr Spencer's travels, looking at the routes to Brazil and America. After some discussion on the topic, Grace took her charge down to the conservatory and showed her some of the wonderful, exotic vegetation there that had come from overseas. Going by the copperplate legends on the wooden nameplates there were plants from India and Kashmir and Brazil, and others from African and Arabian countries. One day soon, Grace went on to suggest, they could bring their sketch-books into the conservatory and render some nice pencil drawings of some of the plants.

Back in the library there was only time for Sophie to gather her things together and then the maid was there saying that Mr Fairman had arrived to fetch his daughter.

With Sophie in her hat and cape once more and carrying her drawing, they went downstairs to find Mr Fairman standing in the hall. He too, as Sophie had done earlier, was looking up at the domed glass ceiling high above.

'I've had a chance to have a real look this time,' he said as Grace and the child went down the stairs towards him. 'It's quite magnificent. One would never guess that such monumental treasures are hidden away like this in some little insignificant English village.' He nodded in affirmation of his words, then turned to Sophie as she skipped towards him. 'Well,' he said, crouching before her and kissing her cheek, 'have you been a good pupil?'

'I think so, Papa.' She looked enquiringly at Grace who stood nearby at the foot of the stairs.

Grace said at once, 'Oh, she has indeed, Mr Fairman – the best pupil I could have wished for.'

'There, you see, Papa? I *have* been good.'

'I'm very glad to hear it.'

'And I did this for you . . .'

Sophie held up the rolled paper that was her drawing. He took it from her, unrolled it and looked at the drawing of the baby lying amid the bullrushes. 'It's beautiful. Very beautiful indeed.'

Sophie raised her eyes and flicked a glance of pride at Grace. And then Mr Fairman was rolling up the picture again and straightening. 'I'm intrigued,' he said, looking up. 'Those figures on the wall of the gallery up there.' He pointed with the rolled-up drawing. 'I noticed them when I came for dinner. What are they?'

'They're characters from the opera,' Grace said. She realized that she was feeling a little self-conscious in his presence; a little awkward. She kept talking. 'Would you – would like to see them?'

'I would indeed. D'you think Mrs Spencer would mind?'

'Oh, I'm quite sure she wouldn't object. I'll lead the way, shall I?'

The three of them walked up the curving staircase to the second floor where the three figures were situated in a gallery that ran almost clear around the wide hall. The figures were not quite life-size, but extremely imposing, nonetheless. Grace, Mr Fairman and the child stopped in front of the first one. Set in a niche was a statue of a tall man in Elizabethan garb, one hand on the hilt of his sword, the other hand held in front of him. He was a picture of male beauty, and looked out over the high drop down to the floor below with a wide smile.

The second figure was that of a rather desperate-looking young girl with one hand clutched to her breast and the other at her side holding a knife. She looked to be wearing a nightgown, and there were dark red stains on the side of the skirt and on her sleeve. The third figure was of an ugly, misshapen man with a jester's hat. Bent at the spine, he looked out over the drop with a leer, one hand held on his belt. There was no left hand; it had been broken off halfway up the forearm.

'Oh, dear, he's had an accident,' Mr Fairman said,

looking more closely at the arm that ended abruptly. 'What happened to his left arm?'

'I don't know,' Grace said. 'I asked Mr Spencer and he said it was broken off years ago. Unfortunately the piece has been lost – otherwise it could have been put back.'

'I don't like it,' Sophie said. 'Not this one. He's so ugly.'

'Yes, he is rather, isn't he?' said Grace.

'Who are they supposed to be?' Sophie asked.

Grace looked at Mr Fairman, smiling. 'Do you know, sir? Can you guess?'

'Oh, I see,' he said, 'this is my lesson for today, is it? A general knowledge quiz, is it? Well . . .' He looked at the three figures one after the other. Then with a nod at the third, broken, one, said, 'It's Rigoletto, isn't it?'

'Who's Rigoletto, Papa?' Sophie asked.

'A famous character from the grand opera. A cruel man – the main character in an opera by Giuseppe Verdi. His opera is called that: *Rigoletto*.' He turned back to Grace. 'So? Did I get good marks?'

'Very good, sir,' Grace said. 'Yes, Mrs Spencer told me it's Rigoletto. Apparently Mr Gresham, who built the house, was a great lover of the opera.' She looked from the man to the other statues. 'And what about the others, sir?'

Mr Fairman stood there, pondering the two figures, looking from one to the other. 'Well,' he said at last, 'I shall assume that they're also characters from famous operas. But which ones?' He studied the figure of the girl with the knife in her right hand. 'Do you know?' he asked Grace.

'Yes,' Grace said. 'I was told.'

'But you're not telling me?' He looked at the figure a moment or two longer, then said, 'Is it Lucia, the bride of Lammermoor?'

'It is,' Grace said.

Mr Fairman nodded his satisfaction. 'It's the knife that betrays it. And she looks suitably deranged.'

'Who was she, Papa?' Sophie said. 'What is she doing with the knife?'

'I'm afraid she's just done something rather dreadful,' her father said. 'But let's not talk about her. What about the other gentleman, Miss Harper? – the fellow with the sword? He could be anybody. I'm afraid I can't guess who.'

'It's Don Juan, sir.'

Grace lowered her gaze to the child. 'Do you like them, Sophie?'

'Not the man with the funny hat, the one whose arm is broken. Nor the lady.'

'No,' Grace said, 'perhaps not.'

Mr Fairman said, 'I wonder what possessed the house owner to install such things. I mean, they're certainly very powerful figures, but they're not that attractive – particularly the one of Rigoletto.'

Grace said, 'Mr Spencer has spoken of getting the Rigoletto repaired. I should think it wouldn't be difficult. It's only ceramic. A good artist could do that.'

'Could you do it?' Mr Fairman asked her.

'I, sir? Oh, no. I draw and paint a little, but nothing to such a standard to enable me to cope with this.'

Mr Fairman nodded, then turned to his daughter. 'Come along, miss, I think we had best be going home.' Briefly he bent and touched at the child's cape and then he was taking her small hand in his.

Grace followed them down the stairs and out onto the forecourt where the hired horse and cab were waiting.

'Up you get, Miss Sophie . . .' With a great flourish, making her squeal, the man picked up the child and deposited her on the carriage seat. Then, moving back across the gravel to where Grace stood on the wide stone step, he raised his right hand to his hat. 'I can't thank you enough,' he said.

'It was a great pleasure,' she said. 'I learned a lot.'

He gave a little laugh at this. 'I'm not surprised. I learn things from Sophie every day. Tomorrow, then?'

'Tomorrow, yes.'

The man touched at his hat again, thanked her again and wished her goodbye. Then, after murmuring a word to the cab driver, he swung himself up into the carriage and the vehicle was moving away, turning on the curve of the drive around the little fountain and heading for the gates. The last view Grace had was of Sophie turning and waving to her.

As the carriage turned out of sight on the bend of the drive, Grace was aware of feeling very glad at the way things had turned out. Notwithstanding her slight sense of awkwardness with Mr Fairman, it had gone well with Sophie. She was altogether such an agreeable child and apart from Grace having enjoyed teaching her, the work had made her feel useful. For so long now she had been only too conscious that she was not fully employed at the house, and the situation had made her wonder how long she could continue to take her wages. Now, though, she felt that she was gainfully employed.

She was standing in the library, having returned there to make sure that nothing was out of place, when there came a knock at the door, and the door opened and Mr Spencer put his head round.

'Ah,' he said, 'I find you all alone. Your pupil has gone.' He came on into the room. He was dressed in a black overcoat, his hat in his hand.

'Hello, Mr Spencer. Yes, sir, Sophie and her father have just driven away.'

'I just got in,' he said, 'and I'm off again within the hour. Soon as the horse is changed. The poor animal must be exhausted.' He looked around him as if somehow the room would show signs of the little event that had taken place there. 'So, how did it go? Was it all right?'

'Oh, yes, sir, it went extremely well. We haven't disturbed anything in the room, I made certain of that.'

'I wouldn't worry about that. So what work did you do? Lessons, I mean.'

'Oh, well, we did English – reading and vocabulary, some geography and also a little drawing and arithmetic. Oh, yes, and we also went for a stroll in the grounds.'

'You packed quite a lot into a short space of time.' He looked around him. 'Did you manage here all right?'

'Oh, yes. Sophie sat at the card table. It worked excellently.'

'What about you? Was the lesson all right for you? I mean – it wasn't exactly something you chose out of the blue, was it? – teaching Mr Fairman's child. You didn't exactly have a lot of choice when it came to it.'

Grace hesitated, then said, 'Well – I can only tell you, sir, that I enjoyed the lesson with Sophie today, and that I'm looking forward to the next one.'

He nodded. 'Well said.' He turned, edging towards the door. 'I must be off. I have things to do.'

The next moment he had wished her a good day and had gone, closing the door behind him.

Grace spent another two or three minutes in the room, then left and went upstairs to her own room.

On entering she found lying on the carpet a letter that the maid had slipped under her door in her absence. She could see at once that the writing on the envelope was that of her aunt.

Grace opened the envelope and took out the letter. The first part dealt with generalities, with her own health and that of Billy and Grace, and then touched upon a subject which, Grace thought, might perhaps have been better left unmentioned. Ending one paragraph, her aunt had written:

. . . and I have in turn to pass on the information received by me from a friend, Mrs Collimore, who assumed that I would

wish to be informed. It appears that Mr Stephen Cantrell has parted from his fiancée. There is no word – as yet – as to the reason, or who has carried out the severing of the tie, but it nevertheless appears to be true. Mr Cantrell is seen in the vicinity of Green Shipton only on his lonesome, while it seems that Miss Shilford is not seen at all. I thought you would be glad to know this, my dear. But whether or not you are actually glad, I do think perhaps it is something you ought to know.

Grace finished reading the letter, read the particular paragraph again, and then stood there with the letter held tightly in her hand. She had tried not to think of Stephen over the past weeks, months. And by not thinking about him she had somehow managed to stifle the hurt she felt within. Besides which she had had all the hundred and one diversions that had commandeered her, all the diversions that had come with leaving the family home and trying to make a new start for Billy and herself.

Billy got home just before five, and after eating a sandwich supplied by Mrs Sandiston went off to join his schoolfriend who lived on a neighbouring farm. He had permission to stay there for an hour and a half, after which he was to come back to the house. Later, following his return, he went down to the staff dining hall near the kitchens and ate the cold supper that Mrs Sandiston provided. When he returned he knocked on Grace's door and found her getting ready for her dinner with Mrs Spencer.

'Now don't you be late to bed,' Grace told him. 'I don't want to come back up and find your lamp still burning.'

When it was time, she made her way down to the drawing room where she found Mrs Spencer sitting in her chair near the fire. The evening had turned surprisingly cool, and it looked as if rain was threatening. Mrs Spencer sat with a warm shawl around her shoulders.

'Make yourself comfortable,' Mrs Spencer said as Grace came forward. 'Dinner will be ready in a minute.'

Mrs Spencer poured sherry for the two of them. As they sat and sipped at their drinks they could hear the sound of the strengthening wind as it rattled the windows. Soon afterwards Jane came in to say that dinner was ready, and the two women got up and went through into the dining room, Mrs Spencer taking her glass with her. Sitting at the table, she finished her sherry, then sat back as Jane served the soup. When the maid had gone away, Mrs Spencer poured wine and said to Grace, 'Well, now, tell me how it all went.'

Over the soup, Grace related the events of the visit and Mrs Spencer nodded her satisfaction at the way things had turned out.

'I'm sure Mr Fairman must have been pleased,' she said.

'Oh, indeed,' Grace nodded, 'he seemed to be.'

'His child has had quite enough upheaval in her short life. First of all losing her mother, and then being uprooted and having to move home. It can't have a calming effect on a sensitive, vulnerable child.' With her soup plate still half-full, Mrs Spencer set down her spoon and pushed her plate away. Then, getting up from the table, she limped to the fireplace and pushed a teetering log more securely into the flames. Putting down the poker again, she straightened and pulled her shawl a little more closely around her shoulders. As she resumed her seat she said, 'Sophie seems a pleasant child, doesn't she? And a bright one too.'

'Oh, yes,' Grace said. 'It's a pleasure to teach her.'

'Well, I do hope she gets something out of it.' She smiled at Grace. 'And you too. Perhaps, Grace, she'll find a friend in you.'

'Well – I hope so, ma'am, indeed. She misses her old friends, she told me so.'

The soup was finished. Mrs Spencer poured more wine for herself – Grace demurred, still having her glass almost full – and rang the bell for the maid. 'Tell me,' she said to Grace, 'does she speak of her mother?'

'She hasn't done so once,' Grace said.

'No, well, I doubt that she remembers her. I understand from Edward that she died some years ago – so Sophie must have been very small. Two at the most, I believe. Apparently, according to what Mr Spencer tells me, Mrs Fairman died of cholera. All terribly tragic. By all accounts she was a very beautiful young woman, and Mr Fairman was devoted to her. I can only go by what Edward tells me, of course, and I don't think Mr Fairman has told him very much. Quite understandably, I shouldn't think Mr Fairman likes to talk much upon the subject – and of course it isn't something one can ask questions about.'

The wind had got up and now began to howl around the house, sending the rain before it in violent flurries that were thrown against the glass. 'Oh, here it comes,' Mrs Spencer said. 'I'm glad I'm not outside right now.' The maid came in and took away the soup plates and then brought in the roast mutton and vegetables and a bottle of claret. Mrs Spencer said to her, 'We'll serve ourselves, Jane,' and the girl left again. As Mrs Spencer poured the new wine she urged Grace to help herself to the meat and vegetables. Grace did so. Mrs Spencer helped herself very sparingly to the food, and only picked at a few tiny mouthfuls in between taking sips of her wine. It seemed to Grace that the time passed slowly, while the food on Mrs Spencer's plate hardly diminished.

'Perhaps what Mr Fairman needs is a wife,' Mrs Spencer said. 'After all, it's time enough if it's been four or five years.' Another sip from her glass. 'The trouble is, so often a man is loath to take a similar step if he's been happy once. It's no recipe for happiness if you find a man measuring all new relationships by the first, successful one. I'm sure Mr Fairman's child will be a lot happier, too, when she and her father have moved into a house of their own. It can't be easy staying in furnished rooms the way they are. No matter how luxurious they might be it's not the same as having your own place. One needs to be able to put down roots, to call a place one's own. It isn't necessary to have a palace.' She waved a hand, taking in the room, the house. 'This place here – one doesn't need a place this size in order to be happy. Have you ever been over it, Grace? Have you ever been over the house?'

Grace swallowed the last of the vegetables she had taken, then shook her head. 'No. You showed me over a part of it when we first came here, but other than that, no.'

'You haven't been over the east and west wings? Well, there's no reason you should. Though if you want to look at it one day I'll be very happy to show you around. There's nothing much to see – rooms with dustsheets over a lot of forgotten furniture, and many other rooms that have not even been finished. Can you believe that? They're not even finished. Some rooms are without fireplaces, without plaster on the walls. Edward has dreams, I know, of finishing it all off and opening up all the rooms. He'd love to have weekend parties here, with all the carriages and servants coming and going, but that's just a dream.' She gave a sigh. 'I don't know – the very notion of employing enough servants to keep it open and functioning is beyond me. I don't know how people managed. Those house parties with people coming for the weekend, in the shooting season and so on. Can you imagine it – just two people living here and having all this space? One's whole time could be spent in administration. As I say, I think my husband might like a more socially orientated life, but it's not for me. He'd probably like having all the guests for a weekend, but not I. I never was accustomed to it, and I don't think I could ever be now. It's too late. Before we came here five years ago I lived comparatively modestly. I never dreamed of having such a home; and inheriting it came as a complete surprise to me. The paper mill as well. But Edward loves it. He loves to be involved in business. And what would I have done without him to run things for me?'

'Mr Fairman wanted to see the figures in the niches,' Grace said. 'I took him and Sophie up to see them. I hope that was all right.'

'Oh, of course. And did Mr Fairman find them interesting?'

'Yes, he did.'

Mrs Spencer shook her head. 'I don't like them. Not at all. I can't imagine how anyone could. Except my husband.' She smiled indulgently here. 'He loves the things, and swears one day he'll get the broken one repaired. Have you ever been to the opera, Grace?'

'Never, ma'am.'

'Have you not? Oh, my dear, you've missed something wonderful. Well, the next time there's a touring opera company coming to Redbury we shall go. I'd love to go, though it's no use my asking Edward. He can't stand it.'

The meat course was finished, and Mrs Spencer rang the bell for Jane to clear away. As they waited, Mrs Spencer turned towards the windows where the rain continued to spatter on the pane.

'I do hope Edward isn't riding in some open carriage somewhere,' she said. 'I didn't want him to go off anyway, but he must go. There's nothing for it but that he must go. He's never at rest. He must be overseeing things all the time. If it isn't the soap factory in Milan it's the paper mill here. And he can't bear to delegate. It's as if he doesn't trust anyone else to do their job. It's no wonder he gets irritable at times.' She shook her head and gave a deep sigh. 'But that's the way he is. There's no changing one's nature.'

'Did you inherit the soap factory also, ma'am? – if I may ask?'

'No, that was my husband's. He's owned that since he was a young man.' She said nothing more on the matter, and Grace could not ask.

The maid cleared away the dishes and then brought in the dessert, a little pastry with raisins and strawberry conserve. Mrs Spencer would have nothing of it for herself, but Grace took a little and ate it slowly while her mistress continued to talk and sip at her wine. There was something different about Mrs Spencer tonight, Grace thought. It was not only the amount of alchohol she was consuming – a phenomenon that Grace had not observed before – but there seemed to be something rather melancholy about her mood, a little sadness about the mouth, in the droop of her eye.

They had coffee in the drawing room, with which Mrs Spencer took a little brandy. And now Grace could clearly see that her employer was somewhat affected by the wine she had consumed. It showed in her slightly languid movements, in the deepening of her voice. The conversation was punctuated by little silences that Grace did not know how to circumvent, and in the end they either resorted to small talk or fell into silence.

Putting down her coffee cup, Mrs Spencer picked up her brandy glass and got up from her chair. Taking her cane, she moved to the window and stook looking out at the wild, wet night. Beyond her head Grace could just make out the heads of the waving treetops against the night sky.

With her back to Grace, Mrs Spencer said, 'It gets lonely here, you know, Grace. All these rooms, all this space – it doesn't help, you know. It doesn't help at all.'

Chapter Eleven

On some days Sophie would arrive and depart by hired cab; on other days her father might bring her and call to take her home when the day's lessons were finished. But whatever varied arrangements were made, the child had her lessons, arriving at ten every day. She was a willing and very able pupil, and Grace found teaching her no chore. Not only did she find it rewarding in the sense that Sophie was obviously learning and enjoying the process, but it also made her feel useful again. And knowing the feeling of being worthwhile, and having something so worthwhile to do, lifted her spirits enormously, and she could only wonder at the difference when she contrasted it with how she had felt before. Just going along from day to day, helping Mrs Spencer when it was required, or sitting with her for company – they were useful acts, but they were not enough in themselves to make Grace feel that she was doing anything that really mattered. Were it not for Billy's needs, she would long since have begun to consider her situation. Now, though, with Sophie coming for lessons on Monday through to Friday, Grace's whole outlook took a change for the better.

On the Tuesday of the second week Sophie arrived in the carriage with her father at the reins. Grace, going to the landing window that looked out over the forecourt, could see Mr Fairman as, holding his hat, he jumped down onto the gravel. Sophie, she noticed, stayed in her seat where she was.

Grace got down into the hall just as the maid admitted Mr Fairman. When Jane asked if she could take his hat, he said there was no need as they were not stopping. As Mr Fairman smiled at Grace who had stopped at the foot of the stairs, Grace said:

'Is Sophie not coming in, sir?

'On the contrary, we've come to see if you'll come out.'

'Go out?'

'A little excursion.' He gestured over his shoulder. 'I've hired a carriage for the day, and I thought perhaps it wouldn't matter so much if she misses a few lessons today. I've told her I'm taking her on a little jaunt, and I suggested that you might like to come along.'

'Well – where to? Where would we be going?'

'I haven't told Sophie yet.' Here he put a finger to his lips. 'But we're going to see our new home.'

'Oh, sir,' Grace said, 'that's wonderful.'

'Yes. I've signed a contract on a house and with luck we shall be moving in in three or four weeks. I want to have a few little alterations made, change a bit of this and a bit of that, but generally it's very suitable. And I know that Sophie will like it. She has seen it, once – when we went to give it a quick look-over a couple of weeks back. And she expressed a liking for it then – so at least I know she'll be pleased. And now,' he added, 'I thought we might find out if Sophie's teacher likes it also.'

'I'm being invited along to see it?' Grace said, the surprise in her voice.

'Yes, ma'am,' he smiled broadly. 'That's why we're here. Please say yes.'

For a moment she was at a loss for words, then she said, 'Well – I'll have to fetch my cape and my hat. And I must let Mrs Spencer know – I must ask her permission. Just in case she wants me for anything. But it'll only take a minute. I'm sure it'll be all right.' Turning, she started up the stairs.

The first thing she did was go to Mrs Spencer's studio where her employer had been working for the past half-hour. Grace tapped on the door, and on the call of 'Come in', stepped into the room. Mrs Spencer was not at her easel but was sitting at the window, vaguely gazing out over the lawns.

'Yes, what is it, Grace?' She turned as Grace entered the room.

'Please, ma'am, Mr Fairman and his daughter have arrived, and wish to know if I'd like to accompany them out on a little trip.'

'What, no lessons today?'

Grace smiled. 'It seems not, ma'am. I understand he's in the process of buying a house, and is anxious for Sophie to see it. He's very kindly asked if I'd care to go along.'

'And do you want to go?'

Grace hesitated briefly before answering. 'Well,' she said, 'if it's all the same to you, ma'am. It's a very pleasant day. And it might be nice to take a little carriage ride.'

'Then you must go, of course you must.'

Grace had not seen a great deal of her employer over the past few days. Not in fact in any great way since the evening they had had dinner together. On the following day Mrs Spencer had come down with a cold, and as was her wont at such times, tended to keep to herself and avoid social company. Today was her first day back in her studio, but it didn't look as if she was getting very far.

As if to endorse the impression that Grace had gained, the woman sighed and gave a slow shake of her head. 'Yes, you go on out and have a good time, Grace,' she said. 'I certainly don't need any help today. It's one of those days when I can't even seem to help myself to any good purpose.' She waved a hand towards her easel with the part-finished canvas upon it. 'I haven't made any progress so far today, and it doesn't look as if I'm going to. I think

209

I'm just not in the mood. And it's no good sitting here, waiting for inspiration to strike.' She waved her hand again, this time in Grace's direction. 'You go on out and enjoy the sunshine. Perhaps we'll talk or have some tea later on, when you're back.'

'Is there anything you'd like me to get for you while I'm out?'

'No, nothing, my dear, thank you.' She gave a little sigh and turned briefly back to the window again. 'What I need can't be bought.' She turned back to Grace, a sudden smile, too bright, too quick, lighting up her face. 'Go on, Grace, go on and enjoy your youth. Enjoy it while you can, for it won't come again.'

Downstairs, Grace found the hall empty, then on opening the front door saw Mr Fairman standing beside the horse. He smiled as Grace approached and held out his hand to help her up into the carriage beside his daughter. Seconds later, he was in the driving seat and the carriage was crunching away across the gravel towards the road.

The house of their destination was situated just off the Corster road on the way to the village of Upper Callow. Mr Fairman pulled up the horse at the entrance and turned to Sophie at his side.

'This looks a likely place,' he said. 'Shall we go in and have a closer look?'

'Papa,' said Sophie, 'this is the house we saw the other week. And I liked it so much more than the others we saw. I told you.'

'Yes,' he said, smiling, 'I remember that you did.'

Early Victorian, the house stood back from the road with a circular carriage drive in front and a paved stable yard at the rear. There were flowerbeds and lawns leading to kitchen gardens and a small orchard right at the back. 'Enough space but not too much,' Mr Fairman said, '– not too much space that a man should be intimidated by it, but enough to enable him to take a breath. After all, I'm an architect. I just need good light and a decent drawing board, not acres of paddocks.'

'Is there room for a girl to have a pony, Papa?' Sophie said.

'A pony?'

'Just a small one?'

'Oh, we'll have to see about that.'

The house had a white stucco façade over sand-coloured brick. And while not vast, it was large enough, with just the right number of rooms – rooms that were spacious for the most part, with high ceilings and decent-sized fireplaces. It had a good, welcoming wide hall, and a fine staircase leading up to rooms that looked out over meadows and copses, and, over to the south, the village of Lower Callow.

One of the upper rooms was papered with a design of butterflies of all kinds, making a beautiful, if somewhat faded, display as they danced around the walls. Sophie was enchanted, and tried to see how many varieties she could find. Moving on to another room some minutes later they found two framed pictures leaning against the wall near the window.

'Can we see them, Papa?' Sophie said, and Mr Fairman picked up the outermost picture and held it before her. It was a rather faded mezzotint of Franz Hal's painting known as *The Laughing Cavalier*. Mr Fairman set it down and picked up the other. As he turned it towards Sophie she drew in her breath and said, 'Oh, the poor angel. What happened to him?'

The framed oleograph showed a slim, near-naked young man lying prostrate on a rock set in a blue sea, with beautiful snow-white wings spread out beneath him. About the still form water nymphs had gathered in the water, some reaching up to him in wonder and curiosity.

As her father leaned the picture against the first one,

Sophie crouched down before it. 'It's so beautiful,' she said. 'Is the angel sleeping?'

Grace said, 'I don't think he's an angel, Sophie. I think it's Icarus, it must be.'

'Yes, of course,' said Mr Fairman. 'It can be no one else.'

'Who is Icarus?' Sophie said. 'And why is he lying there asleep with the ladies watching him?'

Mr Fairman caught Grace's eye across the child's head and said, smiling, 'And I suppose the schoolroom can be wherever you happen to be, can't it?'

Grace smiled back fleetingly then lowered her glance to Sophie and bent beside her.

'The story of Icarus is an ancient myth,' she said, 'and –'

'What's a myth?'

'Well – let's just say for now that it's a very old story from ages past.' Here she flicked a brief, self-conscious glance at Mr Fairman, as if seeking approval. Then back to the child: 'And the myth about Icarus comes from Greece. Icarus was the young son of an architect – just like your papa. But his name was Daedalus.'

'Daedalus? That's a funny name.'

'It is, isn't it? Unfortunately Daedalus made the king of Crete, King Minos, very angry, and the king imprisoned him and his son Icarus in a tower.' Grace broke off here and turned her glance again towards Mr Fairman. 'Am I getting it right so far, sir?' she said.

He nodded, giving a grave smile, his eyes not leaving her own. 'Faultless, so far as I can tell.'

Grace felt herself blush a little under his gaze and quickly looked back at the picture.

'So what happened to them, miss?' Sophie said.

'Well, Daedalus – Icarus's father – decided they should escape, and so he made wings for them both of wax and feathers – and they escaped and flew away.'

'Oh, good, that's good,' said Sophie.

'Ah, but –' Grace shook her head, 'sadly it didn't go well. Icarus flew too high, he flew too near the sun, and the heat of the sun melted the wax of his wings.'

'Oh, dear.' Sophie's hands moved to her cheeks. 'So what happened to him?'

'Well – with his wings so damaged, poor Icarus couldn't fly, and he fell into the sea – and was drowned.'

Sophie gave a little wail, and leaning closer to the picture said, 'So Icarus isn't asleep, he's dead.'

'I'm afraid so.'

'What a sad story. The poor man.' Sophie gave a deep sigh, then looked at her father. 'Can we keep the picture, Papa?'

'Yes, I don't see why not. But we'll leave it here for now, shall we? It'll be here waiting for you when we move in.'

'When we move in?' Sophie said.

Mr Fairman looked from her to Grace and back again. 'Well?' he said to the child. 'What do you think? Shall we move in?'

'You mean it, Papa?'

'Of course. It's ours now.' Finishing his words he gave a *whoop* and caught her and lifted her high into the air, and she squealed out, her small shrill voice echoing out of the room and through the empty house.

When he put her down she turned around excitedly in the room, and then started towards the door. 'Where are you going?' her father said.

She turned in the doorway: 'To look at the butterflies again,' and with a little chuckle of pure pleasure went out of the room.

As Sophie's footsteps receded along the landing, Grace gestured to the picture of the fall of Icarus and said, 'I don't like to tell her such sad stories.'

He nodded. 'I know what you mean, but often they're unavoidable. And there are times when they shouldn't be avoided. At some time in their lives children have to make a start facing reality.' He smiled. 'Even if it comes in the shape of a Greek myth.'

Grace picked up the picture and held it before her. 'It really is quite beautiful,' she said. 'What will you do – hang it on Sophie's wall?'

'If that's what she wants.'

Grace continued to look at the picture.

'Are all your lessons so interesting?' Mr Fairman said.

Grace gave a little laugh, born of embarrassment. She lowered the picture. 'Sir, it's unkind,' she said. 'You're teasing me.'

'Teasing?' he said. 'No, never more serious. I could wish you could be my daughter's teacher for always. I would be well content.'

Grace did not know how to respond, and took refuge once more in the picture, saying, 'Well, let's put poor Icarus back . . .' and moved to place the picture on the floor again. Mr Fairman forestalled her, however, and reached out, saying, 'I'll take it, shall I?'

As Grace moved to hold the picture up to him it somehow slipped in her grasp and almost fell, but even as it shifted so precariously Mr Fairman's hands were swiftly reaching out and catching it, grasping it securely. And in the act of clutching the frame, his left hand closed tightly around Grace's own right one, her small hand smothered by his large one. And they had to remain like that for two or three seconds while he quickly adjusted his other hand to take the weight and so relieve her of it. As he withdrew his hand from over her own she realized that she was holding her breath, and with the warmth of his hand gone she was aware of the cool air again upon it. She had been so conscious of his touch, the closeness of his touch, and could not force herself to raise her eyes to his. With her glance lowered, she heard him say:

214

'Well – I'll put this away safely to keep it out of the sunlight.' For a moment his voice sounded slightly hoarse. 'Otherwise,' he added, 'the colours will fade.'

Looking down she saw that he was placing the picture face inward in a shadowed part of the room and away from the window's light.

'There,' he said, straightening, 'shall we join Sophie amid the butterflies and get on our way?

Back in the carriage, Mr Fairman spread his arms wide, fingers outstretched. 'It's a wonderful day,' he said. 'Don't you think so, Miss Harper?'

'Oh, indeed I do. I just wish my brother could be here to share it with us. He would love an outing like this.'

'Well, he'll have one before too long.'

'Where is he now, miss?' Sophie asked.

'He's at his lessons.'

'Perhaps where you should be, young lady,' Mr Fairman said. 'But no, maybe not today.' He looked upwards. 'Look at that April sky. I think we should go and have a little drink to celebrate, don't you?' He addressed his words to Sophie, and she said, 'Yessss!' and spread her arms in an echo of his own gesture. 'What do you think, Miss Harper?' he said.

'Yes,' Sophie said excitedly. 'Oh, miss, say yes.'

'Oh – well, thank you,' Grace said. 'Of course I'll be very happy to celebrate with you.'

They drove off then, back onto the road. Not going on the road on which they had arrived but on a different route, the one leading to the village. And half a mile along they came to an inn, and Mr Fairman drove the carriage into the stable yard and there helped the pair down onto the cobbles. The mare he led to the water trough and stood stroking her shoulder as she drank deeply of the cool water.

'Now,' he said, when the horse was watered and secured, 'let's get a little refreshment.'

They took seats in the noon sun on benches at the side of the inn, and eventually a young maidservant brought a tray with three slices of venison pie, a glass of ale for Mr Fairman, sarsparilla for Grace and lemonade for Sophie.

'Well, now,' Mr Fairman said, when the maid had left them, '– let us drink to our new home, shall we?'

He held up his glass as he spoke, and Grace and Sophie raised their glasses also. 'To our new home,' Mr Fairman said, and Grace said, 'To your new home,' feeling very happy for the pair, and Sophie cried, 'Yes, yes, to our new home,' and clinked her father's glass with her own. She turned then to Grace. 'Oh, clink my glass, miss,' she said. 'You have to clink my glass too.'

Grace did so, and Sophie laughed and said, 'And now you have to clink Papa's glass as well.' She turned to her father. 'It's only fair, Papa.'

Mr Fairman chuckled, and briefly met Grace's eyes as he said, 'Then of course we must.' And with Grace lowering her glance from his own, touched his glass to hers.

'When shall we move in, Papa?' Sophie asked as she ate her pie. 'When can we go to live there?'

'In a few weeks. We have to get the place tidied up a bit first. But don't worry, the time will pass soon enough.'

'And will I still be having my lessons, Papa? Shall I still be going to see Miss Harper?'

'Well, I don't know,' he said, giving a little glance towards Grace. 'That of course depends on Miss Harper – whether she's still happy to teach you.'

'You are, miss, aren't you?' Sophie said, a little note of anxiety in her voice. 'Miss, tell me you are.'

'Yes, Sophie,' Grace said. 'Yes, of course I am.'

*

From the inn they set off on the road to Berron Wick. There would be no time left for lessons today, Mr Fairman said, adding, however, that it didn't do any harm to take the occasional day off in a good cause.

They drove along the road between meadows where cows grazed, and where lambs played in the spring grass, grass of the freshest green starred with the white and yellow of dandelions, buttercups, celandines and daisies. As they neared a crossroads they saw ahead of them a colourfully painted gypsy caravan parked on a narrow strip of land beside a hedgerow. The horse, freed from the shafts of the vehicle, stood some yards away, tethered to a tree, eating hay, while a gypsy woman sat on a stool, her back to the caravan, eating something out of a bowl. Two small children with dirty faces, a boy and a girl, sat eating beside her, and a man, his brow covered by a red kerchief, sat on the sloping shafts of the vehicle, smoking a clay pipe. All four persons eyed the three with dark, piercing watchful eyes as they approached.

'Look, Papa,' Sophie said in a loud whisper as they drew closer, 'they have birds hanging from the walls.' As she spoke she pointed towards three birdcages hanging from the side of the vehicle. Each cage had a bird inside it. 'Can you see them, Papa, the birds?'

Even as Mr Fairman nodded and said, 'Yes, I can,' the woman put down the bowl, rose from her seat and in one sweeping movement picked up a wide wicker basket that had lain beside her feet – obviously in readiness for whatever travellers should come her way. Holding the basket against her side she came forward into their path.

'G'arternoon t' ye, sir – young ladies,' the woman said. Her hair was coal black and grew low on her tanned brow, while her eyes beneath the black eyebrows flashed brilliantly in the sun. She wore golden hoops in her ear-lobes, and a colourful shawl over a white blouse. Her long skirt was black with red ribbons threaded above the hem, revealing broad, naked feet. Holding her basket of pegs and paper flowers she made a dramatic sight.

'Now, sir,' she said, turning and walking beside the carriage, striding out with her strong legs, 'some nice pegs for the missis – or some pretty flowers for her.'

Mr Fairman slowed the carriage, saying to his companions, 'I'm in a good mood today,' adding, 'Would you like some flowers, Sophie? And you, Miss Harper? They do look very pretty.'

Grace replied with thanks but turned down the offer, feeling slightly uneasy in the gypsies' presence. But Sophie said yes, she would love some flowers, and her father brought the carriage to a halt.

The gypsy woman was right there beside them, at once holding up the shallow basket with its contents for examination. Sophie chose some roses in pink and more in yellow, and added to these some pink carnations. While the coppers were passed over in payment, Grace's eyes focused on the birds in the rough little wooden cages, just a few feet from where they sat.

'Are you sure you wouldn't like some of the flowers?' Mr Fairman said to Grace, and she replied, 'No, really, thank you all the same.'

The gypsy woman spoke up at this. 'No, it ain't the flowers what's caught the young lady's fancy, sir – it be the birds.' She spoke directly to Grace now, smiling up at her, showing large square teeth, very white against the dark tan of her skin: 'Ain't that right, miss? It be the beautiful little birds.'

'Is that so?' Mr Fairman said, looking into Grace's eyes. 'Do you fancy the birds?'

'No. Oh, no.' Grace spoke with a little passion. 'It's not that way at all.'

'Are you quite sure?'

'Yes, indeed! Please – oh, please – may we drive on?'

Mr Fairman looked at her closely for a moment, studying her expression, then turned and said to the gypsy woman, 'Thank you, ma'am, there'll be nothing more today.' Then, without pause for further conversation, he flapped at the reins and said to the mare, 'Come on, Aggie, let's be off.' And tipping his hat to the woman he drove the carriage on.

They drove on in silence until, some hundred or so yards further on, the road rounded a bend. Then, looking back and seeing that the caravan was now out of sight, he brought the vehicle to a halt. Turning in the seat, looking closely at Grace he said, frowning: 'Miss Harper, what is it?'

'Nothing, nothing,' Grace said, turning her face away from his gaze.

'Come now,' he said, 'you spoke with passion back there, and were so eager to quit the scene. Why? What was the reason?' He paused briefly, then gave a nod of his head and said quietly, 'Of course, it was the birds, wasn't it?'

Grace said nothing, and only wished for the matter to drop.

'It was the birds, wasn't it?' Mr Fairman said again.

'Yes.' Grace nodded. 'Yes, it was.'

Now Sophie spoke up. 'See, Papa, you were right, it was the birds.' Then to Grace, 'But Miss Harper, why? Didn't you like them?'

'What? Oh, of course I liked them,' Grace said. 'I just can't bear to see them caged that way. That poor song thrush, and the oriole, and the other little bird. Why do people do it? Those birds will never sing, not caged like that. They should be free and singing over the hills and the woodland, not held in those awful little cages, without room even to spread their wings.' As she spoke tears welled in her eyes, and she raised her hands and wiped them unceremoniously across her cheeks. 'I'm sorry,' she said, 'for carrying on so.'

While Sophie looked at her with sympathetic eyes, Mr Fairman was studying her, a frown on his brow.

'You must not apologize for such sentiments,' he said. 'You are quite right to feel as you do.'

Another moment, and then he was handing the reins to Grace, saying, 'Just hold on to the horse for a second. She won't run away with you.' And then he was climbing down onto the road and walking back in the direction in which they had come. Grace and Sophie, turning in the seat, watched as he walked out of sight.

'Where is he going, miss?' Sophie said.

'I've no idea,' Grace replied.

Six or seven minutes later they saw him again, his tall figure coming into sight around the screen of oak and bramble at the roadside. And they saw that in his hand he carried the three birdcages that had hung from the caravan's side.

Reaching the carriage he held up the cage containing the thrush, saying to Sophie, 'Here, take it, there's a good girl, and give it to Miss Harper.' And Sophie gingerly took the birdcage from him and put it into Grace's hands. The other two cages he carefully placed in the well of the carriage, then climbed up and sat down at Sophie's side.

Grace sat with the birdcage on her knees. Like the other two cages, it was a crude affair, the bars were coarsely cut sticks, the base made of some rough hewn piece of wood, the crown woven of thin pieces of willow. Inside it the bird cowered, its speckled breast heaving, so cramped for space, and unable to get away from the perceived threat with which it was surrounded. Grace was reminded of the two exotic little birds in the conservatory at Asterleigh House. They were accustomed to their prisons by now, she thought – not like this plain-looking little songbird.

'Mind your skirt with the cage, miss,' Sophie said. 'You'll get marks on it.'

Grace said, 'That's all right, the marks'll come out,' but speaking absently, only trying to see how the cage opened.

And then she saw that one of the bars could be lifted clean out, and she held the cage a little higher in the air, and pulled up the bar, pulled it clear. At first the bird did not see the way to freedom, and so Grace turned the cage so that the opening was away from her and the bird, perceiving her as the enemy, naturally moved away. And, moving, he saw the opening, and in one breathtaking little hop and scrabble, was through the bars and out into the space of the world.

Grace watched its swooping flight, and hoped for a moment that it might pause in its flight, perhaps just to stay for a moment on the branch of that hawthorn, but it did not. In just a couple of seconds it had gone from her sight.

Sophie had sat watching with her hands to her mouth, hardly daring to breathe. And then she turned to her father as if looking to see in his expression that Grace had done right. And seeing his smile, she grinned and pressed her hands together.

'Now you, Sophie,' her father said. 'Now it's your turn.' And he took up the cage holding the golden oriole and held it in front of his daughter. 'I'll hold the cage,' he said. 'You do the rest.'

While the bird fluttered inside the cage, Sophie began testing the bars to see which one came loose, and locating it, said with a little gasp of pleasure, 'I've got it, Papa.'

Mr Fairman turned the cage so that the opening faced away from its captors. 'Don't take too long, darling,' he said, 'the poor creature is very afraid.' And Sophie, with one smooth move, lifted the spar clear. The bird saw its way to freedom at once, and in a little flurry of gold and black was through the opening and winging away out of sight.

'Now you, Papa,' Sophie said. 'It's your turn now.'

Mr Fairman took up the third and last cage, and as he did so Grace said, 'Ah, it's a skylark. They need all the space in the world.'

221

Mr Fairman located the loose spar and turned the cage appropriately. Then, with a whispered, 'Wish him well, ladies,' he removed the spar and lifted the cage even higher. And the skylark, without a second's hesitation, was through the opening and swooping straight up into the blue, blue sky, as if trying to reach the sun.

Sophie's lessons continued throughout the rest of the week in their usual way, though she was usually conveyed to and from Asterleigh House in a hired cab. Except on the Friday, the day of the week's final lesson. On this occasion Mr Fairman came to collect her from the house when her lessons were over for the day.

Grace accompanied the pair out onto the forecourt where the carriage stood. After Mr Fairman had lifted Sophie up into her seat, he turned to Grace and thanked her for all her work.

'Though we might not have a full week next week,' he added. 'We have a visitor coming from London for a week. So Sophie, lucky Sophie,' he looked up and smiled at Sophie as he spoke, ' – might have one or two outings.'

'Who is it, Papa?' Sophie asked. 'Who's coming to stay? Is it Miss Lewin?'

'Yes, it is. I heard from her today. She's arriving on Sunday.'

Sophie gave a little cry of joy. 'Oh, that's splendid!' Then to Grace, 'We sometimes get to do special things when Miss Lewin comes to see us. Miss Lewin lives near us in London – or rather where we *used* to live.' Turning back to her father she added, 'But where will Miss Lewin stay, Papa?'

'She'll be staying at a hotel in Corster,' he answered. 'She won't have that far to come and visit us.'

Sophie said, 'Once with Miss Lewin we visited the Crystal Palace, and another time we went to the zoological gardens. Papa, shall we be going somewhere nice?'

'We'll see,' he said. 'I shouldn't wonder.'

'Oh, good!' Sophie said. 'Do you know where we'll be going?'

'We'll have to see.'

'Somewhere nice,' Sophie said. 'And Papa – when we go, can Miss Harper come with us?'

He looked at Grace, and as his eyes met hers, she lowered her glance. 'Well,' he said, 'we'll have to see when the time comes. Maybe Miss Harper will have other things to do.'

The next morning, Saturday, Billy brought Grace a letter that had just arrived in the post. It was from Stephen.

> *Dear Grace,*
> *I learned from Mrs Tanner where you are now living.*
>
> *You might have heard that my circumstances have changed. I would like to see you. Please write and let me know if we might meet. I have to be in Berron Wick on Thursday the 3rd May, and with your permission I'd like to see you then. I could either come to Asterleigh House or meet you somewhere nearby. Whatever is agreeable to you I'll fall in with. I should be grateful if you would let me know your response as soon as possible so that I can make any necessary arrangements. I need hardly add that I am aware that in many eyes perhaps I don't deserve your consideration. But I hope you will at least see me and let me speak to you – for old times' sake if nothing else.*
> *Yours,*
> *Stephen Cantrell*

Grace read the letter through several times, sitting in her little chair beside the window in her room. Billy, standing nearby, watching her, as always sensitive to her moods, looked at her expression and said, 'What is it, Grace? Who is it from?'

She turned to him as if coming out of a dream. 'What? Oh – it's from Stephen. Mr Cantrell. You remember him, don't you?'

'Yes, of course. We haven't seen him for a long time.'

'No, we haven't.'

'Why is he writing?'

'He – he wants to see me.'

'What for?'

Grace paused, shaking her head. 'I don't know, Billy. I don't know.'

Grace went back to Stephen's letter repeatedly over the weekend, so many times that in the end she had learned most of it by heart. The questions came silently over and over. After all these months, why was he writing? Why did he want to see her?

Freed from the schedule of teaching Sophie, who, she surmised, was occupied with their London visitor, Miss Lewin, Grace spent more time with Mrs Spencer over the days immediately following. In part, it seemed to Grace that Mrs Spencer was aware that she, Grace, might be somewhat at a loss without the responsibility of her teaching post and perhaps called upon her now out of a sense of kindness. But Grace also had the sense that Mrs Spencer, with her husband being so much away from the house, was truly glad of her company. So they spent their time sketching together, playing the odd game of chess, working on their embroidery or general sewing, and chatting in a desultory fashion. On one occasion Grace joined Mrs Spencer at the piano, where they worked – not altogether satisfactorily, but with good humour – on a piece for four hands.

So often Grace thought of Stephen's letter, and tried in her mind to compose a reply. But she was never able to. She simply did not know what to say. And so she left the words unformed and unwritten.

On Thursday, it being market day in Corster, Grace decided to go into the town to buy some things for Mrs Spencer, Billy and herself.

As Rhind was off with Mr Spencer, and Mr Johnson appeared to be well occupied with the horses, Grace walked to Berron Wick and took the train.

Arriving in the town – busy as usual for a Thursday – she consulted her list and set about her errands, buying for Mrs Spencer coloured silks and a couple of paintbrushes. While passing along the busy street from the small draper's she encountered Mr Timmins, who had come into the market to sell some of his livestock. They stopped to talk for a minute and he asked after her welfare and that of Billy. Afterwards she went on her way.

At one point in her shopping she saw the back of a tall man's form, and was reminded at once of Stephen. It was not he, but the likeness was sufficient to bring him into her mind. And through her mind ran once more the contents of his letter. She must reply to it. But what should she say? What did she want to say?

When at last her shopping was done she decided she would drink a little tea before starting back to Asterleigh. She was crossing the street when she heard over the noise of the people a child's voice calling her name, and, turning, she saw Sophie come dodging through the crowd towards her.

'Sophie, what a surprise!'

Grace bent to her and Sophie, smiling broadly, pressed Grace's arm. 'We came to the market too, miss,' she said.

Looking over Sophie's head, Grace saw Mr Fairman standing near a stall on the edge of the milling crowd. Their eyes met and he smiled at her through the moving heads. She saw his mouth shape a greeting, and murmured some words in return. Then Sophie was pulling at her arm, saying, 'Come, Miss Harper, come and see Papa,' and Grace allowed herself to be drawn across the cobbles to where Mr Fairman was standing.

'Miss Harper!' he said. 'How nice to see you here. Though I suppose it shouldn't be seen as so much of a surprise, since it seems that all of Wiltshire has come to market today.' He looked down at Sophie. 'And Sophie loves to come here. She likes to see the animals in the cattle market.' He grinned, smiling down at his daughter. 'Even the smell doesn't put her off.'

Sophie spoke up, saying, 'We're just going to have some tea, miss.' She looked up at her father. 'Papa, can Miss Harper come and have some tea with us?'

'Oh, no, really,' Grace began to protest, 'I really couldn't dream of intruding –' But Mr Fairman said quickly, 'Of course – what an excellent idea. Although perhaps you have other appointments, Miss Harper . . .?'

'Well, no,' Grace said, 'I have not,' and had she continued she would have had to admit that she herself had been on her way to get a little refreshment. 'Then you must come with us,' said Mr Fairman, and as she half-heartedly protested again, added: 'Oh, come on – you have time to join us for a little cup of tea, surely.' And Grace, feeling that she had protested quite enough, could only give a nod and murmur words of acquiescence.

Grace expected then that they would all three move off, but Sophie said, 'We have to wait just a minute for Miss Lewin. She's gone to buy some lozenges from the sweet-shop.' And Grace felt her spirits sink. She should have remembered that Mr Fairman and Sophie had their guest from London, and should also have realized that Miss Lewin would in all likelihood be accompanying them to the market. For a moment she felt words of protest and excuse coming to her lips but she forced them back; it was too late to do anything about it now, and Mr Fairman was smiling, gazing off into the crowd and saying, 'Ah, here comes Miss Lewin now.'

Miss Lewin came to them out of the throng, a tall, slim young lady wearing a grey cape trimmed with sable over a dark blue dress. She carried her reticule and umbrella in one hand, and in the other two small packages. On her head she wore a neat little toque trimmed with ribbons and a bird's wing.

Reaching the little group who stood waiting for her, she took in Grace's presence with an interested glance, then turned, smiling, to Mr Fairman, as if asking for information on the newcomer. Mr Fairman at once produced the introductions: 'Miss Harper, this is our friend from London, Miss Lewin. Miss Lewin – Miss Grace Harper, Sophie's teacher.'

As Grace murmured 'How do you do,' Miss Lewin gave a wide smile and said, 'How do you do, Miss Harper. How very nice! Sophie has been telling me all about you.' Her face, Grace thought, was strikingly beautiful with fair skin and finely arched eyebrows framed by black hair.

'I just suggested,' Mr Fairman said, 'that Miss Harper joins us for some tea, and I'm happy to say that she's agreed to come.'

'Well, that's splendid,' Miss Lewin said, adding with a little laugh, 'The more the merrier.'

Mr Harper said to Grace, 'When we've settled on a place, I'll leave you ladies having your tea while I complete a little business with my solicitor. It won't take me long.'

They went to a little teashop in a side way leading from the high street and, looking in, saw that they could get a table without having to wait. At once Mr Fairman turned to Miss Lewin and Grace, saying, 'If you'll excuse me, then, ladies, I'll just pop back into the high street. I'll join you here in ten minutes.'

'Well, don't you dare make it any longer than that,' Miss Lewin said, 'or we shall send the search party for you – not to mention the Bow Street Runners.'

Mr Fairman laughed, touched Sophie's cheek, put finger-tips to his hat, and turned and started away.

The two women and the child went into the teashop and sat down at a table, Grace and Sophie on one side, Miss Lewin on the other. When the waitress had come over with her notepad Miss Lewin said, 'Now, ladies, you must tell me what you'd like,' and after ascertaining what was required said to the waitress that it would be a pot of tea for three, and one lemonade. 'And any little treats?' Miss Lewin asked. 'Perhaps a pastry or some sandwiches?' Grace declined, but Sophie, seeing at the next table a youth eating some sponge cake confection with cream, whispered to Miss Lewin that if it was all right she would like some of the same. Miss Lewin gave the order to the waitress, then turned to Grace. 'Are you sure, Miss Harper,' she said, 'that you wouldn't also like some cake or a pastry?' and before Grace had a chance to refuse again, said to the waitress, who was already turning away, 'Bring two of the cream sponges, please.' Grace raised a hand in protest and opened her mouth to speak, but the waitress had already gone.

'Well, that's done,' Miss Lewin said, and gave a little sigh, as if she had accomplished a feat. 'Now we can relax.' Taking off her gloves, she addressed Sophie. 'And if your papa doesn't take too long he might get back to have a cup of tea before it gets cold.' Putting a slim hand up to check on her hat and hair, she looked around the crowded interior of the teashop. 'Well,' she said, lowering her voice to a murmur, 'what a quaint little place.' Then she added, 'And how – unusual. I have to say that I've been here in Corster a few days now, but I'm sure if I stayed a lifetime I'd never get used to living in such a place.' She turned to Sophie. 'Do

228

you like living here, Sophie? Right down here in the country?'

'Oh, yes, I do, miss,' Sophie replied. 'It's very different from Kensington, but it's lovely. There's so much to see. There are foxes and squirrels and rabbits and – oh, all kinds of creatures. The other day when we were out with Papa we bought some birds in cages, a song thrush and –' Here she quickly turned to Grace. 'What were the other two, miss? I've forgotten their names.'

'One was an oriole, a golden oriole,' Grace said. 'The other was a skylark.'

'That's right – a golden oriole, a skylark and a thrush. Oh, they were lovely.'

'Oh, caged birds can look beautiful in the right setting,' Miss Lewin said, 'though I don't think of thrushes and skylarks as being particularly attractive. They might have a nice song, but I don't think they'd set off a room to any great advantage. Give me a pretty little parakeet or bird of paradise any day. They might not be able to sing, but they look beautiful. I'm rather surprised at your papa buying such dreary-looking creatures. I should have been with him; I'd have talked him out of the purchase.'

'Oh, but we didn't buy them to keep,' Sophie said. 'We bought them to set free.'

'You did what?' Clearly Miss Lewin did not understand. 'You bought them to set free?'

'Yes.' Sophie giggled, still thrilled at the memory. 'Papa bought them from the gypsy woman, and we opened the cages and let the birds fly away.'

'You opened the cages and let the birds fly away.' Miss Lewin repeated the words with some deliberation, as if weighing them up. 'How very bizarre.'

'Oh, Miss Lewin, it was lovely,' Sophie said. 'We watched them fly up into the trees. They were gone in a trice.'

'Is this so?' Miss Lewin turned to Grace with the raising of a finely arched brow. 'I'm sure Sophie wouldn't – couldn't – invent such a thing – but it just seems so very odd.' There was no humour in the rather perplexed smile that touched at her pink lips.

'Yes, it's just as Sophie says,' Grace said, and added, smiling, 'It was a wonderful moment. I wouldn't have missed it for anything.'

'No, I wouldn't have missed it for anything, either,' Sophie said, happy to agree with Grace. 'It was wonderful.'

'Wonderful, eh? Well –' Miss Lewin gave a little shrugging smile, 'to each his own.' And now she gave a little laugh. 'I can see that your papa has let the country air go to his head.' She paused a moment, and the smile on her mouth became one of indulgence. She put her hand across the table and briefly touched Sophie on the tip of her nose. 'I think it's splendid that you've taken to country life so well. And you deserve to have some pleasure, you dear thing.'

Sophie said, 'When we move into our house Papa's going to buy me a pony.'

'Ah, when you move into your new house. Yes, your papa told me of it. And he's taking me to see it tomorrow. D'you think I shall like it?'

Sophie nodded enthusiastically. 'Oh, yes, it's a lovely house. It's right in the country – with only trees and meadows around. You'll love it.'

'Shall I indeed?' Miss Lewin's light little laugh came again. 'I'm not at all sure that I'm suited for a life in the country.'

'Oh, yes, miss, yes! You could be,' Sophie said. 'You just haven't been here long enough yet.'

Miss Lewin gave a little nod and a smile. 'Well, perhaps. Perhaps the place could grow on me, though at the moment it doesn't feel so much like a hundred and twenty miles from London, but more like a thousand. It's like a different country.'

'Don't you care for Corster?' asked Grace. She herself had never thought to question anything about the place. It was there, and that was that. Like the Rock of Gibraltar, she might have said, or the Sahara Desert, some things are as they are; they are to be accepted and cannot possibly be changed. And being so it was more or less fruitless even to name a place's values or lack of values.

'Oh, it's not that I don't care for it,' Miss Lewin said. 'It's just that, as I say, it's so very different. This place, this little teashop,' she waved a hand, taking in the crowded interior with its patronage of the usual townspeople, 'it's so – quaint. And the shops here in the town. I tell you, I brought money with me in the expectation of perhaps buying a new gown, but after seeing what's on offer here I shall save my money till I get back to Bond Street. There's nothing here that's been fashionable in the last ten years.'

Grace could not help but feel a little affronted at the criticism of a place that was so close to her. 'But if you went to Redbury,' she said, 'you would find fashionable shops. I wouldn't necessarily expect to find high fashion in a market town. I doubt the townspeople would expect to find it either. In any case it suits them the way things are.'

'Oh, it's not only the lack of fashionable shops and stores in such a place,' Miss Lewin said. 'That's just a part of it. It's just all so –' and here she dropped her voice almost to a whisper '– parochial. I mean – wandering around this town centre. One can get all dressed up to make the excursion – but for what purpose? There's so little to see that it's all over in fifteen minutes. One's covered the whole place before one's taken a second breath.' Here she lifted her hand and touched at the tip of her nose with the back of her fore-finger. 'And I have no wish to be indelicate – but the smell when one goes anywhere near the livestock – ! Dear God,

I've never known anything like it. And I should never forget it, I can assure you of that. Oh, dear, no. And as for walking –' she laughed again here, a gentle little sound amid the hum of voices and the chink of the china, 'well, I've never before had to be so careful of where I tread.' She shook her head. 'You can't tell me that you find such a thing attractive, surely?'

'Well, of course not,' Grace said. 'But it's a part of life here. It's a market town, after all. Wiltshire is rural. This is what you get in a market town.'

'But the smell. Is it like that all the time? Surely not.'

Grace allowed herself a little smile. 'No. Only on market days. But as I said, it's a part of it. One accepts it.'

Miss Lewin put her head a little on one side now, looking curiously at Grace, as if Grace had said something quietly outrageous. 'You accept it. I see. Well, rather you than me.'

Grace said nothing to this. She did not know what to say. She had never met anyone quite like Miss Lewin before, and although there was no denying that the young woman was beautiful, Grace also found her very proud and not a little unsympathetic and – and foreign.

Miss Lewin turned in her seat and with a frown gave an impatient glance over towards the door leading to the kitchens. 'I wonder how long it takes people to make a pot of tea,' she said. 'I should have told the girl I'm only here till Saturday.' Then, turning back, she said to Grace with a little sigh, as if putting behind her a rather dispiriting subject, 'But anyway, enough of all that . . . How do you enjoy teaching our dear Sophie?'

Grace was on firmer ground here and she said without hesitation, 'Oh, excellently. I enjoy it very much. In fact, if I told you how much I enjoyed it, Sophie might get a swelled head.'

'You hear that, Sophie?' Miss Lewin said to the child. 'We wouldn't want that, would we?'

Sophie laughed and shook her head, her straw hat shifting on her curls.

'And have you been teaching long?' Miss Lewin asked.

'For several years now,' Grace said. 'Until last summer I spent some time teaching two little boys, the sons of a doctor in Green Shipton, the village where I was born, and where I lived before I moved to Berron Wick. Before that I was teaching a little boy who –'

'Well, indeed you have been busy,' Miss Lewin cut in, then added, 'I can't imagine the life of a governess. I'm sure it must be very trying at times, particularly if you have the wrong pupil. I have to say, I do sincerely admire you for it.'

Grace was not sure how to take this, but she was saved having to think of a response, for Sophie cried, 'Oh, here comes Papa,' and turning, Grace saw Mr Fairman coming in at the door. Weaving between the tables, he came across the room towards them.

'Well,' he said as he took off his hat and sat down next to Miss Lewin, 'that didn't take long, I'm glad to say,' then added, looking at the empty table, 'I thought you'd be halfway through your tea by now.'

'Oh, don't talk about it,' Miss Lewin said with a weary air, rolling her eyes. 'The service is impossible.'

'Not to worry,' Mr Fairman said, 'she's busy, poor girl. Market day and all that.'

'It just needs management,' Miss Lewin said. 'After all, they know that market day is coming. If it comes every week, it hardly takes them by surprise.'

Just then the waitress appeared again and now approached them with her laden tray, and in just a few moments, with little breathed excuses for the delay, was setting down the tea things. She placed in front of Sophie one of the plates holding the sponge cake, and held the other in her hand, looking from one to the other of the adults. 'Oh, it's for the lady here,' Miss Lewin said with a smile, indicating Grace, and the plate was dutifully set down.

The waitress went away, and while Sophie wasted no time in starting to make inroads on her cake and lemonade, Miss Lewin poured the tea.

The tea was handed around, and Grace had made no attempt to start on her cake. Miss Lewin was not slow to notice this, and said with a little note of urgency, 'Oh, do eat, Miss Harper. Don't stand on ceremony.'

Grace felt her cheeks burning, at the same time sensing the eyes of Miss Lewin and Mr Fairman upon her. The slice of cake was quite large. Of a soft, airy, yellow-coloured sponge, it was in two parts like a sandwich, its filling made of some white creamy substance. Its surface was covered with a deep, light-textured cream decorated with half-sections of glacé cherries. It was the last thing on earth that Grace wanted to eat.

She took a sip of her tea, took off her gloves, and then, taking up her fork, dug it into the cake and began to eat.

'Did your business go all right?' Miss Lewin said to Mr Fairman over her teacup. 'It didn't take you long.'

'No, I didn't expect it to,' he said. 'And yes, it was fine. I merely wished to pay a bill. And people never take long about it if you're offering them money.'

Miss Lewin smiled. 'Well, I might say that I've been learning quite a lot in the little time you were away.'

'Oh?'

'Yes, I've been learning what it's like to live in a country town. And learning just what adjustment is needed. And apparently you have a feeling for wild creatures.'

He frowned. 'I beg your pardon?'

'Sophie and her teacher here were telling me about your buying the birds and releasing them,' Miss Lewin said. 'Oh, dear, Kester, I did wonder if the country air might have gone to your head. I do hope not. Tell me there's hope for you yet.'

Grace, eating her cake, registered the sound of his name. Kester. An old name, a derivation of the older name Christopher, she had not heard it in many years. She did not look up but continued to nibble at her cake.

Miss Lewin went on, 'I've been rather hard on your new home town, I fear.' Here she turned to Sophie. 'Is that true, Sophie? You're going to tell your papa that I've been a little over-critical, is that so?' Without waiting for an answer she added, 'Well, you must excuse it if I have been.' She chuckled. 'I'm new in town and one has to make allowances.' She set down her teacup and, gently laying one small hand over Mr Fairman's large one as it rested on the cloth, gave it a pat and a gentle squeeze. 'But I can learn,' she said, 'in time. One is never too old to learn.'

Grace watched as Miss Lewin's hand moved from Mr Fairman's and settled again beside her cup. And then came Miss Lewin's voice again, this time directed at Grace.

'Miss Harper,' she said, 'you've dropped cream down the bodice of your dress. Oh, you poor thing.'

Grace, feeling so self-conscious, abruptly leaned back from the table in order to see the damage caused, and in the process sent her fork clattering to the floor.

'Oh, dear – there goes your fork too,' Miss Lewin said – as if Grace were already not well enough aware. And with a little laugh: 'What on earth shall we do with you?'

Hot with humiliation, Grace had frozen; her fork was on the floor, a little drop of cream was on the bodice of her dress. What more could go wrong? With a murmured 'Excuse me,' she took her handkerchief and wiped off the cream. At the same time the young waitress came by and, stooping, picked up the fork.

'I'll get you another one, miss,' she said.

But Grace had had enough. With as much dignity as she

235

could summon, she gently pushed away the plate holding the half-eaten cake. 'Please don't bother,' she said. 'I don't want any more.'

How Grace sat through the remaining time in the teashop she could hardly have described. If they were twenty minutes in number then they seemed more like so many hours. She had thought they would never end. But at last the bill was paid and the four of them were trooping out into the street again. Once there, Mr Fairman asked Grace if she would care to accompany them to their lodgings, telling her that he would get a cab to take her back to Asterleigh. She thanked him but declined, saying that she was happy to take the train, and in any case had to get back without too much further delay.

And so she said goodbye to Mr Fairman and Sophie. And also to Miss Lewin, who, clasping her hands in front of her, said what a pleasure it had been to meet Sophie's teacher, and how she hoped that one day in the future they would have the opportunity to meet again.

And thirty-five minutes later Grace sat on the train heading for Berron Wick and from there the short walk to Asterleigh. And with each mile covered, Grace felt greater relief; she was so glad to be out of the situation she had just left. She had felt patronized, humoured and humiliated, and never wished to see Miss Lewin again.

Back at Asterleigh House, she found that Billy had just returned from school, and had been given some tea and cake by Mrs Sandiston. Grace sat and talked with him for a few minutes about his lessons, then excused herself and went into her room.

There at her little table she sat with Stephen's letter before her. Over the past days, and even earlier that same day she had pondered on how best to respond. There had been times when she had even considered not answering the letter at all.

She drew towards her her writing pad and pen and ink, and then wrote:

> *Dear Stephen,*
> *I thank you for your letter, which I was most surprised to receive – as you correctly guessed I would be. You asked if we might meet. I have no idea of the purpose for such a meeting, but for old times' sake I am happy to tell you that I am agreeable. I would prefer it if we did not meet here where I am presently staying, however, and would like to suggest that on Thursday, the proposed day of your visit, we meet in Berron Wick itself. If you would care to meet me at the crossroads near the Lamb and Flag inn at, say, 4.30, we could perhaps take a walk if the weather is fine. If it is not, then we might have some tea in the Lamb – which is where I shall wait for you if the weather is wet.*
> *Yours,*
> *Grace Harper*

As she had written she had seen Miss Lewin's eyes resting on Mr Fairman's face. It was an image she could not get out of her mind. She thought also of the way Miss Lewin had addressed him as Kester. Most clearly of all, however, was the image in her mind of how Miss Lewin had laid her hand over his own on the white cloth. And he had not, Grace recalled, removed his hand from her touch.

These images were in her mind as she wrote out the envelope and sealed the letter inside.

Without delay she left the house to post the letter.

Chapter Twelve

On Monday morning Sophie came back to Asterleigh
House to resume her lessons. Standing at the library
window on the first floor, Grace saw the carriage pull up
before the front of the house, and watched as Mr Fairman
lifted Sophie down. She waited then for the sound of the
ring at the door, but when it came remained where she was.
During the first days of the lessons she had gone down
herself, but this time she waited while Jane went to let the
child in. A minute or so later, standing well back, half-
hidden behind the curtain, she saw the carriage, with Mr
Fairman at the reins, driven away.

A tap at the library door and the door opened, and there
was Jane with Sophie, Jane saying, 'Miss Sophie for you,
Miss Harper,' and then Sophie coming almost skipping into
the room.

As the door closed behind the maid, Sophie said
animatedly as she took off her hat and cape, 'Oh, Miss
Harper, it seems so long since I was here last. It's been a
whole week.' She gave a theatrical sigh. 'I'm glad to be back
at my lessons. I missed them.'

'I missed them too,' Grace said.

'Did you? Truly?'

'Truly I did.' Grace smiled and gave a little nod of
emphasis. 'So we'll get to work at once, shall we?'

Later as they came to the end of the English lesson,
Sophie, observing that she had done well in the spelling,
said happily, 'There, miss, I got them all right. Did you

think I might forget everything while I was away from my lessons?'

'No,' Grace said, 'I knew you wouldn't forget.'

'No, I wouldn't forget,' Sophie agreed, then added, 'Anyway, I didn't entirely go without lessons last week when I wasn't coming here.'

'You still had some lessons? Oh, how was that?'

'I had lessons with Miss Lewin. I did spelling with her – but not such hard words as the words you choose. Her words were quite easy. And I had drawing too. Though I have to say she's not as good at drawing as you. She can't draw faces and people and ponies like you. She can only draw flowers and trees. But they're quite good, even so.'

'Well – that's splendid.' A pause and then, 'Did Miss Lewin go back to London?'

'Yes, she went back on Sunday. Papa and I took her to Corster to see her off on the train.' She rolled her eyes high in her head, and said admiringly, 'Oh, she had so many trunks and cases. And all just for a *week*.'

Grace did not know what to say to this. 'Do you think she enjoyed her stay with you?' she asked.

'Oh, she didn't stay with us, miss. She stayed at the hotel.'

'Yes, of course, I realize that.'

'Yes, she stayed at the hotel. But she came to see us every day.'

Grace asked, 'And did you – enjoy it? Miss Lewin coming to visit you?'

'Oh, yes. I got to spend a lot more time with Papa. And we went out on most days when the weather was fine in the hired carriage.'

'Well, that's nice. Where did you go?'

'Oh, well – we went to see our new house. But I think I told you about that, didn't I? When we were in the teashop.'

'Yes, as I recall, you did tell me. And did Miss Lewin like it, the house? I'm sure she must have done.'

'Oh, yes, she liked it very much. She said anyone would be happy to live there, especially when it was improved. That's what's happening to it now – it's being improved. The painters are in, painting the walls and the doors and windows and everything.'

'How exciting.'

'Yes, and it will be finished soon and we shall move in, and have all our own furniture again. That will be nice.'

'Indeed, that will be very nice. What else did you do when Miss Lewin was visiting you?'

'Oh, well, we went on a picnic – though the weather was rather too cold. And on another day we went to Redbury. Have you ever been to Redbury, miss?'

'Yes. It's a very nice city.'

'Oh, it is. We got the train. Oh, that was so exciting, miss. I love going on the train. Do you like going on the train?'

'Yes, I quite like it.'

'I love it. We went to the theatre while we were there, and saw a play. Which Papa and Miss Lewin called an operetta. Which means they sing a lot of songs. I don't remember what it was called, the play, but it was very nice. There was a lot of singing. Oh, lovely songs – and a lot of funny people all dressed up. It was supposed to be all happening in Japan. There was a man in it called the Lord High Executioner, and a very pretty lady called Yum Yum. Lots of the ladies had lovely dresses and they all had fans. I slept in a little cot in Papa's room at the hotel, and Miss Lewin stayed in another room.' She sighed with pleasure at the memory. 'Miss Lewin wore the loveliest gown to the theatre. Oh, she looked so pretty. She knows a lot about the theatre, Miss Lewin does. I think she goes a lot when she's in London. She says theatres are very nice in the provinces but they're not the same as in London. She said that one

240

theatre in London is all lit with electric light. Did you know that, miss?'

'I think I read about it,' Grace said.

'And she says the next time she comes here to Corster we can go to Redbury and go to the theatre again.'

Grace heard herself say, in a strange, bright voice, 'So she's coming back some day, is she?'

'Oh, yes. She says she wants to come back very soon, as soon as we've moved in. She says she'll help Papa choose some nice things for the house.'

'Well,' Grace said, 'that sounds very nice. You must tell me more about it all at some time. But for now,' she picked up a book from the table before her and opened it, 'shall we begin our geography?'

In the afternoon when there came the ring at the bell, signifying that Mr Fairman had arrived to take his daughter home, Sophie put on her hat and coat and, wishing Grace a goodbye, hurried down the stairs. Grace, standing just within the room, with the library door open, could hear Mr Fairman greeting his daughter and asking if she was ready to leave. Moments later there came the sound of the front door closing and Grace moved to the window and watched as the carriage drove around the still fountain. Only when the vehicle had moved out of sight did she turn from the window.

The following day Sophie was back, and once more Grace remained in the library while the child was admitted to the house, and again later when she made her departure. As on the day previously, Grace had not been able to bring herself to meet Mr Fairman. And she taxed herself with it. How could she, she asked herself, hide like a coward, afraid to see him face to face, afraid even to be seen by him?

On Wednesday Sophie came by hired cab and was

picked up by the same driver when the day's lessons were over. Seeing the elderly man coming up to the front door, Grace felt a sense of relief that it was not Mr Fairman. At the same time she knew a slight feeling of disappointment.

On the following day, Thursday, Mr Fairman was back behind the reins. And although with one part of her being she had hoped to see him there, still she did not go down to greet him, either when he brought Sophie to the house or when he came to take her away. And once again from the library window she watched their departure from the grounds.

Still standing there by the window some minutes after the carriage had left the drive, she felt in turmoil. It was as if her mind were without direction. And as for her feelings – they were like a foreign language that she could not read. In the end she did her best not to allow herself to dwell upon those unformed, unidentified emotions; it did no good; they only seemed to take her deeper into confusion.

She turned, moved from the window. In less than an hour and a half Stephen would be waiting to meet her at the inn.

As any fool could have told her, she said to herself as she got ready for the meeting: Stephen was the answer to the question. To all the questions.

He was not writing to her out of the blue merely to resume a correspondence, she told herself. He wanted more than that. He wanted more, too, than a mere companion for walks in the country, more than an opponent for games of chess. But being circumspect as he was, and not wishing to be crude in his approaches, he had given hardly anything away in his letter.

She took a final look in the glass, adjusted the beaver-trimmed collar of her cape, touched at her hat one last time, and turned away. At the door of Billy's room she knocked.

There was no answer, but going downstairs she found him in the kitchen with the cook. The kitchen maid had the afternoon off, and Billy was helping the cook with the vegetables. Taking the boy to the side, she told him that she was going out for an hour or so. Where was she going? he asked, to which she replied that she was to meet an old friend.

'Who?'

Not answering his question, she said, 'I'll be back later.'

'What time?'

'Probably around six o'clock. I can't be too late – I'm to have coffee with Mrs Spencer.'

The day, though sunny, was without any great warmth and there was a chill breeze coming from the west. She was glad of her cape and scarf. As she neared the arch leading to the inn yard Stephen came out of the inn's doorway, his hat in his hand, and came to a stop a few yards before her.

'Hello, Grace.'

'Hello, Stephen.'

'I saw you from the window where I was sitting,' he said. 'I saw you coming along the road.' He looked very handsome in his chesterfield coat, and with his tanned complexion – evidence of his time in the sun. He gestured back to the door of the inn. 'Would you like to go inside for a drink – some tea or coffee, or whatever you'd like?'

She looked up at the sky. 'Could we walk a little?' she said. 'It's not that warm, but it looks as if it'll stay dry for the time being.'

'Of course.'

They set out together in silence, walking a yard apart, as if careful of any closer proximity. They made their way along the main street of the village, past the blacksmith's, the little post office, and on to the end of the road where the garden of the last cottage gave way to meadowland, and the road ended in a stile, on the other side of which the way continued with merely a footpath.

After crossing the stile they continued on. Their conversation was composed only of small talk. They spoke of the weather, and then he asked how she had been, and asked also after the welfare of Billy. Grace told him what news there was.

At the far end of the meadow was another stile, beyond which on one side of the path a little woodland began. The ground ahead looked slightly damp, and Grace, careful of her boots, did not wish to go on further. On reaching the stile she came to a halt and turned.

'Shall we stop here?' she said. 'I don't want to walk too far.'

A wild flowering cherry grew close beside the stile, its lush pink blossoms just breaking out of bud. Stephen reached out and took one of the flowered branches in his hand and drew it towards him. Holding the branch close to his nose he drew in the scent and gave a little sigh of pleasure.

'It's so beautiful,' Grace said.

'Oh, indeed it is.' He let the branch spring back to its natural position, then, looking directly at Grace, said awkwardly, 'Thank you for agreeing to see me, Grace.'

She gave a little shrug and a smile, dismissing his thanks. 'Please . . .'

'I so wanted to talk to you. I need to talk to you, Grace. I was afraid you might refuse to see me.'

'I wouldn't do that.'

'No? Perhaps you might think it's what I deserve.'

She smiled a little more warmly here. 'I don't know what you deserve, Stephen. As far as I know you're a good man. I'm sure you deserve only what is good and right.'

'I *am* a good man, Grace,' he said earnestly. 'Although like any man I make mistakes.' He gave an ironic shake of the head. 'Oh, I make mistakes all right.'

Grace said nothing. All around them were the sights and sounds of nature: sparrows cheeped, blue tits and black-birds were busily gathering nest-building material, a butterfly danced by, and the leaves of the yew tree beside the flowering cherry moved gently in the breeze. Stephen remained silent for a moment or two, then went on, 'You probably heard about me and Miss Shilford, did you?'

'Well,' Grace looked off into the distance, avoiding seeing whether or not his eyes were upon her, 'I did hear something. My aunt wrote to me. But who knows if what I heard was true? You know how gossip is.'

'You heard that Miss Shilford and I had – well – had come to a parting of the ways, did you?'

'Something like that.'

'Well, it was true enough.' A little pause. 'You see – while I was away at sea on this last voyage we both somehow –'

Grace broke in at this point: 'Really, Stephen, you don't have to tell me. If things are painful to you, then –'

'No,' he said. 'I want to. I want to tell you. You have to know.' He took a deep breath. 'I want to be completely honest with you, Grace. Miss Shilford ended our – our friendship, our understanding, I must tell you that. But I can also tell you that it came as a relief to me. I don't know –' he shook his head as if in bewilderment, 'I think that when we first met, Victoria and I, I was – well, somewhat bowled over.' He looked at Grace now, a self-deprecating smile touching his mouth. 'Does that sound really foolish? I'm sure it does. But I'm trying to be honest. I suppose I'm trying to get at the truth for my *own* sake also. At times it's been so bewildering, I don't mind admitting.'

Silence fell between them, then Grace said: 'When did this happen – your separation from Miss Shilford?'

'Very soon after I got back from the West Indies. Just weeks ago. I can't be sure, but I rather think that perhaps someone else had come into her life. Not that she ever hinted at such a thing, but . . .' His words ended in a shrug.

'Oh, Stephen, how sad for you. What a great shame.'

'No, it's all right, really it is. As I said to you, it was a relief. The news came as a relief. When she told me, trying not to let me down too harshly – well – all I could feel was relief. I was glad. It sounds awful to say it, but it's the truth.'

'And does Miss Shilford know of your feelings? Does she know how you felt about the parting?'

'I don't think so. I didn't tell her, certainly. I merely wished her happiness in whatever she chose to do and with whomever she chose to share her life. Who knows, perhaps she might have gleaned something of my feelings when I didn't cry and beg her to give it another chance. I have no way of knowing. But I did not. I didn't ask her to reconsider. Of course I'm also glad that, feeling as I did, I was let off so lightly.'

'I suppose you must be,' Grace said. 'What would you have done if she had not done as she did? What if she'd been happy to continue in your relationship, and only wished to go ahead with the marriage?'

'I don't know. Had I ended it myself, against her wishes, it would have been a dreadful scandal, I have no doubt. And I've no doubt either that it would have been very distressing, for both of us. So I don't know. Perhaps I wouldn't have had the courage to end it myself. Does that sound like a confession of great weakness? Perhaps it does. But it's the truth.'

'No, it doesn't sound like weakness. I do know that sometimes it's so much easier to take the line of least resistance.' A moment's pause, then she said, 'Do you know why you were happy to have the friendship end?'

'Yes – it's because I had discovered as time went on that – we were not suited. It's as simple as that.'

'But you couldn't see it at the start?'

'No, I couldn't. But that's often the way, isn't it? Sometimes people get off to the wrong start but end up finding they have so much in common. At other times you start off thinking everything is wonderful – and then things just don't work out. That's what happened with Victoria and me. At first everything was fine, and it was only as we spent more time together that our differences became apparent. And on my last leave ashore I realized the truth. We were not meant for one another. I won't go into all the little reasons that made me come to such a conclusion but it's enough to say that I did. When we met I suppose it was in all the glamour of the situation of being on board ship together. And she was so attractive, so elegant.' He gave a little nod. 'But to make a metaphor, I suppose even in the finest of voyages one reaches the time when one has to put one's feet back on shore again.' He sighed. 'And that's what I did. And what she did. And I suppose I can only be relieved that it turned out the way it did – with neither one of us being hurt.'

'Have you seen Miss Shilford since this happened?'

'No. And we have no plans to meet again. And now –'

He broke off, and Grace followed the line of his gaze and saw a couple approaching, a young man and a young woman, from the woodland path. Grace and Stephen stood aside as the pair clambered over the stile and stepped down onto the other side. When the two were gone out of earshot, Stephen continued:

'Grace, I was about to say that – that I was sorry for what happened between you and me. It should never have happened as it did. Perhaps I should blame it on the tropic sun. Whatever it was, it was wrong. I'm sorry I made such a mistake, and I'm so sorry if I hurt you.'

Behind him, on the horizon, Grace could see that dark clouds were gathering, and she was aware of feeling a sharper chill in the air. She registered the facts only with a part of her mind. Stephen had stopped, as if waiting for her to speak, to respond, but she kept silent. After a moment he went on: 'I know that there were no promises made between us, on either side. And there was no – understanding, either. And perhaps when it all comes down to it you didn't necessarily expect anything more from our friendship – other than what there was. Perhaps it was simply *that* to you – a friendship. I know that's how it started out between us, but . . .' With a little shake of his head he let his words trail off, as if the right words eluded him.

Grace said, 'You speak of what the relationship was for me – or may have been. What was it to you, Stephen? Perhaps that's more important.'

'To me. Ah – to me, yes. I was aware that you were a warm, intelligent young woman, a very pretty young woman. And I know now that my feelings for you were strong. But were they love? No, I don't think that they were love – any more than were your feelings for me. But that's not to say that that is not what they could become. I do know that my feelings are stronger for you now than they have ever been. And perhaps that's one thing that time does.' He paused. 'It does take time for love to grow, Grace. Do you not agree?'

'Perhaps,' she murmured.

'And I wrote to you as I did, Grace, to ask if you would consider giving me another chance. Will you?'

'Another chance – for what, Stephen?'

'To be something more to you. Something more to you than a mere – friend. And a chance to let that friendship grow between us. A chance to allow your own feelings to develop – as I think they could. For I know you liked me, Grace. And I hope you like me still.'

They stood in silence, a silence broken after moments when Stephen, turning, raising his eyes and seeing how the clouds were gathering, said, 'Oh, dear, I think we're in for a shower. Perhaps we should start back.'

They set off back the way they had come, moving side by side, a yard apart, along the footpath that dissected the meadow.

As they walked, Grace's mind was in turmoil. This was what she had hoped for, she realized, but never had truly believed could happen. So many times soon after the break with Stephen she had tormented herself with dreaming that he might end his new relationship and come back to her. But in spite of her brave thoughts she had never entertained any real hopes that it could come to be. And yet it had. And not only had it happened, but now he was here beside her, and he had just spoken words of reconciliation that she herself in dreams might have composed.

As the clouds grew darker overhead they quickened their steps. The rain began to fall as they drew near to the inn, and they made the last few yards in a dash.

They stood just within the small foyer from which opened the public and saloon bars, and watched as in seconds the rain came teeming down, bouncing off the steps and darkening the earth and stones of the road.

'Well,' Stephen said, 'I think we might be here for a few minutes. Would you like a drink of some kind?'

There was no option: they had to remain for a while, in which case they must take some refreshment. 'A little tea would be nice,' she said.

Moving through the saloon bar, they found another room opening from it, a small private bar, and they went in and sat at a small round table. From the barman Stephen ordered ale for himself and tea for Grace, and while they waited to be served he took off his coat and hat. Grace kept her cape on; she somehow doubted that they would be long in their present surroundings. Avoiding Stephen's eyes, she looked around her. She had been living on the edge of the village for some months now, but this was the first time she been inside any of the inns in the locality. She was glad of the fact that there was no one else in the room.

After a minute the barman brought Stephen's ale and said to Grace that her tea would be only another minute. Grace thanked him and he went away. Through the window that faced onto the stable yard at the rear she could see the rain still falling, but up above the May sky had already begun to clear, the sun shining through the dark clouds.

'Perhaps it's not going to keep up after all,' Stephen said.

'No – it looks promising.'

At any moment, she thought, the conversation would be returned to its former subject, and he would ask for an answer to his question, his request for another chance. And now that the opportunity had come, the chance that she herself had hoped for, she did not know what she would say. She must think it through, and she must be careful in her answer. What was her situation? she asked herself. She must try to be sensible about this. Her situation was such that she was a single woman with a dependent younger brother to care for. She had no doubt that Stephen appreciated her situation, and was well aware that wherever she went Billy would have to go with her.

How fine it would be, she thought, to be loved by one man, and to love him in return. To have a home of her own – which of course would be a home for Billy too. A home of her own, where she could feel secure and no longer need to be dependent on charity – or any near-charity of the kind that currently came from the Spencers. A home of her own where she would make up her own curtains and embroider the pillowslips and antimacassars, and cook and bake in her own kitchen for her own family; cook and bake not only for her husband and for Billy, but for a child of her own too.

'What are you thinking about?'

Grace turned at the sound of Stephen's voice, watched as he raised his glass to his lips and took a sip of his ale.

'All kinds of things,' she said. 'You, me, Billy, the future.'

'Ah, the future . . . Tell me, Grace, after what I said, do you think I have any part in it – your future?'

When she did not answer he added, 'I'm hurrying you. I'm sorry; I don't mean to. You should have time to think about it.'

'I'm not sure, not even now,' Grace said, 'what it is you're offering.'

'My friendship. But you know that already.'

'Yes.'

'And my hope is that we can have a – an understanding.' He had lowered his voice considerably now. 'I feel very deeply for you, Grace, I realize that now. And I hope in time that you will come to feel the same for me. And if it should happen – then I hope we can make other plans. Marriage.'

He had spoken the words.

'Yes, marriage,' he said. 'I would look after you, Grace, you could be sure of that. And Billy too, until he's able to fend for himself. I'd see he was all right. He would have a home with us.'

She had no chance to reply at that moment, even had she wished to, for the barman came with a tray and placed the tea things before her. As the man turned, Stephen watched his departure then said, his voice still low:

'What do you think, Grace?' Then with a wretched little smile, 'Are you going to put me out of my misery? Please tell me what you think.'

A ray of sunlight cut through the leaves of the rowan tree in the yard and touched her china teacup. She saw that the rain had stopped. Through the window she could see that the dark clouds had almost vanished and in their place the sky was infinitely blue. She knew what her answer must be.

'Stephen,' she said, 'I'm so sorry.'

Back at Asterleigh House Grace wiped her boots and let herself in at the back door of the house.

As she went through into the rear passage, Mrs Sandiston came to the kitchen door. 'Ah, you're back, miss,' she said. 'Will you be wanting some dinner? There's some nice cold ham if you'd like some.'

Grace thanked her and said she would like just a little, and would come down to eat in half an hour. Going on through, she went up the stairs to her room where she took off her hat and cape. She felt restless, and as if she had not done enough walking it was almost all she could do not to begin pacing the floor. The meeting with Stephen had left her with no peace of mind at all.

She looked at the clock, it was almost 6.15. Billy would have had his dinner by now. She took off her boots and changed her clothes, washed her face and stood before the glass to put her hair in place again. In a while she would go downstairs to have her own dinner and then later go and join Mrs Spencer for coffee. Jane would come for her when it was time.

She stood before the glass, but saw herself only with the surface of her consciousness. She kept hearing Stephen's voice, the echo of his words, and her own words that she had uttered at the end.

'I know what it must have taken for you to come here today and offer these things to me, Stephen,' she had said. 'And I'm just so sorry to disappoint you. But I've come to the conclusion that it would never work.'

'Oh, Grace –' he had broken in, but she had stopped him, saying: 'Please. If I don't speak now I might never have the courage again, and I have to say what I feel.' The little teapot and milk jug, all the tea things, had remained before her on the table, untouched, unheeded. 'I was a little like you, Stephen,' she went on. 'But in the opposite way.

252

Whereas I thought I cared for you quite deeply, I realize now that it was not so.' Here she lifted her hand in a little gesture for understanding, in a little plea for him not to be hurt. 'That sounds so cold, I know, but it's not intended to be so. I'm only trying to speak the truth – what I feel. And I like you, Stephen, I like you very much. And I admire you also. But I realize now that my feelings for you didn't run any deeper than that. I think I was merely in love with the notion of having a – an understanding with a fine person – such as you are. It was not love. And I don't think it ever could be.'

And she had got up from her seat a few moments later, there at the small round table in the private bar, her tea still untouched. She had stood up, and then reached down to press his hand. And he had grasped her hand in his and murmured with quiet urgency that she should not be hasty, and asked her if they could not go on together for a while, for in time she might change her mind. But no, she had said, she would not change her mind. And it would not be fair of her to prolong the situation. Her mind was made up.

And she had left him then – 'No, please don't get up,' and had gone out into the rainwashed air.

Now, giving a last touch at her hair she stepped away from the glass. A minute later she was outside and making her way down to the kitchen.

When she had eaten she went back upstairs and moved along the landing to Billy's room. A tap at the door and he called, 'Come in,' and she went inside.

'Did you have your meeting?' Billy asked. He was sitting at his little table cutting out shapes to make a model house.

'Yes, I had my meeting.'

'Oh.' He stopped in a movement with the scissors and looked at her a little more directly.

'What is it?' Grace said. She thought she could see the faintest look of panic in his expression.

'You've been to see your Mr Stephen.'

'Mr Stephen Cantrell. Not my Mr Stephen. What's the matter?'

'Nothing.'

'Tell me what it is.'

'I told you, it's nothing.'

'Billy . . .'

Then, the words almost bursting from him, he said, 'Does this mean you'll be getting married?'

'*What*? What gave you that idea? Who said anything about getting married?'

'That's what Mrs Tanner always said. She said one day you'd marry your Mr Stephen.'

'Well, I shan't be doing anything like that.' She moved closer to him, looking into his face, shadowed a little as he sat with the window behind him. 'Why are you concerned about me marrying Mr Cantrell?'

'Not only him – anybody.'

'But – but why?'

'Well, you'd have to leave, wouldn't you? You wouldn't stay here any longer, would you?'

'Well, I –'

'You wouldn't, would you? Not if you were married. You and your husband would have a place of your own.'

'Well, yes, that's true . . .'

'So, what would happen to me? Where would I go?'

'Billy . . .'

'I couldn't stay here, could I?'

She remained looking down at him. 'Well,' she said, 'I'm not marrying anybody so you and I are not leaving here. And whenever we do decide to leave it will be for some nice place that's just right for both of us. I can promise you that.'

'But Grace –'

'I promise you, Billy,' she said. 'I will never leave you. Never.'

It wasn't till almost nine o'clock that Grace, having been summoned by Jane, left her own room to go down to the drawing room where Mrs Spencer was about to have her coffee. Grace did not want to go. She felt somewhat melancholy tonight, a little low, and having had a choice would have chosen to remain in the solitude of her room. There was nothing for it, though, but that she must go to spend a little time with her employer; it was what she was there for. With Mr Spencer away on business again, Grace's company was needed.

At the drawing room door Grace tapped, listened for Mrs Spencer's voice and went in. She found her sitting on the sofa, her silver-topped cane leaning against the arm. A bright fire was burning in the grate. She appeared to be dressed a little more casually than usual, wearing a very simple dress with a little woollen jacket against the chill, and on top of this a shawl.

'Ah, good evening, Grace,' she said. 'Come and sit down. Jane will be bringing the coffee any minute.' There was a half-full decanter and a sherry glass on the low table before her, and after she had spoken she picked up the glass and took a little sip. 'Spring's not here yet,' she said as Grace sat down, 'not by a long chalk. Some of these evenings feel more like December, don't you agree? And I seem to feel the cold so. One needs a little something to warm the blood. Will you have something, Grace? A little brandy with your coffee perhaps?'

'No, thank you, ma'am, the coffee will be fine.'

'Are you warm enough?'

'Yes, thank you.'

'And what sort of day have you had? You had your pupil as usual, did you?'

'Yes, I did.'

'And how is Sophie getting on?'

255

Grace talked for a minute about Sophie's lessons, and her progress, then Mrs Spencer, said, 'It will be very nice to see them settled in their own home. He's an extremely nice man – and his little girl is so sweet. They deserve some happiness. They've had a visitor here from London, I gather, for about a week, is that so?'

'Yes. A friend of Mr Fairman's. Miss Lewin, her name is.'

'A very elegant and beautiful young lady too, according to Jane. She saw them in Corster when she was out on an errand for me last week. What do you suppose? Do you think we're about to hear the sound of wedding bells?'

At that moment came a tap at the door, and then Jane was coming in with the tray of coffee which she set down on the low table in front of her mistress. When the maid had gone again Mrs Spencer said to Grace: 'Grace, would you like to do the honours?' and Grace moved to the sofa and poured the coffee for the two of them. Her own cup she took back with her to her chair.

Mrs Spencer sipped from her cup, then said, 'Jane said she'd seen you walking towards the village this afternoon. I hope you didn't get caught in the rain.'

Grace smiled. 'Fortunately I managed to miss it. I got into shelter just in time.'

'Well, that's good. I do hope the good weather isn't too far away. Well, certainly all the signs of spring are here even if it is so cold – the daffodils all out, and the cherry blossom; the birds nesting. I'm just so glad the winter is behind us. I so hate the long nights and the short days and the bleak skies.'

'When we have some warmer days,' Grace said, 'perhaps we can go out with our sketchbooks and paint-boxes.'

'Yes, perhaps we can.' But Mrs Spencer spoke without enthusiasm. 'Perhaps we can.'

Grace began: 'Also, when the warmer weather comes we –' but Mrs Spencer overrode her, not rudely, but as if she was preoccupied to the point of being momentarily unaware. 'Even if we don't go painting,' Mrs Spencer said, gazing off, looking into the fire, 'it would certainly be nice to get out of the house for a while. I don't get out enough, my husband tells me, and perhaps he's right. Perhaps I should make more of an effort. After all the carriage is there, and Mr Rhind or Mr Johnson can be there if I need a driver.' She took a sip from her sherry glass. 'Rhind is always there for Mr Spencer.' She turned to Grace now. 'I don't think you like Mr Rhind, do you? I somehow got that impression.'

'Well –' Grace did not know what to say, and so said nothing, taking refuge from the awkwardness of the moment in stirring her coffee.

'Not everyone does. Like him, I mean. He does not inspire liking. He is not an eminently likeable man. Although at times I'm sure my husband must think he is. Heaven knows, Rhind is loyal and faithful enough. Where Edward is concerned, there's no one more faithful.'

'I rather gathered that,' Grace said tentatively.

'Then you gathered correctly.'

Grace said, having wondered so long, 'Has Mr Rhind been in Mr Spencer's employ for long? I rather assumed that he has.'

'Oh, for a considerable number of years now. My husband was a young man when they met. They both were, though Rhind is a few years older. Exactly by how much I don't know.' The sherry glass was empty and Mrs Spencer refilled it from the decanter. Her coffee seemed to be more or less forgotten. Grace divined in the woman's mood some lowness of spirit – as there was in her own, and thought that if she, Grace, were asked to give some kind of emotional comfort, then she would be ill equipped to provide it.

'They met, so I understand, as I say,' Mrs Spencer picked

up a napkin and dabbed at her mouth, 'when they were both young men. Apparently Rhind was in a spot of bother over something. Something in which he was in trouble with the police. I don't know the ins and outs of it, and it's of no importance now, but I believe what happened is that Edward helped the man out of the particular spot he was in. And, loyal man that he is, Rhind never forgot it. He seems to have spent all these years supporting my husband in whatever way he thinks necessary. I do believe that if Edward asked him to jump off a bridge he would do it. There's nothing, I think, that Rhind wouldn't do for him.'

'I've never been quite sure what Mr Rhind's exact role is,' Grace said.

'That's an excellent question,' said Mrs Spencer. 'I'm not sure that I can answer it precisely. Let's just say he's a kind of factotum. Whatever Edward wants him to be he will be. He's his valet, his driver, his groom, his just about everything.' She put the napkin down on the table before her. 'Would you like some more coffee, Grace?'

Was it possible that her mistress's words were a little slurred? Grace wondered. 'No, thank you,' she said. 'I still have some.'

Mrs Spencer gestured to an area behind the sofa on which the chess set lay on a marble-topped table. 'We must get back to our games at some time,' she said. 'We haven't played in two or three weeks now.'

Grace had been at the disposal of Mrs Spencer for most of the time when Sophie had not been having her lessons, but her employer had not called on her beyond the odd occasion, and none of those periods had lasted any great length of time. It was almost as if for the time being she preferred her own company.

'We must do more sketching together as well,' Mrs Spencer said. 'And more painting. I'm afraid I've neglected my painting somewhat – which is a shame as it can be a great comfort to me.' She was silent for a moment, then added, 'I met my husband through my painting, did I ever tell you that?'

'No, you didn't.'

'Yes, that's how we met. I had some of my paintings on show in an exhibition in Swindon and he happened to see them. And bought them, can you believe? So that's how our correspondence began – and then he asked whether I had more paintings available. So he visited me and – and well, that's how it all began. Just think, just by chance he happened to be in Swindon at the time my paintings were on show.' She smiled at the memory.

Grace said, 'Perhaps I've been spending too much time with Sophie. I should be spending more time with you, ma'am. We could make other arrangements if you like. Perhaps Sophie should come in only for half the week.'

'No, no,' Mrs Spencer said quickly, 'the arrangements are fine as they are. You teach the child. I like the thought of her coming here. The same with Billy. I like the thought of his living here. At least this house serves some purpose, instead of just standing here like some great mausoleum.' A brief pause and she added, 'I never wanted to come here.'

Hearing such words, Grace was curious. But she dared not enquire further, feeling as it was that Mrs Spencer might well think she had already volunteered more than enough.

'Are you sure you won't have some more coffee, Grace . . .?'

'No, really, thank you.'

Mrs Spencer nodded, sipped from her glass and went to replace it on the table. She misjudged the placing of it, however, and caught the rim of the glass's foot on the edge of the table. In a moment the little amount of sherry that was in there had spilled over the table's surface. Quickly Grace hurried over and with Mrs Spencer's napkin dabbed at the spilt liquor. 'It's all right, Grace,' Mrs Spencer said as Grace mopped up, and then, 'I don't know what's the matter with me tonight.'

'I'd better go and get a cloth,' Grace said, looking at the table, but Mrs Spencer said, 'No, don't go to any trouble. It was only a drop and there's no harm done.'

'Shall I get you a clean glass?' Grace said, holding the empty one.

'Oh, good heavens, no, don't bother to do that.'

Mrs Spencer made no attempt to take the empty glass from Grace, and after a moment Grace picked up the decanter and refilled the glass. Setting glass and decanter down on the table she moved back to her own seat. Silence fell in the room, silence but for the occasional crackle and snap from the fire. Mrs Spencer sipped from her newly charged glass and into the quiet said, 'I used to live in Swindon. Did you know that?'

'I believe someone told me.'

'You believe someone told you, eh? Oh, yes, I'm sure the gossip about me has gone the rounds.' She took another sip from her glass. 'Yes, in Swindon – and I lived in a very modest house. Oh, very modest. Small in comparison to this. But it suited me. I was settled in my life, and I never thought I would move. I had no reason to. But then I married and we moved here.' She gave an ironic smile. 'I had one maid where I lived before, and now look.' Her gaze wandered off again, as if her thoughts were elsewhere, then, turning back to Grace, she said: 'What do you want to do, Grace?'

'What do I want to do? I don't understand.'

'With your life. What do you want to do with your life? I mean, here you are – How old are you now, twenty-one?'

'Yes.'

'Twenty-one years old. You have your life before you. Don't waste it.'

'No,' Grace said, 'I won't,' and thought how foolish her words had been. It was a wonder Mrs Spencer hadn't laughed aloud. And truth to tell, if she had thought for a moment on Grace's situation, she probably would have done so. Here was Grace, at twenty-one, spending her days either teaching a small child or working as companion to a lonely woman – and she could spend years in the same employ without the chance to meet anyone or change her position. And that very day what had she done? She had turned down what in fact amounted to a proposal of marriage, with security for the rest of her days. But then, she had had no choice. Quite simply, it had not been right.

Mrs Spencer, still thinking on Grace's answer, said, 'Indeed, no, you must not,' then gave a sigh and raised her head and looked about her. Returning her gaze to Grace, she added, 'Are you satisfied with your room, my dear?'

'With my room? Yes, indeed. It's very nice, thank you.'

'Well, if not, then there are plenty of other rooms in the house.' Mrs Spencer waved a hand, as if taking in the other rooms. 'That's one thing there's no shortage of – rooms. And Billy? Is he happy with his room? I should have asked long before this.'

'Oh, he loves it. He's never had such a room before.'

'He's a good boy. He'll be in bed asleep now, right?'

Grace smiled. 'I hope so.'

'It's such a good thing he's got you. Without you, what would he do? With no parents and no home? It would be the workhouse, I've no doubt. Or he'd be sleeping rough, begging for his food, perhaps doing the odd job to earn a crust. And with his – his injury he'd be limited as to what he could do. Thank God he's got you.'

Grace said, 'Yes, he's got me.' She did not want to dwell on such a theme.

Mrs Spencer took a sip from her glass. It was already half-gone. Grace wondered what she did with her time all day. While she, Grace, was teaching Sophie, what was Mrs Spencer doing? She didn't spend all her time painting, Grace knew that much. In fact, as far as Grace was aware, she was spending less and less time at her easel and sketch-book. The portrait begun of Grace remained unfinished; it had been two or three weeks since Mrs Spencer had asked her to sit for it. She had been passionate about it at the start, but no longer, it seemed. Like the rest of her painting. Like the games of chess they had enjoyed. And it seemed a very long time since Grace had heard her mistress playing the piano and singing her favourite songs from the operetta. Things were different, Grace thought. In just a few months things seemed to have changed.

Mrs Spencer sat with her sherry glass in her hand, eyes half-closed, her gaze in the direction of the fire. On a small table just behind the back of the sofa an oil lamp cast its soft light, making a pale nimbus around the woman's hair. A little sigh came from her. Grace took in the drooping eye and softened jaw line and thought how tired she looked. There was no longer any trace of youth in her face.

Mrs Spencer put a hand to her mouth as she yawned. 'I'm so pleased you could come and see me tonight,' she said. 'I've been feeling a little melancholy. But I'm sure that's often the way when you have a husband who works all hours God made.'

Grace said, 'I'm almost always about the house, ma'am, if you want me.' Then she added, 'At any time, day or night.'

'Thank you, dear. I appreciate that.'

Mrs Spencer looked away again, gaze towards the fire, eyes half-closed. Silence fell in the room. In the quiet Grace could hear the singing of the burning wood in the grate, the faint sigh of the wind in the tree outside the window, its branches tapping now and again upon the pane. One of the burning logs toppled into the glowing ash, a little too close to the edge of the grate, and Grace looked at Mrs Spencer as if to ask, *Shall I attend to the fire?*, but saw that there had been no reaction, and realized after a moment that the woman was asleep.

Quietly, Grace got up from the chair, moved to the fire and, taking the poker, pushed the burning log back into a safer position. Carefully setting the poker down again, she moved back to her chair.

Grace sat there, unmoving. She did not think to look at the clock until some considerable time had passed, and then she saw that it was close on eleven. Mrs Spencer must have been asleep for at least twenty minutes. Grace did not know what to do. She could not just get up and leave her mistress there. And on the other hand, she did not feel that she could go and rudely awaken her. So she stayed where she was, and all the while Mrs Spencer remained sitting there on the sofa, her chin lowered to her chest, eyes closed, her empty sherry glass held in her lap between her hands.

The fire in the grate was burning lower. Should she, Grace wondered, put on more wood? Or would Mrs Spencer, on waking, see this as a liberty, a step too far?

And then suddenly, Mrs Spencer was awake again. As if nothing had happened she opened her eyes and lifted her head, saying a very little 'Oh,' of surprise to find that she had been sleeping. 'Oh, dear,' she said, turning, finding Grace still in her chair, 'Grace, I think I must have dropped off for a minute. How rude. Please forgive me.'

'You're tired, Mrs Spencer,' Grace said. And then, 'Wouldn't you like to go to bed?'

Mrs Spencer nodded. 'My dear, I think I would.' She became aware that she was still holding her sherry glass, and she leaned forward a little and carefully placed it on the table. Then, leaning to her left, she took hold of her cane. Grace got up and moved to her to help her up from the seat.

At once Mrs Spencer put up her free hand, palm out, stopping Grace in her movement.

'It's all right, my dear. I can do it myself. I'm quite capable.'

'I'm sorry,' Grace apologized.

'That's all right, that's quite all right.' Pushing herself up from the sofa, and with the support of her cane, Mrs Spencer got to her feet. 'My leg bothers me a little tonight,' she said. 'Sometimes it does that. Not often, but occasionally. Tonight it does. It's as if I have no strength in it. There's nothing I can do about it. It will pass in time. Tomorrow it'll be all right again.' She bent slightly and rubbed at her thigh. Then, turning to Grace, she said, 'Is Billy ever in pain? In discomfort?'

The question took Grace by surprise, and she found it a little shocking. How much did people know? she sometimes wondered. She was about to say, *Yes, at times he is.* But she simply said, 'He doesn't complain. He never has.'

'No, I doubt that he would. He doesn't strike one as that kind of a lad.' A brief moment of silence between them, then Mrs Spencer said, 'I was hard on you both on that first day when you came bringing my paintings in their new frames. And you know why, of course, don't you?'

Grace did know, but she kept silent.

Mrs Spencer went on. 'I'm sure you do – you're a sensitive person. Well, it was because of my leg, wasn't it? You and your brother – you just stared at my limping across the room. It made me angry, as you no doubt noticed. And then, of course, I saw that young Billy also had a slight disablement.' She was silent for a moment, then she added, 'My leg – my condition – it didn't come from any accident. Not like Billy. Did you know that?'

'No,' Grace said. She had wondered often, but had never dared ask knowledge of it of any of the servants.

'No, I had infantile paralysis,' Mrs Spencer said. 'I was

just coming up to four. I remember hardly anything about it. All I really remember is lying about so much and then growing up with a game leg and a limp.'

Grace was at a loss for words. She wanted to say how sorry she was, but did not dare, for fear such sympathy might be thought impertinent.

Mrs Spencer went on, 'So no dances for me, I'm afraid, when I was a young girl. In fact, very little of any kind of physical activity. But I should think Billy knows about that too. Oh, when I was growing up I saw the other girls going off to their soirées, going ice skating when the lake was frozen over, but not me. Ah, well.' She pressed her lips together and then added with a sigh, 'But it's no good standing here talking about it. It's all a part of history now. Nothing to be done about it, and I'm not complaining. I've had my share of good times in spite of all that.' She turned and started to move away, then added, looking over towards the fireplace, 'I must see to the fire before I go,' and Grace said at once, 'Leave that to me. I'll look after that. Let me walk with you to your room first.'

Mrs Spencer said, just a trifle defensively, 'Well, I don't need it, of course,' then added in the same breath, 'but at the same time I'm always glad of your company, my dear.'

Grace walked with her to the door, opened it for her and followed her mistress out of the room.

There was one little gas light palely burning in the hall, another on the first-floor landing, and a third on the second floor. Looking up, Grace saw that the top of the cupola seemed to fade into a hazy darkness above the rail that ran around the gallery, the three figures in their niches looking ghostly and half-formed in the pale light. Mrs Spencer, stopping at Grace's side, followed the line of her gaze and looked upwards.

'Dear God,' she said, 'this is such an ugly house.'

'Oh,' Grace said quickly, hardly able to believe what she

had heard, 'but there are so many lovely things here. The high, ornate ceilings, the tall windows . . .'

'Oh, some of the rooms are all right.' Mrs Spencer gave a grudging nod. 'Some are quite attractive in fact. But the house itself – it isn't beautiful – it's ugly. There's no other word for it. My husband loves it, though. In his eyes it's the finest place on earth. I would never have chosen to come here. But that's what you do.' She gave an ironic smile. 'Such things will a wife do.'

They moved on over the carpet of the hall, Mrs Spencer seeming to limp a little more and to lean a little more heavily on her stick than usual. When they reached the stairs she stopped, her free hand on the newel post, looked about her and said with a sigh, 'No, I don't think this has ever really been a home to me. And if truth be told, I think I would have been happy to let it stand empty. I never wanted it in the first place. I didn't even know my uncle – my uncle who left it to me. I never met him in my life.' She gave a little shake of her head. 'Look at this place. One doesn't need a hundred rooms in order to be happy. And I certainly don't need such a place in order to be happy with Mr Spencer. Sometimes I think it doesn't make him happy either. In a way it does but – it just eats up the money. It's like some monstrous hungry animal. No matter how much money is spent on it it's never satisfied. And now my husband is talking of having electricity installed throughout.'

She stood there for a moment in silence then turned to Grace as if having just remembered her presence. 'Take no notice of my meanderings, Grace. Sometimes I talk to myself, and sometimes I talk too much. I shouldn't complain, I know. I've nothing to complain about.'

She took the first step and side by side they moved steadily up the wide stairs together to the first-floor landing. There Mrs Spencer turned towards her room.

'Thank you, Grace,' she said. 'And now you go on to bed. I'm sure you must be tired.'

'I'll see that the fire's safe first.'

'Yes, put the guard up.'

'Good night, Mrs Spencer.'

'Goodnight, Grace.'

Mrs Spencer turned away and opened the door to her bedroom. As Grace made her way down the stairs the hall clock struck twelve.

Chapter Thirteen

The following week Sophie was brought to and fetched from Asterleigh House by hired cab. The lessons proceeded as usual; the child worked hard and still seemed happy and contented with the arrangements. On three of the evenings Grace went to see Mrs Spencer. On the Tuesday they began a game of chess, but Grace could see that Mrs Spencer's heart was not in it, and before long it was abandoned. For most of the rest of the time they chatted and worked with their needles, Grace sewing and mending clothes either for herself or Billy, and Mrs Spencer at her embroidery. Most of Grace's evening time, however, was spent with Billy. During the whole week she saw nothing of Mr Spencer.

Then, on the Friday, Mr Fairman himself brought Sophie for her lessons. On this occasion, having seen their arrival from the library window, Grace expected to see the carriage drive away again. But it did not happen. Going to the library door she got there just as Sophie came along the landing towards her. Sophie wished Grace a good morning, then added that her papa had gone to call on Mrs Spencer for morning coffee. Forty minutes later there drifted up the sound of a horse and carriage moving on the gravel, and Sophie got up from her chair at the table and ran to the window. 'It's Papa, driving away,' she said, and waved, trying to attract his attention. 'Ah, he doesn't see me,' she sighed. 'Still, he'll be back soon.'

A minute later came a tap at the door and Jane was there, asking if Grace could go and see Mrs Spencer in her studio.

Grace left Sophie working and went along the landing to her mistress's studio where she found her standing with her face to the window. She turned as Grace entered, and Grace could see at once that it was one of her better days. She was not, however, dressed in her smock for painting. Beside her on the tall easel was the unfinished portrait of Grace.

'Hello, Grace,' she said as Grace entered, then with a gesture towards the canvas, 'I've been showing your portrait to Mr Fairman. I mentioned to him that I'd begun a painting of you, and he was most insistent that I show it to him.' She looked back at the painting, head a little on one side, studying it. 'He seemed quite taken with it, and said I should set about finishing it.'

Grace stood beside her mistress and looked at the picture, seeing herself gazing out from the canvas frame.

'Edward has said often that I should finish it,' Mrs Spencer went on. 'He says it's one of the best things I've done,' and corrected herself with a little laugh, ' – or rather, one of the best things I've *almost* done.' She turned to Grace. 'What do you think?'

'Oh, I like it very much, ma'am. And you know I'll be happy to sit for it again whenever you like.'

'Yes, I have no doubt of that, my dear. And an excellent sitter you were, too.' She sighed. 'But do I have the energy right now? That's the question. When I work on a canvas this size it's a different matter. I can't sit down to it at the smaller easel, the way I do when I paint one of my still lifes. For something like this I have to be able to walk to and from the easel. Not so easy with my leg.' She stepped back from the painting, eyes narrowed, studying it. 'Well, we shall see.' She turned then, almost full circle, looking about her at the room. 'I haven't worked in here in – oh, it seems ages,' she said a little wistfully. 'For years I couldn't wait to get to my painting every day. But these past months – I don't know – I don't seem to have had the urge that I once did.' She moved to her painting table on which stood her jar of brushes, the little container of linseed oil, the larger one of turpentine, the old rag that she used to wipe her brushes on, and her palette – the latter covered with different hues of paint smears, just as she had left it. Seeing it all, Grace reflected that when she had first come to the house eight months earlier it would have been inconceivable that such a thing could happen. Time had changed things.

'Anyway,' Mrs Spencer turned back to Grace, ' – I didn't ask you come here just to hear me go on about my painting. I had another reason.' She paused. 'You left Sophie at work, did you?'

'She's doing some arithmetic. Simple addition and subtraction.'

'Well done.' She gestured towards a wicker chair standing nearby. 'Please sit down. I won't keep you long.'

Grace sat, and Mrs Spencer sat in the old grandfather chair, the one that Grace had sat in for her portrait.

'Now . . .' Mrs Spencer said, 'as I said to you just now, I didn't drag you out of your lesson with Sophie merely to ask your opinions on my painting. The reason I asked you is because I've just been having a little chat to Mr Fairman, and he's asked me if it will be possible for you to go to his house and teach Sophie once he's moved in.'

'Well – yes, I suppose so.'

'Good. He's going to speak to you about it when he comes back to collect her this afternoon, but I thought I'd mention it to you first. He says he also would like your assistance in another way.'

'Oh?'

'He would like you to help, so I understand, in the placement of all the ornaments and pictures and such things in the house.'

'But – but why me?'

'He says he wants someone with an artistic eye. Going by what Mr Spencer tells me, Mr Fairman's wife would have revelled in it. An artistic woman, by all accounts. But, Grace, you don't have to do it. I merely told him that as far as I was concerned you would be perfectly free to help out. But of course you're not obliged to.'

Grace would so much rather she had not been asked. But how could she refuse? What reason could she give?

'If you'd rather not,' Mrs Spencer said. 'If you have some reason not to, then it's better you say so.'

A pause, then Grace said, 'If there's some way I can help Sophie and Mr Fairman then I'm happy to do so. So long as it's perfectly all right with you.'

Mrs Spencer smiled and gave a little nod. 'Yes, of course. Thank you, my dear. Mr Fairman will be very pleased.'

It was not easy for Grace to concentrate on Sophie's lessons after the meeting with Mrs Spencer, and she was a little anxious when the time came for Sophie's lessons to come to an end.

She was so attuned to the sounds of Mr Fairman's arrival that she could not have missed hearing them. First came the sound of the horse-drawn carriage on the forecourt and then the ring at the front doorbell.

'It's Papa,' Sophie said. 'He's a little early this afternoon.'

When Sophie was dressed in her light cape and hat, Grace escorted her to the stairs. There was no longer any point in trying to avoid Mr Fairman. She had already agreed to help him at his new home, so she must face him and get used to the situation. And she comforted herself with the knowledge that it wouldn't be for much longer, for once they had settled into the new house Sophie would be enrolled in school and would no longer have need of a governess.

As she and Sophie walked down the stairs Mr Fairman

turned from looking at a painting on the wall and started towards them. He met them at the foot of the staircase, his hand coming out towards Grace in greeting.

'Ah, Miss Harper, how nice to see you again. It's been some days.'

'How do you do, sir.'

Mr Fairman turned to address his daughter. 'Sophie,' he said, 'would you be a good girl and sit here in the hall for a few minutes while I have a private word with Miss Harper? We shan't be long.' He gestured to a bench beneath the window. 'Sit over there, if you will.'

Obediently Sophie moved to the bench and sat down, hands clasped in front of her. Mr Fairman turned to Grace. 'Miss Harper, could we go somewhere and talk for a minute?' Then without waiting for an answer he added, 'I'd suggest we walked outside, but you're not dressed for it and the day is not overly warm. What about the conservatory? I'm sure Mrs Spencer wouldn't object if we went in there for a while.'

'We can go outside,' she said, drawing her shawl more closely about her shoulders. 'I shan't be cold.'

He smiled. 'As you wish.'

Grace moved to a hook beside the door and took down the front door key that hung there. Fairman moved to the front door, opened it, then said to Sophie, 'I'll come back for you in a minute.'

Grace stood on the gravel while he closed the front door behind them. He was right, she thought, the day was not warm, and she pulled her shawl more closely about her. He came to her side and they set off slowly over the gravel, walking along on the forecourt with the house on their left. After they had moved just a few paces, Grace said, 'Mrs Spencer's already spoken to me about your moving. I told her I'd be happy to help in any way if I can.'

'Oh,' he said in a tone of disappointment, 'I didn't want

the request to come from her. I wanted to speak to you myself.'

'It's quite all right. There's no harm done. She was thinking of me.'

'And quite right too. I didn't know what to do for the best. I approached Mrs Spencer first as I didn't want her to think me presumptuous. After all, you're here to help her, not me and Sophie. I'm already deeply in your debt, what with all the lessons you're giving Sophie. So much so that I don't know how I can ever repay you.'

'It's nothing,' she said. 'Sophie is an excellent pupil, and if I can help her with her learning then I'm happy to do it.'

'Even so . . .' He paused. 'So – so you're agreeable to coming over to Birchwood House to help us out a little, once our things are moved in?'

'Yes. Though I'm sure I don't know how much use I can possibly be.'

'Oh, you can be a great help,' he said, 'a great help, make no mistake about that. We have so many things – paintings, sculptures, lamps, so many *objets d'art*. And it'll be so useful to have another pair of eyes when it comes to the placing of the various bits and pieces.'

'Well, as I said, if there's any way I can help, I'll be only too glad to.'

They had reached the end of the house, and they came to a halt, standing on the gravel, a few feet away from one another.

Mr Fairman said, 'Our furniture and effects are to be delivered next Friday. The painters will be gone by then, and all the carpets will be down. I should think the following Monday would be a good time to begin putting the things in order. What do you think about Monday? Could you come then? Would that be convenient?'

'Yes, I should think that would be all right.'

'I thought perhaps Sophie could have her lessons during

the day as well. She'll get bored with nothing to do, so if she's set some of her school tasks she can get on with them while we try to get the place in order. Sophie's nurse will be there too, so she can help us out in various ways as well. I would guess it'll take about a week. But you help out just as long as it suits you. I'll send a fly to meet you at the station each morning, and take you back again at the end of the day.'

Grace nodded. 'Yes. That sounds fine.'

They stood in silence. Then, increasingly conscious of their proximity, Grace made a move to turn and start back towards the house. At once Mr Fairman said, 'Don't go – not for a moment.'

Grace stayed. After a second he said, 'Why have you been avoiding me?'

She could not bring herself to speak.

'You have,' he said. 'I'm sure you have. Ever since the day when we saw you at the market you've avoided me. I bring Sophie here for her lessons and you're nowhere to be seen. Neither when I arrive nor when I depart. Why is that? It's not as it used to be. Why? Is it coincidence? Or have I done something to offend you?'

'No, not at all,' she said.

'I'm glad to hear that, at least. But then, why have you been avoiding me?'

Now she remained silent. In fact, had she spoken and tried to speak the truth she would not have had much of an answer to give him. For she was still so much in the dark. All she was primarily aware of was a sense of turmoil, almost familiar now – and all connected with him. And somehow Miss Lewin was there in the picture too.

A sharp, keen wind came around the side of the house, ruffling Fairman's hair and blowing at Grace's skirts. 'Come,' he said, 'it's too cold to stay out here,' and he put his hand under her elbow in a gentle urging to move away.

274

She needed no second such gesture. Side by side they made their way back to the front door where Grace let them back in with the key.

'So,' he said to Sophie as they entered the hall, 'Miss Harper's going to come over to Birchwood and help us with our moving. Isn't that splendid?'

When, nine days later, Grace arrived at Birchwood House she found it newly papered and painted and the carpets and furniture in place. After setting Sophie some school-work to complete at a little table in one corner of the drawing room, Grace set about helping Mr Fairman in the task of arranging the various artefacts that still remained packed away. They had help in the shape of Sophie's nurse Nancy, a young maid from the village, and a general carpenter-cum-handyman. Other than a number of larger paintings, most of the items were still stored in several tea chests. As the time passed, the paintings were hung on the walls and the artefacts were taken out of their wrappings. Newly dusted, and polished where necessary, the clocks, the lamps, the ornaments, the silver, the glass and the china were set out in their newly chosen places.

At the end of the afternoon Grace was sent back to the station in a cab. She was glad to see the end of the working day, finding herself somewhat exhausted from having been on her feet for so many hours.

She was back again the following morning, and the task was resumed. And so it went on for four days when, on Thursday afternoon, Mr Fairman pronounced the work finished.

The house looked complete now. Grace had rarely known such coming and going: the seemingly endless round of unpacking, dusting and polishing and then finding the right sites for the various items, whether the item in question was a porcelain statuette or a pan for the kitchen. Sometimes it took more consideration and several tries before the right home could be found for a particular piece, but in the end everything had been found a place.

And Grace would have had to admit that she had more or less enjoyed the experience, though she had still, at times, found herself less than easy in the company of Mr Fairman. She could not have explained why, but she was only aware that she was more at ease with him when others were present, such as the maid or the nurse, and she did not feel – as she sometimes did – the unaccustomed focus of his concentration.

She ate lunch each day with him and Sophie, sitting in the dining room, the three of them, and served by Emma the new maid. And there were moments at such times when they laughed together. Mr Fairman would relate some anecdote that would set Sophie giggling and before long Grace would be brought into the laughter, unable to resist.

While there on one occasion Mr Fairman spoke again of finding a school for Sophie, and although Sophie protested, saying that she was very happy having Miss Harper as a governess, and would like to continue to do so, it was pointed out by her father that such a situation could not continue. Miss Harper, he made clear, was teaching her only as a special favour, and would soon have to return to her main task, the help and support of her employer, Mrs Spencer.

When Grace set off back to Asterleigh at the end of that Thursday, she found that although she was glad that the task was finally finished, she was also sorry that her time at the house had come to an end.

On arriving at Asterleigh late that afternoon, she thanked the cab driver and made her way round to the rear of the house. Billy came to her from the stables as she walked across the yard. He had been helping Mr Johnson with the horses, he said, and then asked whether she would be going back to Mr Fairman's house the next day. No, she told him; her work at the house was finished; tomorrow Sophie would be coming back to resume her lessons at Asterleigh.

She left Billy to his work then and went into the house. As she drew level with the kitchen door she saw Mrs Sandiston at work at the table. The cook looked across the room and greeted her, going on to say that Mr Spencer was back.

As she moved towards the rear stairs Jane came from the front of the house. Grace wished her a good evening and Jane returned the greeting, though in a rather half-hearted manner. Briefly Grace wondered at the girl's coolness, but then Jane was saying:

'I've just come from Mrs Spencer, miss. She was asking me if you were back yet.'

'Do you know what she wants me for?'

'No, I don't, miss. She's up in her sewing room.'

Grace went on by and into the hall and along the passage to where the sewing room was situated. There she tapped on the door and a moment later heard Mrs Spencer's voice calling to her to enter. She went in and found her mistress sitting by the hearth. There was a small fire burning in the grate.

As Grace moved across the room, Mrs Spencer said, 'Hello, Grace, I was just asking Jane if you were back from Upper Callow yet.'

'I just saw her. She said you were asking for me.'

Mrs Spencer pulled her shawl more closely about her shoulders. 'Look at me, Grace,' she said, ' – a beautiful May day with fine weather and here I am sitting by the fire. I just can't seem to get warm these days. Did you just get in?'

'Just a minute ago. Can I do something for you, ma'am?'

'Yes, you can. Mr Spencer's back, did you know?'

'Cook just told me as I came in.'

'He got back this afternoon. I wanted to ask you if you'd mind doing my hair for me tonight. Would you mind?'

'Of course not. I'd be glad to. What time d'you want me?'

'Say in an hour? About half past six – quarter to seven?'

'In your room?'

'Yes, in my room.'

'I'll be there.'

Grace let herself out, moved along the landing and started down the stairs. Only a few steps down and she heard her name called from above her. Looking up, she saw Mr Spencer looking down from the gallery on the top floor.

'Grace,' he said, smiling, 'how nice to see you.'

'Good evening, sir,' she said.

'You've been out all day, is that so?'

'That's correct, sir.'

'I just got back, this afternoon.'

'So I hear, sir.'

'And I hear you've been over at Upper Callow for most of the week giving Mr Fairman the benefit of your artistic tastes, is that so?'

She smiled. 'That's putting it rather grandly, I think, sir.'

'I'm sure it's not.' He paused, then added, 'Perhaps while you're here you might like to give *me* the benefit of your artistic tastes.'

'Are you serious, sir?'

'Never more so. Come on up, will you?'

Turning, she started back up the stairs, and continued on until she reached the gallery two floors above. There she found Mr Spencer now standing beside the niche holding the figure of Rigoletto the court jester.

'It's our friend here . . .' Mr Spencer said as Grace approached. He gestured towards the stooped figure in the alcove. 'I want to get him repaired. I wish your talents ran to sculpture as well as painting.'

Grace smiled. 'I could wish they did as well, sir. And I'm not sure that I know so much about painting either.'

'That's it, Grace – modest as ever.' He turned back to the figure. 'I know he's not the most handsome fellow, but he belongs here. And I'd like to make him whole again. As he is, he detracts from the others. Trouble is, we don't know what form his missing hand took.' He turned back to Grace. 'Have you any ideas?'

'I'm afraid I haven't, sir.'

'You don't even like him very much, do you?'

She said nothing.

'Come on,' he said. 'I shan't be offended if you tell me the truth. Confess it, you think he's ugly, don't you?'

'Well – yes, sir, I *do* think he's ugly. But my thoughts are of no relevance whatsoever.'

'That's not so at all. I wouldn't have asked your opinion if I didn't value it. But anyway, your liking or disliking him has nothing to do with his missing hand.' He turned back to look at the figure. 'I'll have to look for a sculptor who can do the right kind of work.' He stepped back a little, head slightly on one side, looking at the figure appraisingly. 'He'll look as right as rain once he's complete again.' He turned back to her. 'Anyway, that aside, tell me what you think of Mr Fairman's house?'

'Oh, I think it's very fine, sir. And now that the furniture and everything else are in place it looks quite splendid. I'm sure he'll be very happy there.'

'Well, let's hope so. He could do with a little happiness.'

The next morning Mr Fairman brought Sophie for her lesson and came up to the library with her.

'We want to invite you out, tomorrow,' he said, and Sophie, almost hopping with excitement, said, 'Papa, let me tell it.'

'Go on, then.'

'Papa says if the weather is still good we can go for a drive. Will you come, miss? Please say yes.'

Grace was considering whether or not to accept when Mr Fairman said, 'This would include your brother. If you think he'd like to come, we'd love to have him. I hope you can both come. I've hired the horse and trap.'

'Will Billy come, miss?' Sophie asked. 'Will you ask him?'

'We'll come by for you both around two o'clock,' Mr Fairman said. 'And you won't have to bring anything but yourselves.' He paused. 'So – what do you think?

'Thank you,' Grace said. 'I'd love to – and I'm sure Billy would also. Of course, I shall have to get Mrs Spencer's permission, but I don't think she'll object.'

Mrs Spencer did not object – on the contrary, she expressed pleasure at the idea – and the trap called at Asterleigh just on 2.15 the following day. Billy, sitting on the bench outside the back door – he would not have dared wait at the front of the house – had waited eagerly for news of the appearance of the trap, and as two o'clock had approached had become almost anxious. But then Grace had come out to him, and he had run around the side of the house to where the trap waited on the gravel.

When all the greetings were over, Mr Fairman helped Grace up into the trap with Sophie, then said to Billy, 'Now, young Billy, perhaps you'd like to ride beside me on the box, would you? And we'll leave the ladies to their talk.'

Billy needed no second asking, and in a trice Mr Fairman had hoisted him up and then climbed up beside him.

'Well,' said Mr Fairman as he took up the reins, 'we're off to Marshleigh Abbey, is that all right?' and with a flap of the reins and a click from his tongue, they were off.

Marshleigh Abbey was situated some four miles away, between Little Berron and Marshleigh. The building had been mostly destroyed by fire some fifty-odd years earlier and now, long deserted by its religious erstwhile inhabitants, remained solely as an occasional venue for picnickers and ramblers and courting couples. Where it had once served only in the matter of privation, self-sacrifice and gravitas, now it served only in matters of pleasure.

On reaching the site Mr Fairman jumped down and led the horse through a gateway to a wide stretch of green between the building and the lake's shore. The area had once been a spacious lawn, but now it grew wild and overgrown with weeds of every kind. Here, to one side, Mr Fairman halted the mare and helped the passengers down and took the hamper from the box and set it down on the grass. He also took down a couple of rugs. Releasing the mare from the shafts, he hitched her to a slender silver birch. He'd bring her some water soon, he murmured to her, and then turned and, calling to the others, set off across the grass.

There was not another soul in sight, and they chose their picnic place in the shade of some shrubbery at the edge of the lawn where the grass had been kept cropped by the rabbits. Here Mr Fairman put down the hamper and spread out the rugs, partly in the shade and partly in the sun. Before them, the former gardens sloped down to the lake, its long-abandoned boathouse on the right almost hidden by the encroaching weeds. Behind them the roofless shell of the old abbey reared up against the blue of the May sky, its paneless windows like blind eyes. After watering the horse, Mr Fairman asked if anyone would care to go and look round the place, and at once Sophie and Billy spoke up with eagerness, saying they would like to go.

'Miss Harper,' Mr Fairman said, ' – what about you? Will you come too?'

'What about our things?'

'They'll be safe here.'

And so, with Mr Fairman leading, the quartet made their

way into the ruined shell of the old building. A few of the lower rooms were intact, and looked barely touched by the consuming fire, their floors and window frames unmarked even by smoke. Other rooms had been completely destroyed, so that not even the joists remained, and the little party could only stand awed on the thresholds and look into the chasms where once floors had lain and wonder at the fierceness of the blaze. Their steps carefully placed, and only venturing into those areas that Mr Fairman deemed safe, they continued to explore for some thirty-odd minutes, when Mr Fairman suggested that they might now have had enough. Grace and Sophie at once concurred. Their skirts so hampered their movements in the more confined spaces, many of which were choked with encroaching plant-life – brambles, cow parsley and other wild plants – added to which it seemed that they could not touch any surface without getting smeared with soot. Billy, however, was eager to continue, and as they made their way back to the chosen picnic spot he pointed up at the tall tower with the turret reaching into the sky, and said he would like to climb the circular staircase to the very top. No, it was too dangerous, Grace said at once.

'But, Grace,' Billy said, 'there's nothing to be afraid of, and I'd be careful, really I would.'

'No, I couldn't think of it,' Grace said. They had reached the sheltered place by the shrubbery and she picked up one of the rugs and opened it out. 'We're going to have some tea and some lemonade. Come on.'

'Ah, but Grace . . .'

'Maybe another day,' she said, and realized even as she spoke how foolish were her words. At once Billy said, 'There won't be another day, Grace, you know there won't.'

At this Mr Fairman said, 'He won't come to harm, I promise.' He wiped his smut-stained palms one against the other. 'I'll be with him and I'll make sure it's safe.'

Billy, his face lit up, turned to Grace. 'Oh, Grace, can I?'

'What do you think, Grace?' Mr Fairman said. 'Would it be all right?'

He had called her by her first name. She looked at him, seeing his slow smile, the small crease in his right cheek. 'Well . . .'

'Truly,' he said, 'I'll look after him.' He turned to Billy. 'We'll look after each other, Billy, right?'

Billy grinned. 'Yes, sir.' Then to Grace, 'Is that all right, Grace?'

And Grace smiled now. For years she had been denying her brother pleasures that other boys his age took for granted. For years she had been watching over him, afraid of his risking further injury. Now, seeing him with Mr Fairman, she felt she could relax in the knowledge that he would be safe. 'Yes,' she said. 'Yes, of course.'

Mr Fairman nodded his satisfaction while Billy gave a little *whoop* and grinned. 'Good, then we'll get off,' said Mr Fairman. 'Come on, Billy.' With Billy beside him he took a few steps away, then paused to say over his shoulder, 'Perhaps you two ladies could get our tea ready in the meantime. I've no doubt that we shall be thirsty when we get back.'

A moment later he and Billy were heading back towards the ruined building. Grace, standing with the tartan rug spread out on the grass before her, watched them go, seeing Billy, small and slight and limping, walking by the side of the tall man. She continued to watch them as they reached the entrance to the ruined building and disappeared from her sight.

'Shall we, miss?' Sophie's voice came interrupting her thoughts, and she turned to where the child stood beside the hamper. 'Shall we get the tea ready?'

'Yes.' Grace turned her back on the building, and gave Sophie a wide smile. 'Yes, let's get tea ready for when they come back.'

After they had gone down to the edge of the lake to wash their soot-stained hands they opened the hamper and took out a chequered cloth. They spread it out on the grass and then took out the plates and cups and set them out. Turning to face the ruined building, Grace looked at the tower. There were narrow slits of windows in the walls and she gazed at them one by one hoping perhaps to catch a glimpse of Billy going past as he climbed the stairs. But there was no sign of him. Dragging her glance away, she took the other rug and spread it out on the other side of the cloth.

'Now – it's all done,' she said to Sophie. 'All we need are Billy and your papa.'

As she finished speaking there came a shout, her name being called: 'Grace! Grace!' but in happy, excited tones, and turning, raising her head, she looked up to the top of the tower and saw Billy and Mr Fairman standing there. Mr Fairman's tall figure was clearly to be seen, while Billy's head was only just visible above the parapet.

She waved back, and Sophie waved too, and then came Billy's voice, calling again: 'Can you see me all right, Grace? Look at me! I'm right up here.'

'Yes,' she called back, 'I can see you. You're so high up!'

'I know.' His tone was full of pride. 'It's marvellous, Grace. You should come up too.'

She laughed. 'Thank you, but I don't think so.'

And at this she could hear Mr Fairman's laugh coming briefly over the intervening green of the shrubbery. And then his voice, calling to his daughter: 'Can you see us, Sophie?'

'Yes, Papa,' Sophie's voice rang out in the soft air. 'I can see you both.'

Billy's voice came again: 'We're coming down now, Grace.'

'Good,' Grace called back. 'We've got the tea almost ready.'

A final wave from the top of the tower and then the heads of Mr Fairman and Billy vanished from sight again.

Several minutes passed and then Billy's voice came once more, but this time from the lower level of the earth, his voice moving rapidly closer as he ran limping towards them over the grass. Turning to him as he approached, Grace could see Mr Fairman behind, walking at his steady pace.

'Oh, Grace!' Billy yelled ecstatically, 'it was wonderful. It was just wonderful. Those stairs, they're like a corkscrew, and they go up and up to the very top. And once you get up to the top you can see for miles and miles. It's marvellous. You should come up and see for yourself. Oh, Grace!'

Looking past him, Grace smiled at Mr Fairman as he came to a halt beside the rug. 'Thank you,' she said, 'so much.'

'There's nothing to thank me for,' he said. 'I enjoyed it as much as Billy did. And maybe Billy's right – maybe you should go up there and see for yourself.'

Grace laughed. 'Thank you, but I shall take the word of you two men.'

Mr Fairman laughed along with her, then, turning to Billy, said, 'Young Bill, come on, let's go down to the lake and wash our hands, shall we? Get rid of all this soot. And as the ladies have set out the refreshments we'll have something to eat and drink when we get back.'

As the two of them moved away together, Sophie said, 'Perhaps we should have gone up to the top of the tower as well, miss. Next time we'll go up as well, shall we?'

Grace smiled. 'Maybe, maybe. We'll see.' She watched as her young brother and the man stopped at the water's edge. And she knew a sense of happiness that she had not known in so long. Part of it stemmed from Billy's joy – joy at the fact that he had accomplished something physical, and something that Grace herself, through her protective instincts, would have denied him. To see his happiness as he had hurried towards the tower, to hear it in his voice as he had called to her over the parapet; she had not heard such pleasure in his voice before. Another part of her happiness came from the very presence of Kester Fairman. She knew it, without doubt. Watching as he walked beside Billy, his frame so tall beside that of the boy, she felt a warmth, a completeness that took her by surprise.

And then Sophie said, in words that would shatter Grace's peace: 'I had a letter from Miss Lewin today, miss. She's coming back to Corster soon.'

'Oh?' Grace heard herself say. 'Well – that's nice for you.'

'Yes, her letter came this morning. D'you know, I never had a letter before in my life.'

'Well – that must have been exciting.'

'Yes, she asked if we had completely moved into our new home, and said that she's looking forward to seeing it now that it has all our things in it. And Papa said again that I must go to school. He's been to see two schools. He says I shall make friends there, have schoolfriends my own age. Which is true, of course. But what would be nice, miss, is if you could come to the school and be my teacher. Wouldn't that be good?'

'Yes,' Grace heard herself say, 'that would be good.'

She heard a sound from above, the honking cries of wild geese, and looking up saw three of the birds, majestic in flight, skimming overhead, necks outstretched, strong wings beating the air. Their cries were plaintive, and seemed to touch a chord within Grace's heart. She watched the birds until they had flown out of sight, then lowered her glance and took in the sight of Mr Fairman and Billy coming towards them from the lake.

She felt suddenly lost. What was she doing there? she asked herself. She could see no future for herself, or for Billy either. They were just marking time while she chased shadows and let her life slip by.

And then Billy and Mr Fairman were close, Billy running towards them, the man following. Billy threw himself down on the rug at Grace's side and Grace saw the joy in his face.

Chapter Fourteen

It was close on six o'clock when Mr Fairman hitched up the horse again and they moved back to the trap. As they got in he looked at Sophie and said, 'We have here one tired little girl who will be relieved to get home and have a nap.' Sophie protested, but her protests were clearly half-hearted, and as soon as she and Grace were aboard she pressed up to Grace's side and closed her eyes. 'We'll go by way of Upper Callow first,' Mr Fairman said to Grace. 'We'll let Sophie off in the care of her nurse and then I'll take you on to Berron Wick, if that's agreeable.'

Reaching Birchwood House in Upper Callow, Mr Fairman drove the trap into the stable yard and helped the passengers down. Sophie, having been close to sleeping in the rocking of the trap, now became wide awake again and eager to show off her new home and possessions. Standing on the cobbles, she tugged at Billy's sleeve. 'Billy, would you like to come and see my rabbit? Her name is Mrs Cottontail.' Then to Grace: 'Will you come and see her, miss?' Then back to Billy: 'Will you, Billy? Come and see my rabbit.'

'Can we, Grace?' Billy looked at Grace, and Grace looked at Mr Fairman. He nodded. 'Yes, indeed, do so – unless you're in a hurry to get back – are you?'

Grace shook her head. 'No, not at all.'

'Good, we'll let Sophie show the way, then, shall we?' The mare gave a snort, and Mr Fairman turned to her and said, smiling, 'What is it, Carrie? Are you bored standing here? You don't want to be left on your own? Or are you thirsty? Or is it that you want to get back to your true master? Is that what it is? Oh, Carrie, like all females – it's not always easy to tell what you want.' He said to Sophie, 'You take Billy on down to the orchard while I give Carrie some water. We'll catch you up.'

'Come on, Billy,' Sophie said. 'I'll show you our garden too. We have so many flowers and so many fruit trees.'

Sophie led the way, skipping across the yard to the rear garden and the path leading down to the orchard. Grace was uncertain for a moment as to whether she should go with them, but then Mr Fairman said to her, 'Come on, let's get Carrie a drink, shall we?' With his hand on the mare's bridle he led her clopping across the cobbles to the trough. It was almost dry and putting his hand to the pump he drew some cool fresh water. The mare gave a little whinny, then took a step forward and, lowering her head, began to drink.

'There,' Mr Fairman said, 'that's better, isn't it, old girl?' He stroked the mare's neck as she drank, then turned to Grace. 'There – you see? Sometimes needs can be satisfied so easily, so simply.' He turned back to the horse and, leaning forward, said in a loud whisper into her ear, 'If only it were that easy with people, Carrie – what do you say?' He stood with his back to the house, the horse between him and Grace. 'We shall be getting our own horse and carriage next week,' he said, 'and Carrie here can go back home to her own stable.' He patted the horse. 'You'll be glad of that, won't you, old girl? All these unfamiliar hands on the reins, I doubt that it's pleasant.' Then, almost in the same breath he said to Grace, 'Thank you so much for coming today.'

'Oh, it's been splendid,' Grace replied. 'And it's a day Billy won't soon forget.'

'You think he really enjoyed himself?'

'And still is. You must have seen it for yourself.'

'Yes – but it's good to have it confirmed.' He paused. 'And what about you?'

'Oh, thank you, yes – I had a lovely time too.'

'Well, I'm so grateful to you for coming. It's meant everything to Sophie. Without you it wouldn't have been the same.'

A little silence between them, and Grace said, to cover the quiet, forcing a lightness into her voice, 'I suppose we'd better go and see Mrs Cottontail, hadn't we?'

She half-turned, as if on the point of moving away, then Mr Fairman said, 'Why are you in such a hurry?'

'In a hurry? I'm not in a hurry.' She smiled, but saw that his own expression was serious. 'I'm not in a hurry,' she said again.

'What is wrong?' he said.

He had come out with the question so bluntly, and for a moment she wondered if she had misheard. 'Wrong?' she said. 'Nothing is wrong.'

'Grace.'

He had again called her by her given name. 'Really,' she said. 'Why should anything be wrong?'

'I know very little about you, but I think I know enough of you to be able to tell that.'

Grace shook her head: 'No, really . . .'

He shrugged, then, stepping to the carriage, took out the hamper and the rugs. 'Might as well get rid of these. Give them to Emma.' Opening the rear door of the house, he carried the things inside. Grace stood on the flags alone for a minute, and then he was reappearing. 'Would you like something to drink?' he asked. 'My cook's got some lemon and barley if you'd like some.'

'No, thank you.'

'Well,' he said, 'I'm sure Billy and Sophie won't need asking twice.'

They saw that the mare had drunk her fill now, and Mr

Fairman said, 'Had enough, Carrie?' and took her bridle and led her to the side where he secured her to a stanchion. 'She'll be all right here for a while.' To the mare he said, 'We'll get going again before too long, Carrie, then when you come back you can have a nice rest. You'll have earned it today.' Then, turning to Grace, he said, 'Come on, then, let's go and join the children. I can see you're hopping to go.'

Feeble words of protest sprang to her lips, but she held them back. There was something disturbing about his manner towards her at times. It was something in his way and his words that made her almost tongue-tied, so that she feared answering, afraid to say the wrong thing and be left appearing foolish.

Without looking at her, he turned and started across the yard in the direction taken by Sophie and Billy. Grace stepped out at his side. They walked in silence for a dozen yards or so, then he came to a sudden halt and turned to face her. She stopped before him, just two yards away.

'I would like to talk to you,' he said. 'Will you allow that?'

'Well – yes, of course.' Why would he wish to talk with her? And what about?

'I asked you just now what is wrong, but you didn't answer. I would just like to know what it is,' he said. 'Have I said something to offend you? To upset you?'

'No, sir.'

'There is *something*. I know there is. You've been – constrained – since our picnic. Billy and I, we came back from our climb up the tower stairs and you were – different in some way.'

Grace looked away. She could feel his gaze upon her, burning like sunlight focused through a glass, and she could not meet his eyes with her own.

'Well,' he said, 'if you won't tell me, then you won't tell me.' He sighed. Then, almost clumsily changing the subject,

291

he added, waving his hand across the near landscape, 'God, this place is getting so overgrown.' He was referring to the formal garden, once green lawns, herbaceous plots and clipped box hedges; now, flourishing in the warm May weather and in parts overgrown almost to the point of wildness. 'A few more months and it'll start to look like the Abbey grounds,' he said with a smile. 'But I'm getting a gardener in a week or so, and he'll soon have it licked into shape. I shan't worry about it.'

From some distance ahead of them there came the sound of Sophie's voice ringing out on a laugh. Mr Fairman nodded towards the sound, grinned and said, 'They're having a good time.' He sighed again, this time looking directly at Grace. 'Shall we, then? Go and see Mrs Cottontail? Though we don't really have a choice.'

The path took them through the rest of the formal garden, through a spacious kitchen garden and into the orchard. In the centre of the orchard a swing hung from a high apple bough, and nearby on a rough trestle bench stood a rabbit hutch with a grey rabbit in it nibbling on dandelion leaves. There was no sign of the children.

'Where are they?' Grace said, and Mr Fairman said, 'Oh, they won't be far away,' and then the next moment there came Sophie's voice excitedly calling as she ran towards them from the little thicket at the orchard's foot: 'Papa, Billy found a bird's nest, a robin's nest! Come and see.' Billy was right behind her, and laughing along with her as she clutched at her father's hand.

The four of them, with Sophie and Billy leading, made their way from the orchard into the copse, and there Billy, a finger to his lips, moved silently ahead to a shrub in between two silver birches. Coming to a halt, he turned back to face the others, and then beckoned to them. The three moved forward and Billy parted the leaves and exposed the little nest with two chicks in it, the little

292

creatures immediately freezing in their actions, cowering down in the nest.

'Wonderful,' Mr Fairman breathed, 'but let's leave them; let's not disturb them any more.'

Quietly the four moved away from the nest. When they were some distance away Mr Fairman said to Sophie and Billy, 'We wondered where you were. We got into the orchard and there was your rabbit but no Sophie and no Billy.'

'I'd shown Billy Mrs Cottontail,' Sophie said, 'and then we went into the copse, exploring. That's when Billy found the nest. He knows just what to look for. He knows how to find them.'

'He was brought up in the country,' Mr Fairman said. 'He's had experience. You were brought up in London.'

'Papa,' Sophie said, 'Billy and I are thirsty. Can we go and get something to drink?'

'Of course,' he said. 'Mrs Lovegrove knows we're back. I just saw her, and she's got some nice lemon and barley water, if you want some. Go and see her. We'll come and join you in a minute.'

A moment later he and Grace stood in the copse watching as the two children made their way through the trees in the direction of the house. Grace said, 'Sophie is settling into her new home so well, so quickly.'

'Oh, indeed.' He stood, looking off. The children's voices could be heard still, though fading in the soft evening air. 'It's just grand for her to be here in the country.'

'And she tells me she'll soon be going to school.'

'Yes, we've been discussing it. She realizes it can't go on with you giving up your time like this – much as she enjoys it.'

'It's a pleasure for me to do it. It's very – rewarding.'

'Well, that's nice of you to say so. But you have a life of your own to live.'

Do I? Grace thought, in her mind echoing his words. And what life is that? 'Yes, of course,' she said. 'But I'm happy to help with Sophie's teaching as long as it suits you both.'

'Thank you.'

'But it will be good for Sophie, I've no doubt – going to school. She'll make friends, mix with others her own age.'

'That's what I tell her.'

'She seems to like it so, living here in the country.'

'Oh, she loves it. I don't think she misses London at all. And – well, I think the country is the right place for a child, I've come to that conclusion. And you're right – she's settling in so quickly.'

'And what about you?' Grace said. 'Are you settling in to your new home?'

'I? Oh, yes. I'm sure we're both going to be very happy here.'

The voices of the children had faded to silence. Grace said, 'It's been wonderful to see Billy having such a good time today. Such times, they don't often happen.' She raised her head a little, looking around her. All about grew trees and shrubs and wild plants of so many varieties. 'This is such a beautiful spot. So peaceful.' She suddenly felt infinitely sad. Watching Billy walk away in Sophie's wake, moving eagerly among the trees, she had seemed to see a difference about him. It might have been her imagination, but she seemed to see a different kind of movement in his walk, as if there was a little spring in his limping step that was not there before. Today, for him, had been something wonderful: he had climbed the tower, he had run in the grass, and he had made a friend in Sophie. For him it had been something of a beginning. While for herself the day seemed to mark the beginning of an ending. There was talk of Sophie going off to school, so there would no longer be any need for the child to visit Asterleigh House. And it was likely, therefore, that Grace would never see Mr Fairman again, for the only times he would be coming to Asterleigh House would be on those infrequent occasions when he came to visit the Spencers. But in any case, she had learned today, Miss Lewin was returning to Corster . . . And Mr Fairman had asked her was there anything wrong.

The leaves rustled in the breeze, from high above in the treetops came the evening call of a blackbird. The shadows were lengthening. Grace said, 'I shall have to go and see Billy in a minute. Then we should think about starting back for home, I suppose.'

'Billy's fine,' he said. 'Any minute now he and Sophie will be served some large glasses of lemon and barley – and a few other good things if I guess right. Don't worry about him.'

'I don't worry about him.'

'I think you do, Grace. But he's stronger than you think.'

'You don't understand . . .'

'I understand that he's your young brother and that you are all he has in the world. You feel totally responsible for him, it's natural. And especially with the – the injury, to his leg.'

'What about that?' she said quickly, a little sharply. 'What are you saying?'

Surprised at her tone, his eyes narrowed slightly, and he frowned. 'I'm not saying anything about it. I don't even know what you mean. What I'm saying is that with the injury to his leg he might be perceived as a little more – dependent – and that's bound to bring out the protective feelings in an elder sister.'

'No,' she said quickly, 'you don't understand – about Billy,' and the tears welled up in her eyes, swimming, glistening in the low evening sun.

'*Grace*.' He stepped forward, reaching out, one hand briefly touching her wrist before drawing it back to stay clenched before his chest.

His sympathetic gesture, the note of deep concern in his voice as he spoke her name, the very fact that he had spoken her name – all seemed to force wider the little break that he had made in the dam that held in check her defences. And the tears spilled over onto her cheeks.

'Oh, my dear Grace.' With his words Mr Fairman stepped closer still, and this time when he reached out for her he let his hand close around hers, and held it there. 'My dear Grace, what is it? Tell me what it is. What is it about Billy? Please – tell me.'

'I cannot.' She shook her head. 'I just – cannot.'

'Grace –'

With a sudden gesture she moved her hand so that his touch fell away. With her hands moving to her mouth as if she would physically stop herself from speaking, she said in a little burst:

'His injury. It's all due to me. I did it to him.'

On its southern side the copse ended on the slope of a gentle hill, and the trees and shrubs gave way to rolling fields, fresh and green with new barley. Grace, turning, almost hurrying from Mr Fairman's side, had come to a halt beneath a silver birch. Mr Fairman came following in her footsteps, and now came to stand a yard away. As he faced her she turned her head, so that he saw only her lowered profile, the tears running down her cheeks.

'Tell me about it, Grace,' he said at last.

She said nothing for some seconds, then she said, 'We don't talk of it, Billy and I. It's as if we have this – agreement. The subject – it's never mentioned.' She paused. 'It's made such a difference to his life. Before it happened he was like any other boy his age, running, climbing, doing everything boys do. But then that happened.' She raised her eyes a little and looked off, as if seeing the past go by her gaze. 'Our mother was alive then. Billy was five, just five. It was in the summer, June, a beautiful day. I had taken him out to go fishing. Our father had promised to take him, but then had had to back out because something had come up. So I said I would take him. Pappy had made Billy a fishing rod, and provided him with a little tin can with worms in it he had dug from the garden. We had also a glass preserves jar that Mama gave us – this was for the fish that Billy would catch. And we had sandwiches and cold tea for when we wanted our dinner – oh, yes, and I had a book and my parasol and a little rug. We had it all planned.'

She fell silent, and in the quiet they could hear the blackbird singing, so close he seemed. Mr Fairman said nothing to prompt her to continue, but just stood close by, his eyes fixed on her face. After some moments she went on.

'We were heading for a brook not too far away, near Coleshill. But we never got there. And never have I tried to go back there since. We had only reached one field away. As we went towards a stile Billy ran on ahead and climbed up onto it. As I came up I saw that they were haymaking in the field beyond. Billy sat there watching the men at work. As I got to him he moved over to let me pass, and I did so. Then I got a few yards further on and looked back and he was still sitting there, dreaming, watching the men with their scythes. I went back to him, and said, "Come on, our Billy, or we shan't catch any fish," but he didn't seem to hear me or to be paying attention.'

She paused, her eyes closing in anguish, and then continued on, sometimes speaking haltingly, and at other times letting the words come out in a rush.

'And, just – just in fun,' she said, ' – I made a kind of – kind of playful little snatch at him – as if I would catch him in my arms and drag him away. And he laughed – and I can hear his laugh to this day: the laugh of a small, happy boy – and ducked from my hands. And in ducking, trying to evade me, he fell backwards. He lost his balance and fell backwards. And his laughter became a scream. He fell only part-way off the stile. His leg was caught up and prevented him from falling to the ground. The men dropped their scythes and came running at his scream. They only took seconds to get to us.'

She looked briefly at Mr Fairman. He stood silent, hanging on her words.

'That was it,' she said, looking away again. 'The younger of the two men took him down and carried him home, I walking at their side. He was so kind, the young man. He wept as he walked; even now I can see the tears in his eyes. When we got home Pappy called the doctor. Billy's leg was broken in two places and – as you can see – it never set properly.' She turned and looked him in the face. 'I ruined his life,' she said, then turned her face away again.

'Don't say that.'

'It's true.' She stood looking out, standing in the tree's shade. To her fancy, facing out over the gently rolling fields was like being on the edge of the world. 'I am so selfish,' she said.

'You? Selfish?'

'Yes. Here have I just been thinking only of myself, all afternoon, and Billy will never be right. How can I imagine, even for a moment, that I have dilemmas, difficulties . . .? When there's that boy . . .'

'I meant what I said,' he said, 'I think Billy's stronger than you think.'

She looked at him at this, frowning. 'He never refers to it. He's never once reproached me.'

'He knows it was an accident. He knows how much you regret it.'

'Even so.'

Her voice was full of unshed tears, and her eyes briefly closed again, shutting them in. He moved to her, closer, and reached out, his hand touching her shoulder. He began to

298

draw her towards him. For a moment she allowed him to do so, then she froze and then stepped away, shaking off his touch.

'I'm sorry,' he murmured, apologizing for the liberty.

'No,' she said. 'Oh, please. I couldn't bear that also.'

'Bear what? What do you mean?'

'Miss Lewin will be here soon, and soon Sophie will be going away to school.'

'Miss Lewin? What has she to do with anything?'

'Sophie told me. Miss Lewin is coming back to Corster.'

He nodded. 'Well, I understand that's what she told Sophie in her letter. But it was the first I heard of it.'

Grace looked directly at him at this. 'Isn't it so?'

'As I just told you, it didn't come from me. That's what Miss Lewin has written to Sophie, but it's come purely from herself.' He paused, then added, 'There's been no invitation from me.' Another pause. 'And nor is there likely to be.'

'But Miss Lewin –'

'Miss Lewin may say whatever she wants, and I have no control over her tongue or her pen. But I can assure you of the truth. Can I put it more plainly than to say that she means nothing to me?' He studied Grace's expression as if reading the response to his words, then added, 'There was a time when certain people thought perhaps there was something between us – and Miss Lewin has probably been among those people – but I can assure you that I was not among them.'

'But she came to stay in Corster – to visit you and Sophie.'

'It was not by invitation. Except by her own.'

They were words Grace had longed to hear, but still she could scarcely believe she had heard them. 'Is that true?' she said.

'I wouldn't lie to you, Grace.'

'No, of course you would not.'

'But please tell me – why are you so concerned about

Miss Lewin, and about Sophie going away to school?' He added quickly, 'I don't know whether I dare interpret your words the way I would like to.' He paused. 'Do I dare to, Grace?'

'Sir?'

'I don't want to sound immodest, but is it possible that your – your attitude towards me has something to do with Miss Lewin?' He paused. 'Do I dare to think for one moment that you have some fondness for me?'

And Grace said, almost on a cry, 'Oh, Mr Fairman, please don't ask such a thing lightly. You wouldn't do so if you knew what it means to me.'

Now he moved towards her again, and reached out to her again, and grasped her shoulders and turned her towards him. And this time when she moved as if to pull away he held her. 'Don't,' he said. 'Don't draw away, for I shan't let you go.' He paused, 'Unless you tell me you want me to.'

She did not speak. She remained there as his arms wrapped more closely around her, drawing her to him, nearer. She was aware of everything that was happening and almost of nothing. She could hear the sound of the blackbird singing his evensong; she could feel the texture of the man's waistcoat; beyond his head the sweeping green of the barley field in the dying light; she was aware too of the smell of him, a mixture of his tweed waistcoat, his cotton shirt, the scent of his skin and his hair oil. She knew all these things, yet at the same time her knowledge of it all seemed to be almost swept aside by his presence and what was happening. All at once his mouth was on her own, his lips pressing hers, tenderly at first and then more strongly. And it was a revelation, the kiss, his holding her. Nothing like it had ever happened before, and she felt the utmost desire to give herself up to it. When at last he released her, she stood with her mouth a little open, gasping slightly at the shock of it all.

'Oh, Grace,' he said, and his hand came up and touched at her hair, at her cheek, 'I've wanted to do that for so long.'

On the road back to Berron Wick Grace relived the kiss. She sat in the trap with Billy beside her, but felt some kind of invisible attachment to the man in the driver's seat. And so many times he turned and looked at her, and caught her eye, and made some little murmur of words – though he did not need to seek her attention, for always she was waiting for him to turn, for him to look at her. And now all her life was changed.

When they reached Asterleigh House, Mr Fairman drove the trap around to the back of the house and pulled up in the stable yard. Billy and Grace got down and solemnly Billy thanked the man for all his kindness during the day. Mr Fairman told him it had been a pleasure. 'And what shall you do now?' he said to Billy.

Billy gave a little laugh. 'I shall go to bed, sir.'

Mr Fairman laughed too. 'I should think you need it. Which is your room? Can we see it from here?'

Billy stepped back a little and raised his arm, pointing up. 'There, sir, the third one from the end, on the second floor.'

Kester Fariman looked up. 'Ah, yes. Well, you have a nice outlook, over the stable yard.'

'Yes, sir.'

'Is it a nice room?'

'Very nice. Though not as big as Grace's. Hers is the next but one on the left.'

'Ah, I see.'

Billy said goodnight then, and Grace said, 'I'll come in and see you in a minute,' and he went into the house.

When he had gone, she and the man stood looking at one another.

He said, in a voice that only she could hear, 'I want to kiss you, Grace,' and she smiled at the secret and the happiness, knowing that she wanted it too, and that it would almost certainly happen if they were quite alone and free from the possibility of being observed.

'Well,' she said, 'I must go in.'

'Must you?'

'I must.'

'Then I shall see you on Monday.'

'Yes, on Monday.'

Upstairs on the second floor she went into her room where she washed, and changed into her old day dress. Then, feeling refreshed, she went along the landing to Billy's room and knocked on the door. At his voice she went in and found him in his nightshirt, just getting up from saying his prayers. She watched as he got into bed and then sat on the coverlet beside him.

'Don't you want any supper?' she asked.

'No, thanks. I ate so much.'

'So I noticed.' She smiled. 'And did you have a good day?'

'Oh, Grace, yes.' He gave a deep sigh of pleasure. 'It was one of the best days of my life.'

'Really?'

'Yes. Grace, you should have come up to the tower with us. You'd have loved it.'

She smiled. 'I'm not so sure that I would. I'm not fond of heights.'

'Oh, it was quite safe. It was so exciting. I'd like to go there again some day.'

'Well – maybe one day we will.'

'Mr Fairman said he'll take me.'

'Well, that would be nice.' She smiled. 'You go to sleep now.' She leaned over and kissed his cheek. 'Goodnight, our Billy.'

'Goodnight, our Grace.'

From where Grace sat at her open window she could see the sun sinking lower, going down beyond the stable roof in a blaze of rose and gold, backlighting the tall elms and throwing them into stark relief. Returning from Billy's room to her own, she had paced the floor for some minutes and then forced herself to sit. But she had felt no sense of resting. And even now after all this time she had not.

The night was warm, and the sweet, summer-scented air drifted in. Her room was in darkness now, and she struck a match and put it to the wick of the lamp. A moth, attracted by the light, flew in and fluttered about the glow. Loath to attract more, she got up to pull the window in a little. And then, looking down, she saw a figure in the yard below. A man stood looking up at her window. At first it was hard to tell whether it was Kester or Mr Spencer – they were much alike in colouring and build. She stood unmoving, looking down at him. And then, his right arm came up in a salute, and he turned his head so that she could see his face. It was Kester. After a moment's hesitation she put up her own hand. Then, the next moment, he was turning, taking the mare's bridle and leading her out of the yard.

Chapter Fifteen

Although much of the work was done as regards
unpacking and placing all the artefacts in the house it was
arranged that Grace would still go to Birchwood House to
teach Sophie for a further week, so that Grace could lend a
hand should it be required. And she could hardly wait for
the time each day for the cab to pick her up. Each morning
she stood ready and waiting at the library window,
watching for the carriage to arrive, and as soon as the ring
came at the door she was down the stairs, fighting the urge
to hurry, nevertheless forestalling the maid: 'It's all right,
it's my cab to take me to the station,' and was away out of
the door. Her greatest fear was that Mrs Spencer would at
the last minute send some message to ask her to remain at
Asterleigh House or get her to undertake some errand that
would prevent her going. Fortunately it never happened.

And so the days passed. In Birchwood House Grace taught
Sophie in the little room set aside as a schoolroom, but
always there was the knowledge that Kester was in or near
the house. And he seemed always to be around somewhere.
Nothing, she hoped, would be evident in front of the child
or the staff, but his devotion was there, nonetheless. And
sometimes there were those stolen moments when they
found themselves truly alone, perhaps when Sophie was
working on an assignment and Grace was helping Kester
with some project concerning the house.

*

On the Monday morning as Sophie worked at an arithmetic exercise Kester lightly tapped on the door and came into the room. On his appearance Sophie at once said, 'Papa –' but he put a finger to his lips and she grinned, nodded and continued with her work. Grace was sitting at a little table where she had been reading a book on English history. She put the book down as Kester came into the room, and murmured softly to him, 'Have you come to join our class, sir?'

'No.' He shook his head, his voice equally quiet. 'Though perhaps it's not a bad idea. I might learn something.'

Grace smiled, and he spoke again, starting, 'One thing you could –' in his usual tone, and now Grace put a finger to her lips. He halted in his speech, glanced about the top of the table at which she sat, then, taking a piece of paper from a pad in front of her, picked up a pencil and wrote the words: *Tell me about yourself. I know hardly anything about you.* And Grace took up her pencil, and wrote beneath the words: *There is little to tell, and a very small piece of paper would suffice.* And he nodded, smiled, and took the paper away with him.

Later, when Sophie and Grace had gone to get some lunch, Grace came back alone to the classroom and found Kester sitting in her seat at the desk. 'Now,' he said, 'pay attention. I have a few questions for you.' Grace stood there smiling, and he said: 'So, Miss Grace Harper, what do you want out of life?'

And Grace said, 'Just one thing. To be happy, sir.'

On the Tuesday, when the lessons were over for the day, he brought her some flowers, a spray of lilac and a red poppy.

On Wednesday morning Sophie showed Grace a photograph of her mother. 'She was beautiful, miss, wasn't she?' Grace took the silver-framed photograph and looked at the lovely face of the young woman there. 'Yes, indeed,' Grace replied, and looked for sadness in the child's face. All she could see was a slight wistfulness. Then she realized that the child had been so young when her mother died that she would hardly have remembered her.

Kester was around the house so much. That same Wednesday he came into the schoolroom and announced: 'Come on, enough of work for today. Right now the subject is sport,' and led them outside onto the newly mown lawn where he had set up croquet hoops. They spent the rest of that afternoon playing croquet.

Afterwards, just before Grace was due to return to Asterleigh, and Sophie was with the nursemaid, Grace said to Kester: 'Sophie – today she showed me a photograph of her mother.'

Kester gave a nod and lowered his head a little, and Grace suddenly had misgivings about bringing up the subject. But then Kester looked at her with a sad smile touching the corners of his mouth. 'Sophie doesn't remember her,' he said.

'I thought that might be the case,' Grace said.

'She was so young when her mother died. All she has of her is a photograph.'

On Thursday the three of them went into Corster to look around the market place and do a little shopping. In a bookshop Kester bought Grace a small book of Keats's poems.

Later, while Sophie was taking a little sleep in the nursery Grace sat looking through the book.

'You must know some of the poems,' Kester said.

'*Ode to a Nightingale*,' she said, 'I always loved that.'

'Ah, yes.'

'Have you ever heard a nightingale's song?'

'No, never, not to my knowledge. I doubt that we had many in Kensington. It's a beautful song, isn't it?'

'Oh, yes. So beautiful.'

'Keats died in Rome, did you know that?'

'No, I didn't.'

'In a little room at the foot of the Spanish Steps. He died in the arms of a good friend, Joseph Severn, and is buried there in Rome. He made no claim to making his mark on posterity and requested to have written on his gravestone: "Here lies one whose name was writ in water." Can you believe that? His poems will live on for ever. They must.' Then he added in the same breath, 'Oh, Grace, I would like to take you to Rome. I would show you the Spanish Steps, the Coliseum, all the sights there. I would like to take you to Venice too, and to Florence.'

With a little sigh Grace put up a hand in protest, as if the things he was saying were not to be borne. And he said:

'I would. I would show you everything; I would take you everywhere.'

And stepping towards her he wrapped his arms around her and kissed her on the mouth. 'Grace, Grace,' he said, 'I love you so much.'

That Friday night Grace lay in her bed and thought back over all the things that had taken place over the week. How had so much happened in so short a time? That Kester Fairman should find that he loved her – it was a miracle. And a miracle too that she had found love in this man. How miraculous it was that two people, born far apart, should come together and discover that they had been meant for one another.

On the Saturday Grace came into the house after posting a letter to Aunt Edie and was going through the hall when Jane came to her and said that Mrs Spencer had been asking for her. She was in the sewing room, the maid added. Grace went there at once and found Mrs Spencer sitting in her armchair with her sewing in her lap. On the small side table was a tray bearing tea things. Grace had not seen her for two days.

'Ah, Grace, there you are.' Mrs Spencer put aside her embroidery frame and indicated the seat of the chair facing her. 'Come and sit down a minute.'

Grace moved to her and sat down. In spite of the warm day there was a bright fire burning in the grate.

'Would you like some tea?' Mrs Spencer asked. 'This will be cold, but we can get Jane to fetch a fresh pot.'

'No, thank you, ma'am. I had some not long ago.'

Mrs Spencer nodded acknowledgement. With a sigh she said, 'It's been so quiet here, with you away teaching little Sophie, and Mr Spencer off in Milan.'

'Is he due back soon?'

'This evening, I'm glad to say. I do wish he would give up the factory there, but he won't hear of it. It makes so much travelling for him. He gets exhausted, and it tries his temper.' She took in Grace's light shawl. 'Are you warm enough, my dear? The sun has been bright enough today but with such a keen wind there's been little warmth in the air. I need this fire.' She smiled at Grace. 'Well, tell me how you've been, my dear. I haven't seen you in two or three days. Is all going well with your teaching?'

'Yes. There's a little schoolroom now, which Mr Fairman has created. It's very nice, and will do so well for Sophie until she goes away to school.'

'Has Mr Fairman decided on a time for that?'

'He mentioned September – when the new school year begins.'

'And does he expect you to teach Sophie until that time?' There was a slight note of concern in the tone.

Grace said quickly: 'No. He's spoken of finding another governess for the meantime.'

'It won't be easy to hire one just for a matter of months.'

Mrs Spencer studied Grace for a second then said, 'What about you?'

'Me?'

'Is Mr Fairman not tempted to offer the post to you?'

'Oh – such a thing was not mentioned. I don't think it would be.'

'Why not? You are a governess, after all.'

'I know, but – I suppose Mr Fairman acknowledges that I'm employed here, with you. He wouldn't wish to – disturb your arrangements.'

'Perhaps so. But as I say, you are a governess. And you'll be looking for work as a governess. I assume you will, anyway. But one thing you will not be doing is staying here with me for ever, will you? You don't see a long-term employment here, do you?'

'Well, no . . .'

'For your sake I hope not. I know you have Billy to care for, but, even so, you can think of better things than being stuck here for years on end. As much as I enjoy your company, Grace, I do realize that it will not be mine indefinitely. I know there must come a time when you'll want to move on. And I invited you here with that knowledge. I never imagined for a moment that it would last any great length of time.'

Grace said, 'I have enjoyed my time here, Mrs Spencer. Very much so.'

'Well, I'm glad to hear that, and I've enjoyed having you here. But there has to be more to your life than this, my dear. At the moment it's a little more exciting and interesting for you while you're teaching Mr Fairman's girl, but that won't go on, will it? She'll either get a new governess or go to school – or both. And then it'll be just you and me again. And I'm getting older, and you surely don't look forward to spending your life as companion to some ageing, increasingly irascible old woman.' She paused. 'Besides, what about Billy? What are you going to do about his life?'

Grace looked down at her hands. 'I don't know,' she murmured. 'He's a clever boy, good with his grammar and creative things. I'd like to think that there's something he could do when the time comes.'

'Oh, no doubt about that. He is a very clever boy, and he's a fine little artist too. Were he from a wealthy background, I can see him being sent off to study art, perhaps going to art school. But one has to be realistic. His prospects are limited.'

'He should be able to get a job as a clerk when he leaves school. If he applies himself it shouldn't be too difficult.'

'Yes.' Mrs Spencer nodded, 'I can see that happening. But you've a little time yet. Two or three years at least. Though those years will fly past, you can believe it.'

'Oh, I'm sure of that.'

A little pause, then Mrs Spencer said, 'What about you, Grace? What do you want out of life? Where do you see yourself going?'

Grace did not answer.

Mrs Spencer put her head a little on one side. 'But some questions have to be faced. They need answers. One can't get on by ignoring them.'

'No, I realize that.'

'You're twenty-one years old. It seems so young in one way. But you should beware. Give it another three years or so and people will start to regard you as a spinster. Another two or three years on top of that . . .' She spread her hands, palms out, 'and practically all your chances will be gone. You wouldn't want that to happen to you.'

'No.'

'Get yourself in that situation and you lose all opportunity to *choose*. As the old saying has it: you can spend so long looking round the orchard that you end up picking up the crab apples.' A momentary pause, then she added, looking off into the greenery, 'I left it very late before I married. Oh, very late indeed, as you'll probably know. But I was lucky in my husband. Not all women are lucky in such circumstances.' She turned back to Grace. 'Is there no one, Grace? No one at all?'

Grace did not know how to respond and lowered her eyes to her hands again. And feeling Mrs Spencer's gaze upon her, kept her glance lowered. And too long.

'Well,' said Mrs Spencer, 'it looks as if I have my answer.' A pause. 'Do I?'

Grace looked up now, but could not find words of response.

Mrs Spencer gave a little nod. 'I see that I do.' She smiled. 'And can you tell me any more about it – this – this *interest* of yours?'

Grace said nothing, and Mrs Spencer tilted her head, peering in a quizzical way into Grace's shadowed face. 'Well, now, don't tell me I've hit upon a secret, have I?' Her tone was playful, teasing.

Grace looked up and gave a little groan. 'Oh, ma'am . . .'

And seeing Grace's grave expression, Mrs Spencer said, frowning slightly in concern and sympathy, 'Oh, don't take it amiss, what I say. I don't mean to take it lightly at all. If you've met someone, found someone, then that is wonderful.' Then she added, 'Or rather, I *hope* it's wonderful. Are your feelings – reciprocated?'

Grace gave the very faintest nod, but made no sound. Hardly could she meet the other's eyes.

'That is excellent, Grace.'

'Yes,' Grace said, unable to suppress the smile of happiness that touched her mouth, 'my whole life is changing, ma'am.'

'I can see. I knew there was something different about you. I could tell.' She sighed. 'Oh, I do hope everything will work out well for you. Is there any reason it shouldn't?'

Now Grace said, answering the question she had asked herself a hundred times: 'No, I don't think so. I don't see why it shouldn't.' And knew such relief at hearing the answer on her own lips.

Mrs Spencer gave a little chuckle, a sound touched with sympathy. 'I'm very glad to hear that. Though you're not being very forthcoming, I have to say.' She pressed her lips together, and slightly narrowed her eyes. 'I'm thinking,' she said. 'Or rather I'm trying to think. I'm trying to think who it could be. After all, you have so little opportunity to meet anyone. You're either here, or you're spending your hours with Sophie and –' She came to a halt, and then gave a slow nod. 'Of course. Of course. I should have realized right away. There is only one person it could be. Heavens, how slow I am.'

Silence between them, and there came to Grace the ticking of the clock. It seemed strangely loud in the quiet.

Mrs Spencer said, 'Yes, indeed, how slow I am. And all this has been going on practically under my nose, and I wasn't aware of it.'

Grace looked at her at this, trying to read Mrs Spencer's expression. Was there a flicker of a look of displeasure, of having been betrayed, something that said she had been used? But no, no such thing. The woman smiled. 'And certain things become clear to me now,' she said. 'And make me wonder why Mr Fairman was so anxious for you to go to his home and help him sort out his bits and pieces. Could it possibly have been more for the pleasure of your company?'

Grace could feel herself blushing. Mrs Spencer observed it and said, smiling again, 'I don't mean to tease you or embarrass you.' She studied Grace for some seconds' silence, then gave a little sigh and said, 'Well, I do hope this is a good thing, Grace.'

Grace felt a little rush of panic at the woman's words. Why should it not be a good thing?

Mrs Spencer went on, 'Mr Fairman is a little older than you, though I don't think that matters in the slightest. Nine or ten years, I should think. Though to my reckoning age differences are overrated. He also has a child, though that's no problem either, for you're well acquainted with his daughter and are fond of her. You are, I assume?'

'Oh, yes,' Grace breathed. 'I am indeed.'

'I thought so. By all accounts the child is so eager for her lessons with you, and that makes it clear enough.' She gave a nod. 'He's a personable man, too, and a talented one. I'm sure you agree.'

Grace nodded.

'According to what I've heard, he's designed some splendid buildings. Mostly in London, I believe, although I think he's done work throughout the country. Have you seen any of his work?'

'Only in pictures. There are some photographs I've seen. They're very impressive.'

'Oh, he's a talented man, there's no doubt. And attractive in so many ways.'

A little silence. Mrs Spencer seemed to be thinking things through. Then she added, 'Even so, I think you must be careful here.'

'Be careful?' Grace's heart beat momentarily more strongly. 'I don't understand.'

'I wouldn't want to see you hurt, Grace.'

'Well, no, but . . .' Grace let her words falter and fade.

'I mean it. I would hate to see you hurt. This is a man who's been married. A widower. He's a man who's been through a great deal of pain and anguish with the loss of a much loved wife. A wife who, clearly, he was very happy with. No new wife can be a replacement for what he's lost.' She added quickly, 'I didn't mean it to sound like that. I'm

313

sure he would never see you as such – a replacement. I'm just saying that this is something a new wife could never be – no matter who she might be.' She sighed. 'To follow in the steps of someone so – loved – must be a very difficult task. Which is not to say you are not up to such a demand.'

Grace heard herself saying, 'I know so little about his wife. He doesn't speak about her. He doesn't want to, I'm sure. And I can't press him.'

'Of course he doesn't want to speak about her. And one can't blame him. I'd be surprised if he did.'

'Sophie showed me a photograph. She looked to be a very beautiful young woman.'

'So I understand. She was half-Italian, did you know that? My husband met her, but that was years ago, just before her death. Sophie was very small. Only about two years old, I believe.'

'And that was about the time that Mrs Fairman died?'

'That's right. Mr Spencer met them on the way out to Italy, he told me. He was going out there on business connected with the soap factory, and met them on the train. The Fairmans were travelling to Naples, where Mr Fairman had secured a commission. It's very sad. That would have been only weeks before his wife died.'

Grace hesitated for a moment, then asked, 'Do you know the circumstances of her death?'

'I believe I told you that she died of cholera.'

'Cholera, yes, I remember.' Grace had read enough in the newspapers over the years to learn what a deadly and dreadful disease it was.

'Such an awful disease,' Mrs Spencer said. 'There have been numerous outbreaks of it in southern Italy over the years, and apparently there was one touching Naples while the Fairmans were there. And sadly, tragically, Mrs Fairman contracted it. I believe by drinking from an infected glass. It's carried in water.' She shook her head.

'It's so tragic. That's all it can take – something as simple as that – a drink from an infected glass. After her death Mr Fairman brought his daughter back home, to safety. Mrs Fairman, poor woman, would have been buried there, of course. Her body wouldn't have been brought back – not with her having died from such a disease.' She gave a little shudder. 'That poor woman. I understand that death from cholera is a particularly horrific one. And so little Sophie is left without a mother.'

Mrs Spencer turned to Grace, looked at her almost piercingly for a moment, and then reached out and laid her left hand on Grace's wrist. 'My dear, I think you could be the person that Mr Fairman needs.' She paused for a moment. 'Tell me, do you love him?'

'Oh, yes, ma'am.' Grace caught her breath as a little surge of excitement rose in her. 'Oh, yes, ma'am, I love him.'

The weather was exceptionally fine on Sunday and that afternoon Grace and Billy went out for a stroll together. They had returned and were walking through the stable yard when they came face to face with Mr Spencer. He had, Grace learned, returned the previous evening from Italy. Until this moment Grace had not seen him in several days.

'Well, good afternoon, Miss Grace, Master Billy.' He came from the stables and was wearing riding breeches and jacket.

They returned his greeting, and Grace asked if he had enjoyed his ride.

He nodded. 'Oh, indeed, but hardly the thing after a good lunch. Mrs Sandiston always seems to excel herself when I get back from a trip away. I think she thinks I don't get fed while I'm out of England.' Then, turning to Billy: 'Billy, would you be kind enough to excuse us for a moment? I'd like to have a private word with your sister . . .'

'Of course, sir.' Billy nodded quickly, and with a murmured word to Grace: 'I'll see you later on,' moved to the rear door of the house and disappeared inside.

Mr Spencer turned from watching Billy's departure, and said to Grace, 'Have you got a minute or two to spare?'

'Yes, of course.' She wondered what it was that was so sensitive it could not be said in front of Billy. 'What is it, sir?' she said.

He regarded her gravely in silence for some moments, then with a shake of his head, said, 'We can't talk here. Let's go inside, shall we? We'll go up to the library.'

He opened the back door and Grace passed through into the passage. After that he began to lead the way up the stairs to the first floor. And all the time Grace followed in his steps she asked herself what was the reason for it all. What could he possibly have to say to her that was such a seemingly grave matter? Was she, unknowingly, guilty of some error that had caused displeasure in the house? The thoughts, the search for possibilities, ran through her mind, but she could settle on nothing that could give any likely answer.

Reaching the library, he ushered her in and closed the door behind them. 'Sit down, please, Grace.' He gestured to a chair near the fireplace and she sat down.

He remained standing before her for some moments then moved away to the window. Turning from her, looking down on to the forecourt, he said, 'You're still enjoying teaching Mr Fairman's young daughter, I understand.'

'Yes, sir, very much.' His words had bordered on small talk. She continued in her bewilderment.

'So my wife was telling me.'

Grace waited. After a moment he turned back to face her and went on:

'Grace – nothing of this is easy for me to say, please believe me. I hope you do.'

When he finished speaking he looked at her as if expecting an answer. She merely said, frowning, 'Yes, sir.'

After a few moments of awkward silence he went on, 'My wife also tells me that – oh dear, Grace, this is so difficult . . .' He took a deep breath, then said, 'My wife tells me that you have – formed an attachment – to Mr Fairman.'

Grace drew a breath to speak, but before she could do so he added, 'You may think it's no business of mine, and in fact it is not, but for your sake I feel I have to speak.'

Grace, remaining silent, became aware of the beating of her heart. Almost always she felt in his presence some lack of ease, but this feeling now was quite different; now alarm and panic touched her.

He went on, 'My wife tells me that when she learned of your – your affection for Mr Fairman she told you that she would not wish to see you hurt . . .'

'Yes, sir, that's correct . . .'

'And nor would I wish such a thing.'

'I am aware,' Grace said now, 'of the situation, sir. I am aware that Mr Fairman is a man who has been hurt, has suffered tragedy, and I don't expect to replace his late wife, but I –'

'That's not what I meant,' he said, interrupting her words. 'What I want to do – though it gives me no pleasure – is to prepare you – if this is at all possible. Though there is no good way of breaking bad news. In the end, however the news is said, it still has to be said.' He broke off here and looked at her with his eyes narrowed slightly, as if trying to read her responses in her expression.

'I take it you are serious about your relationship with Mr Fairman?' And here he held up a hand, palm out. 'And please, don't think I'm being impertinent. I am not. This is, believe me, vital. You are serious about your relationship with Mr Fairman?'

'Yes, indeed.' Grace nodded, frowning. 'Absolutely.'

'And Mr Fairman – do you infer that he also is serious about this?'

'Yes.' Grace's heart was beating fast now.

Mr Spencer nodded. 'May I ask if the subject of marriage has been brought up . . .?'

'Well – no. No, it hasn't.' She wanted to say, *But it will be, of course it will be.* 'No,' she said again, 'it hasn't been mentioned. But – it is understood, sir. I'm sure it is understood.'

'Have any promises been made?'

'I haven't asked for promises. I wouldn't ask.'

'May I ask how long you have been aware of your feelings for this man?'

'For – for some weeks now.' Putting a hand to her cheek, she said quickly, 'Sir, I find this line of questioning somewhat embarrassing. If there –'

Once again he broke in, now saying, 'I'm sure you do, but please, don't take it amiss. You won't feel the same once you hear what I have to say.' A little silence, then he said, 'You've been told, I gather, of his wife dying in Naples of cholera some few years ago.'

'Yes. He's never spoken of it, but Mrs Spencer told me. He's rarely spoken of his wife.'

'That's understandable.'

'It is indeed.'

'Not for the reasons you might think.'

Grace frowned again. She was increasingly bewildered by his words, and her feeling of dismay grew stronger.

He paused for a second, as if weighing his words, then said, 'Have you wondered why his wife is not buried in this country? Why her body was not brought back here for burial?'

'Well, with a death from cholera, I understand that such an act would be unthinkable.'

'There is that, of course, which is quite true. With a death

318

from cholera the important thing is to get the victim buried, and prevent further harm.'

Grace wondered how he could talk so about the death of a young woman, then he said:

'What if I told you that his wife did not die of cholera at all.'

'What?' She spoke the word almost inaudibly. What was he saying? What was he suggesting?

'Did you hear me?' he said.

'Yes. But I don't understand . . . This can't be so. Mrs Spencer told me that – where would she have gained such information?'

'From me, mostly. But there, I didn't know the truth.'

'I don't understand. I don't understand any of it.' Grace's heart was pounding. She felt she was going to hear something terrible, and wished suddenly that they could put back the clock, that this conversation had never begun. 'I don't understand any of it,' she said again.

Suddenly his expression was all kindness and sympathy. 'No, of course you don't. And why should you? You're young and innocent. How on earth should you have experience of such a thing in your life? How often can such a thing happen? For a girl to love a man who is mourning a dead wife, only to find that the wife is not dead at all.'

It might have been that the room spun around, and Grace would not have noticed. She frowned, not truly understanding what was being said to her. It was as if she registered an error on the man's part, and it would be only a matter of seconds before he corrected himself. But the seconds ticked by and he did not. Then, her heart thudding in her breast, she said:

'This can't be so.' A little laugh came, a hollow sound of disbelief. 'It can't be so. Did you say that Mr Fairman's wife is still living? It can't be.'

'I'm sorry,' Mr Spencer said. 'I'm so sorry to tell you. But you had to know.'

'No,' she said, 'there is some mistake. Mr Fairman's wife died in Naples, in the early 1880s. She died in a cholera outbreak, and was buried there.'

'She didn't die of cholera. She didn't die at all. As far as I know she's still alive and well.'

'It can't be true,' Grace protested. 'It can't be.'

'There is no mistake about this.'

Grace got up from her chair and moved to the door and stood before it, hands clasped into fists, knuckles pale, at her mouth. She looked as if she had halted in her tracks on the way to making her escape. Mr Spencer stood behind her, his back to the window.

'I take no pleasure from having told you these things,' he said. 'I hate to see your hopes dashed like this.'

She could not speak, could not trust herself to speak.

After a moment he went on, 'I first met Fairman and his wife when they were on their way out to Italy. I was going to Italy also. But where they were heading for Naples I was going to Milan. They had their small daughter with them. I stopped in Milan and they stopped there also for a while, and we got to know each other better. We had some pleasant dinners and went to the theatre. I remember he was on his way to undertake an architectural commission. He hadn't gained the success he's gained since, I might add – not by a long way. He was very eager for work, to make his name. His wife was a very beautiful young woman, so beautiful. She was part-Italian, and I believe had family in Italy. Her name was Bellafiore.'

'Beautiful flower,' Grace said dully.

'Beautiful flower, indeed. And as I say, she *was* beautiful. I think they'd only been married a little over three years.'

He came to a halt, then moved over to Grace and put a

hand lightly, briefly, on her shoulder. 'Grace, come and sit down. Please.'

After a moment she turned. He gestured to the seat she had previously occupied and she sat in it again. Although her outward expression was relatively calm, inside her breast there was the greatest turmoil.

'I'll tell you the rest of the story,' he said. 'As I say, we became friends, Fairman and I. There we were, not too far apart in age, two ambitious young men who had come up the hard way – but now had all the world before us,' he laughed here, ' – or so we thought. And we had other things in common as well. Not least the fact that he knew Corster, having stayed there when he was younger. So – we said we would keep in touch. He would contact me when he and his wife were back in London, and then I should go and stay with them.'

'And did you?' she heard herself say.

'He never wrote. And after a time I thought, well, that was it – another of those ships that pass in the night. I thought not a lot more about it, and there were no hard feelings. Things were happening to me, I might add, so I had plenty to occupy my time. I met Mrs Spencer, and we married, and moved here to Asterleigh House. Oh, my own life was very full.'

'How did you know about – about Mr Fairman's situation changing . . .?'

'Well, I was going up to London – oh, it was some time later – four years or so, and I found myself right in the area where he was living – in the very street – and on the off-chance I called at his address. He was at home, and he invited me in. He made no mention of his wife, and there was no sight or sound of her whatsoever. As a matter of fact I don't recall even seeing a photograph of her. It seemed to me that she was no longer a part of his life, and I was very hesitant to ask about her. When I did eventually mention her he spoke of her having died. I had guessed at something like this, some tragic happening. I didn't go into it any deeper, however; I could see it made him very uncomfortable. Later I heard from somewhere that she had died of cholera while they were staying in Naples on their trip. I never did speak to him of it directly, of course. It isn't the kind of thing one does.'

'But – but you say that it's not so – that his wife did not die of cholera.'

'She did not.'

'But – how do you know this?'

'Because I've seen her myself.'

'You've seen his wife?'

'Yes.'

'Where? How?'

'I saw her in London.'

'You remembered her? You recognized her after all this time?'

'Yes, I did, and of course I recognized her name.'

'Bellafiore.'

'It isn't a name that one comes across commonly.'

Grace's hands worked agitatedly in her lap. The whole thing was like some nightmare, and still she kept telling herself that there was some mistake. Mr Spencer was mistaken, that was the only explanation for it all.

'You met her in London, you say, and you recognized her name.'

'Yes. I had an appointment with a business client. We met for drinks in a hotel and to discuss our business matters. He said that when our meeting was over he was meeting someone for dinner. I gathered of course that it was a certain young lady. Then she arrived and we were introduced. Even before I heard her name I knew her face. I could never forget such a face. She was not going under the name of Fairman, but another name that I can't remember.

322

An Italian name, I recall. And then he addressed her as Bella – and that confirmed it. Bellafiore.'

'You're absolutely sure of it? It was Mr Fairman's wife?'

'Absolutely. And *she* knew *me*, I could see that.'

'How do you know?'

'I could tell. I could see the recognition in her eyes. It was almost immediate. And after all, it hadn't been so long, and I wasn't changed so much.'

'What about her? Was she changed much?'

'A little. She was still beautiful, though it looked as if the intervening years had not been too kind to her.'

'What was she to your friend?'

'He was not a friend – a business colleague, that's all. I don't know what she was to him. I didn't ask.'

Grace sat there in silence. There were no further questions she could ask, not of Mr Spencer. He had told her all that was necessary. After several moments she got up and started across the room. Mr Spencer moved towards her.

'I'm sorry – to have given you such news. Such distressing news.' He shook his head. 'I'm really sorry, but you had to know.'

She opened the door in silence and passed through. On the other side she turned and said, 'I have to go out. I have to get to Upper Callow.'

'You're going to see him?'

'If Mrs Spencer should ask for me, will you tell her I'll be back as soon as I can?'

'I'll tell her. How will you get there?'

'I'll walk into the village and take the train.'

'Mr Johnson is off on an errand but Rhind is around. He will take you.'

'No, really, thank you.'

'I'll call Rhind. He's got nothing much else to do.'

Grace opened her mouth to protest once more, but said nothing. What did it matter how she got there?

323

Ten minutes later she was in the carriage and Rhind, having helped her in, was climbing up into the driver's seat. He had already been given directions by Mr Spencer, and with a questioning glance at Grace, flapped the reins and started away.

No word was exchanged between herself and the man, and they rode in complete silence for the short journey to the station. When they arrived Grace was getting out even as Rhind jumped down and moved to her. She thanked him, hardly without looking at him, and hurried into the station. There she bought her ticket and moved to the platform to wait for her train. When it came in she climbed on board and sat back in her seat. Her palms were damp and her heart was thumping.

On arrival she took a fly from the Upper Callow station and reached Birchwood House fifteen minutes later. There she paid the cab driver and stepped across the gravel to the front door and rang the bell.

Grace's ring was answered by the new young maid Emma who welcomed her with a smile saying that Mr Fairman was in the back garden. 'Would you like me to tell him you're here, miss? Or will you just go through?'

'Is he alone?'

'Yes, miss.'

'Then I'll go through, thank you.'

Grace went through the hall towards the rear of the house and out at the back door. Crossing the first lawn at the rear, she moved around a privet hedge and saw Kester there before her, crouching over one of the herbaceous borders with a trowel.

Seeing her approaching figure in the periphery of his vision he turned and, seeing who it was, beamed with pleasure. 'Grace! What a lovely surprise.' He tossed down the trowel and got to his feet. 'Sophie's in her room, having her afternoon nap.' He was in his shirt sleeves, with a pair of old, stained corduroy trousers, and a battered felt hat on his head. His fingers were grimy from the soil in which he had been working.

Grace's answering smile was pale, barely moving her mouth. Seeing him now she could scarcely believe what Mr Spencer had told her. How could it be true what he had said?

'Grace –' Kester held out his hands as if expecting her own to reach out to him. But they did not and, frowning, he let his hands fall back to his sides. 'Grace,' he said, 'is there something wrong?'

Lowering her eyes, unable to meet his gaze, she said, 'This is something that you will know better than I, Kester.'

'Grace? Grace, look at me.' He waited till she had raised her eyes, then said, 'Tell me what it is. Please.'

It was all she could do not to weep. She glanced quickly around to ensure that she could see no one in earshot, then said, 'I believed you loved me, Kester.'

'You believed I loved you? I *do* love you.'

As if he had not spoken, she said, 'You told me you loved me. You let me believe that – that what we had was something to last. You never said it in so many words, but you knew that I inferred as much. You knew it, didn't you?'

'It's what I wanted you to believe. Because it was the truth.'

'Ah,' she said, 'the truth. Now we come to the truth, do we?'

'Grace,' he said, his lips barely moving, 'what is happening? Tell me what it is.'

'I believed,' she said, 'that in time we would marry. I believed that you would be mine, and I would be yours. We would make our home together, the four of us. We would be happy together. For you loved me, and therefore you

325

would want to marry me.' She paused. 'Was I such a fool to believe such a thing?'

'No, you were not.'

'Really? That's something, then, I suppose.' She turned away, and then immediately looked back at him. 'You know why I'm here, don't you?'

He hesitated for a moment, then said, 'No, I don't.'

'No? No? Think about it, Kester. Think about it.'

She gazed into his face and saw his skin grow paler. She nodded. 'Yes, I think you do know why. And that gives me the answer I must have. It isn't the answer I wanted, but I think it's the only one I can get.' A little sob burst from her lips. 'Oh, Kester!'

They stood on the grass, some four feet apart, hands hanging down at their sides, tears streaming down Grace's cheeks, Kester's face white.

'I spoke of your wife,' she said, 'I even made a reference to her – her death, and you said nothing to disabuse me of my misapprehension.'

Kester remained silent.

'You have not been widowed, Kester, have you?' Grace said at last. 'Your wife, little Sophie's mother, is very much alive.'

His face looked deathly pale, and for a moment her heart reached out in sympathy. But she held herself in check; she did not move.

'It's true, isn't it, what I say?'

'Grace –' he began.

She broke in, cutting off his words, 'It's true, isn't it? It's true.'

'Yes.'

'There was no death from cholera, was there? There was no illness at all. It was all a lie. It was a lie, wasn't it?'

Silence. Somewhere, unheard by either one, a bird sang in the beautiful afternoon.

'Wasn't it?' Grace said.

He nodded, the barest gesture.

'I was sorry for you,' she said. 'I saw you as having suffered a tragedy, having lost your wife in the most dreadful circumstances – and it was all a fraud. And you let me go on, making a fool of myself. Yet you were mourning no one. Did it give you amusement, seeing me behave like a fool?'

'Never. Never even suggest such a thing.'

As if he had not spoken she went on, 'I expect you saw me as some poor, naïve creature who hasn't the sense to come in out of the rain. Is that how it was?'

'Never,' he said. 'Please, don't.'

'Oh, I want to believe you,' she cried. 'I want to, but I – I've been on such a fool's errand.'

'Grace –'

'Don't you see? How can I believe anything any more?'

'Grace, I must talk to you. Please.'

'What is there to say? You are a married man. You have a wife, living in London.'

'Who told you this? How do you know it?'

'Does it matter? It's not important how I know. I *know*, that's what counts. And thank God I found out – before I got in even deeper and made an even bigger fool of myself.'

'Grace, I can tell you about it, I –'

'You can tell me about it? What is there to tell? You've lied to me. You said you would never lie to me but you have. And you didn't care about me. In the end you would have had to tell me, and what then? Was it not enough for you to break my heart? Did you want to ruin me as well?'

'Grace, please –'

'There is nothing more to say, Kester. Nothing at all.'

'No, it's not so,' he said. 'There are many things to say. It isn't exactly the way it looks.'

'It looks very clear to me,' she said. 'You let me believe

you were a widowed man, when in fact your wife is very much living.'

He said reluctantly, 'There is more to it than that, Grace.'

'More? Whatever it is, does it change the situation?'

A little silence, then he said, 'No.'

Another silence. He stood looking at her, and she stood with her eyes downcast, fixing on her agitated fingers. Then she said simply, 'I loved you, Kester. For the first time in my life I loved. And I loved you.'

'Oh, Grace –' taking a step forward, 'don't put such words in the past. Don't say it like that, I beg you.'

'What else can I say?'

'Grace, to hear those words from you. You never spoke them before, and now when I hear them you're speaking of something in the past. Grace, please.'

'And what of you?' she said. 'What were your feelings for me? Did you love me as I thought you did, hoped you did? Or was this some kind of game? And did you play the same game with Miss Lewin?'

'Don't bring her into this. She has no part in my life.'

Sadly, Grace shook her head. 'And I'm afraid that I have no part in your life either.'

She turned then and started back over the grass, around the trimmed privet and onto the first lawn. Seeing with a glance over her shoulder that he was following, she said, 'Please, don't come with me.'

'But I can't let you leave like this.'

'Please.' She stopped and turned to face him. 'You must tell Sophie that I'm sorry I cannot give her lessons any more. You can find some reason. I'm sorry to be leaving her, but there's nothing else I can do.' She paused, then said, 'Goodbye,' – avoiding his gaze – and turning again, hurried around the side of the house.

PART THREE

Chapter Sixteen

Grace could recall little of her walk back to Asterleigh House from Berron Wick station that late afternoon; so little of it stayed in her memory that it might just as well have happened to someone else. It did not matter that the occasional carriage driver slowed to offer her a lift along the road, or that others, younger men in a group, called out provocative comments; if she had been aware of them in the first place, she did not care enough to heed them.

By the time she got back to the house it was after 6.30. On arrival she went straight up to her room, praying as she did so that no one would appear to say that Mrs Spencer required her presence. All she wanted was to be alone. She wanted to see no one, no one at all.

Lying on her bed, on her back, the tears ran down the sides of her face onto the pillow. She would never be happy again, she knew.

Later, she went along the landing to her brother's room and tapped on his door. He called out to her to come in and she entered and found him stripped to the waist and drying himself. He had just got in, he said, from helping Mr Johnson with the horses. She could smell the stable on him. He looked at her closely, seeing the redness in her eyes, the puffy flesh around them. 'Grace,' he said, 'what's the matter? Why are you upset?'

'I'm all right. I just came to see how you were.'

'I'm well, very well.'

'I haven't seen you all day.'

'No, after Sunday school I put on my old clothes and went straight to help Mr Johnson. Grace, what's wrong?'

'I shan't be going to Birchwood House any more,' she said.

'Not going to Birchwood? Why?'

She shook her head. 'Oh, Billy, don't ask me to talk about it now.'

He gazed at her. For the first time in his life he saw her completely at a loss. At all other times she had been able to cope. Whatever difficulties had come their way she had somehow managed to deal with them. But now here she was, looking lost.

'Is it to do with Mr Fairman?' he asked.

'Yes. I shan't be going to teach Sophie again. Mr Fairman and I – we shan't be meeting again.'

'Did you – quarrel, Grace?'

In spite of her sorrows she smiled at his naïvety. 'That's one way of saying it.'

On Monday morning Grace had her breakfast and then stayed in her room. Mrs Spencer would, of course, as would the maids, wonder why Grace was not being picked up from the house and driven to the station as on other days. After some consideration Grace went downstairs and asked Jane where Mrs Spencer was. On being told that she was in the drawing room, Grace made her way there and tapped on the door. A moment later she was entering the room.

'Grace,' Mrs Spencer said, 'I've been wondering about you. Clearly you haven't gone to Upper Callow.'

Grace said, 'No, I'm not going this morning.' A little pause, then: 'I shan't be going again. That's what I came to tell you.'

Frowning, Mrs Spencer looked at her for a moment, then said, 'Come and sit down, Grace.'

Grace did not want to, but she could not refuse, and she sat in the chair across from the sofa.

'Something has happened, hasn't it?' Mrs Spencer said.

After a moment Grace said, 'Things – are not the same. I shan't be going there again.'

'I gather that this is all to do with Mr Fairman?'

Grace nodded.

Mrs Spencer nodded also. 'And I can guess what's happened. You went to see him after talking to Mr Spencer, is that right?'

'Yes.'

Mrs Spencer sighed. 'I hope I'm in no way responsible for the unhappiness you're suffering. But you had to know. I told my husband of your news – that you and Mr Fairman were approaching a – an understanding, and that you were so happy – and then he told me. He told me what he told you – that Mr Fairman's wife is still very much alive.'

Grace hung her head. She could find no words.

Mrs Spencer went on, 'I couldn't understand why Mr Spencer hadn't told me before, after all, he had known for several weeks.' She gave a little shrug. 'Men and their loyalties. He had determined to tell no one, he said, until he had spoken to Mr Fairman himself about it – not that it was any of my husband's business.' Another little shrug. 'Anyway, it's done. And you had to know. Having that knowledge, Grace, he couldn't keep it to himself and see you get hurt.'

The clock ticked into the silence between them.

'And it turned out to be the truth, I'm guessing. Am I right?'

'Yes.' Grace's voice was the merest whisper.

'Oh, dear. What a sad business. When my husband told me that you had gone over to Upper Callow to see Mr Fairman – well – an outcome like this was certainly a

333

possibilty.' She paused. 'Can you tell me anything, my dear? Can you tell me what happened?'

'I put it to him,' Grace said. 'I put it to him – what Mr Spencer had told me – and he admitted that it was true. His wife is – he is not a – a widower.'

'What a dreadful shock for you.' Mrs Spencer sighed. 'Until that moment, when my husband told me, I had thought that Mrs Fairman had died some years ago. I believed the story of her having died of cholera. There was no reason I should not. I must admit that at first, when my husband told me of having met her in London, I was dubious. I thought he must have made a mistake. But now he's been proved correct.'

Tears filled Grace's eyes and she put up a hand and roughly wiped them away.

'What is to happen now, Grace?' Mrs Spencer said.

'What is to happen? I don't understand.'

'What are you going to do?'

'What can I do? There is nothing to be done. Mr Fairman and I, we shall not meet again. And that is something I must think about. I don't want to risk running into him at the market or other places so – perhaps we should think about moving on, Billy and I.'

And now tears rose in Mrs Spencer's eyes and glistened there. 'I'm angry about this,' she said. 'Why should a man lie so much? And why on earth did he ever have to come here in the first place? Why couldn't he have stayed in London? If he had, there wouldn't be all this heartache.'

There was a letter from Kester on Tuesday, asking Grace if she would agree to see him; could he call at the house to see her? She did not reply but wept and put the letter aside. On Saturday came a second letter, asking again for a meeting. And again she did not respond.

From that time on, Grace tried to put her energies and

her thoughts into her work, such as it was. And whatever it was it could only depend on the wishes and requirements of Mrs Spencer, who seemed to be very much aware of Grace's needs and did what she could to help. Over the following days, Mrs Spencer called on Grace to a degree that she had not for some considerable time; they played chess, and with the weather brightening and growing warmer, they took their sketchbooks out into the woodland and onto the heath. They played the piano together also, and sat over their sewing and tapestrywork. And for Grace everything was just another diversion, and she knew that the calls upon her time were for just such a purpose. But she was glad of it. There were times when she wanted nothing but to lie in a dimly lit room and give herself up to her misery, but she did not, and when the aching desires had passed she was glad of the responsibilities of her work.

Billy was so understanding too, and did all he could to alleviate his sister's unhappiness. And she accepted his efforts and was grateful for them, and in a way they helped also. As did Mr Spencer's understanding. He said nothing in so many words to Grace, but he showed – in the little time he was there about the house – that he understood her unhappiness and regretted it and wished her well.

And then came word from Mrs Spencer: she had heard from Mrs Sandiston that Kester Fairman was planning on leaving Birchwood House. Grace knew moments of panic on hearing the news, and doubted the veracity of it. And then came another letter from Kester:

Birchwood House
Upper Callow

Dear Grace,
    I have so much regret that you could not bring it upon yourself to see me. I have so much I could tell you. Though

perhaps nothing of it would persuade you otherwise in your determination.

My purpose now in writing to you, is to tell you that I am leaving the area. I do not wish to compromise you in any way, and also I do not wish to cause you the slightest embarrassment or misgiving – which I am well aware could happen if we were to encounter one another while moving about in the vicinity. Therefore, as I say, I am leaving Birchwood. It is too late to find a school for Sophie this year but I have found a school for her for the new school year in September. In the meantime she will come with me when I leave here this weekend. We will spend a little time on the coast and then she will stay with one of her aunts. She is not happy at the prospect of leaving Upper Callow – or indeed, at losing all opportunity to see her friend Miss Harper – but there is no alternative. For myself, I only want to get away from the area, the scene of so much recent happiness and unhappiness. I cannot ever regret the former, but the latter, which I have brought to you, will be a matter for the deepest remorse for the rest of my life.

Sophie misses you. As do I. I wish you well in your life, and please do not think it presumptuous, but please understand that if ever you need my help you can depend on

Your true friend,

Kester Fairman.

The days passed, in the meadows the buttercups and vetch were in bloom, as on the hillsides were the gorse and broom. In the high grass at the roadside the poppies and the moon daisies stood tall. Grace went from day to day, and became less employed in her duties with Mrs Spencer than before. Now, as the time went on she found herself for a greater part of each day with little or nothing to do. She was available to help Mrs Spencer at any time, but now there simply was insufficient call on her services.

And what was Mrs Spencer doing with her time? Grace wondered. She was sure that her employer was no longer working in her studio at her painting. Nor did she go outside in the fine weather – though there were numerous opportunities – with her sketchbook and pencils. There were no more games of chess, no more backgammon; no more sounds of the piano issued from the drawing room, and the mallets and the rest of the croquet paraphernalia lay forgotten in the box in the garden shed.

On some occasions when Mr Spencer was away on business Grace would be asked to dinner or coffee with Mrs Spencer. But they were not happy, carefree times. On the contrary, there was the strange sadness about her employer that Grace had noticed on occasion before. But now it seemed stronger; now it sat with Mrs Spencer like a shadow. Whether it was brought on by her employer's increased drinking, or was a result of it, Grace did not know. But it was there.

There was no word of Kester Fairman now. Soon after receiving the letter from him, Grace had learned that he and Sophie had left the house and gone away. Where they had gone to, she did not know.

The summer wore on, and Billy, faithful to his earlier interests and loves, found work with a local farmer and helped in the haymaking and then the bringing in of the harvest. And each evening he returned to Asterleigh House suntanned and exhausted, but happy, and Grace longed, for his sake, for his contentment to continue. For herself, in her resignation over Kester, she felt wretched, and the days dragged by with no breath of happiness or joy to distinguish one from another.

October came in with a cold snap and there were cases of influenza reported in the newspapers. When it came to the area of Berron Wick Mrs Spencer was one of the first victims.

And now, finally, Grace felt she was useful again. Mrs Spencer lay in her bed, prostrate, her head pounding and a dry cough hacking at her lungs. Mr Spencer was away and not expected back for two days. At Grace's insistence, Mrs Spencer finally agreed to sending for the doctor, and Jane went with a message for Johnson to ask Dr Ellish from Berron Wick to call at the house.

Dr Ellish turned out to be small and elderly and, where Grace was concerned, with a rather offhand, cold manner. 'Who are you?' he asked as Grace opened the door to meet him on the landing.

Grace hesitated before answering, 'Mrs Spencer's companion.'

'What?' the doctor sniffed as he strode past her into the bedroom. 'She's in need of a companion?'

Ten minutes later, while the doctor was still there, Mr Spencer returned. Being told by the maid that Mrs Spencer was ill, he hurried up the stairs to find his wife with a raging fever and the doctor in attendance.

'How long has she been ill?' he asked Grace, who replied that it had been three days.

Dr Ellish, who had had Mrs Spencer as a patient since her arrival in the area, said it was such a severe case that he feared the infection going to the lungs. That, he said, would be a most serious complication.

Mr Spencer was due to leave again a few days after his arrival but had Rhind go and send off a telegraph to say that he would be detained for a while. He could not, he said, leave while his wife was so sick.

But Mrs Spencer's illness did not pass swiftly. After five days her condition had worsened; there was a marked rise in her temperature, her pulse rate became very rapid, and her breathing sounded painful and difficult in the extreme. A strange dusky red colour came to her lips, cheeks and ears, and Dr Ellish looked at the varied symptoms and nodded. They confirmed his fears: as he had been afraid might happen, a new infection had taken hold; severe bronchial-pneumonia had set in.

For days and nights Mrs Spencer lay prostrate, a steam kettle gently hissing away near her pillow, and throughout it all Grace and Mr Spencer attended at her bedside. Mr Spencer had calls on his time for business in Corster and Redbury, and on those occasions his wife's care was left solely in the hands of Grace.

When Dr Ellish came Grace could tell from his demeanour that he regarded Mrs Spencer's condition as very grave. When he had gone – saying that he would return in the evening – Grace tapped on the bedroom door and, on hearing Mr Spencer's voice telling her to enter, went into the room. She found him sitting at his wife's bedside. He got up and, beckoning to Grace, moved to the other side of the room.

'I don't want my wife to hear,' he said in a whisper as Grace came to stand beside him. 'But I have to tell you that Dr Ellish regards the situation as very serious.'

'Oh, sir,' she said at once, 'I'm sure she'll be all right. We'll give her all the best care we can and –'

'There's so little anyone can do,' he said. 'Her fever is so high – it doesn't seem to go down. And there are no real medicines to fight something like this.'

He turned away, and Grace saw a tremor go through his shoulders. 'Sir,' she said, 'I'll do everything I can to help you.'

'I know you will. I know.'

The next morning Mrs Spencer's fever had abated, and the doctor, calling on her just after eleven, declared that he thought the worst was over and that she was on the way to recovery.

Grace and Mr Spencer took turns in watching over her, and it was clear to both of them that her temperature was down and that she was getting better. All she needed now, Dr Ellish said, was careful nursing and continuing rest.

A further three days and Mrs Spencer's condition had visibly improved even more, and Dr Ellish gave his opinion that she was well out of danger.

Mr Spencer came out of the bedroom after spending some time with his wife and said to Grace that he felt that he might now safely make his long delayed trip to Italy. What did she think? he asked her.

'Of course madam would rather you stayed with her, sir,' she said, 'but I have no doubt that she's going to be all right now. The doctor has every confidence in her situation and she's making headway every day. Anyone can see that.'

So Mr Spencer rapidly made his new arrangements and a day later was ready to go. At 1.30, with Johnson waiting on the forecourt with the carriage to take him to the station, Mr Spencer, dressed for his journey, came from the bedroom down the stairs to Grace who stood in the hall.

'I leave her in your care, Grace.'

'Yes, sir. And don't worry – she'll be all right. I'll take good care of her.'

'I'm sure you will.' He half-turned and glanced up the stairs towards the first floor. 'She's quite calm and peaceful now. I told her I'll be back in just over a week – by which time I shall expect her to be on her feet again.' He gave a grave smile. 'Though Dr Ellish says this is a little too much to hope for after such a serious illness. It'll take a couple of weeks yet, I understand. But the important thing is that she's improving all the time.'

He wished Grace goodbye then, and she watched as he left the house. When the front door had closed behind him, Grace turned and went upstairs.

Tapping lightly on the door, she let herself in and moved quietly to the bed.

'Hello, ma'am.' She came to the bedside and looked down at Mrs Spencer who lay with her upper body propped against the pillows. 'Mr Spencer has just gone.' As she finished speaking there came, as if on cue, the sound of the carriage moving away across the gravel of the forecourt.

Mrs Spencer, also hearing the sound, gave a little nod. 'Yes. But he'll be back in a week or so.'

'Yes, ma'am.'

Mrs Spencer gave a wistful little smile. 'I do so hate it when he goes away, Grace.'

'I know that, ma'am.'

'I'm selfish; I'd like him to stay here all the time, but of course I've always known that wasn't possible.' She sighed. 'I'm afraid we can't always have what we want, can we?' A brief pause, then she added, 'I think you know that as well as I do, Grace.'

Grace said after a moment: 'How are you feeling now, ma'am? Is there something I can get you?'

'Not right now, dear, thank you very much. I just had a little chicken broth – which I didn't really want, but took just to please Edward. He was so insistent. That will be enough for a while.'

'Would you like me to read to you?'

'That would be very nice. Shall we carry on with *The Woodlanders*? Though Mr Hardy can get rather gloomy at times.'

So Grace took up the book she had been reading to her mistress, and continued at the part where they had last left off. She had only been reading for some ten or so minutes, however, when she realized from her mistress's breathing that she was asleep. Letting her voice fade to a gentle murmur and then to cease altogether, Grace softly closed the book and put it aside.

Later that afternoon, with Mrs Spencer awake again and having eaten a little vanilla junket, Dr Ellish returned and remarked at how relieved he was that Mrs Spencer seemed now to be mending well. When he left it was with the words that he would come back in two days, though this, he seemed to imply, was merely a formality; with the right care, Mrs Spencer would have no further real need of him.

That evening Mrs Sandiston prepared a little game soup and set it on a tray with a thin slice of bread and butter. Grace took it up to Mrs Spencer's room, tapped on the door and let herself in.

'Cook's sent you a little treat, ma'am,' Grace said. 'A little soup for you. Help you get your strength back.' She set the tray on a small table to one side. Mrs Spencer still lay propped against the pillows, and Grace moved to help her sit up a little more. 'Would you like a little?'

'No, thank you, Grace,' Mrs Spencer said, 'I don't think I want any.'

'It's Mrs Sandiston's special recipe,' Grace said, and added, smiling, 'You wouldn't want to upset her, would you?'

'Heavens, no, I wouldn't want to do that. I'd better have a little, I suppose.'

So with Grace's help Mrs Spencer ate a little of the soup and a few bites of the bread. Then, moving her head from the offered spoon, she said, 'No more, Grace, thank you. I couldn't manage any more. I'm just not hungry.'

'But you know you have to eat, ma'am. Just a little more – and it'll help you get stronger. You've lost weight over the past days.'

Mrs Spencer leaned her head back on the pillow. 'I just don't want any more. I haven't got any appetite. Maybe later I'll have something.'

Grace set the tray back on the table and resumed her

chair at the bedside. Leaning a little closer to her mistress she said, 'Aren't you feeling too good, ma'am?'

'Not too good, no. Though I shouldn't be surprised, I suppose. Perhaps I was expecting too much.'

'Perhaps so.'

'I don't know, I just feel so – so very weak. I have no energy whatsoever.'

'Hardly surprising, ma'am – you've just come through pneumonia. You were very sick.'

'Yes.' Mrs Spencer nodded. 'I find I've got a bit of a headache too.'

Grace reached out and took Mrs Spencer's wrist and felt for the pulse. Checking it with the clock, she said, 'It's a little fast,' and then touched the back of her hand to the woman's forehead. 'You have a slight fever again. Still, I've no doubt it'll go down again very soon.'

Grace read to Mrs Spencer for a while then, but it was clear that after a few minutes the woman was taking nothing in. 'I think you've had enough of Mr Hardy this evening,' Grace said, and Mrs Spencer gave a little nod and forced a smile.

'Shall I leave you now, then, ma'am?' Grace said.

'Thank you, Grace, I shall be all right. Another good night's sleep, like last night – that's all I need. I'll be as right as rain in the morning, you'll see.'

'You send Jane for me if you need anything, will you?'

'I will, don't worry.'

'Goodnight, ma'am.'

'Goodnight, Grace.'

Grace turned, but was halted briefly by Mrs Spencer's voice.

'And Grace?'

'Yes, ma'am?'

'Thank you – for everything.'

*

343

After Grace had breakfasted in her room the next morning she took her tray down to the kitchen. As she moved back along the rear passage Jane came to her to say that the mistress was not at all well. There was urgency in the girl's voice, and Grace at once went up to the first floor, tapped on the door and entered the room. Jane followed in her steps and came in, closing the door behind her.

The change in Mrs Spencer's appearance was startling. As Grace moved across the room to the bedside she could already see the beads of perspiration standing on the woman's forehead, and see the pale, waxy look about her flesh.

'Ma'am,' Grace said, sitting on the bedside chair, 'how are you this morning? Jane tells me you're not so well again.'

'I don't understand it,' Mrs Spencer said. 'It doesn't make sense. I was doing so well, the doctor said so. He said now it was only a matter of time before I was really well again.'

'And I'm sure it will be.'

'I have this – this nauseous feeling in me now, Grace. All the time, I feel as if I want to be sick.'

Grace turned and caught Jane's eye and the maid moved to the washstand and brought back a basin. Grace took it from her and set it down on the bedside table. 'We're prepared now,' she said. Turning back to Jane, she said, 'I think we'll be all right, Jane. Thank you so much. I'll come and call you if we need anything.'

'Yes, miss.'

When the maid had gone and closed the door behind her, Grace sat and looked at her mistress. The woman's breathing seemed a little laboured, and once again Grace noted the perspiration standing out on her forehead. Mrs Spencer made no murmur as Grace took up her wrist and checked her pulse. It was faster than ever. She could not understand it; everything had been going so well.

And then, suddenly, Mrs Spencer was opening her eyes and sitting bolt upright in the bed, her mouth opening as she retched. Grace snatched at the bowl and held it beneath the woman's chin, her other hand coming to the back of the woman's head. Mrs Spencer brought up a little viscous-looking fluid and then sank down again. Grace got a piece of flannel from the washstand, dipped it in cold water, wrung it out and then gently wiped Mrs Spencer's forehead. The woman gave a little sigh of relief and thanked her. 'I'm sorry to give you all this trouble, Grace,' she said. 'I'm hardly ever ill, and here I am making up for the past, isn't that it?'

'Something like that,' Grace said.

The minutes passed. Mrs Spencer's breathing continued laboured, and still Grace sat at the bedside, her eyes upon her mistress. And after an hour Mrs Spencer was once again retching into the bowl, and Grace was mopping her brow.

'I think I must send for Dr Ellish,' Grace said as Mrs Spencer, exhausted, sank back onto the pillows. 'He'll know what to do; I confess I don't.'

'But he's due to – come back tomorrow anyway,' Mrs Spencer said. 'The poor man is – so busy. Perhaps we should let him have his rest.' Her speech seemed now strangely affected, Grace thought, the words a little slurred and halting.

'Even so,' Grace said, 'I think we should send word to him.'

'No, no – leave it for now. See how I am later on.'

But later on Mrs Spencer's condition had clearly worsened still further and Grace looked down at her with growing horror and dismay. The woman had vomited several times, and now lay with a pounding head and a mounting fever.

'It's no good putting it off, ma'am,' Grace said. 'I'm going to send for Dr Ellish.'

This time Mrs Spencer did not protest. 'W-well, if you think so, m-my dear.'

'Yes, I do. I shall go and see Mr Rhind or Mr Johnson this minute.'

Downstairs, Grace made enquiries and was told that Johnson had left the house on an errand, but that Rhind was in his room over the stables. She quickly made her way there and rapped on his door. He took his time about answering it seemed to her and she was raising her hand to knock again when the door opened and he stood there glowering. Beyond him she could see his room, his bed, the washstand, clothes hanging on hooks, boots side by side under a side table.

'Yes?' he said, making it clear through his tone that he did not care to be interrupted in whatever he was doing.

'I'm sorry to trouble you, Mr Rhind,' Grace said, 'but I have to ask you if you will please go and fetch Dr Ellish again.'

His expression had changed slightly at her words, his usual look of arrogance mixed with contempt being brushed aside by some other expression. Concern? Grace could not tell. 'It's the missis, is it?' he said.

'Yes, it is. Please tell him that she's taken a turn for the worse, and that I don't know what to do.' She added hastily, 'Would you like me to send a letter?'

Witheringly he said, 'No, you don't need to send any letter. I'm perfectly capable of conveying a message.'

'Thank you. I'll tell the mistress you're on your way.' She turned and left him, and made her way back across the yard and into the house again.

Entering the bedroom once more, she found that Mrs Spencer had pulled herself up in the bed and vomited into the bowl, though having eaten so little, there was little that she could bring up. Grace mopped her brow and set the bowl – covered with a cloth – back on the side table. 'I saw

Mr Rhind, ma'am,' Grace said. 'He's going for the doctor right now.'

'Th-thank you.'

Grace laid the folded, damp cloth across the woman's forehead. Mrs Spencer's drooping eyes momentarily brightened and she gave a little smile and a sigh of pleasure. 'Oh, Grace, that is so g-good.'

Jane knocked on the door some forty minutes later to say that Rhind was back. Dr Ellish had not been at home, but Rhind had left the message for him.

Dr Ellish arrived just on five o'clock. As he came up the stairs to the first-floor landing Grace said, 'Oh, Doctor, thank goodness you've come.'

Clearly taking her relief as a comment on the lateness of his call, he said haughtily, 'I got here as quickly as I could, miss. I do have other patients to see to.'

Embarrassed, Grace let this pass, and told him what she could of Mrs Spencer's condition.

In the bedroom he examined Mrs Spencer. Grace, standing by, watched as he took her pulse and temperature. She could see the dismay on his face. After studying his patient for a moment or two in silence, he said, 'You know, this won't do at all, Mrs Spencer. You were doing so well, I thought. And we were sure the worst of your illness was behind you. You were starting to make a good recovery. Now you've made a nonsense of my prognosis.'

He made no comment on the cause of Mrs Spencer's apparent relapse, but merely left instructions with Grace to see that her mistress was tended every minute, that cold compresses should be used to keep down her temperature, and that she should be kept calm. He would, he said, return first thing in the morning.

When the doctor had gone, Mrs Spencer said, 'You'll stay here with me, will you, Grace?'

'Of course, ma'am,' Grace replied. 'I'll get Jane to bring some blankets, so I can make up a bed on the couch.'

'Thank you. I'll be all right come the morning.' Mrs Spencer sighed. 'I wish Edward were here.'

'We can write to him, ma'am, at his hotel in Milan.'

'It would take so long to get there. I shall be well long before he receives it. Best not to disturb him.'

With some sheets and blankets supplied by Jane, Grace made up a bed for herself on the narrow sofa, and eventually, after seeing Mrs Spencer settled as well as she could be, she got into her little bed and tried to sleep. It was a long time before she dozed off, however, and then she did not sleep for long. She was awakened by the sound of Mrs Spencer crying out. Quickly Grace got up from the couch and moved to her mistress's bedside. In the dull glow from the nightlight Mrs Spencer lay tossing, her mouth opening and closing.

Grace pulled on her dressing gown, turned up the wick on the lamp and brought it back to the bed. Setting it on the bedside table, she bent over the sick woman. Now, in the brighter light, she could see the perspiration running down Mrs Spencer's face, and touching her hand felt her skin cold and clammy. Mrs Spencer reacted to the touch and, eyes still closed, turned her face vaguely in Grace's direction.

'E-Edward . . .'

'It's Grace, ma'am. It's Grace.'

'Grace . . .' Mrs Spencer's eyes fluttered open and then closed again.

'Can I get you something, ma'am?'

Mrs Spencer turned her head on the pillow. 'W-we don't need to live th-there,' she muttered.

'Ma'am . . . ?' Grace murmured.

'The house is too big. M-much too big. We don't need a-anything like that. Oh, Edward . . .'

The woman was rambling, and Grace did not know what to do. Glancing at the clock above the fireplace, she could just make out that it was a quarter to five. Dr Ellish had said he would be calling later in the morning. Should she send for him sooner? To Mrs Spencer she said, 'Shall I send for Dr Ellish again, ma'am? What shall I do?'

For a moment Mrs Spencer's eyes fixed on Grace's face in something near concentration, then, her attention wavering again, she tossed her head and said, 'Asterleigh is too b-big. And s-so much work needs to be done to it. The expense. And I was r-r-right. Edward, I was – was right – it's like a bottomless pit. It'll take all the m-money we care to throw at it and s-still want more.'

'Ma'am . . .'

'Y-yes, still want more. You'll have t-to work all hours – and then what will there be to show for it? And even then . . .'

'Ma'am,' Grace said, as the woman's voice trailed off into silence, 'I think I should send for Dr Ellish.'

'Who's that speaking . . .?'

Mrs Spencer opened her eyes now and turned her face to Grace again. 'Grace? Is that you?'

'Yes, ma'am. Shall I send for the doctor?'

'Oh, Grace, I w-wish Edward were here. Is he here? Is he in the house?'

'No, ma'am, Mr Spencer left on Sunday. He's gone to Milan. He won't be back till early next week.'

'Milan? What's he d-doing in Milan?' And then a nod. 'M-Milan, yes, of course. The soap factory.' She looked directly at Grace now, focusing on her. 'The soap factory, Grace. He won it. Can you b-believe it? Mr Spencer won his soap factory – in gambling, when he was a young man.' Her glance swivelled away then, seeming now to gaze at nothing.

'Ma'am – can I get you something?' Panic touched at Grace's heart; she felt helpless and useless.

'You know – you c-could sell that b-business, Edward. Make soap in England.' And now Mrs Spencer had turned her face away again, talking to the shadows at the other side of the bed. 'You c-could sell it, then you wouldn't have to be running around so much. You could spend more of your time here. And if the house is s-so important to you it would suit you better.'

To Grace's consternation Mrs Spencer now seemed to be trying to raise herself up in the bed. Quickly Grace moved to prevent her. 'Lie back, ma'am, please do.'

And then the woman's eyes fluttered and closed. 'Oh, Edward, sometimes you can be so sweet,' she sighed, 'but at other times I'm not enough for you. I know I'm not.' She lay back on the pillows, a tear running down her cheek.

Grace took Mrs Spencer's cold hand in her own and felt for the pulse. It seemed even more rapid than before. The woman had lapsed into silence again, and Grace sat there as the minutes dragged by, waiting for daylight and the sound of the doctor's carriage on the forecourt.

Dr Ellish came into the house just after nine. He entered the room and strode quietly to the bed. He took Mrs Spencer's pulse and temperature and stood there in grave silence. Grace knew that Mrs Spencer's temperature was down, but her pulse rate was up, galloping. She looked at the doctor as the seconds ran one into another. Eventually, plucking up all her courage, she said:

'Sir – sir, if you should wish to call in anyone else, we can get the groom to ride off with a message. He'd go at once.' Then, realizing that she might have gone too far, she said, 'What I mean, is . . .'

As her words trailed off, the doctor was turning his head slowly to her. 'If I should wish to call in anyone else? And who would this anyone else be, may I ask? Did you perhaps mean another medical doctor?'

Grace, remaining silent, turned from his furious, withering gaze.

'I think you need have no worries, miss,' the doctor said in a low voice. 'If I thought for a moment that a second opinion was required I would do something about it. It most certainly would not be a matter for discussion with you.' He held up a hand. 'But no more. We have a sick person here. One who needs your attention.' He picked up his bag and started across the room. At the doorway he turned and said, 'I shall be back in an hour. I'll bring a little laudanum to help with the fever. In the meantime, make her a little tea, and try to get her to eat something. A little soup, perhaps, or some bread-and-milk.'

When the doctor returned an hour later he found Mrs Spencer writhing in the bed, plucking spasmodically at the sheets while her eyes rolled in her head and unintelligible words stammered from between her dry lips. The doctor was able to do nothing for her, and fifteen minutes later she was dead.

Chapter Seventeen

On a cold and damp November afternoon, Grace and Billy stood side by side at Mrs Spencer's grave in the yard of the local church. The newly erected stone at the grave's head bore the simple legend:

DEARLY BELOVED
SACRED TO THE MEMORY OF
ELEANOR ALICE SPENCER
2 MARCH 1837 – 31 OCTOBER 1888

It was a Saturday, there was no one else about, and the place was silent. Billy carried flowers, chrysanthemums from the gardens of Asterleigh House, kindly cut by the gardener. The flowers left on the grave at the time of the funeral were dying, and Billy stood silently by while Grace discarded them and refilled a pot with fresh water. When the new flowers were in place she straightened and bowed her head and said a silent little prayer. At her side, Billy did the same. Afterwards he opened his eyes, turned to Grace and said:

'She was so nice to me, Grace.'

'Well, she liked you.'

'She gave me her second-best watercolour set.'

'I know she did. She admired your talent, too.'

'And she gave me pocket money.'

'She was a very kind lady.'

Grace bent and adjusted one of the blossoms in the pot,

then, straightening, said with a sigh, 'Well, I don't know how much longer we shall be able to come here.'

'What d'you mean?' Billy said.

She didn't answer his question, but took from her pocket a sealed envelope. 'We must go back by way of the letter-box,' she said. 'I have this to post.'

They made their way out of the churchyard and set off along the lane to where the post box was set in the churchyard wall. Billy held out his hand and Grace gave him the letter and he ran off and slipped the letter into the slot.

'I've written away for a position,' she said when he returned to her side.

Throughout the autumn days since Mrs Spencer's death, Grace had pored over the classified advertisements in the newspapers searching for a suitable post. Ideally, as she had wished before, she would have liked a resident position where she could also take Billy, but she knew that such a place was an impossibility. The next best thing would be to find one where she would be employed on a daily, visiting basis, and find rooms for Billy and herself somewhere not too far away from her place of employment.

Now Billy was looking at her in surprise. 'To go and work somewhere else?'

'Yes.' They walked on along the lane, back in the direction of Asterleigh House.

'But – but why should you want to do that?' Billy said.

'Because I no longer have a job here. My job was as companion to Mrs Spencer. But now that she's gone . . .'

'Did Mr Spencer say you have to get another job?'

'No, he's hardly ever there, and when he is he's so busy, anyway, what with one thing and another. He's so distracted – he probably doesn't even notice that we're around half the time. But it can't continue like it.'

'You could ask him.'

'No, no. You must realize, I've been paid some of my wages in advance but after that I can't go and ask for more. Ask for more for doing what? It's all right for you, you're going to school and working at your lessons, but I don't have any work to do. Oh, I find things to keep me occupied, but it's not what I'm paid to do.'

'But Grace – if you get a new position it'll mean we have to leave the house.'

Grace was silent at this.

'Oh, Grace,' he said, 'don't say we have to leave Asterleigh. If we leave we might have to go and live in that place where all the bugs were in the bedding and –'

'No,' Grace said sharply, 'we shan't be going back there, have no fear of that.'

'Or some place even worse, perhaps.'

'I won't allow it.'

'I don't want to go away from here, Grace.'

'We haven't got a choice, Billy.'

He said nothing to this and, turning, she saw that tears had filled his eyes. She stopped in the middle of the lane, put out her arms and drew him to her. 'Oh, Billy, don't cry. Please don't cry.'

'Grace, we don't have to move again, do we? I like it so much at Asterleigh. Everyone is nice to me. And at school, too. Oh, Grace –' he turned to her now with a pleading look, 'I'll work really hard, I promise I will. I really will. I'll do better at school, and I'll help in the house more and the stables. I shall –'

'It's not a matter of your having to do better; you're doing very well. Everyone thinks so. It's just that – we can't stay here.'

'But I shall have to find a new school.'

'Please don't cry, Billy.'

'I – I'm sorry. I'm being silly.'

'No, you're not. I understand how you feel.'

After a while his tears dried. He took Grace's hand, and together they walked back to Asterleigh House.

A few days afterwards Grace saw Mr Spencer – which was not a frequent occurrence given his busy schedule. She was in the library when he came into the room, clearly not expecting anyone to be there. Following the funeral he had kept away from almost everyone. Further, he had been away from the house so much. Standing at the shelves with a book and a duster in her hand, she turned at the sound of the door opening and saw his tall figure enter the room. It was three weeks after the funeral.

'Mr Spencer, good morning.'

He looked around at the sound of her voice. 'Hello, Grace . . . I just came in for a book. I won't disturb you for long.' He moved to one of the shelves and took down a small volume. Turning back to her, he registered the duster in her hand, and said, 'What are you doing?'

'Oh, I'm just – trying to make myself useful. As well I can.'

'You're dusting books?' His tone was a little incredulous.

'Well – Jane and Annie have enough to do between them. And it has to be done.'

'I suppose it does. But I didn't expect to see you doing it.'

'I have to do something, sir.'

He nodded. 'No doubt.' He stood there in silence for a moment, as if considering the situation, then said, 'I suppose many things around here have changed now.'

Grace said nothing, and at a loss, put the book on the shelf and took down another one. And almost at once Mr Spencer said with an irritable wave of his hand, 'Oh, Grace, put the books down for a moment, please.'

She did so, and stood there, silent.

'I'm sorry,' he said. 'It's just that – oh, I can't stand all the – the changes that have taken place. Everything is so

355

different in so many ways. Now that my wife is gone I – oh, I don't know – it's just all so different.' He turned his face away and stepped to the window overlooking the fore-court. 'I miss her so,' he added gruffly.

Grace nodded.

'I can't describe it,' he added after a moment. 'She was always here. We came into this house together. We first set foot in it together. Not that long ago. But long enough for her to make her mark, to be a part of the whole place.' He turned to face her. 'She was a lady, Grace. She had no title, but she was a lady, through and through.'

'There's no doubt about that, sir.'

'No. And thank you.' He shook his head. 'It's not the same without her, I don't mind saying.' He looked from Grace's face to the feather duster she had put down on the shelf beside her. 'And here you are dusting books in the library, because you can't find anything better to do.'

'As I said, sir – I must do something.'

'Yes. What is the good of being a companion, if there's no one to be a companion to? – is that it?'

'Something like that.'

'Yes. But you were not meant to be a lady's companion at any rate, were you? Not that you didn't do your work very well, I'm sure. With your intelligence you're much more suited to being a governess. You wouldn't want to go as companion to any other woman, would you? I'm sure it must be a tedious job, and have few rewards. I'm never sure of a companion's place in the hierarchy of a household. Perhaps something akin to that of a governess. It's commonly said that they're between places – neither a part of the family, nor one of the servants. Have you had difficulties like that?'

'I can't say I have, sir.'

'Well, that's all to the good, then. Though I don't doubt it can be hard at times, being a companion. And particularly to some women. Always having to be agreeable, so many times having to bite your tongue, never to have a contrary opinion.'

'If I may say so, sir, it was always very easy being with Mrs Spencer.'

'Was it?' He put his head a little on one side, considering her. 'Was it really?'

'Yes. I think we had a – a good understanding.'

He nodded. 'Doubtless you did. I know that my wife could have her difficult side at times, but get past that and you saw the real person there. Which was what you no doubt did. Well, she liked you, Grace, I know that much. And my wife thought a great deal of your brother too.'

Grace smiled. 'Yes, sir, I know. She was very kind to him. Very kind. And he misses her too.'

'Mmm. And Billy hasn't had the easiest time of it, has he?'

'He's been a lot happier over recent months, sir – apart from the – the loss of Mrs Spencer. Since coming here he's been getting on well at school, and he's made friends in the area. It's done so much for his self-confidence. And Mrs Spencer – she helped him.'

'That pleases me,' he said with a little smile. 'And it would have pleased my wife too, to hear you say such a thing.' He gestured towards the duster. 'Though I doubt she'd be pleased to see you doing this work.'

'I often did work like this, sir, when the mistress was alive. Mrs Spencer didn't always want help from me. I don't like to be idle, and it's a big house to care for.'

'I know that.' He looked off into the distance beyond the window.

Grace said after a moment: 'I'm looking for a new position, sir, though I don't suppose that will come as any surprise to you.'

He turned to her. 'Well, it shouldn't, should it? As I said

357

just now, how can you be a companion if there's no one to be a companion to? What have you done about it – going after a new situation?'

'I've been answering advertisements in the papers.'

'And have you had any promising responses yet?'

'Not yet, sir, but it's early days.'

'What are you going for? A governess, I presume.'

'Yes, sir.'

'Of course.' A brief pause. 'It's a shame you lost your little pupil, Mr Fairman's daughter.'

Grace turned her face away, and he quickly added: 'But that's not something you wish to be reminded of, I know. I never had a chance to say it before, but let me say now that I'm very sorry things happened there in the way they did. Have you heard anything of Mr Fairman and his daughter?'

'No, sir.'

'No word at all? No, I haven't either. But there you are – that's the way things go sometimes – sad to say.' He sighed. 'But anyway, that's all in the past. What is pressing for the present,' he said, 'is that you have to find some employment you'll enjoy. Unfortunately I don't know how I can help you.'

'I shall manage, sir, somehow. I don't have any choice.'

'How does Billy feel about it, the likelihood of your leaving?'

'He's not happy about it. He loves it here. He has his school nearby, his friends. He has his own room here in the house.' She smiled. 'He never had such a room before.'

'He helps out too, I know – in the stables and the scullery, when he can.' He smiled. 'He's like you, Grace – he doesn't like to be idle.' He hesitated a moment longer, then moved back to the door. 'Well, I'll leave you to your work – whatever you choose to do.' In the doorway he turned. 'But please bear in mind – that you don't have to go. I'm sure we can find a way.'

When he had gone, closing the door behind him, Grace thought back on his words. It would be so good to be able to stay on in the house, she thought. Not to have to uproot Billy from all that he had become familiar with. But what alternative did they have?

On a Saturday just before Christmas Grace achieved positive results from her endeavours and found employment with a family in Little Berron, less than three miles from Berron Wick. Her employment was to begin early in the new year.

At Asterleigh House she told Billy of her success – which she had learned of that morning by letter.

'Grace, I don't want to leave here,' he said.

'I know you don't. But we don't always have choices. We can't stay on when I have no work to do here.'

Billy remained silent. She had come upon him in the stable yard as he came back from the woodland beyond the paddock. Over his shoulder he carried a sack containing bits of dead wood, kindling for the kitchen stove and copper.

'Billy,' she said, 'try to understand, will you? If we could stay I would love it, for your sake. But as things are we just can't.'

He nodded and sighed. 'All right. But it won't be till after Christmas, will it?'

'No.'

He nodded. 'Good.' A little pause, then he added, 'I'm sorry for making a fuss, Grace.' He hitched the sack more securely in place and turned away. 'I have to put this stuff in the stables so it'll dry out.'

In the house Grace made her way to the drawing room and tapped on the door. Mr Spencer's voice called for her to enter, and she pushed open the door and went in.

He had been in the house for most of the week and, so

Mrs Sandiston said, was to remain there over Christmas. Grace found him sitting by the crackling fire, some papers spread out on the low table at his side. The smell of pipe tobacco hung in the air. He looked up and smiled as she came into the room.

'Grace, hello. To what do I owe this pleasure?'

'Do you have a moment, sir?'

'Of course I do.' He set down the paper in his hand. 'Come in and sit down.' He gestured to the sofa, the place where Mrs Spencer had been wont to sit. Grace sat down.

'I won't keep you but a minute, sir,' she said. 'It's just that I've had a satisfactory response to one of my applications.'

'So you're going off as governess somewhere, are you?'

She nodded. 'I've been offered a place in Little Berron.'

'I see. Well, that's not too far away. What sort of a job is it? Whose brat are you to teach? Or are there more than one?'

'There are two children, sir. A boy of seven and a girl of eight. Adam and Frances Kellas. They're the children of Mr Kellas, a barrister.'

'I've heard of him. And I believe he has a fine house. Well, barristers are wealthy men, so I hope he's paying you well, is he?' He waved a hand. 'Don't answer that; it's none of my business.'

'I'm happy to tell you if you like, sir.'

'I just told you, it's none of my business. Have you met the children?'

'Yes, I have – when I went for my interview with Mr Kellas.'

'And are they misbehaving monsters?'

Grace shook her head and smiled. 'No, sir. They are – spirited children, but they seem no worse than others of their age. I'm sure we shall get along perfectly fine.'

'That's something, then. So, what does this mean?'

'What does it mean?'

'Yes. I mean, so what are your immediate plans?'

'I'm due to begin work in the new year – as soon as the Christmas school holidays are over.'

'And?'

'So –' she shrugged. 'So I must look around for rooms for the two of us.'

He nodded, picked up his pipe, leaned closer to the fireplace and tapped the bowl against the side of the coal scuttle. Then he took tobacco from a pouch and packed it into the bowl. He looked into the packed bowl, pressed the tobacco down with his forefinger, then said, 'Of course you don't need to go anywhere, you know.'

'Sir – ?'

'I mean to say, why the devil can't you stay where you are? Why on earth d'you need to go scampering off like this?'

'But – but sir, I have no place here.'

'Of course you have a place here. And Billy has a place here.' He looked again at the pipe in his hand and then set it down on the papers on the table. 'Tell me,' he said, 'why don't you have a place here?'

'Well, as you said yourself, how can I be a companion if there is no one to be a companion to? I'm redundant in the very truest way.' She spread her hands, palms up. 'What else can I do, sir? I have to find employment and accommodation elsewhere. We spoke about this some weeks ago.'

He nodded. 'And since that time I've been thinking more about the situation. And now, now that you've brought the matter to a head, so to speak, you're concentrating my mind. And I've come up with a solution. And I have to ask, why in the devil's name do you have to go and find rooms somewhere else in order to teach a pair of children? Why on earth to do you have to tear your young brother away from all the security he knows in order to stick him in some ghastly rented room? Will he be able to keep on at Culvercombe school?'

'I don't know, sir. It depends on where I find rooms for us.'

'Well, there you are – you might have to take him out of his school and send him off to a different one where everything and everyone will be strange to him. Is that what you want?'

Grace said, 'No, but if there's no way around such an arrangement . . .'

'What if there is? Why on earth can't you stay here. You have clean rooms, good food, you have –'

Grace broke in: 'Sir, you don't need to remind me of all the good things and the advantages at Asterleigh. But we can't stay, we simply can't. Not while I'm working some-where else.'

'I should have realized, of course. You've got your pride, haven't you? You've always had your pride.'

Grace said nothing.

'Well, I'll tell you what,' he said, 'and don't give me an answer right away. But think about it and then let me know your conclusion. Supposing – supposing you pay me rent? How would that be?'

'Rent, sir?'

'Rent. You've heard of rent – payment for the use of property. Say a shilling a week? How would that be?'

When Grace said nothing, he added, 'And if Billy cares to, he can continue helping out as he does now.'

'And that would –'

'That would allow you and Billy to remain here, and keep your pride as well.' He paused. 'And if you wonder why I'm suggesting such a thing, it's because, for one thing, you cared for my wife in her illness. Indeed, you cared for her throughout the time you were here. I know that much. Also, I can't bear the thought of you both going into some squalid lodgings as you did before you came here. And besides which, having you stay here – it's what Eleanor would have wanted. It's what she would have done. She would want an arrangement like this. Except that she wouldn't allow you to pay rent. But I'm quite sure that if I don't agree to such an arrangement as that then I can't see you accepting.'

Grace frowned, opened her mouth to speak again, but he cut in. 'Don't give me a negative answer now,' he said. 'Save your answer for later, once you've had a chance to think it over. But think about it carefully. If you have sense – which I don't doubt you have – you'll agree it's the best thing for both of you.'

Upstairs, she went to Billy's room. Finding it empty, she left a note for him and went to her own room along the landing.

He came to her a little under an hour later, freshly washed and changed from his work in the yard.

'I've been to see Mr Spencer,' Grace said to him. He sat on a small footstool near the bed. 'I told him that I've been offered a position in Little Berron.'

Billy hung his head. 'I've been thinking,' he said. 'I can still go to school in Culvercombe if we live in Little Berron.'

'But it's miles. Besides, we might not find rooms in Little Berron. It might be further out.'

'I shall manage.'

She hesitated for a moment, then said, 'Well – anyway – it might not be necessary.'

'What d'you mean?'

'I just told you that I went to see Mr Spencer, and – he told me that we might stay.'

'We can stay? He said so?'

'He's suggested an arrangement whereby I pay him rent. That way we wouldn't be accepting his charity.'

Billy waited a moment then said, 'What did you tell him?'

'I haven't told him anything yet. He didn't want my answer right away. He asked me to think about it. So –' she shrugged, 'I thought we'd best talk it over before I give him an answer.'

'What do you think, Grace? Please say yes. Tell him yes, will you?'

'I know that's what you'd like.'

'It would be so much better. We could keep our nice rooms, and there wouldn't be any question of my changing schools.'

'He said if we stay you could continue to help out around the stables and in the gardens. How does that sound?'

'Does that mean we can stay?' he said.

She smiled. 'If you want it so much.'

Later that day Grace went to see Mr Spencer, and told him that she was pleased to accept his offer of continuing accommodation for herself and Billy.

'What a wise decision,' he said.

In the second week of December Grace received a Christmas greeting card addressed in a child's round, careful handwriting. There was no return address on the card or the envelope. The card bore a picture of robins and holly, with snow falling against a frosty window. The message said:

Dear Miss Harper,

I am writing to wish you and Billy a very merry Christmas and happy new year. Papa and I are well, and hope you are too. I am going to school now, here in Redbury, and I quite like it, though I wish you were still my teacher. With love and best wishes from
Sophie
ps: I hope you still remember me.

Oh, Sophie, Grace silently cried as she pressed the card to her heart – how could I forget you?

In spite of the lingering sadness over Mrs Spencer's death and the ending of Grace's association with Kester Fairman, she looked upon that Christmas at Asterleigh as a relatively happy affair. With the matter of their living quarters decided, at least for the time being, she could see Billy relaxing in the knowledge that he need have no worry about having to move on. Even so, Grace still harboured some vague feelings of uncertainty. A part of her mind still placed so much value on her independence, and she sometimes told herself that perhaps it would have been better had she obeyed her instincts and found furnished rooms for herself and her brother. That way she would maintain her independence and be beholden to no one. But she had made the decision to remain where they were, and for Billy's sake if for nothing else for the time being the decision would stand.

In January Grace began her work teaching Mr Kellas's children.

The Kellas family lived in an attractive, rambling red brick house on the edge of Little Berron, with views over woodland and the distant ford. Mr Kellas was a serious man with a grave demeanour – essential to him in his work, Grace assumed – while his wife was jolly and outgoing. While Mr Kellas was ordered, neat and meticulous, Mrs Kellas was carefree and casual. To Grace the house seemed always to be in disorder; no matter how much the maid swept and tidied, in no time at all the muddles would begin to form again. At times Grace wondered how the husband and wife could always be in agreement with one another, but they seemed to be so, and always behaved affectionately to one another. Their two children, Adam and Frances, seemed to follow in their parents' characters, the boy like his father, the girl like her mother, but whereas the parents produced harmony together, the children were frequently at odds. Still, they were well-behaved children in the main, and Grace was pleased to teach them. She knew, however, that it would not be for long, for already there was talk of their going to school in a year or two.

In the meantime, though, Grace enjoyed her work. On short, cold winter's days she travelled sometimes by coach and sometimes by omnibus. On warmer days, however, she took advantage of the good weather and walked. The exercise was good for her, she reasoned, added to which, she saved on the fares.

And the days and weeks went by, and the winter-cold branches eventually sprang their buds and blossomed, and the birds sang and the foxes took up their strange crying and the trees took on their full canopies. Spring was there, bright, and lush and green.

As the weeks passed, and spring gave way to summer, during the long summer holidays from school Billy spent hours working in the gardens and the stables. Grace's holidays were not so long, for the Kellases required her to teach their children throughout the summer all but for three weeks in July and August when the family went to the coast.

Generally, for Grace, it was an uneventful time, and the weeks followed one after the other with little to mark them as remarkable in any way.

But then in the autumn she heard the first breath of gossip.

On a Saturday late in November the maid, Jane, was leaving. By the time she was ready to make her departure, just after eleven, her replacement, Effie, had already arrived, preparing to take up her duties. Grace did not know the details of Jane's dissatisfaction with her position; she was only aware that it was a factor in her leaving.

According to Annie, the kitchen maid, there had been a disagreement between Jane and Mrs Sandiston, and Jane, hard to please at the best of times, had given notice. Now, this Saturday morning, with her hat and cape on, she swung out of the kitchen for the last time. Grace stepped into the rear passage just as Jane emerged, and moved to her.

'Oh, Jane,' Grace said, 'I was hoping to catch you before you left.'

Jane turned to her. 'I've only got a minute.'

Her manner was sullen, and Grace, taking in the redness about her small eyes, thought that she might have been crying.

'I came to say goodbye and to wish you luck,' Grace said.

Jane put her head on one side for a moment as if studying her, then said with an ostentatious tone of gratitude, 'Well, how very kind of you. How very nice of you to spare the time to come and see me off.'

Her tone took Grace by surprise. She could see hostility in the girl's face. 'Jane, I mean it,' she said, ' – I came down to wish you good luck for the future.'

'What does my luck matter to you?' Jane said. 'You never cared a fig about my feelings since the moment you got here. If you'd only tell the truth you'd say you're glad I'm going.'

'Jane, that isn't so at all. How can you say such a thing?'

'How can I say such a thing? Oh, Miss Sweetness – listen to her, like butter wouldn't melt in her mouth.'

'Jane,' Grace said evenly, 'I don't want us to quarrel. Can't we part as friends?' With her last words she tentatively put out her hand.

Jane looked at the hand and curled her lip. 'I'm not going to shake your hand just to make you feel good,' she said. 'That's what you'd like, isn't it? Well, you're going to be disappointed. It was never the same for me after you

367

arrived.' She shook her head, lips compressed, as if she had difficulty forming the words she wished to speak, then she spat out: 'I used to do Mrs Spencer's hair before you came.' Roughly she brushed past Grace and flounced to the door, then, reaching it, she turned and took a step back to stand before Grace again. 'Companion,' she sneered. 'People like you – governesses, companions, you think you're such a cut above the rest, don't you? But you're no better than the rest of us. You're only a servant, after all. Companion, huh. What I'd like to know is, if you're a companion, what are you doing here now? Mrs Spencer's dead. She've got no need of a companion any more.' She paused. 'Unless it's not *Mrs* Spencer you're companion to.'

With her final words she swung about, moved back to the door and stormed out into the yard and away.

Grace stood with white face, her lips pale. She heard a sound, and, turning, saw Mrs Sandiston standing in the kitchen doorway, wiping her hands on her apron. Grace put her hands to her face. Mrs Sandiston stepped forward.

'I wouldn't worry about that,' she said. 'She's not a happy young woman. And I'm afraid you put her nose out of joint. Put it down to that.'

Grace couldn't speak. Lowering her eyes, she gave a shake of her head, and murmuring, 'Excuse me,' hurried along the passage and up to her room.

An hour later Grace was in her room when she saw Mr Spencer draw up in his carriage in the stable yard. In seconds she was through the door and starting down the stairs.

'Mr Spencer . . .' She called to him as she saw him moving towards the stairs.

He stopped as she came towards him. 'Is it important, Grace? I have to go out again soon.' He had his coat on and carried his hat.

'Please – it'll only take a minute.'

He nodded, stayed there waiting, but Grace said, 'Oh – not here, sir, if you don't mind.'

'Fine.' He turned and stepped towards the drawing room and opened the door. 'Please . . .' He held the door open and Grace stepped through. He followed her and closed the door behind them.

'Would you like to sit down?' he said.

'No, thank you.' Wasting no time, she said, 'Sir – I thank you so much for allowing Billy and me to stay here over the past year . . .' She came to a halt. He waited a second then said, prompting her:

'Yes? Go on.'

'I – I'm sorry if I sound ungrateful, sir, but – but I shall have to look around for other accommodation for us.'

'What on earth for?' He looked astonished.

'Well, I . . .' Her voice trailed off.

'What for? Tell me. Are you leaving your position in Little Berron?'

'No, it's not that.'

'Then, what?'

She shook her head. 'Oh – I don't want to go into it. Can't we just say that I have to leave – with great gratitude for everything, I hasten to add – but nevertheless I have to leave.'

'No, we can't just say that. I want to know why.'

She gave a little groan. 'Sir – please, I –'

'Tell me,' he said.

'I saw Jane a little while ago . . .'

'Ah, yes, Jane – I understand she gave in her notice. Has she left?'

'An hour ago.'

He shrugged. 'Well, I doubt her absence will be that much mourned. If Mrs Sandiston's opinion is anything to go by, she was more trouble than she was worth. Anyway, what's she got to do with anything?'

'Mr Spencer – I really don't want to go into this . . .'

'I don't think you've got much choice. Just tell me what it is – or I shall begin to imagine all kinds of dreadful things.'

'It *is* – dreadful.'

'Oh?' He frowned deeply. 'Come,' he said, 'tell me now.'

Unable to meet his eyes, Grace said, her gaze in the direction of the window, 'Jane made a comment to me just before she left . . .'

'Yes . . .?'

'Yes – and she made the implication that – this is very difficult for me – the implication that there is – is more to my relationship with you than there actually is.'

'Are you serious?' His frown was heavy as thunder. 'What did she actually say?'

'It isn't so much what she said, sir – it was her clear implication. She made it very clear that she thought there was some relationship between us. Other than what there is.'

He was silent for a moment, then he said, 'Do you think she truly believed it?'

'I'm not sure about that, sir – she may simply have been trying to hurt me – to score a point – but it's obvious that the thought has gone through her mind.' Then, seeing nothing else for it, she told him what Jane had said.

'I see,' he said. 'And now what is going to happen?'

'Well – I see nothing for it but to leave, sir. I can't stay on here if there is this kind of gossip starting.'

'I could say, of course, what does gossip matter if there's nothing in it? – but we all know that it can do great harm.' He took out his watch, looked at it and put it back. 'I'm sorry, Grace, but I just have to go. I have to rush out again. Can we talk about this later?'

'Of course, sir, but –'

'We'll talk about it later.' He was already moving back to the door. 'I'll send you word tomorrow. We can talk then.'

In the afternoon of the following day, the new maid, Effie, came to Grace's room with a message asking if she would go and see Mr Spencer in the conservatory in half an hour.

At the appointed time Grace left her room and went downstairs. Entering the conservatory she found Mr Spencer standing looking out over the rear garden. 'Ah, Grace,' he said, turning at the sound of her step. He moved towards her. 'Would like some tea? I can send for some.'

'Not for me, thank you, sir. I had some not long ago.'

'Right.' He nodded. 'Sit down, please.' He gestured to the wicker sofa and when Grace was seated took the chair facing her. 'Thank you for coming down,' he said.

Grace smiled, but said nothing. He looked around him. The varied fragrances of the plants were in the air. 'My wife loved this part of the house,' he said. 'All these plants.' He gave a deep sigh. 'Life has to continue, doesn't it? Sometimes we have no idea how, but it does.'

There was a silence for several moments. Then Mr Spencer leaned forward, his forearms on his knees, his hands clasped.

'I have to talk to you,' he said.

Grace said nothing, waited.

'I was distressed to hear what you had to tell me yesterday,' he said. 'That foolish, coarse girl. How dare she speak to you like that? Well – good riddance.'

His eyes burned into her own, his gaze seeming to search her face – for answers to which there had been no questions. 'I have to talk to you,' he said again. He reached out his right hand, took her left hand and drew it towards him. Then, clasping her hand between his own, he said, 'Grace, I want to marry you.'

Silence. For a moment Grace thought she had not heard correctly. But he was holding her hand, and leaning urgently towards her.

'Grace – you heard what I said.'

She nodded. 'Yes.' She merely breathed the word.

'This business with Jane – her saying that stupid, cruel thing – it was awful for you – though at the same time it has made it possible for me to say what I want to say. She's forced my hand, so to speak. I suppose I should be grateful to her, in a way.'

'Sir –' She began to withdraw her hands, but with the slightest pressure he renewed his hold on her.

'Please – let me tell you,' he said. 'Your telling me what you have heard and that you might have to leave – it gives me no choice now but to speak out. If I don't then you'll go away and I shall never have the opportunity – and I shall have lost something very precious to me.'

'Mr Spencer –'

'No, no – not *Mr Spencer* – *Edward*, you must call me *Edward*.'

'Sir – please . . .'

'Edward.'

She shook her head. 'I – I cannot.'

He paused. 'As you wish.' He released the pressure on her hand and she withdrew it and sat back, holding herself upright in the chair.

'You look as if you're poised for flight,' he said. 'Relax, Grace, please.'

'Relax,' she said with irony in her voice, '– oh, you've made it impossible for me to relax.'

'I'm sorry. I know it's come right out of the blue. You obviously had no idea of how I feel. How could you?'

She said nothing.

'My wife,' he said, ' – God rest her soul – has been gone over a year now, and – oh, Grace, I cannot deny love if it comes to me. You do understand, don't you?'

'Yes.'

'How could I? We have no say as to how love comes, and who it touches, and when. Or do you think we do?'

'No.'

'No, we do not.'

Silence fell. Grace did not know where to look. She could not look him in the face, and at the same time she felt self-conscious looking elsewhere in the room. A few moments more and then he said:

'I meant what I said just now. I want to marry you.' A pause. 'I love you, Grace. I love you. It's as simple as that.'

She raised her head now, turning to look at him, trying to find words to say, but he held his hand up, palm towards her. 'Don't say anything right now, as I fear I might not like what I hear. Please – just think about it. I might just add that neither you nor young Billy will want for anything – anything at all. This house will become your home – your real home.' He lowered his hand. 'But enough for now. It's too much for you to take in, I'm sure. I'll ask you at a later time for your answer.' He stirred in the chair. 'I shall let you go back to your work now. But please think on what I've said this afternoon.'

Grace got to her feet, and he stood up also. She gave him a brief nod, and then turned and walked away.

In her room she lay back on her bed, thinking of what had passed.

This house will become your home, he had said. Your real home. Neither you nor Billy will want for anything – anything at all.

The words had brought almost a sense of relief. Not for herself; she wanted nothing for herself. But for Billy. For Billy she wanted everything that was good. And to see him with a settled home, security, never the fear of wanting – was there anything more that she could ask?

373

And she had no doubt that Edward Spencer would be true to his word.

But she did not love him.

Such thoughts were still going through her mind a week later when she and Billy were walking in the grounds of Asterleigh House.

The sun was bright, but there was a strong breeze. On that Sunday after church Grace had called to Billy, and together they walked through the gardens down to the orchard. The trees were bare. As they walked beneath the leafless branches she thought of that earlier time, that summer, when she and Kester had walked beneath the apple boughs.

She must come to a decision. Jane's words still rang in her ears, and she constantly asked herself whether the implication had been voiced elsewhere. But the fact that Jane had uttered it was enough, and Grace could feel her cheeks burn with shame simply at the memory.

So, she must leave. She must find another home for Billy and herself.

And then again the words of Edward Spencer came back to her. His proposal of marriage. And again she was torn.

'Grace, look at me.'

The words, interrupting her thoughts, came from Billy as he sat in the fork of a gnarled old apple tree.

'You be careful you don't fall,' she said, moving forward and looking up at him. She would have much preferred that he did not do such things, do anything that might endanger him, but she could not forbid him such pleasures. The more physical things he could do like other children and the more risks he could take, then the less his consciousness of his disability.

'I shan't fall,' he said. 'I've climbed up here hundreds of times.'

'Have you now? Well, don't cause any damage to the tree.'

'I shan't. Mr Spencer knows I climb them.'

And then another voice came, saying, 'Yes, indeed he does,' and, turning, Grace saw Edward Spencer moving towards them through the trees.

'And he can do no harm,' the man added as he came to a stop a few feet from Grace's side. 'Particularly in that tree – the poor thing's too old to bear fruit and is half-rotten.' He looked from Billy to Grace. 'I saw you from the window, heading in this direction, and thought this might be a good time to catch you, and perhaps talk to you further.'

Grace guessed what was coming, but could say nothing. She flicked a glance between Edward Spencer and Billy. Mr Spencer said:

'Perhaps we can leave Billy to his climbing and take a stroll.' He looked up at Billy. 'Is that all right with you, sir? Shall we leave you to your monkey business for a while?'

Billy gave a whoop of joy. 'Yes! I shall climb all the trees!'

'Well, just you be careful,' Mr Spencer said.

'I will, sir.'

'We don't want any broken necks.'

'I'm going to build a den in the summer,' Billy said. 'I could build it in the copse.' He pointed off. 'Would that be all right?'

'Of course it would be all right.'

'If you like I could show you the spot where I'm going to build. Shall I?'

'In a while, perhaps. Right now I want to talk to your sister.' Edward Spencer smiled at Billy then turned to Grace.

'Can we walk a little . . .?'

He stepped away as he spoke, and Grace nodded and fell in step beside him. When they were out of earshot of Billy, Mr Spencer said:

'I have to ask if you've given thought to my question to you. Have you?'

Grace hesitated, then said, 'Yes,' though knowing that even as she spoke she was no nearer an answer.

'I meant everything I said,' he murmured, not looking at her but looking ahead. They walked very slowly. From behind them they heard Billy give a little yelp of pleasure as he continued in his games. Mr Spencer said, 'I do realize that you may not love me.' Then he added quickly: 'That you do not love me. I should think that would be closer to the truth.' He came to a stop, and Grace halted at his side. 'But you could love me in time,' he said. 'I know you could.'

A wind had grown stronger and up beyond his head the dark apple boughs moved and sighed. 'Tell me you'll marry me, Grace,' he said. 'It would make me so happy. And I swear to you that you'll never regret it. All I ask is that you give me a chance.' He paused. 'Can you give me an answer, Grace? The answer I need?'

Before Grace could say anything in reply, there came a loud cry from over to her right, from where they had just come.

'Billy,' she gasped, and, gathering up her skirts, turned and ran. Edward Spencer, starting just a second behind her, quickly overtook her, and she watched as he dashed ahead of her among the trees and knelt at Billy's side.

Seconds later she came to the foot of the old apple tree where Billy lay, silent, unmoving, Edward Spencer bending over him.

'Billy – oh, Billy,' Grace breathed as she knelt in the cold grass. She touched his face, his shoulder, but he did not move. 'Billy,' she said, in a louder voice now, trying to reach him through the shield of his unconsciousness. 'Billy, wake up!' Her heart was pounding in her breast. He was dying, she thought; he was dead. But no, for when she put the back of her hand to his mouth she could feel the faint warmth of his expelled breath. At the same time Mr Spencer was feeling the boy's pulse. Then, giving a nod, he said, 'He's all right. I think he's going to be all right . . .'

'No, no, he's not all right. He's not moving.' Her voice sounded shrill in her ears, ringing out among the bare branches of the surrounding trees.

Mr Spencer turned to her. 'Be calm,' he said in a low voice. 'We'll look after him.' Gently he felt with sensitive fingers about the boy's neck and then, with a little nod, bent lower and gently scooped him up into his arms. 'Come, we'll take him to the house.'

With Billy cradled in his strong arms, Mr Spencer strode back towards the house, Grace hurrying along at his side.

They went in by the servants' entrance, and up in Billy's room Mr Spencer gently laid the boy down on his bed. Then, straightening, he said, 'We must fetch the doctor. I could send Johnson but – no, I'll go myself. It won't take but a minute to saddle the horse.'

He spent no further time on the matter, but turned and moved towards the door. 'I'll be back as soon as I can,' he said, and a moment later he was gone.

Grace sat at Billy's bedside, watchful for any sign of his returning consciousness, or any other change in him. There was none that was discernible to her. The time dragged so slowly by and she wondered where Mr Spencer and the doctor could be. And what if the doctor was out on other calls – as he could so easily be? What then? She sighed and bent again towards her brother. 'Billy,' she whispered to his bruised face, 'wake up. Please wake up.' But there was no response.

It was almost two hours before the doctor came. Grace was aware of footsteps on the landing outside and then the door opened, and Mr Spencer was ushering in a tall, olive-skinned man and following him into the room.

'Dr Ellish was already out,' Mr Spencer said, 'but fortunately I managed to get Dr Mukerjee from Liddiston. He very kindly agreed to come out.' Then to the doctor he added, 'This is Miss Harper, the young boy's sister.'

The doctor gave Grace a nod as he moved towards the bed.

Grace and Mr Spencer then stood by while the doctor examined the boy, all the while murmuring little words to himself, which Grace could not quite catch. Then, when his examination was over, he turned to Grace and Mr Spencer.

'Well, the boy is concussed,' he said. 'There's no doubt about that. Though I don't think it's any worse than that. I've made a tactile examination of his skull and there doesn't appear to be any depressed fractures.' He was a handsome man with thick black hair. He nodded his finely shaped head. 'I'm sure he's going to be all right.'

Grace felt such relief at his words that tears sprang to her eyes. But still the fear was there. 'But – but how long is he going to be like this?' she asked. 'He's been like it for two hours. He doesn't move; he doesn't open his eyes.'

'I think you can only be patient,' the doctor said. 'He'll be all right, I'm sure. He'll come round. In the meantime you must just keep him warm, and keep him lying on his side. You might find that when he wakes he won't care for bright lights, and also that he'll feel a little nausea – so have a bowl handy. Other than that . . .' he spread his hands, 'he's in God's hands.'

The doctor left soon afterwards, saying that he would call again that evening. Mr Spencer showed the man out to his carriage and then came back up to Billy's room.

'He seems like a good man, Mukerjee,' he said.

'Yes, he does.' Grace nodded. She much preferred the Indian to Dr Ellish.

'It was Dr Ellish's wife who suggested that I go to ask Dr Mukerjee,' Edward said. 'Apparently he's fairly new in the area.'

A little pause, then Grace said, 'Thank you so much.'

'Oh – it was nothing.'

'No, you did so much. You rode out for the doctor yourself.'

He shrugged. Grace opened her mouth to speak again, when there came a sound from Billy's bed. She turned quickly to look at her brother. His eyes were open, he was frowning with an expression of irritation.

'Billy . . .' Grace breathed, quickly bending to him.

The boy mumbled something and then closed his eyes and drifted away again. Grace put a hand to her throat and looked at Mr Spencer. 'He spoke,' she said. 'He spoke and he had his eyes open.'

'I saw,' the man said. He gave a nod. 'He'll be all right now, you'll see.'

That evening, after the doctor had visited Billy again and made his departure, Edward knocked at the door of Billy's room. Grace called for him to come in and quietly he entered and closed the door behind him. She was sitting, as before, in a chair beside the bed. Mr Spencer took the only other chair in the room.

'He's sleeping,' Grace whispered.

'So I see.' The man's voice was low, like Grace's.

'Though he was awake a little earlier,' she said. 'Not that he said much. Still, it's all to the good.'

'Yes. Dr Mukerjee is sure he'll be all right now.'

'Yes, he told me that.'

'Such a relief for you. You were frantic.'

'I'm afraid I was.'

'And how are you now?'

'I'm better, thank you. Much better now.'

'You've had nothing to eat for some time.'

'I'll get something soon. I'm not that hungry.'

They sat for some moments without speaking, and in the

379

silence they could hear the sound of Billy's steady breathing. After a while Mr Spencer got to his feet. 'I'll leave you alone. If you want anything, just come and get me. I shall be in the library.' He started towards the door.

'Wait – one moment, please . . .' Grace got up and moved to him, reaching him as he stood with his hand on the doorknob.

'Yes? What is it?'

They still whispered.

'I didn't really get a chance to thank you,' she said. 'I don't know what I would have done without you.' She kept seeing the man before her as he had carried Billy's unconscious body; as he had laid him gently on the bed.

'And I,' he said, 'didn't really get a chance to ask you my question again. You know what question I had in mind.'

She nodded after a moment. 'Yes.'

He smiled. 'But this isn't the time either, I know that.' He paused, glanced towards the bed and then back to her face. 'When do you think would be a good time to ask you again?'

She did not answer; she could not.

'Of course you can't answer that question,' he said. 'If you could, I would have no need to ask the other one, the all important one.' Another little pause. 'I shall ask you again tomorrow. And you know what the question will be?'

'Yes.'

'Fine.' He smiled gently and inclined his head a little. 'Until tomorrow, then.'

A second later and he was letting himself out of the room and the door was quietly closing after him. She did not hear his soft footfalls as he made his way back along the landing.

For some moments she remained standing by the door, then she moved back to the bed and sat down on the chair. Billy was still sleeping. She leaned over and put her mouth close to his ear. 'Sleep well, Billy,' she whispered. 'You're safe now. Nothing will hurt you now.'

No, nothing would hurt him now. He would recover soon from his fall and would be as well as ever. The doctor had told her, and she had to believe he was right.

She sat back in her chair in the silent room, and in her mind Edward Spencer's words went over in her brain. Tomorrow he would ask her again the question he had asked her before. And why should she not marry him? she asked herself. There was no longer any other man in her life, and although she did not love him she could tell herself that in time she would come to do so. She turned a little and took in Billy's sleeping form, and saw him once again held in the man's arms as they had hurried through the orchard. Billy – he would be well cared for, too.

Yes. She knew now what her answer would be.

Chapter Eighteen

The wedding would take place in April, the couple decided. It would not do for Grace to be married from the same house in which her husband-to-be also lived, so she arranged to stay with her Aunt Edie in Remmer Ridge for the last month of her life as a single woman, and be married from her little cottage. Billy would remain where he was, and continue with his schooling, seeing Grace just at weekends until she moved back, as Mrs Edward Spencer, to Asterleigh House. It was also necessary for Grace to quit her post as governess to the Kellas children, and after working a month's notice, this she did.

She arrived at Aunt Edie's home, Widmore Cottage in Remmer Ridge, in early March, travelling by carriage driven by Edward Spencer, who, after seeing her settled in with her aunt, set off back to Asterleigh.

Aunt Edie, already excited at the prospect of the coming wedding, was further thrilled when, during Grace's first week in residence, it was decided that they should make an excursion to Redbury to buy Grace's wedding dress and trousseau. Edward had made Grace an allowance to buy clothes and things for the wedding, and at the end of their day's shopping she and her aunt came back to Remmer Ridge not a little exhausted. And even then their work was not done, for it would be necessary to return to the city to collect the wedding dress when the alterations had been completed.

Each Friday during her month's stay, Grace left her

aunt's house to go to Asterleigh, in order to see Billy and spend some time with Edward. She spent the night there and returned to Remmer Ridge on Saturday afternoon. On Sunday morning she accompanied her aunt to the little local church for the morning service, the church where, very soon, she was to be married.

The time passed swiftly by, and then came the week of her wedding. On the Monday of that week there came a letter from Kester. Sent from an address in Redbury, it had been forwarded to her from Asterleigh House. In it he wrote that he wanted to see her, and would like her permission to come to Asterleigh to visit her.

Grace was in a quandary. She did not know what to do. With her impending marriage to Edward there was no question of allowing Kester to visit her at Asterleigh – in any case she was not there to see him – and she certainly could not receive him there once the wedding had taken place.

Why, why she asked of the heavens, was he asking to see her again, coming back into her life like this? Just when she was starting to get on with her life – after such upheaval and uncertainty? Now here he was, writing to her, asking to meet, upsetting her equilibrium and making her doubt her every action.

As she pondered on his request she thought several times that she might just ignore his letter, simply not respond at all. But he had written in such a heartfelt-sounding tone that such a notion could not sustain for long in her mind. She knew that, if it were at all possible, she would have to see him. But there, she could not think how it could happen. And then her aunt was saying to her, 'My dear, when you go to Redbury on Wednesday for your fitting, shall you need me along? My arthritis is giving me trouble again, and I'm sure you can do without me, my dear.' And of course Grace said yes, that she would happily go alone. After all, it was just for the final fitting and to bring back the dress.

And then, before the idea had had a chance to grow cool in her brain she had written a short letter to Kester saying that she must be in Redbury on Wednesday, and that if he was free on that day she could meet him at 11.30 in the foyer of the Royale Hotel. She chose this meeting point as it was fairly close to the draper's that was supplying her wedding dress. As soon as the letter was finished and sealed, she posted it off.

On Wednesday morning Grace set off to catch the train, arriving at Seager's, the draper's, well before eleven.

Trying on the dress once more, it was decided that one single further minor modification was required, which could be done during the next hour. So, saying that she would return later, Grace left the seamstress to her work and went back out into the city streets.

She reached the hotel before 11.30, and found Kester waiting for her when she entered the foyer. Watching for her, he saw her at once and came towards her with hand outstretched. Immediately her heart began thumping in her breast; all sense of ease that she had been feeling swiftly gone. That she should see him again, after all this time . . .

'Grace . . .' He took her hand in his, warmly, briefly pressed it. 'Oh, Grace, how are you?'

Tentatively she shook hands with him, sensing the familiar feel of her hand in his. And then he was releasing her. 'I'm very well,' she said. 'And how are you?' She could not bring herself to speak his name. She felt awkward, so ill at ease.

'I'm well, I'm well,' he said. 'And Sophie also. And how is Billy?'

'He's very well too, and getting on at school.'

'He'll have grown so much since I last saw him.'

'Oh, yes, indeed. He grows apace.' A pause while Grace

sought for something to say, then she said, 'Your letter came from an address in Redbury.'

'Yes, that's where we're living now. But I'm hoping that we can return to Birchwood before too long. I don't think that would embarrass you now, would it?'

'No – not at all.'

A little silence fell between them, then he said, 'Shall we have some tea or coffee or something?' Briefly he glanced around them. 'We could have some here or find somewhere else.'

'Yes, let's go somewhere else . . .'

'As you wish.'

They went outside together and turned onto the main street, walking along until they came to the sign of a teashop hanging over a doorway. 'Will this do?' he said.

'Oh, indeed.'

He opened the door to the teashop and Grace preceded him into the interior where they were shown to a small round table in a more shaded area towards the rear.

After a brief consultation with Grace, Kester asked the waitress to bring them some tea.

'So,' he said when the waitress had left with their order, 'what brings you to Redbury today – and on your own? You are on your own, aren't you?'

'Oh, yes.' She took off her gloves. 'I'm just here to – to do a little shopping.'

He smiled. 'It must be a special kind of shopping to bring you all this way. Though going by the look of you, you haven't done it yet.'

'No.' She spread her empty hands. 'I have to go back to the draper's in an hour.'

'Ah.' He nodded. A brief silence fell between them, and Grace became aware of the other voices in the room as they chattered over their teacups and pastries. Why on earth was she here? she asked herself. She had come to accept the reality of her decision to marry, but here was Kester, whose very presence jeopardized her peace of mind, and undermined her confidence in the choice she had made. How could he do such a thing? Why could he not simply stay out of her life? He could in no way bring her happiness – no happiness at all could come out of their relationship – whatever that relationship might be.

'Is Sophie enjoying her school?' she asked.

'Yes, she is. Very much. Though she's a day pupil, so she's not away from the house for so long. I don't think I could bear it for her to go away as a boarder.'

'I can understand that.'

The silence fell between them again. There were many questions that Grace would like to have asked, but she could not. After a moment Kester said:

'I heard that Mrs Spencer died.'

'Yes, that's correct.'

'Very sad. She was an extremely nice woman.' He paused. 'What did she die of?'

Grace hesitated, then said, 'The doctor said it was pneumonia – which started as influenza.'

He shook his head. 'How very sad. I only met her a couple of times, but I did like her so.'

'She was a fine woman. And she was so kind to my brother. We owe her a great deal.'

'Poor Spencer – he must miss her very much.'

Grace said nothing.

'So, what are you doing now?' Kester said. 'Are you and Billy still staying at Asterleigh? Presumably not – as you were employed by Mrs Spencer . . .'

'I've been teaching in Little Berron,' she said. 'The two children of a solicitor. But still staying at Asterleigh. Billy too. It's good for him – having a sense of security. He's so used to it now.'

The waitress brought the tea to them, set it out on the table and went away again.

'Would you like to pour?' Kester asked. Grace silently did so. Kester slowly stirred his cup and said, lifting his gaze to Grace:

'I hurt you, Grace. I'm so sorry.'

Avoiding his eyes, she lowered her glance to her cup. 'Well – that's in the past now.'

'Is it?'

'We get over things.'

'I'm not sure I like hearing that.' A pause. 'Do you mean it?'

'Oh, Kester,' she shook her head distractedly, ' – I'm not sure I know what I mean.'

A long pause in the conversation. Grace self-consciously sipped her tea, while Kester stirred his again.

'I owed you explanations,' he said after a few moments.

'No. No, it's all right. It's in the past.'

Abruptly he reached across the table and briefly touched her hand. 'Don't. Please don't say that.'

'It is, Kester. You know it is.'

'Grace –'

'We can't go back.'

He picked up his cup, then immediately set it down again in the saucer and pushed it away from him. 'I don't want this,' he said. Looking up, looking directly into her eyes, he added, 'I have to talk to you.'

She did not know how to respond. There was such passion in his eyes.

'I have to, Grace,' he said. 'I must.'

After a second or two she said carefully, 'What is it you want to say?'

'Not here. We can't talk here.'

'But –'

'Can we go outside? Please – I have to talk to you.'

Only a moment of deliberation, then she nodded and began to put on her gloves. 'Yes, of course.'

He stood up, took some coins from his pocket and placed them on the table near his cup and saucer. 'Shall we go?'

'I don't have that long,' Grace said as they went outside in the air. 'I have to get back to the draper's.'

'It won't take that long – what I have to tell you. But it has to be said.'

With him taking the lead, they walked together along the main street. There was a little garden over to the side, he said, where they could sit and talk in some privacy.

A turning into another street, and then there before them was the entrance to the public park, and they entered it and moved along a pathway until they came to a bench. Here they sat down. Around them people strolled, lovers and old people, while children and dogs scampered through the spring grass. Grace thought of those earlier times, an earlier spring, when she and Kester had walked together. They had both been happier then. At least she had; she could no longer pretend to know how he thought or felt about anything.

'I can't say here long,' she said. 'I shall have to go soon.'

'Not yet,' he said. 'I have some things I must say to you. They have to be said.'

She waited, their little silence touched by the squeals and shouts of the playing children.

'I love you, Grace,' he said after a moment.

'No, Kester, please. You mustn't say such things.' She clutched at her bag, preparing to rise and move, but he put out his hand and held her arm.

'You must hear me,' he said.

She stayed, but she remained tense, ready to move away.

'Whatever else you believe, please believe that,' he said.

She made no sign that she accepted his words or even that she had heard them spoken.

'Now,' he said, and took a deep breath, 'I'm going to tell you something. It is something I should have told you before. And I would like to say that what I tell you must go no further. You'll understand why.'

She nodded. 'Very well.'

'I never set out to lie to you,' he said. 'But I came to feel so deeply for you. And it came to the point where I knew that if I told you my – my situation, I would lose you. And that I couldn't bear to contemplate.' He gave a rueful little shrug. 'But I lost you in the end anyway, didn't I? I suppose it was inevitable.'

Grace did not look at him, but sat gazing off into the trees on the far side of the park.

'My wife,' Kester said, 'was a beautiful woman. She was –'

Grace broke in: 'Kester, I don't know where this is getting us. I –'

'Please,' he said, 'let me tell you.' He paused, then went on, 'My wife, Bella, is half-Italian. She was born in Florence. Her family still lives there – though she never sees them now. I met her there, in Florence, when I was there studying. And I was drawn to her. As I said, she was very beautiful. I was very young, and impressionable, and I had to have her. So we married, and I brought her back to England, here to a small village near Redbury. Sophie was born just over a year later.' Looking off into the distance, he gave a little shake of his head. 'It wasn't a success, though, our marriage, I'm sorry to say. I could see that before too much time had gone by. I think my life was too dull for her. She was used to more exciting times, used to a more exciting life than that of an architect's wife. So after a time we moved to London. I thought that would improve things, and it did for a while. But it wasn't to last. She seemed to tire of things so quickly. Whatever it was, it seemed not to be long before disenchantment would set in, and whatever

389

novelty she had would lose its allure. I'm afraid that went for me as well as everything else. Oh, yes, it wasn't that long before the love between us died. Her love for me – if she'd ever had any, of course – was the first to go. I don't think it took that long. And my love for her didn't survive every obstacle. Love does not do that.' He turned to Grace at this, as if to affirm his words. 'Love can be a very fragile thing, I've discovered. In some respects, anyway. Sometimes it can withstand all kinds of hardships and buffeting, and at other times it breaks and crumbles away to nothing.' He shrugged. 'Perhaps in that case it is not true love. I don't know.'

A ball, thrown by a child, came rolling across the grass, coming to a halt near Kester's foot. He bent, picked it up and tossed it to the small boy who came running in pursuit. He sat in silence for a moment and then continued:

'Two years after Sophie was born I was offered some work by an Englishman living in Italy, in Naples. Bella was very anxious for me to investigate the job and to accept it. So, as not a lot was happening for me here in England we decided to go and look into it, and to have a pleasant little holiday at the same time. Incidentally, it was while we were on our way out there that we met Edward Spencer. He was travelling in Italy also on business. He seemed to me to be a man of great experience. A little older than I, and quite daring and adventurous. I think his adventurousness came about through his hard upbringing. By all he told me he had not had an easy life of it. Anyway, we became friends, and agreed to keep in touch – though that's by the way, that has nothing to do with my own personal story with my wife.'

On the breeze, from a distance, came the sound of a church clock striking the hour of two. Grace knew that she must soon go back to the draper's, but she could not leave just yet. She must hear him out.

'No, Spencer had nothing to do with my own story with my wife,' Kester said. He gave a deep, short sigh, then went on, 'We got to Naples and I had various meetings with the potential client, and as a family we had some pleasant excursions. Sophie was too young to appreciate the change of scene – but Bella loved being there.' He paused. 'And unfortunately, while we were there and I was having meetings with the Englishman she was having meetings with a certain gentleman.'

A silence fell, and Grace said, 'Someone she knew?'

'No, no one she knew. A stranger. He was an opera singer. We met him one night in a restaurant after the opera. We had been to the opera that evening, and we had seen him perform. And as I say, we were in the restaurant having a light supper, when he came in with friends. He drew us into his conversation, and once he knew that we had seen his performance and enjoyed it, he invited us to join him at his table. I didn't want to; I thought we should get back to Sophie who was at the hotel with the hired nurse, but Bella was keen to take advantage of the moment. Well, as it turned out, it was to become more than a moment. I won't go into all the detail – I don't know a lot of it myself – but suffice to say that Bella and the man were soon meeting in secret. And so it turned out that when I said it was time for us to move on and return to England, Bella said she would not. She wanted to stay on, she said, and then she told me of having fallen in love with the man.'

'She was prepared to let her child go?' Grace said, a note of incredulity in her voice.

'Well, at first she said that I must leave Sophie with her, but I refused flatly. So then she said that she would remain in any case. I pleaded with her – to think of both of us, but nothing would change her mind. So I told her that I would take Sophie back to London.'

'And that's what you did,' Grace said.

'Not immediately. At first I thought that with time I could change Bella's mind.' Here his mouth was touched by a bitter smile. 'You'll notice that my love for her had not yet been destroyed, and I was still hopeful of reconciliation. So although Bella left the hotel and went off with her lover, Sophie and I remained, while I tried to do what I could to win Bella back. It was no good. She was totally infatuated with the man, and nothing I could say or do made any difference. And then, then I learned of a cholera outbreak in the city. People were dying. And with that I didn't hesitate. I had to protect my daughter. So straight away I packed our bags and brought her back to England.' He fell silent and sat looking off over the grass, but his focus was far away, as if he was seeing nothing but memories.

'Of course,' he said moments later, 'I didn't mention to anyone what had happened. No one at all. How could I? I couldn't possibly admit to such a thing. I remember telling the maid that her mistress would not be returning yet. And soon after that the maid left and was replaced, so I had no need to lie or go into the matter further. I hired a nurse for Sophie and we tried to get on with our lives. Sophie missed her mother, of course, but Bella was never the most caring and affectionate of mothers. Some women are just not. At the same time, children are very adaptable, and I honestly don't think Sophie missed her mother for too long. Well, if she did,' here he spread his hands in a little gesture of helplessness, ' – then it's something I deeply regret. Not that I could do anything about it. Not a thing.'

He turned and looked at Grace now. 'I did the best for Sophie that I could do,' he said. 'And I know I've made mistakes, but I did the best I could under the circumstances.'

Grace gave an almost imperceptible nod. 'I'm sure you did.'

Kester was quiet for a moment or two, as if gathering his thoughts, then he went on: 'It didn't last, her affair with the singer. I don't think I expected it to. Not that I knew anything about it at the time. I didn't hear anything more of her for some while. Years went by. And then she wrote to me. She was back in London, she said, and wished to see me. She asked me if she should come to the house. I wrote back at once saying that she must not. I couldn't subject Sophie to any kind of – of drama. I told Bella that I would meet her. Which I did. We arranged to meet at Victoria Station. She was already there when I arrived. I noticed a change in her at once. And it wasn't simply that she was older. There was a greater difference in her – one that had nothing to do with the time that had passed. She was still good-looking, but no longer beautiful. She was like a flower when it's nearing the end of its season. Faded, overripe. We went into a hotel, to the bar there, and over drinks she told me her story. It didn't all emerge easily; it came out in fits and starts, and bits and pieces. But I put it all together – which wasn't difficult – and what a wretched story it made.'

He had turned his face away from Grace now, looking off again, seeing scenes from the past.

'The story that I gathered was that she and her singer had parted after a time, and she had gone with a new friend. She didn't name him and I didn't ask. It wasn't important. This one didn't last either, and it wasn't long before she was on to the third. She was drinking too. This much was evident when we sat in the bar. She was well accustomed to drinking, I could see that.' He paused, took a breath. 'But the worst was yet to come. It soon became apparent, no matter what words she used to try to hide it, that she had been . . . that she had been . . . selling herself.' He closed his eyes tightly, hanging his head. 'There's no other way of putting it. She had become – she was no more than a . . . a common prostitute. Imagine, she was making a life for herself – if you can call it that – in that way. With any man

– indiscriminately.' He lifted his head, opened his eyes and turned to Grace. 'I don't know how I can tell you this. And I can only say that you must never, never repeat what I say.'

'Never,' Grace said. 'I promise you.'

He nodded, was silent a moment, then said, 'And can you believe that she wanted to come back to us? I think she had the notion that if she said she was sorry and begged forgiveness, I would take her back, and once more she could be a wife to me and a mother to our child. Oh, make no mistake, I was cured of love for her by then. There was no chance that such a thing could happen.'

'Did you tell her that?'

'Yes. Though I think she found it hard to accept. I don't know. She was – is – such an actress. She's always been able to turn on the tears. In the beginning she was able to melt my heart – but in time I was cured of that too.' His words came to a halt.

'Where is she now?'

'She's in London, somewhere. I want her to keep away from Sophie and me. This is the reason we left London. She is the reason. I gave her money on two or three occasions, but I said she must never come to the house. But that wasn't enough for her, the money. She wanted her old life back too. She didn't give up on it. And in spite of my warnings she came to the house. Fortunately Sophie was out with the nurse. As soon as I saw Bella there at the door I took her away. She protested, but I didn't care. I gave her money again, and I told her that if she ever came to the house again she would never get another penny. I made it clear, too, that her life with us was over. She had other ideas, though, and came to the house again. That was when I decided we must leave London and come to the country.'

'Sophie, of course, knows absolutely nothing,' Grace said.

'Oh, my God, no. God forbid. She must never know. I let

it be understood that her mother was dead, that she had died of the cholera while we were in Naples. I have no regrets about lying, and I would do it again if necessary. I shall continue to do it for as long as I need. I have my daughter to think of. And she must never, never, know what her mother was – is. She's just a child now, but one day she'll be sought in marriage to some fine young man. And I want the best for her. Only the best is good enough for her. And I will not have her mother – or anyone for that matter – ruining her chances. She continues to believe that her mother is dead, and that suits me. Better that than the truth. The truth would destroy her and all her chances of happiness. And as long as I have the power I will never allow that to happen.'

For a brief moment Grace thought she could see in his eyes the glisten of unshed tears. But he turned his face away from her again.

'So now you know,' he said. 'Now you know the reason I could not offer you marriage. And the irony is that I cannot even consider a divorce. As difficult as divorce is I would have chosen it rather than lie and be tied to her for ever. But a divorce would create such a scandal, and all the truth would come out about my wife, and that would be enough to finish Sophie's chances in life. She would have no future at all. So you see, I have to stay married. I think the best I can hope for is that Bella does not come to bother us here. My work has suffered, of course, having to move like this – but if it protects Sophie's future then that's all that matters.'

Grace was silent. She could think of nothing to say. She had never imagined that his story could be anything like this.

A drop of rain fell on her cheek, and she suddenly realized that the skies had darkened.

Kester muttered, 'It's starting to rain,' and, reaching out, took her hand and drew her from the seat. Side by side they walked quickly over the grass towards the exit, and even as they moved out onto the street the rain stopped.

'Hardly even a shower,' Grace said.

They walked in silence for some moments, then Kester said, 'You said you had to go to a particular shop.'

'Yes, the draper's, Seager's.'

'What are you doing after that? Returning to Asterleigh House?'

'No – I'm staying with my aunt for a while. My Aunt Edie in Remmer Ridge.'

'You wanted a little change of scene, did you?'

When she did not answer, he said: 'I don't know whether I should have told you all that. All that about my wife.'

'I'm so glad you did.'

'Yes. I had to, anyway. You had to know.'

Although the rain had stopped for now, the skies still looked threatening.

'I'll walk with you to Seager's,' Kester said.

She wanted to protest, but she could not find the words without giving too much away. So, keeping silent, she assented.

When they got to the nearest entrance to the draper's shop, Grace turned to Kester and said, 'I'll finish my shopping now . . .'

'I'll wait for you,' he said. He pointed to the teashop on the other side of the street, the one they had visited earlier for such a brief time. With an ironic smile he added, 'It looks as if I'm bound to take some tea in there after all.'

Again Grace wanted to protest, but there were no words that she could find, even if she could have found a reason.

'All right,' she said. 'I'll join you in a little while. But then I must catch my train.'

'How long will you be?'

'Oh, twenty minutes perhaps. Half an hour.'

She turned then and went into the store and made her way to the department where they catered for bridal wear. The alterations were complete, she found, and once more she tried on the dress. In a small dressing room she stood before a full length glass, and saw before her a young woman in a long bridal gown with a veil made of the finest handmade lace. She was a bride. 'Is there something wrong, miss?' asked the middle-aged female assistant, adding with a little laugh: 'You look almost a little sad.' 'No, no, everything is fine,' Grace replied. 'Miss – if I might suggest,' said the assistant, ' – why not step outside where the light is better? You'll get the full picture then . . .' And Grace nodded acquiescence, and, with the woman holding up the skirts of the dress, moved out of the dressing room into the shop proper, and there stood in front of a different glass, briefly lifting the veil so that it framed her chestnut hair. 'Everything is fine,' Grace said, and the woman ohed and ahed over the dress and twitched at the skirt and the veil. Grace thanked her. Back in the dressing room she took off the dress and changed into her own street clothes. And the dress was wrapped and boxed, and the balance of her money was paid over and she left.

Outside the store, on the threshold of the teashop she hesitated. What purpose would it serve to see Kester again? As much as she wanted to see him, it could do no good whatever. In fact, she told herself, it could only do harm. Her feelings had not changed towards him, she realized that, but they had no future together; he had a wife, and no matter how much he might wish to, he could not, would not, give her up.

But then her steps were leading her into the teashop, and she looked around in the shaded interior and there was Kester, sitting at the table next to the one they had previously occupied, standing up as she turned and saw him, gravely smiling at her.

She reached his side and sat down on the chair he pulled out for her. The tablecloth was still bare. 'Have you ordered anything yet?' she said.

'I ordered some tea. Just a minute ago. I only just got in here myself.'

She set the box containing her wedding dress on the empty chair beside them, and began to take off her gloves.

'I saw,' he said. His words came out bluntly.

'What?'

'I saw you – in Seager's.'

'What?' she said. 'I don't understand. You say you –'

'I saw you – in your wedding dress.'

She opened her mouth but no words came.

'I saw you,' he said again. 'I saw you wearing your wedding dress.'

There was nothing for her to say. She was only aware that she regretted his knowing. Though of course he would have to have learned of it at some time.

'You're getting married,' he said,' and I never knew.'

She looked down at her cup.

'I never dreamed,' he said. 'It's the last thing I could have foreseen.' He paused. 'Why didn't you tell me straight away?'

She could give no answer to this.

He sighed. 'But of course, why should it not happen?' he said. 'Just because I've been moping about, thinking about past things, that's no reason to think you might not be doing the same. Look at me, Grace, please.'

She raised her head now, turning to face him.

'Am I to learn who it is?' he said. 'Who is the fortunate man – the most fortunate man who has so quickly captured your heart?'

'Listen –' she said. And then stopped, unable to continue.

'Yes, go on,' he said.

A few moments, and then, unable to put the moment off

any longer, she said, 'I – I am to marry Mr Spencer. On Saturday.'

Silence followed her words for several moments, and during the time Kester looked at her with a half-frown on his brow. Then his mouth moved in the shadow of an ironic smile. 'Mr Spencer. Edward Spencer.' He shook his head. 'How could I possibly have guessed such a thing?' He leaned a little closer to her. 'I can't get over the sight of you there in the store. There I was, wandering in, just killing time while I waited for you, and suddenly there you were, in your wedding gown. I didn't know it was you immediately. I just saw a girl in a veil come out of a small room and stand before a glass. And there was something about her figure, her carriage. And then she lifted the veil and I saw her face . . .'

'Kester . . .'

'But not the happiest face, I have to say. You were not smiling as a bride should smile. Not in my reckoning, anyway. And I wonder if Mr Spencer is smiling. No doubt he is. And indeed, why not? His wife has not so long been dead, but here he is about to walk down the aisle again. And this time with a beautiful and captivating young woman.'

She looked at him in horror. 'Stop. Please stop.'

'Ah,' he said, 'I'm in danger of being indelicate, am I? I'm sorry about that. Well, I suppose I should be congratulating you. Yes, indeed! My congratulations to you. And to Mr Spencer also.'

The sarcastic tone of his words was like a knife to her flesh. But she could find no words to say.

'Well, I'm glad you've found love,' he said after a moment. 'I suppose I should be glad of that. After all, I couldn't offer you anything more than that. And sometimes it isn't enough.' He paused. 'And *have* you found love?'

Grace hesitated for just a moment then reached for her gloves.

'Was that a difficult question for you to answer?' he said. 'It shouldn't be. There should be only one answer and it should be given immediately, without a moment's pause. Do I take it that you have not? That you have not found love – or at least that there is some doubt as to whether you have?'

With her gloves on, Grace picked up her bag and began to rise from her seat. At once Kester reached out and took her arm, staying her.

'If you're not marrying him for love, Grace, then what are you marrying him for?'

She felt tears of anger, shame and humiliation well up, stinging her eyes. 'I can't be forced to sit and listen to this,' she said, her nostrils flaring, and still holding her bag, she went to remove his fingers from her wrist. At the first touch of pressure from her hand he released her and held up his hands, like a man demonstrating that he is unarmed.

'I give up,' he said. 'Oh, Grace.' He slowly shook his head.

And now that she was freed of his grasp, Grace sank back into her seat, her head turned away from him so that he should not see her tears.

'Grace Harper,' she heard him whisper, as he leaned closer to her. 'Grace Harper, soon to be mistress of Asterleigh House. And is that what you wanted?' A brief pause. 'What are you after, Grace? Are you running towards something, or making your escape? I think it's the latter.' His voice was bitter. 'And you're flying very high, Grace. So high. Are you ready for such a flight? Be careful. Remember Icarus. Don't go flying too close to the sun.'

She could bear no more. Now when she rose she brooked no hindrance – not that he made any attempt to prevent her move. Her bag on one arm, the box holding her wedding dress under the other, she turned and went out onto the street.

Chapter Nineteen

The October night sky was a vast, deep blue canopy, anchored low in the west by one gleaming star. Standing at the drawing room window, Grace looked up at the sky, at the star and gave a little falling sigh of sadness. How incredibly wide was the whole universe. And what possible significance in it could her own being, her own self and her own problems have? Nevertheless everything had to be dealt with; no matter how small one might be in the great scheme of things, one still had to go on; the whole universe could be sliding across the emptiness, but still every living thing in it continued on its fated way, to eat, to mate, to live.

Illuminated by the light of a candle set on a small table nearby, her face was dimly reflected in the window pane, the face – shadowed alabaster – almost of a ghost, lit from beneath so that the hollows of her eyes were dark and her hair lost its colour and faded into the shadows behind.

How quickly the time passed, she thought. Here it was October, six months since her wedding. She so rarely thought of that day, those moments when she had stood at the altar with Edward at her side, and they had made their vows to one another. Since that time there had been occasions when she had asked herself whether she was happy – as if it really mattered, she had then admonished herself. For she had not necessarily been expecting happiness from this marriage; happiness was not what she had been seeking when she had entered into it. At best she was sometimes content with her lot, and she would be content with that.

One difficulty Grace had with her life at Asterleigh was keeping herself occupied. In the past she had had Mrs Spencer to assist, and at other times her teaching. Now she was mistress of the house and there was almost nothing for her to do. She missed her teaching but had to acknowledge that that part of her life was gone for ever. During the summer months she had decided to take up her painting again, and this she had done, trying to settle herself in Mrs Spencer's studio and using her easel, palette, paints and brushes. It had not felt right, though; the place was still so much the late Mrs Spencer's own, and Grace felt ill at ease, like a conscience-stricken trespasser. Mrs Spencer's things were all around her, all her finished and unfinished canvases – even the unfinished portrait of Grace herself, standing tall, leaning against the wall by the window. So she had given up the idea of painting, at least for the time being. And as there was nothing to do in the matter of the running of the house – not with the capable hands of Mrs Sandiston at the helm – Grace found that she spent her days reading, sewing, embroidering, riding the grey mare around the paddock or playing the occasional game of patience. Soon, she told herself, ironically, she must begin to take up charity work. On one occasion she had spoken to Edward about finding some respectable employment somewhere, but he had reacted angrily. 'It's enough that I have to work,' he said. 'Certainly no wife of mine ever shall.'

Edward's behaviour had come to surprise her in several ways, and not to the good. He had changed since their marriage. Whether fundamentally or merely on the surface, the result was the same. In the past, from the time of their early meetings to the time of their wedding, he had always been kind, solicitous and showing understanding. But now such days seemed for the most part to be over, and though at times he could be tender with her, those times seemed few and far between. Perhaps his kindness and warmth had merely been part of an act designed to win her over – and now that she was his he was simply reverting to his true nature, giving up the charade. But she had the feeling there was more to it than this. Perhaps the answer would come in time. But whatever it was, the answer, she had to put up with the manifestation of his demons. So often she found him difficult and unapproachable; sometimes having to tread so warily if he was not to be offended or enraged. But surprisingly, on some occasions when he did become angry it would follow that he would apologize for his behaviour and plead for forgiveness. At times there was no knowing how to deal with things.

A little earlier this evening she had gone to the kitchen and made herself a cup of tea. Now she sipped from the cup as she gazed out into the night. All the servants had gone to bed; Billy too, long ago; to bed in his same room, the one he had been given on first arriving at the house. Edward had offered him a different, larger room, but Billy had insisted that he was happy where he was. For Billy there had been slight changes, of course, since his sister's marriage, but not so great that he found his life very different. In essence it was not, on the surface, anyway; he continued with his schooling, and his associations with his schoolfriends, and even – purely out of choice because he liked to be occupied – giving the occasional help in the kitchen, the garden and the stable. The one main difference in his life – which Grace was aware of if not he – was that he had security. And that was what mattered.

Where the servants were concerned, Grace had expected greater changes in her relationship with them; and great changes there had been, but those changes had not been such that she was unable to deal with them. Before her marriage, Edward had told her, he had gathered the house servants together and informed them that he was to marry Miss Harper, the late Mrs Spencer's former companion. They already knew, of course, as the banns had been called in the church of St Michael's in Remmer Ridge. So they were prepared for and expecting the information. And Grace had pictured him as he had stood before them, his glance daring the very slightest critique or expression of disapproval. And so, when she had returned to Asterleigh House, she had returned as Edward's wife, their new mistress. Since then, in respect of her being mistress of the house, everything had gone well; there had been not a hint of anything untoward in the servants' manner or behaviour. Indeed, they knew their master well enough to know that were there such they would not last a minute longer in their present employment. If anyone had some-times felt at a loss in the new mistress-servant relationship it was as often as not Grace herself, for she had at first found it difficult to give instructions to those with whom she had formerly been almost on the same level. Mrs Sandiston for instance. But that lady had immediately established herself in the new relationship, at once acknowledging Grace's superior social station. Grace was grateful for it.

Now, turning her head and looking at the clock on the mantelpiece above the flickering fire, she saw that it was almost 10.30. She yawned; she was tired. She would like to go to bed, but she could not, must not; she must wait up for Edward. She had learned early in their marriage that he expected her always to be awake and alert when he returned home late. On an early occasion when she had gone to bed before he had come in he had entered the bedroom calling for her, irritable and angry, demanding that she awake and give him attention and company. Afterwards he had apologized: 'I'm sorry; forgive me. But I've been travelling all day, and the thought that kept me going was the knowledge that you would be waiting for me at the end of the journey. You can't imagine how dispiriting it is to find that there is no one there.' And she had kissed him and told him that she simply had not known, but that she would in future always be there.

So there she sat, while the moon moved across the sky and the tea grew cold in the cup.

In the kitchen Mrs Sandiston had left a cold plate for him – chicken and ham with pickles, potatoes and, to follow, a cold fruit dessert. Everything must be ready for him – that was another thing Grace had learned.

Today Edward was travelling back from Italy, from Milan, where he had been for a few days seeing to the business of the factory there. And he always came back exhausted from such a trip. And although he complained about it, he could not let it go. 'People always get dirty,' he said. 'That's something you can rely on. People always need clean clothes. Soap will never go out of fashion.' Grace herself had tentatively touched on the subject of his selling the factory, but he had become angry, questioning her right to give an opinion in the face of her ignorance, and she had quickly backed away from what threatened to be a confrontation.

There had been several such incidents of late, she reflected, and she had not known how to respond. He was at times like a spring that could be released by the slightest vibration, set off by almost anything. And yet again she wondered at the reasons for his sensitivity. Could it be partly to do with money? He was desperate to make money, it seemed to Grace, and generally his businesses were doing less well than he hoped or needed. When money did come in, so much of it went in expenditure on the house. 'The house must be finished.' He had said the words to her more times than she could remember. And when money permitted, the plasterers would come in, and the painters and the carpenters, and another room in the house would be a little closer to completion. 'But we don't need the other rooms to be finished,' Grace had said. 'We have plenty of room for all our needs.' And it had been the wrong thing to say, for who was she to know better than he, particularly where the matter of the house was concerned?

So she had learned to hold her tongue in matters of the furbishing of Asterleigh, and learned not to be surprised when she heard banging or hammering from the direction of some distant, unused, unfinished room.

And in order to pay for the developments certain cost-cutting measures must be applied. It came to Grace eventually that the completion of the house was the most important thing in Edward's life – more important at times, she thought, than she herself.

And yet, strangely, he never stinted on her clothes or her carriage. And she eventually realized why: she, Grace discovered, was in a way to him like a part of the house itself. Perhaps she was like a possession also, and as such he wanted her always to look her best, and to be shown in the best setting. So he might suggest cutting back on certain items such as food, and wages for his workers, but at the same time Grace, as befitting the wife of a prominent man, must always be well dressed and a credit to her husband.

Mrs Spencer had believed that the house had driven him, and Grace had no doubt that she was correct.

Yes, it was the house. This had not been apparent to her at the very start. After their marriage they had spent just one night at Asterleigh and then had gone to London for two weeks on their honeymoon. And he had been kind and considerate and caring, and she had thought that a marriage without love on her side might not be such a bad thing after all. They had gone to the opera and the theatre. But Grace had soon learned that it was not because he enjoyed such things but because they were part of the lifestyle that he aspired to. And he soon learned, even then, what he could get away with. When discussing a visit to the opera house it was: 'Oh, not Wagner – he takes too long. He's much too great a piece to take out of life. Find something shorter, that won't send me to sleep. And preferably where the soprano doesn't sound like a cat on heat.'

It took a little while, but before too long Grace learned of the scope of Edward's aspirations. He never said as much, but in time she divined that his aim was to be on equal terms with those on a social scale above. He professed so many times not to care for position, but it became very clear that his ambition was to join those who enjoyed by right and birth a plane on a stratosphere above his own. He was resentful of old money, Grace discovered, yet all his efforts, with every breath he took, was to that one end, to be one of them.

'Look at you,' he had said in admiration and with great pride while they were on a trip to Redbury some months after their marriage, '– you'd show them all up – all the lords and ladies in the kingdom.' Grace had been trying on a gown in a dress shop and had come out of the dressing room to show off the gown to Edward. 'You must have it,' he had said. 'You look wonderful.' But Grace had protested, 'Edward, it's an extravagance we can't afford. When do we get invited to a ball or a soirée?' And his face had darkened and he had exclaimed, 'My wife will be a credit to me, no matter what the occasion.' And so the dress had been bought, and hung now in the wardrobe, never worn since that first fitting.

'What I want, and what I plan,' he had said on that night after their return from Redbury, 'and what I intend to have, is to live a better life than this. The time isn't ready yet, but the time will come, and come soon, when we can hold up our heads with all the gentry around here – around anywhere. We shall have grand balls and I shall show you off –

and I'll be the envy of all those namby-pamby bluebloods who think they're so grand. And you shall give afternoon teas to the wives of the gentlemen, and we shall have croquet parties, and archery and tennis, and in the winter we'll go skating on the frozen lake, and afterwards everyone will come back here to get warm, and we shall serve hot rum punch.'

And she had nodded yes to all he said, for she had learned by this time that it was unwise to deny the possibility of any of his dreams.

'And,' he had said, 'I want a son. A son to carry on my name and my blood.' He had kissed her, passionately. 'Give me a son, Grace, and you'll make me the happiest man.'

Now, picking up her cup, she drank from it. The tea was cold. As she set the cup back in its saucer she heard the sound of a carriage, and looking from the window again, saw the lights of carriage lanterns as the trap, driven by Rhind, came up the drive.

On a much earlier occasion when Edward was returning home she had seen Rhind as he was about to set out to meet his master at the station. 'But what if he's not on that train?' Grace had said to Rhind. 'Then I shall simply wait for the next train, ma'am,' Rhind had said.

Now she moved from the window and sat beside the fire, and minutes later heard the front door closing and then Edward's steps crossing the hall. Seconds later he was entering the room, closing the door behind him and coming towards her.

'You waited up for me,' he said after he had embraced her and kissed her.

'Of course.' Their words were a charade, she said to herself; they both knew that she was never again likely to do otherwise.

With a groan and a sigh of relief he threw himself down

409

onto the sofa. 'Please, Gracie,' he said, and lifted his right foot.

Grace eased off his boots. 'Your supper's in the pantry,' she said as she handed him his carpet slippers. 'Shall I get it for you?'

'Thank you.'

'Will you eat in here?'

'Yes, I will.'

Grace set a place for him on a small table by the piano, and poured him a glass of wine. As he preferred, she sat not too far from him as he ate.

'I was tempted to eat something on the train,' he said, 'but it looked such disgusting muck I managed to resist it.' When he had finished the meat he poured himself another glass of wine. 'That's better,' he said, smiling at Grace. 'I'm a nicer person when I've eaten.'

'How was it?' Grace asked, when he began to look a little more relaxed. 'How was the business?'

He groaned. 'Oh, God, it gets so trying. It seems that whenever I go back there there's trouble of one kind or another. I really must think about getting rid of it. Sometimes I think it's not worth all the effort, the constant travelling back and forth. If I had somebody there I could trust that would be a different matter, but I haven't, and it's not likely that I shall have.'

Grace removed the tray and placed it on the sideboard. 'Would you like more wine?'

'Just a drop more.'

When she had poured his wine she got the post that had come for him in his absence. 'Will you look at it now?'

He nodded, and Grace took a letter opener and slit the envelopes one by one and placed them before him in a neat little pile. Turning up the lamp he began to go through them, putting some aside immediately and looking at others with interest.

'Ah,' he said, tapping a letter he held, 'this is interesting. I've found a sculptor to mend the figure. It will be good to get that done. He's based in Redbury. He's the only one who answered my advertisement. Still, it'll only need one if the man is the right one.'

Had Grace been more foolish than she was she might have said: why go spending money on a not very good piece of sculpture when you need it for more pressing matters? But she knew that such words would anger him, besides which, having just returned from one of his trips abroad his temper was never the best in any case.

He made love to her that night, taking her with a passion born not only of his feelings for her, but also his hunger after being several days away. And Grace did her best to respond, and tried to say the appropriate words and make the appropriate sounds and moves. And although she was not happy with the situation, he seemed to be. If it was a charade on her part, then it seemed that she was the only one who was aware of it.

When it was over, he lay with his arm across her body and said, 'I shall arrange to go into Redbury and see that artist on Friday. You might care to go in with me, would you? You must have some shopping to do.'

It was her instinct to decline the invitation; there was no particular reason she wished to go into the city. But refusal of his offer would not have been well received, she knew.

'I don't suppose you've been out much while I've been gone, have you?' he said.

'I haven't been anywhere.'

'Then come in with me. I can leave you there to do any shopping you need and I'll meet the artist and then go on to Swindon. I have an appointment there – and the next morning as well. So I shan't be back tomorrow night. I'll stay over. Save all the travelling.'

On Friday the two set out for Berron Wick station with Johnson holding the reins. They started early: Edward, once up and on the move, was never one to tarry, and as soon as breakfast – and hardly a leisurely one at that – was over, he was ready and eager to be on his way. Rhind, he said, would have driven them to the station, but he was already out of the house on various errands.

Arriving in Redbury, Edward walked with Grace to the main street, and then left her there to pursue his business with the sculptor. Grace, on her own, wandered about the shops buying various items. She stopped to have some coffee at one point and then, having made one or two further calls, set off back to the railway station. With luck, she thought, she might make the 12.50.

She arrived on the platform just seconds after the train had pulled in, and was met by a throng of people leaving the train to go into the town. She hurried towards the carriages, and then came to a sudden stop as a man swung out in front of her.

'Kester . . .'

'Grace . . .' He was facing her, having just got off the train. He wore his grey ulster and carried a small case.

Grace stayed there looking at him, unmoving. She could not simply step around him and get onto the train. And he, seeing that this was nevertheless her intention, put out a hand, palm out, and said: 'Don't. Oh, Grace, don't go.'

She remained where she was, while people hurried past carrying their baskets and bags and umbrellas. And along with all the bustle came the sound of the carriage doors slamming, and then, moments later, the guard's whistle. At this Grace took a step forward.

'I should –' she began, but got no further.

And then from beyond Kester's tall form came the sound of the engine starting to get up steam. The decision was made, it was too late for any other course now, the train was leaving the station.

'Thank you.' Kester inclined his head slightly as he murmured the words. And then, 'Oh, Grace, I've been so hoping to see you. I didn't dare write.'

She had said hardly more than three words, and realized that she was almost breathless. She gave a foolish sounding little laugh, and said, 'That wasn't clever, I'm afraid. There isn't another train for half an hour.' They were almost alone on the platform now, and the train was swiftly receding in the distance. 'Did you just get off the train?' Grace said.

'Yes. I've been working in Marshton. So, what brings you to Redbury?'

'Oh, nothing of importance, just a little shopping for this and that.'

He nodded. 'I have some brief business here in the town and —'

'Then I mustn't keep you,' Grace broke in.

'Don't say that. It's such a pleasure to see you again. I can hardly believe it.' A little silence fell between them, obvious and awkward, then Grace said:

'Are you still living here in Redbury?'

'No, we're in Corster. Crescent Gardens, do you know it? A decent enough little villa, I suppose. The White House it's called, though it's not white by any means. Still, it'll do until the lease on Birchwood becomes free again.' He paused a long moment, then added, 'Will you walk with me a little? I have to visit a house not too far away.'

She hesitated, and he, seeing her hesitation, gently touched her arm. 'Please — walk with me.'

As he took a step beside her she found herself turning and falling in step with him. And so they left the station platform and the station and walked together, a little apart, along the street.

'Is it far?' Grace asked as they crossed over at the corner.

'No, just five or six minutes.'

She did not want to leave his side, but at the same time she felt uncomfortable walking beside him. 'If you have business,' she said, 'I shall be in the way.'

'No, you won't, believe me. Trust me.'

Having reached the other side of the street, he came to a stop, Grace halting with him. 'It's just along here,' he said. 'Have you got to get your train so soon?'

'Well . . .'

He read the uncertainty in her voice. 'No, you haven't, am I right?'

'Well, I mustn't be too late.'

'Of course not.'

'Where is your husband?'

'He has several errands to run. Some here in Redbury and then others in Swindon.'

A moment's pause, then: 'Listen,' he said, 'let me do what work I have to do here, and then let's have a drink somewhere and talk. Please don't say no. I have to know about you. How you've been. Sophie still asks after you.'

'How is she?'

'Oh, she's fine. She's absolutely fine.' He turned, and took her arm, and for a few moments she allowed her arm to be held. 'Come . . .'

'What do you have to do here?' she asked.

'There's a house for which I'm to design some alterations. I'm just here today to take some measurements. Then I can get on with the final drawings.'

They came to a stop outside a tall Georgian house. 'Is this it?' Grace said.

'Yes.' He took keys from his pocket.

'You want me to wait here for you?'

'No, come in with me. There's no one there. The place is empty, and it'll only take a minute.'

She hesitated, but on his urging moved behind him as he

414

pushed open the gate and started up the short path to the front door.

'Are you sure this is all right?' Grace said. Her heart was hammering now, and she felt like a child at risk of being caught out in some major wrongdoing.

'Perfectly all right.' He turned the key in the lock and pushed open the door. 'The owners are away. No one'll come in.' He walked ahead of her, opened the door on the left and stepped into a spacious drawing room. After a moment's hesitation, Grace followed. The room had very little furniture in it. The carpet, though clean, was old and worn. 'The owners have just bought the house,' he said. 'All this –' he waved a hand, taking in the spare furnishings, 'is to be thrown out.' He gestured to an old sofa along one wall. 'Why don't you sit down and I'll get this bit of work done and we can leave again. Take your coat off if you like. I shan't be more than fifteen minutes.'

'Well – yes, I will for a minute. Are you quite sure no one will come in?'

'Positive. Please, trust me. They're in France.' He took off his coat and draped it over the arm of the sofa. 'They'll be away for ages yet. Months, so I understand.'

From his bag he took out a notebook and pencil and a tape measure. 'Now I'll leave you here while I get busy,' he said. 'It won't take me long to take these few measurements.'

He went from the room and Grace turned, looking about her. There was a cracked, speckled mirror on the wall opposite, and she saw herself reflected in it, and wondered at the circumstance of her being there. She looked strange, odd in this strange setting, standing there, in a stranger's house, killing time. She wandered around the room. There was little to see. The old paper on the walls was stained and the marks where pictures had hung were clearly evident. There was a chair next to a rather distressed-looking table. At one time handsome, now the table's surface was bruised and scarred. On its once flawless, polished surface were rings left by hot or wet vessels, and someone had carved initials and scratched an obscene little drawing. In the centre of the table stood a cracked pot with a dead plant in it. Beside the wide fireplace there was a bureau with a broken top. She moved on, with every step seeming to be more conscious of her presence there. She could not seem to slow the rapid, heavy beating of her heart.

It seemed to her that she waited in the room a long time, but then at last there came the sound of footsteps in the hall and Kester was coming into the room, rewinding his tape measure.

'All finished,' he said, turning to the sofa near where Grace had been standing, and then swiftly turning about, with a touch of panic in the move at finding her not there. Seeing her standing by the window his face relaxed into a smile. 'There you are. I thought you were going to take off your coat.'

'I shall have to go,' she said. 'I have to get back.'

He set down his measure, notepad and pencil on the table, then moved towards her, coming to a stop a yard away. 'Ah, Grace, I can't believe it, that you're here – that I'm with you.'

She did not move, did not speak.

'Come on,' he said. 'Come and sit down a moment.' He reached out and took her hand in his and turned, drawing her with him. She moved half-reluctantly, her mouth opening to protest, but in the end saying nothing. There was a deep fear in her; it was partly a fear of being disturbed by the owners, and partly a fear of the immediate freedom they faced.

He led her to the sofa, and there stopped. 'Oh, Grace,' he said, 'I can't tell you how I –' and then broke off to add,

416

'Please – oh, please take off your coat and hat. You look as if you're about to take flight.'

'But I can't stay. I have to go.'

'Not yet. Stay a while to talk. Just for a few minutes. Come on, take off your coat, take off your hat.'

She did so, setting them on the chair beside the table.

'That's better. Now come and sit down a minute.'

She sat on the sofa and he sat down beside her.

A momentary pause, then he said, 'The people who own this house, the Clarksons, want me to design a conservatory to go at the back. It's not a huge job, but it's one that I'll enjoy, I think. They want other things done too, nothing really major. There's talk of a spiral staircase and –' He broke off. 'Listen to me rambling on – as if I'm the least interested in such work right now. As if you're interested either.' He reached out and took her left hand and began to peel off her glove. When he had done, she took off the other one. He took it from her and laid both gloves down on the seat at his side. 'Oh, what a thrill it is to see you,' he breathed.

'Kester . . .'

'Don't say anything – not if you're going to say that you must go.' He took her hand and kissed her palm, her fingers curling up against the slight roughness of his cheek. 'I still can't believe it, that you're here, with me.'

He released her hand and his arms came around her, drawing her closer. Bending his head to her, his hand came up and touched beneath her chin, lifting her face to him. His mouth came down upon her own, and she could do nothing, could say nothing that would stop the moment.

The kiss between them was so long that she became breathless, and broke from him to snatch at the air with a little gasping laugh that was half-joy and half-hysteria. His hand brushed around her back and came to touch on her breast. She drew in her breath, her lips apart, and his mouth again came pressing onto hers. She felt his tongue, warm and sweet against her own tongue, and thought that she could never get enough of his touch. They had kissed before, the thought flashed through her mind, but it had never been like this. In the past they had held back, she realized, on her part in a belief that there was a future, and that they could afford to wait. Now she knew they had no future, and that these stolen minutes must last – perhaps for ever.

His hands moved lower and when she felt his touch upon her bare skin she made a little moan of protest. He was heedless, however, and when she sighed again it was purely from pleasure and her protestations were stilled.

They were lying on Kester's coat which he had spread out on the carpet. She sat up, her petticoats awry and her hair over her face. Her dress lay with her coat and hat. As she put a hand up to her hair she felt his hand on her bare back. She turned and bent to him and kissed him.

'Grace, Grace, Grace,' he said.

'Yes? What is it?'

'Oh, Grace, that was the most wonderful thing.'

'Yes. Yes, it was.' She whispered the words in the stillness of the room.

And it had been wonderful, she thought. She had never imagined that she could have found such joy, such pleasure. This was the act that she participated in with Edward, but it could not be the same. Now it had taken place with Kester, and with love, and it was so different, so very different. 'Oh,' she said, 'what it is to love and be loved.'

He gave a little groan at her words and raised his hands to put them either side of her face and draw her to him to be kissed again. 'I love you,' he said. 'Oh, Grace, I love you so much. Do you love me?'

'You must know I do.'

'Tell me. Let me hear the words.'

'I love you, Kester. As I've never loved any man before.'

He sighed, a deep sigh of pleasure, then pulled himself up a little so that his back was resting against the sofa. Then drawing Grace towards him he wrapped his arm around her. She murmured, 'That's better: I'm a little cold,' and he took the loose ends of his coat and pulled them over her. 'I'll make you warm,' he said. And warm, content, she nestled in the crook of his arm, her chin against his bare chest.

'I don't ever want to go back,' she said.

'That's what I want too. For you never to have to go back.'

A little silence, just the sounds of their breathing, then he said, 'I had no right to talk to you like that the last time we met. I was so shocked – to discover that you were to marry.'

'I know. I couldn't bear the thought of you knowing.'

'I couldn't believe it. And that you were to marry Spencer – of all people. But why not? You had every right to try to find happiness wherever you could – for both you and Billy. I certainly couldn't offer it to you.' He paused. 'How is it, Grace?'

'How is what?'

'Your life – your married life. Are you happy?'

She raised her head and looked him in the eyes. 'Of course I'm not happy. But I get by. Besides, I made a bargain.'

'Yes.'

She laid her head back on his chest. 'And I try to make Edward happy. Whether he is or not, I don't know. I think it would take a great deal to make him satisified.'

'You don't love him.' It was half-question, half-statement.

'No, I don't love him. I told you, I love *you*. I'll never love anyone else but you.'

Silence between them again, then he said, 'I have to tell you . . .'

'What? You have to tell me what?'

'My wife . . .'

She sat up now, turning her face to him. 'What about her? Has she been to see you?'

'She – she's dead.'

Her mouth fell open in a silent expression of shock. 'Tell me,' she said, 'what happened.'

'She had been ill, for a long time,' he said after a moment. 'I hardly know how to say it, but – it came from a – a disease, from her way of living. She had no resistance to anything at the end. Her heart was so weakened, I understand, and it was this, finally, that took her. I was there when she died. It seemed to me that she had been holding on – until I got there. She spoke to me a little and then went quite swiftly.'

'When did this happen?'

'Two months ago. I had a letter from her, telling me she was sick. I didn't go at once as I thought perhaps it was just another of her stories, another of her tales to gain sympathy. It was not. This time it was true. I found her in a dreadful state, lying in a workhouse infirmary.'

'Oh, Kester – I don't know what to say.'

'There is nothing one can say.' He shook his head. 'What a wasted life she had. Totally wasted. And to turn her back on love like that. She could have had so much joy, so much contentment. She strove so hard, never being satisfied, and in the end she had nothing of it. She had nothing to show for a lifetime.' His voice cracked on the last word and Grace saw tears glistening in his eyes. 'It's the waste,' he said. 'And how desperately wretched she must have been. All that time. To go through life and never to find anything that could make her happy.' There was a pause, then he sighed and added, 'I can't help but think how ironic it is, now, the situation.'

'What do you mean?'

He shrugged. 'Well, here am I, free at last to marry you, but you're married to another.'

She put a hand to her face, closing her eyes. 'I can't bear to think about it. It's too cruel.'

'Let's not think about it,' he said. 'Let's not talk about it either.'

'No.' Then she added in a little burst of passion, 'These moments have to last me.'

'Grace . . .'

'They do. They have to last the rest of my life.' And now she turned her face away. 'For we can never meet again.'

'Don't say that.'

'You know it's true.' She closed her eyes and the tears spilled out between her lashes and ran down her cheeks. He wrapped his arms more closely about her and felt her tears against his chest. Bending his head, he kissed her forehead, kissed her mouth and kissed the tears from her cheeks.

On her return journey she got a hansom from the station. It was almost seven o'clock by the time she got back to Asterleigh. She found herself walking self-consciously into the house, aiming for a sense of casualness that she was far from feeling. In her mind she felt that the afternoon was written all over her, over her face and over her body, written in the fabric of her dress and in her desperately dressed hair. And she greeted Mrs Sandiston – who happened to be passing through the hall – a little too expansively, and could feel her guilt in her smile.

Up in her dressing room she took off her hat and coat and looked at herself in the glass. She looked just the same. Her dress was unmarked, uncreased; there was no trace that she could see of what had taken place in the drawing room of the strangers' house. But when she lifted her hands to touch at her hair she could trace the faintest scent that was unfamiliar, and Kester was with her still.

She had finished changing, when through the open dressing room door, a knock coming from the door to the bedroom was heard. She called out, 'Come in,' and saw Billy enter and cross the carpet towards her.

He stood in the dressing room doorway. 'I saw you come in. I saw you from the window. You've been out so long.'

'Yes, I had some shopping to do, some errands to run, in Redbury.' It was partly a lie; it was not the whole truth.

'If you'd waited till tomorrow I could have come in with you.'

'I was going in with Mr Spencer. How was school today?'

'It was fine.' A little pause; he put his head slightly on one side and gave her a sideways glance. 'You know, Grace, I reckon you've changed.'

A pause from her before she responded, then she gave a light little laugh and said, 'Changed? Oh, William, what nonsense you talk. Of course I haven't changed. How have I changed?'

He didn't answer.

'Do you mean today?' she said.

'No, lately.'

'Oh.' She felt a little relief at his words, partly afraid that he might have been able to read upon her face her meeting with Kester.

'No, I haven't changed,' she said. 'It's your imagination.'

'Yes, you have.' He thought about it for a moment, then added, 'I can't describe it, I can't explain it. It's as if you're not so – so bright as you were. So often you seem – a little sad.'

'Do I?'

'Yes.' He moved to her and put a hand on her shoulder. 'I haven't seen you really happy for a long time. I don't want you to be sad, Grace.'

'I'm not sad.'

'Really?'

'Believe me.'

That night Grace lay in the wide bed, facing the empty space that would tomorrow night be occupied by Edward. She thought of Billy's words – that she had appeared to him to be unhappy. Happiness . . . What right had she to expect such a thing? And regardless of right, how could she expect such a thing to come to her? Not now, not ever, not without Kester. Kester was denied her now.

She turned in the bed, imagining Kester's arms about her, the sensation of his body upon her own. A long time passed before she slept.

Chapter Twenty

Edward returned the following day just after five o'clock. He was tired, and irritable with frustration. Things had not gone well at the mill, and Grace knew that she must watch her step or risk raising his anger.

At least, however, he had made some progress with regard to the statue. He had met the sculptor, he said, and the man planned to come to the house and look at the piece and then arrange to take it away. Going by what had passed between them, Edward seemed not to think that the restoration would pose any difficulties for the artist.

They dined early that evening. Edward had several drinks before dinner – Scotch whisky and soda – and during the meal drank liberally of the wine. It would affect him, Grace knew, and not for the better, and she was dismayed but not surprised when later, in the drawing room, he eschewed the coffee that was offered and merely poured himself brandy. His dark mood was all due to the businesses, she told herself, and wondered yet again whether he would ever be content. The way he ran from one endeavour to another, she reflected, he was like a juggler with plates spinning on poles, moving desperately between them to stop them from crashing to the ground.

A little later, Edward glanced at the clock and murmured, 'Five past nine. I want to see Rhind before he turns in,' and got up from his chair and started across the room. Grace wanted to say, 'Can't it wait till tomorrow?' but knew that such words would be useless. Instead she said,

424

'Edward, I'm very tired. I think I shall go to bed soon, if you don't mind.'

'Do as you please,' he said shortly, and went from the room.

When he was not back by ten o'clock Grace made her way up to the bedroom and got undressed. Not only did she feel weary, but she felt a headache coming on, and a heaviness at the back of her eyes and nose as if a cold might be developing. She climbed into bed and closed her eyes and lay there waiting for the sounds of Edward's feet on the landing. For a long time he did not come.

She had fallen asleep, and Edward's voice was suddenly there: 'Are you sleeping? Are you? Are you sleeping?'

'What?' She came to out of the fog of her sleep. 'What – what time is it?'

'What time is it? What does it matter what time it is?'

He had been drinking further, she realized. She pulled herself up a little in the bed, trying to appear more alert, and he came forward and sat on the side of the bed, his back to her. 'Did you see Rhind?' she asked, showing an appearance of interest that she did not feel. And quickly he turned so that he could face her:

'What do you care whether I saw Rhind or not? Don't you concern yourself with Rhind. Not that you'd ever want to, would you?' He gave a short laugh. His words were a little slurred. 'I'll say not. You'd like it if Rhind were sent away, far, far away, and never showed his face around here again, wouldn't you?'

She did not answer. He spoke the truth, but she could not admit it.

'Wouldn't you?' he said. 'Well, I'm afraid it's not going to happen. I need him around.' He smiled suddenly. 'And the truth is – he needs me. So I suppose we suit one another. He's for ever grateful to me, Rhind is – and I'm glad of that.

I trust him implicitly where I'm concerned. And there's not many one can say that about. Mind you, he hasn't always been a good boy with other people. But I s'pose you know about that, don't you?'

He would be answered, she realized, and she said, 'Mrs Spencer mentioned something once. She said you helped him out of a difficult situation.'

'Oh, is that what she said?' He nodded. 'Well, she was right. I suppose you could say that being accused of arson was a somewhat difficult situation. Anyway, I got him out of it and he's never forgotten it. Sometimes his loyalty gets a bit – a bit too much in a way, but he's here now – and he's not going away, my dear.' He paused. 'Anyway, why this antipathy towards him? After all, he's only trying to protect my interests. Is that such a bad thing?'

She did not answer.

'Or is it,' he said, 'that perhaps he knows something that you don't know? Or rather, something that you don't know he knows? Is that more like it?'

'I'm sorry, Edward,' she said, 'but I don't know what you're talking about.'

'No, of course you don't. And why should you, when I speak in riddles? Don't worry, my dear, in time all will become clear. Or perhaps it will.' With his last words he swayed, leaning briefly towards her, and she could smell on his breath the liquor he had been drinking.

'You never have liked him, have you?' he said, straightening again and pulling at his cravat. 'You once hinted that he had been insolent to you – right at the start, at that time when I found you on the road and drove you back to Green Shipton. He said to you – what was it? You never would tell me what he said.'

He waited, and Grace said, 'I can't remember. It's so long ago.'

'You remember all right. You wouldn't be likely to forget an insult, I'm sure. I never would, anyway.'

Grace said nothing, but gave a little shake of her head, as if to say, it's of no importance. With Edward in the mood he was in, she must watch her every word, her every expression.

Edward looked steadily at her for a moment, then raised his arm and threw the cravat. It landed on a chair a few feet away. He began to unbutton his waistcoat and shirt, then paused in the action and leaned towards Grace again. 'I have the feeling,' he said, 'that Rhind knows something about you that you're not aware of.'

There was something a little chilling about his words, his tone. 'I told you, Edward,' she said, 'I don't understand. I don't know what you're talking about.'

He smiled, but there was no humour in the expression. 'No, of course you don't, my dear. And why should you? And why should you bother your pretty head about the jealous mutterings of some slightly crazy servant?' He nodded emphatically. 'Oh, yes, I'm quite sure he's half-crazy. But there, he's also very faithful, and that's worth a lot at times.'

'Edward, I'm tired – I think I've got a cold coming on, and –'

'Oh, dear. You're tired and you think you've got a cold coming on. Well, that's too bad, isn't it. You'd better take something for it. We can't have you with a cold, can we? And you'd better stay indoors and not go gallivanting about. No more trips to Redbury for you, not until you're sure your cold has gone.'

What did he mean? 'It's just – my head aches so,' she said. 'I'm sorry I'm not better company. And I know you've had some difficulties.'

'That's not far from the truth.' He continued undressing, draping his clothes over the back of a chair. In the morning, she thought, they would be creased and he would complain.

She lay down again, turning away, and closed her eyes.

427

After a while she felt the mattress dip as he got into bed. Only seconds passed before he reached out for her, roughly taking her shoulder and turning her towards him. 'Don't go to sleep,' he said. 'I'm not tired. I need company.'

His heavy beard had grown so throughout the day and it was rough on the softness of her cheek. His hands too, were rough in the using of her, but there was no sound she dare make other than those that might falsely express a pleasure that she was so far from feeling.

He reached his orgasm quickly and aggressively, and fell away from her, lying on his back, his breath from his exertion coming in gasps that slowly diminished. Grace could hear her own breathing, also a little heavy from exhaustion, and touched too by her shame and misery at the role she had played. She could not help but think of how it had been with Kester. And had that been so recently, that wonderful, magical time – or had it happened a hundred years ago?

She lay for some moments just listening to Edward's breathing. How could it all have turned out in this way? She had never, at the start, thought that it could be like this. It was not the first time, however, she reminded herself with bitter irony, and it most surely would not be the last. Tonight, however, she felt that he had been unusually careless of her own feelings, had been even rougher than he had been during some of the more drunken periods that she could remember.

The minutes dragged by. She had turned on her side now, away from him, her teeth clenched, trying to slow her breathing and capture some sense of calm. She could not, would not complain. She had made her bed, and now she must lie in it.

She could feel tears well under her eyelids and wet on her skin, running down her cheek onto the pillow. It was self-pity, she told herself, and there was no place for such an indulgent emotion in her present life. And yet for a minute or two the tears continued to fall. When they had ceased she could feel them drying on her cheeks.

'I need some water.'

Edward's voice came thick and muttering, and she was aware of him sitting up in bed beside her. She heard the sounds as he groped for matches and then the sound of the match being struck and the hiss of the flare of the flame. Shadows danced on the ceiling as he lit the bedside candle. She heard him drink from his water glass, and then the fall of water as he refilled the glass from the jug. He drank again.

'I can't sleep,' he said. And then, turning to Grace: 'Are you asleep? No doubt you are.'

'No, I'm not asleep.'

'What is it they say? No sleep for the wicked? Well, I don't know if that applies to me, but what about you, Grace?' His tone was heavy with irony, and she could not think of any words to frame a reply.

He pulled himself up further in the bed, and she turned and looked at him as he lay beside her. She found his eyes directed at her, meeting her gaze.

'Well, d'you like what you see?' he said.

'I beg your pardon?' There was something about him this evening that was almost unnerving.

'I thought you turned round to have a look at me,' he said.

She shook her head on the pillow. 'I don't know what's going on with you tonight,' she said. 'There's something – something – I don't know.' And as soon as she had spoken, doubt flashed through her mind; she should have not acknowledged his strange mood; better she had left it without comment.

'There's nothing different about me,' he said. 'Perhaps it's you. Perhaps there's a difference in you.'

'Edward – please. Don't go on like this.'

'Like what?'

'You know what I mean . . .'

He continued to look at her, and she closed her eyes against his ungiving gaze.

'Your looking at me just now,' he said, '– I wondered if it was because you thought we were something alike.'

'Alike?' She was looking at him again now. 'What are you saying? I don't understand.'

'Fairman and I. I heard people say that in some lights they could hardly tell us apart. Same height; same hair colour, almost. Similar build. Did you ever have that difficulty? In telling us apart, I mean.'

She felt herself go cold. Why should he suddenly bring up the subject of Kester? 'Why are you saying this?' she said; then, 'No, I've never thought about it, your similarities.'

'I just wondered.'

'Mind you, we're not at all alike under the skin. Any similarity is purely a surface, physical thing.'

'Of course.'

'Sit up a bit,' he said. 'Let me look at you.'

'Edward –'

'Sit up.'

She did so. He leaned closer to her, peering closely at her in the dim light.

'You look – strange,' he said.

'I'm all right.'

'Have you been crying?'

'No.'

'You look as if you might have been. It's hard to see in this light.'

'What have I got to cry about?'

'Exactly. I couldn't have put it better myself.'

'Edward – why are you being like this?'

A pause, then he said, 'You will love me some day. And

when you do, I just hope I still feel the same way about you.'

They looked at one another in the pale light of the candle, then Grace turned her head away and sank lower again in the bed.

'Rhind was out on errands yesterday,' he said.

'Yes, you told me he would be. Why? What of that?'

'He went to Marshton.'

'So?'

'He got on the train at Marshton, which of course stops at Redbury. And as the train drew out of Redbury station he saw you. You were standing on the platform, talking to my old friend Fairman.'

Grace could feel herself chilled, and the most dreadful feeling of fear swept over her, and so swiftly; her mouth was at once dry, her heart pounding.

'Did you hear what I said?' he said.

'Yes, I heard you.' And surely, she thought, he must hear the hammering of her heart. She wet her lips and was grateful that she was facing away from him, her face in deeper shadow.

'I assumed it was a chance meeting. It must have been – since you only went into the town at my suggestion.'

'Of course it was a chance meeting.'

'You didn't mention it – seeing him.' He touched her shoulder. 'Turn round and look at me, will you.'

'Why should I mention seeing him?' She would not turn her head.

'Do you think about him?' he asked.

'Of course not,' she lied. 'He's part of the past.'

'I hope that's true.'

'Of course it's true.'

'Turn round and look at me.'

She did so now, looking him in the eyes, lying with her gaze.

'What did he have to say to you?'

'The usual things. He asked how I was. He told me of his daughter. He asked after you.'

'How kind.' He paused. 'How long did you talk to him?'

'Oh – some minutes. He said he had an appointment in the town. I got the train back.'

A long pause, then he said, 'You do know you're mine, don't you? You must never forget that. If I ever thought you were unfaithful to me . . . I would . . . I would . . .'

'Oh, for God's sake, Edward.' She tried, daring, to put a note of irritability and scorn into her voice.

'You hear what I'm saying?' he said. 'I hope you do, because I mean it. And if you ever tried to get away from me I would find you. No matter where you were I would find you. And then . . .'

She waited for him to finish the sentence. But he did not. She could feel her palms wet, and she pressed her right hand to her breast; her heart was thudding away again. She turned her body away to lie on her side again, facing away from him, closing her eyes.

'I don't know what I'd do,' he said. 'But whatever it was, it wouldn't make you happy.' He paused. 'Did you hear what I said?'

'Of course I heard what you said.' She must not for one second allow him to think that she was in any way nervous or uncertain.

'What is mine,' he said, 'I do not let go. Ever.'

Dear God, she thought – if he should ask Mrs Sandiston the time of her arrival . . . 'I'm afraid you're rather drunk,' she said.

'Perhaps I am. But that doesn't change anything.' He gave a short laugh. 'It's the wine that does it,' he added, and laughed again. Then his voice serious once more, he said, 'Yes, what is mine is mine. And you'll be mine eventually.'

'I already am.'

432

'I mean your heart and your soul too. Not your body alone.'

A silence fell. She could hear his breathing, and her own. 'I want to go to sleep,' she said. 'I'd rather talk to you when you're sober.'

'No doubt.'

Silence again, then she heard him say:

'I always get what I want sooner or later.'

She did not answer. With luck he would think she was asleep and leave her alone. But it was not to be.

'Did you hear me?' he said. 'You're not asleep, are you?'

'No, I'm not asleep.'

'Well, look around you,' he said. 'And you'll see whether I'm speaking the truth or not.'

She was to get no peace. After a moment she said with a sigh, 'Edward, I'm tired. I'm sorry, but I'm so tired.'

'You can always sleep,' he said. 'You've got no work to do. You lead a life of pure leisure, while I work all hours possible. If I want a little attention I should think I'm entitled to it.'

She turned in the bed now and opened her eyes. 'I'm sorry,' she said, 'I don't always think. I know you work hard. I admire you for it.'

'Thank you, but I don't care to be patronized.'

'No – I mean it.' She spoke the truth now.

'You do?'

'Of course I do. How could I not? Anyone who observes you must think the same.'

'Well, it's true,' he said. 'I do work. And I've had to work, all my life. Since I was a boy. I never had it easy, not like some people. Some people have it handed to them on a plate. Not me. I've had to work and scheme for every penny I've made. And I sometimes think there's no end to it – that I'll never be done.'

She drew herself up a little in the bed and looked at him.

433

He was sitting up, gazing off into the shadows of the room. She could not see his eyes, but she could tell from the position of his body, how he was holding himself, that there was such a great tenseness in him. Lifting a hand, she laid it on his back, through the cotton feeling the cords of his muscles beneath her touch. 'Get some sleep, Edward,' she murmured. She let fall her hand. 'You're tired too. It's so true what you said – you work so hard. You drive yourself so. Please – get some rest. Lie down. Sleep.'

'I can't sleep.'

His words made her think of nights past, nights when she had felt him lying sleepless beside her. Often she had wondered at the demons that were keeping him awake.

'I shouldn't have had to do what I've done,' he said after a moment. His voice was still thick from the wine he had consumed. 'No one should have to do such things.'

'What are you talking about? What things?' She sank back, closing her eyes.

'It's true,' he said after a moment, '– I do always get what I want. I wanted you, didn't I?'

'Did you?'

'I think I wanted you from the first time I saw you, in your father's yard. I was sure to have you eventually, I knew.'

His words brought a chill to her heart, and for a moment she stopped her breath.

'As I said,' he said, 'I always get what I want. Though some things are more difficult to achieve than others. Don't you agree?'

'I don't know, Edward. I don't know what you're talking about.'

'Well, this house for a start,' he said. 'You don't think it just fell into my lap, do you?'

She felt a strange uneasiness that had nothing to do with the conversation of moments before. 'What about the house . . .?'

She felt him, heard him, stir beside her. Then she heard him drink the water from his glass. She had never known him so restless, so sleepless before. 'What about the house?' she said again, though a part of her was telling her not to ask, to leave things unsaid.

'It was always mine,' he said at last. 'Always.'

'What do you mean, it was always yours?'

'It was always meant to be mine.' She heard him take in a breath. 'In God's plan. I'm talking about in God's plan.'

His words were bewildering; and he was making her increasingly uneasy.

'All those people who have it so easy,' he said. 'They don't know what it's like to have to work and graft and scheme and gamble to make headway. I know what it's like. It's what I've always had to do. Nothing fell into my lap, nothing at all.'

The springs creaked as he sat up and then got out of bed. She opened her eyes and in the dim light saw him move in his nightshirt across the carpet. On a small table near the door was a tray holding a jug of water. She watched him as he refilled his water glass and drank from it. 'I've got such an almighty thirst,' he said.

'Perhaps you're coming down with something,' she said. 'There's influenza and colds going about.'

'I haven't got any cold,' he said dismissively. 'I don't get colds. It's the wine; it's not a cold.'

'As you wish. Have it your way.'

'Yes, I'll have it my way.' He drank more water. 'I always do. Sooner or later.' He moved back to the bed, his feet padding softly on the carpet. She heard the sound of his glass being set down on the bedside table, and then felt the mattress sink on his side as he climbed back into bed. 'Like with Asterleigh,' he said as he pulled the covers back over himself.

435

He seemed to want to talk about it, she thought. The house, it seemed to be on his mind.

'No, Asterleigh didn't fall into my lap,' he said after a moment. 'Though it should have done. It was rightly mine.'

'What do you mean? The house came to you with your marriage.'

'Oh, yes, eventually it did. And my wife had got the house because on Joseph Gresham's death everything went to her – being his nearest legal relative. His nearest relative – on paper. Everything – imagine it. Asterleigh, and the land around it, and the mill, everything. It all went to her, his niece – the daughter of his sister – a sister whom he'd barely spoken to in well over twenty years. He didn't even like the woman, by all accounts. They never did get on. So he'd never have any feelings for her daughter, his niece. Are you listening to me?'

'Yes, of course.' She paused. 'If he didn't have any feelings for his niece, why did he leave her everything?'

'He didn't. He left no will – or at least not one that could be found. So everything as a matter of course went to his next of kin – his acknowledged next of kin. And as her mother had already died, that was Eleanor.'

'She told me she couldn't remember anything about her uncle.'

'I doubt that she could. As I say, he and his sister never got on, so he'd hardly have been a regular caller at the house.'

A little silence went by. The house was so still, but then into the quiet came the distant harsh and eerie sound of the barking of a fox. The sudden noise only served to emphasize the silence that surrounded the pair on the bed. 'Why are you telling me all this?' Grace said.

'I'm your husband. A wife should be close to her husband. If she doesn't know what there is to know about him, who should? I'm telling you things.' He was sitting up beside her in the bed, looking ahead of him into the candle-lit dark. 'I might not feel like saying these things again.'

She was growing increasingly uneasy. She could not understand why he was talking in such a way. Although all desire for sleep had left her, she wanted only that he would stop and find sleep for himself.

'I shouldn't have had to do some of the things I've done,' he said after a moment. 'But there are times when you're left with no choice. There's no other way out.' He turned to her, looking her directly in the face. 'You're not stupid,' he said belligerently. 'You can add two and two together.'

'Edward . . .' She put a hand to her mouth. His manner was a little alarming. 'I'm sorry, but I don't know what you're talking about.'

'You don't know what I'm talking about,' he said contemptuously. 'You're not an idiot, and you must have heard the gossip over the years.'

'Gossip? I don't listen to gossip.'

He laughed derisively. 'Well, my God, if that isn't what they all say. And they're the first to listen to any bit of tittle tattle that comes along. Don't play me for a fool, Grace. I'm anything but that, and you know it to be so.'

'I haven't heard any gossip,' she insisted.

'No, well, I s'pose that's because of who you are, who you're married to. You're involved, so you and I would be the last to hear it.'

'I remember my aunt telling me about Mrs Spencer,' Grace said. 'She told me she'd inherited all her uncle's property.'

'And did she tell you anything about Joseph Gresham?'

'Not that I recall. Should she have?'

'He had an eye for the women. Weren't you told that?'

'Oh, yes, now that I think about it. There was something.'

'Well, the way I was told it, his own marriage wasn't up to much. A loveless, childless thing it was.'

437

'And how do you know all this?'

'From my mother. She knew a lot about him.'

'Did you know him?'

'Me? No.' A little pause, and he turned and looked at her. 'You're not getting the picture, are you?'

'What are you talking about?' She turned to face him. 'I told you, Edward, I don't understand what you're saying.'

'No, you don't, you truly don't. Are you that naïve? Perhaps you are.'

'Perhaps I am.'

'Well, to spell it out for you: I'm his son. I'm Joseph Gresham's son.'

The fox barked again into the quiet. And as the echo of the sound died away Grace became aware again of the beating of her heart. It was almost as if she had been anticipating some such revelation from him; that he had been preparing her for such. And perhaps he had. Perhaps all of it tonight had been leading to this.

She did not speak. But at the same time she knew her silence would not end it. After a few moments he said:

'Did you hear what I said?'

'Yes.'

'I'm Joseph Gresham's son.'

'Yes. I heard.'

'Not that he ever recognized me. Certainly not publicly, and barely in reality in any way. Afraid, you see. Afraid of it getting out. The scandal. Nothing was allowed to besmirch his good name. So when I was born there was no whisper of who my father was. It couldn't be allowed to get out.'

'Is Spencer your mother's name?'

'No. She was born Tatten, Ellen Tatten. Spencer was Thomas Spencer, a farmhand who lived nearby. And I suppose he always had an eye for my mother. She was a beautiful young woman, by all accounts – which of course was how she came to attract the attention of Gresham in the first place.'

'So she married Mr Thomas Spencer.'

'Yes. She was pregnant with me when they married. He must have known, of course. But he was so taken with her that he accepted it, her pregnancy, or so I believe. Anyway, he gave me his name, and cared for me as if I'd been his own son. My birth certificate gives his name as that of my father – and I always called him that. I didn't know any better. There were no children born to my mother after me, so I think perhaps this helped to cement the relationship between me and my stepfather. Later, when my mother told me the truth she said that Gresham gave her money when she was pregnant with me – and you can bet your life that this was partly to ensure her silence. I know the rest of her family never knew – her mother and sister, she never told them.'

'How do you know?'

'She told me so. They asked her so many times, but she never told them. She didn't tell her husband, my stepfather, either. I know that; she told me.'

'Did no one have suspicions?'

'Well, of nothing that was near the mark, I believe. People can keep their counsel when they absolutely need to. And I think my mother's relationship with Gresham was unexpected and very brief. I doubt anyone knew of it, other than those concerned. And those who knew weren't talking.'

'When did you learn about – Mr Gresham being your father?'

'When I was eighteen. My stepfather was long dead by then, and it was just the two of us at home. My mother had become ill, and I think she decided I had to know then or perhaps I never would. I suppose she thought that if she waited she might take her secret to the grave. I don't know what good she thought it would do, telling me. I suppose she just thought it was something I was owed. Which I was.'

'What did you think – when she told you?'

'Well, obviously I was very surprised. First of all that Thomas Spencer, whom I'd always thought of as my father, was in fact not. And then to learn that my real father should turn out to have been a rich man, a powerful man. Not like poor old Thomas, poor as a church mouse.'

'Did you believe it – when your mother told you?'

'Why should I not?'

'Well – it's quite a piece of news to tell a young man.'

'Oh, it was that.'

'You must have been very curious about so many things. Did your mother tell you very much?'

'She told me a few things. Of course after her death I thought of so much I wanted to ask her. But that's always the way. I remember I asked her where he was then – my real father, Gresham. She said he'd died when I was ten. And it turned out that he'd acknowledged me to the point where he sent my mother money every year at Christmas. Apparently there was never any letter or note with the money. It was just the money, wrapped in paper, sealed in an envelope. No sender's name or address. I don't know why he chose to send it at Christmas – perhaps he didn't know the date of my birthday. Though I suppose Christmas is as good a time as any.'

Grace could hear the note of bitterness in his voice, and thought perhaps it was not so surprising.

'I remember my mother saying to me that everything should have come to me. Asterleigh, the mill. "It was yours by rights," she said. "You're his only child." Unfortunately it didn't come to me.'

A little moment of silence, then Grace said, 'It went instead to his niece.'

'As I said, he left no will – so it all went to his niece, his niece Miss Eleanor Addison. And she didn't particularly want it. She didn't move into the house. It was too much for her to deal with. She was accustomed to a quiet, very simple life. She was not one for activity and getting about and meeting people, and having lots of servants at her beck and call. No, so she didn't move into the house; she came and looked it over and that was it. She decided to stay put in her little cottage on the outskirts of Swindon.'

'Then who looked after it, the house?'

'Oh, she kept on a couple of Gresham's servants to run the place and keep it from falling down. And her solicitor arranged for payment to be made to them. Like with the mill. She had no interest in that, either. She told me she never even visited the mill. And the place was making hardly anything. I think the whole thing would have collapsed if I hadn't come along when I did.' He turned in the bed and leaned towards her and she could smell the warmth of his breath. His hand touched her shoulder, grasped it for a moment then let go. 'Aren't you going to ask me, then?' he said. 'Eh? Aren't you going to ask me how I got it?'

She kept silent, while a deeper chill seemed to invade her blood and her bones.

'Well,' he said, ignoring her silence, 'it didn't drop out of the sky into my lap, did it?' He hooted a laugh that rang in the room, and made Grace grip the sheet around her. 'I told you just now, that whatever I set my mind on getting I usually get. Like you, when I saw you in your father's yard one day. I saw you and –'

'Edward –' she broke in, 'please . . .'

'What? What's the matter? You think it's a bit indelicate, do you? Well, maybe it is, but on the other hand you should be flattered. It's true – what I set my mind on I generally get. And I set my mind on you.' He gave a deep sigh, reflective, as if looking back over the years and examining the past. 'Yes, I did. And before that I set my mind on Asterleigh.' He was looking directly at her now, his face only inches from her own, as if determined not to miss one nuance of any change in her expression or the tone of her voice. 'But don't run away with the idea that that was easy, because it wasn't. I had to plot and plan for it.'

'Edward – why are you telling me all this?' She did not think she could stand to hear any more. In her heart there was a growing fear, a fear of what other possible revelation she might be forced to listen to.

'Aren't you interested?'

'I don't know why you're telling me it all.'

'I thought you'd be interested,' he said. 'After all, I'm your husband. You should be interested in everything about me – particularly in learning a little about my past.' He paused briefly. 'And I'm not ashamed of it. You don't think that, do you?'

'Of course not.'

He hiccuped, and it sounded loud in the room. She heard him hold his breath, and then hiccup again. He sat in silence until the momentary disturbance had passed, then said, 'Miss Eleanor was not an easy woman to get to know. At least she wouldn't have been in the ordinary way, but I managed without too much trouble.'

'Mrs Spencer said it was through her paintings.' Grace said.

'That's right. But not quite in the way she thought.'

'Oh?'

'Yes. I made all kinds of enquiries about her, and over a short space of time learned a great deal. I found out so much. She kept to herself, I found out, and hardly went anywhere. Her one passion was her painting. You see, that's where a person is vulnerable, did you realize that? In their passions. Find out what it is that drives them, find out the nature and the subject of their passion, and you'll find you have power.'

'Is that what you wanted? Power over her?'

'Well, that's a rather brutal way of putting it, isn't it?' He waited for a moment or two as if she might answer, then went on, 'Yes, her passion was her painting. She'd had no great loves in her life. Due to her damaged leg she hadn't done all those things that girls of her age had done. She hadn't gone to dances and soirées, she hadn't played tennis or gone skating. Even a walk could prove tiring for her, the way her leg put so much strain on her back.' He sighed. 'So there she was – a very inexperienced woman, well into middle age, and seeing nothing before her but a continuation of her life as it was, living alone with just one maid to help out, and spending her days at her easel.'

It was so easy for Grace to see the late Mrs Spencer in her little house, sitting over her easel. She could picture it all, so clearly see the scene.

'Well,' he said, 'aren't you going to ask how it happened? How we met?'

Grace did not need to ask; she had already learned an answer to this. She could recall the exact moment when Mrs Spencer had told her. But Edward was insistent; he wanted to tell her his own version.

'Don't you want to know how it happened?' he said. 'I was no sluggard, I can tell you. No great general could have come up with a better strategy.'

'Tell me,' she said. 'Tell me how it happened, your meeting with her.'

He gave a little sigh that smacked of self-satisfaction. 'Well, by a stroke of luck I found out that there was to be an exhibition of paintings done by local artists – from Corster and the surrounding areas – and one of the exhibitors was to be Miss Eleanor Addison. It was written up in the papers. The exhibition was to be held in Swindon at the town hall.

443

So as soon as it opened I wasted no time in going to see it. I got there on the first day. She had three paintings on show. I bought all three. And it went on from there. I wrote to her and said I'd like to see other examples of her work, and I was invited to call on her.' He shrugged. 'That's how it began.'

'Did you – did you tell her that you knew about her having inherited Asterleigh, and the mill?'

'No. Not at first. I did a little later. I had to. One could not make many enquiries without being informed of it. I mean to say that it was fairly common knowledge, and it would have looked rather suspicious if I'd still pretended not to know.'

'So – you were married.'

'So, eventually, we were married.'

Grace, knowing part of the story, half-feared to continue listening, but heard herself say, 'Were you happy?'

'Me? Happy? I had the house, didn't I?'

She shrank from the callousness of the sentiment, the matter-of-fact tone in his voice. 'Is that all it meant to you?' she said.

'What are you talking about?' His voice rose. 'It was through me that this house was opened up, that it began to be lived in again. It's through me that it's been improved so much. Just look around you at your home – it wasn't like this when Eleanor and I moved in. It was made like this through me. And I'm not only talking about the house. The business too. It was through me that the mill began to show a bit of a profit – though it isn't doing so well now, I grant you that. But I got hold of it, took it out of that useless manager's hands and shook some life into it. And I helped Eleanor herself, too. It was through me that she began to live – I reckon so, anyway. Without me she'd have been stuck in her little house, never leaving it from one day to another. And don't forget that she had me, too. And she

444

loved me. Although I venture to say it myself, her life was a lot richer for having known me.'

Was it? Grace wondered. Perhaps the first Mrs Spencer would have been happier left as she was, growing old with her one servant and her painting. But who was she to say? She had no doubt that Edward had been loved by his first wife.

Throughout all Edward's alcohol-tinged meanderings, his passionate words, there had been something else, other words waiting to be said. And the longer he had gone on the more clearly Grace had felt they were there – just waiting in the dark – though she dare not ask the questions that would bring them into the light. She could not, would not allow herself to search for those questions that lay waiting to be discovered, perhaps merely acknowledged.

'I'm tired, Edward,' she said. 'I'm so tired. Please, let me sleep. We can continue this another day.'

He made no response, though she could hear his heavy breathing continuing unchanging as she turned away from him on her side. She tried to close her eyes, but sleep would not come. And she was still awake when, an hour later, she heard the rhythm of his breathing change and realized that he had at last fallen asleep.

Chapter Twenty-One

A week later the sculptor approached by Edward arrived at the house to look at the figure. Following his examination, the commission was accepted and two weeks later two workmen came to take the statue away. Grace did not observe the undertaking, but heard of it from the maid, Effie, who had been present when the men had carried it down the stairs. Later, gazing up at the high gallery, she looked at the vacant niche and thought how much she preferred it so. She would be happy, she thought, if the unattractive figure was never returned.

Edward did not feel the same way. As she stood there he came towards her from the rear of the house and stopped at her side. Following her glance, he looked upwards.

'So he's gone.'

'It looks strange,' Grace said, 'seeing the niche without the figure. It looks so empty.'

'It does. But it'll be a good job done – to get that restored. The hall will be nearly complete then; it'll look the way it was meant to look.'

Thinking of his attitude towards her, she remarked to herself that he had been morose all week, and had had little to say to her beyond the usual everyday expected words. Certainly there was no reference ever made to his drunken outpourings when he had admitted to courting his first wife solely for possession of the house.

And then last week, he had revealed, he had decided to sell the soap factory in Milan. He had not volunteered the information to Grace; it had emerged when she had asked him when next he would be travelling to Italy. He not been there in some little while, she had noticed, and wondered how the business there was faring.

'I shall only be going back two or three more times,' he had said. 'Soon I shan't have a business there any more.'

He had then told her that he was disposing of it, selling it to one of the major soap manufacturers in the country. The problem with the company was, he said, that he couldn't be there all the time, and that was what was required; it was essential that there was someone present with the right power and the right interest. Without his continuing, unrelenting hands on the reins of the business it had gone downhill. The economic situation in the country had also worked against him, as had the fact of him, the owner, being a foreigner. Further, he had not invested in new machinery, and the existing machines there had long past seen their best days. So, when some of the machines had begun to malfunction – he suspected sabotage, he had said – he had decided to throw in his hand and sell up.

'Therefore soon,' he had finished, in his relating of the story to Grace, 'I shall be staying here most of the time. No more trips to the Continent.' And with a slight, ironic smile, 'And how will you like that, my dear?'

How he had changed, Grace thought once more. Over the months how he had changed. In so many ways. Not only in their relationship, but in his dealings with his businesses too. Whatever flame of enthusiasm had once been there, now appeared to have gone, so that so often he seemed to go about absorbed in a kind of surly melancholy.

He spent the greater part of his days at the mill, and when he was not there he had taken to walking in the fields, or sitting up in his study. And there he would drink, and she, sitting in the room beneath, would hear his footsteps as he paced the floor over her head, drinking whisky and consumed by his devils. On some evenings he would eat alone there, leaving Grace to dine alone in the dining room. On latter days, if the maid let Grace know that the master had asked for a tray to be sent up to his study, Grace would forgo eating in the dining room and herself eat from a tray in the drawing room. As for the night when, drunk, he had told her of his pursuit of Miss Eleanor for the sole purpose of obtaining Asterleigh, no further reference was made to such a time; it might never have happened.

Although in his manner towards Grace he was less considerate, he still insisted he loved her, and at night his passion would often bring him to her side. After he was sated he would turn and fall into an uneasy sleep, a sleep broken by mutterings and ramblings which, to her, would make no sense.

And as the days wore on she told herself that she must get accustomed to the changes, for it was almost a certainty that they would never be as they were again. Kester was out of her life, but Billy was safe and happy. She could bear what she was going through, she thought, and indeed, it was not so bad as so many women had to suffer. She and Edward would get through this desperately bad period, for this is what she told herself it was, and when that was done they could find some measure of happiness together.

But then, she found the seeds.

In the last week of November, Grace learned that Effie, the maid who had replaced the ungracious and insolent Jane, had given in her notice, intending to find a position that was both closer to her sweetheart – apparently he was foot-man at a house near Bath – and better paid. Achieving the latter aim, Grace guessed, would probably not be that difficult; she did not know what wages Edward paid his staff, but she was fairly sure that they would not be over-generous. Grace did not learn directly from the maid that she intended to leave, but from Mrs Sandiston, who mentioned it almost in passing. And then the next day Edward himself mentioned it. Grace had never been given a role in the management of the house as were other wives, but, whether she liked it or not, had to leave it to her husband and the housekeeper. Old habits die hard, she had silently acknowledged; the first Mrs Spencer had not done so, and the pattern had been set with her.

'Seems like the parlourmaid's going to be leaving us any day soon,' Edward said to Grace as they sat over the last of dinner. 'Timpkins, whatever her name is.'

'Yes, Timpkins – Effie,' Grace replied. 'Mrs Sandiston mentioned it to me the other day.'

'So that'll mean another advertisement, more interviews. Christ knows why these girls want to hop, skip and jump from one post to another like this. But they all do it.'

'For one thing, I understand, she wants to be near her young man.'

'What!' Edward exclaimed. 'Dear God, what a reason. But that's the way the world is, I suppose, and ever was. Can you see a man doing that?' He shook his head. 'Women. Ah, well, there'll never be any changing them.'

'Is it such a bad thing,' Grace said, 'to wish to be near the one you love?'

'Oh, Grace,' he said, 'sometimes you sound like the voice of some pathetic novelette. Please – don't say such things when I've just eaten. And be glad I haven't got a queasy stomach.'

Grace said, ignoring this, 'She's a nice young girl, and very obliging. I shall be sorry to see her go.'

'Well, she is going, and she wants a reference. She asked days ago, I'm afraid. I just haven't been able to get down to it.'

Grace thought, this is something that I could do, as mistress of the house. It's my duty as mistress. But she would not suggest such a thing. Such work had always been done by Edward, who would be guided by Mrs Sandiston who would take into account the views of his wife.

'What do you think?' Edward said again. 'Shall we give her a nice reference?'

'Of course,' Grace said, and then realized he was teasing. 'She deserves it, and you can't blame a girl for wanting to better her position.'

'I suppose not. I'll write one for her tonight and leave it on the hall table. You or Mrs Sandiston can give it to her.'

'You're going off first thing in the morning, are you?'

'Of course.'

'Will you be back tomorrow?'

'No, I'll stay overnight. There's so much to sort out.' He sighed. 'It just doesn't seem to get easier. On the contrary, it just seems to get more difficult.'

Grace kept quiet at this; she had heard the same complaint several times recently, and there was nothing new she could think of to say.

The next day Mrs Sandiston came to her asking for Effie's reference. 'Oh,' Grace said, 'Mr Spencer said he would take care of it. He said he'd leave it in the hall.'

But it was not on the hall table, and Mrs Sandiston said, 'Where else would he have left it, ma'am? Effie's hoping to get it off today to the people she's applied to. She's late with it already, I understand.'

'And it's not in the hall, you say?'

'No, ma'am.'

'Well, I can only think that it must be in his study. But I'm afraid I don't have a key.'

'I've got a key, ma'am.'

This was an interesting point. Edward's study had to be cleaned and dusted, but it also had to be safe from intruders and snoopers. There would never be any reason for Grace to go looking in his study, therefore there was no reason for her to have a key. On the other hand, the place would be quite safe where the servants were concerned. Not only, was it assumed, would they have no interest in what was in Edward's study, but even if they had, they would not dare to indulge that interest.

After a moment, Grace said, 'Yes,' trying to make it appear that it was the simplest answer to the problem; certainly not one that would present her with the slightest of qualms. 'Yes,' she said again, 'then perhaps you'd best get your keys and we'll have a look.'

Mrs Sandiston went away and was back within two minutes carrying a bunch of keys on a large ring. She and Grace went to the study and there Grace stood aside while Mrs Sandiston unlocked the door. Then it was Mrs Sandiston's turn to stand aside while Grace entered the room.

Grace had never been in the room on her own before, and it felt strange to go there now. She could smell the distinctive smell of the place, the wood, the leather of the book bindings, Edward's tobacco.

With Mrs Sandiston standing in the doorway, Grace crossed the room to Edward's desk and there looked down at the few items on its surface. On the blotter lay two or three open letters to him, and a hurried survey showed that they were nothing to do with what the women were seeking.

Mrs Sandiston, hearing Grace's sigh, and seeing from her expression that the reference was not there, said tentatively, 'Perhaps it's in the drawer, ma'am.'

And Grace, hearing the words, could not turn to the woman and say, *I must not venture so far; my husband would be most displeased*, could only pause while she steeled herself, and then say, a little too brightly – as if such a request were no more than asking for extra bread for the day: 'Of course, yes,' and immediately pulled on the left-hand drawer. And to her surprise it opened smoothly; it was not locked. But there, Edward expected no one but the maid to ever enter this locked room, and therefore what need was there for secrecy and locks and bolts?

Letters, envelopes, pencils, erasers, pins, two boxes of matches. Grace moved her fluttering fingers over the items that faced her in the drawer, at once trying not to disturb their seeming unordered order, and at the same time investigating the various contents. There was something there that drew her attention, but she passed on, looking for the reference. It was not there. She looked up at the housekeeper, and gave a little shake of the head, sighed, closed the drawer, and pulled on the middle one. Again, unlocked. And there, before her eyes, was a fresh envelope addressed: *To Whom it may concern*. And opening the envelope, Grace took out the page inside and read the words in Edward's distinctive handwriting:

> Dear Sir, Madam,
>   *I have pleasure in recommending to you the services of one Euphemia Timkins who has for the past year plus been in my employ at Asterleigh House . . .*

'Here it is,' said Grace, holding up the envelope in one hand, the letter in the other. 'Success at last.' She put the letter back into the envelope, stepped across the floor and put it into Mrs Sandiston's hand. 'Here – please give it to Effie, and tell her I'm sorry it's been so delayed.'

Mrs Sandiston thanked her, put the envelope into her pocket, then said, 'D'you want me to lock up, ma'am?' standing hesitantly with her keys in her left hand.

A moment passed, a moment that would change Grace's

life, and Grace said, 'Not for a minute or two. Leave the key and I'll bring it down to you.'

'Very well.' Mrs Sandiston nodded, clearly not happy with the proposal, for it was against the usual practice. 'I'll come back and lock up when you're through, ma'am.'

'Thank you – just give me ten minutes.'

Grace stood there while the sound of Mrs Sandiston's footsteps faded on the stairs. She looked down at the desk before her. The centre drawer was still open. She glanced over its contents and then pushed it shut. And then turned her gaze to the drawer on the left, the one she had opened first.

After a moment she gingerly grasped the handle and slid the drawer open.

She stood looking down at the interior of the open drawer, and her eyes moved to focus on the object that had distracted her: an envelope, folded over, with contents that rattled dimly when the drawer was moved. An envelope, unsealed, that had spilled a little of its contents with the shifting of the drawer.

Turning, stepping away, she crossed to the door and silently closed it.

Back before the desk, she looked again at the envelope and the two or three seeds that had spilled from it.

This was what had attracted her – the seeds that had rattled into the corner of the drawer from the envelope's aperture. The seeds had struck a chord in her somewhere.

Tentatively she reached in and picked up the seeds that had spilled into the drawer. Then she took up the envelope in her right hand, tipped it, and spilled a number of the seeds into her palm.

They were quite large, the size of a pea, and of a light brown colour. They looked like mottled beans. Her immediate thought was surprise that such things should be kept in a secluded place like this. What were they, and what were they for? In her experience Edward had never been overly interested in matters horticultural, and she could not entertain the idea that he would be starting now. While the questions went through her mind, there in some other part of her brain a little bell rang again. She stood there with the seeds in her hand trying to think what that something was.

It would not come. After a few moments she tipped most of the seeds back into the envelope and, keeping five or six still in her hand, put the envelope back and closed the drawer.

From the study she went to the kitchen where she found Mrs Sandiston, and told her that the study could now be locked again. Afterwards she went into the sewing room, her little lair, where no one came but she and Billy and the maid. A fire had been lighted and she sat by the fireside and laid the seeds out on the small table at her elbow.

And then as she looked at them it came to her; she knew where they had come from.

At once she got up, left the room and went to the conservatory. It had been long ago that her attention had been drawn to the plant, but she remembered the incident. She rarely went into the conservatory, but now as she entered the smell and warmth swept over her with such familiarity as if it had been only yesterday when she had last been inside. Turning to her right she moved past the stunted palms, the lush green of the ferns with their sweet, sickly scent and then past the wicker chair, the sofa and table. She moved past the spot where on its ornate stand the birdcage had hung – gone now, like the small songbirds, those songbirds that had refused to sing – to a place beside a tall, prickly shrub that in the ripeness of summer had born such strange fruit. The plant she sought was no longer there.

It had been there; she had seen it herself. She could recall Edward's words as she had looked at the plant, telling her that it carried a deadly poison. She could almost see the plant in front of her – very tall, with palm-like leaves, toothed at the edges. She could remember its ripened fruit, too, see again the bean-like seeds. But the plant was not there now. However, there was a space where the plant had stood, so she was not mistaken.

For a moment as she stood there she considered going to see Mr Clutter. He would surely remember removing the plant – if indeed he had been the one to remove it. Further, he would know the name of the plant; he might even recognize the seeds.

But something held her back from going to see him. If she spoke to him there was no knowing to whom he might casually report her enquiry. And then how to explain it? The fact of the place at which she had found the seeds – Edward's private drawer – could put her in a difficult position. For the time being, she thought, she would try to keep things from general knowledge.

And then she remembered the name of the plant – the English name; they had joked about it: the *castor oil* plant. She remembered too that there was in existence a picture of it.

Often when Billy got in from school he went straight to seek out Grace. But not every day. So today, to try to ensure that she saw him without delay, Grace left word with the maid to tell him that she wished to see him. He found her in the drawing room, waiting for him. He was going out again, he told her; to join one of his schoolfriends. Grace said she wouldn't keep him long, and after asking him how school had gone that day, moved at once to the subject uppermost in her mind.

'Billy, you drew pictures of many of the plants in the conservatory, didn't you?'

'You know I did,' he said. 'So did you. Sometimes we drew them together, or I did them with Mrs Spencer.'

'Yes. There was one plant in particular – it's gone now – that we both made drawings of.'

'Which one?' He was impatient to be gone.

'It was a tallish plant near where the birdcage stood. I think it was the castor oil plant.'

'Oh, yes, the castor oil plant.' Then he added, smiling at his own smugness, 'Genus *ricinus communis*.'

'You remember its Latin name even.'

'It was written on the little plate.'

'I threw my drawing away, I'm sorry to say.'

'I've still got mine.'

Grace smiled. 'I was hoping you'd say that. I thought you would. I know you never throw anything out. Can you get it for me – your drawing?'

'Now?'

'Is that inconvenient?'

'I was going out as soon as I've had something to eat.'

'It won't take you long, surely.'

Twenty minutes later Billy was handing Grace one of his sketchbooks, opened to a page showing a drawing of the plant. Grace looked at the sketch of the large plant with its huge, handsome, fan-like leaves and bristly, spined clusters of fruits.

'May I borrow this?' Grace asked.

'Of course. What d'you want it for?'

'I just want to borrow it for a while.'

'All right.' She hadn't answered his question, but he did not pursue it. 'I'm going out now, then,' he said, 'as soon as I've had some tea.'

Left alone, Grace sat looking at the sketchbook page. Beneath the drawing Billy had written the date that he had made it, and also *Ricinus communis* – a name he had obviously copied from the plant's label in the conservatory. After a few moments Grace got up from her seat and, leaving the room, made her way to the library.

It did not take long to find the right book, and soon she had found a page on which was a description of the plant. And there was a small drawing too, not as fine as Billy's but informative, nevertheless.

The article, after describing the plant – to her surprise, she read that some specimens grew to thirty or forty feet in height – went on to say:

> . . . *Although the plants are probably native to Africa and Asia they have become naturalized throughout the tropical world. They are chiefly cultivated in India and Brazil where they are largely grown for their oil in pharmaceutical and industrial usage . . .*

The article then spoke briefly of the plant's poisonous properties. When Grace had read it she read through it again, and on a piece of paper made some notes, after which she closed the book and put it back on the shelf.

The next morning, Grace decided to go to Corster, and eschewing the notion of having Rhind or Johnson drive her, she walked to the station and there caught a train into the town where she bought some silk colours and linen. Having finished her shopping in good time, she set off for the station and there caught the train heading back to Berron Wick. She got off the train, however, when it reached Liddiston, and there made her way to an address in Willow Street, close to the station. According to the card that Dr Mukerjee had given her when he had called on the occasion of Billy's fall, he held surgery in his house on weekdays from ten o'clock until twelve. When she rang the bell at the front door of his house it was close on 11.30.

A maid showed her into the doctor's waiting room on the left of the hall and after Grace had given her name the woman went away, closing the door behind her. There was no one else in the room. Sitting on a sofa, Grace began to glance through a copy of that morning's *Times* that had been left on the coffee table. She did not have to wait long. After just three or four minutes the door opened and Dr Mukerjee stood there in his frock coat, smiling at her in greeting and speaking her name.

'Mrs Spencer.'

Grace gave him her hand. 'Good morning, Doctor.'

'Please, come into the surgery.'

He opened the door to the hall and Grace allowed herself to be ushered through into the room opposite. There beside his desk she sat down.

The doctor asked after Billy's health and after her own. Replying to the latter question, she said that she had been well except for the fact that she sometimes had difficulty sleeping. 'I'm sure it's just a passing thing,' she added, 'but perhaps you could let me have something that would help.'

The doctor asked if she was being kept awake by worries of any kind, and she replied that she was not.

'Do you drink a lot of coffee?' he asked. 'Coffee is a stimulant.'

'I drink very little.'

'Perhaps you need more exercise,' he said with a smile, and Grace, with a smile in reply, said that perhaps she did.

Anyway, the doctor said, he would give her a little chloral hydrate and a prescription for more when it was required. She should take it at night, though she must not, of course, exceed the dose. No, she said, she would not do so. He went out of the room then, and returned a few minutes later with a small bottle of what looked to be fine crystals. He placed it on his desk then wrote out a small label for it and stuck it on the bottle. That done, he wrote out the prescription for her to take to the chemist.

'Just take the chloral in water as directed,' he said as he

pushed the bottle across the desk towards her. Then he looked down at the written prescription. 'Was there anything else?' When Grace said there was not, he signed the paper, blotted the ink and handed it to her with a little inclination of his head. Grace thanked him and said there was no need to send his bill to the house, she would pay it now. He was slightly surprised at this, but covered his surprise immediately and said, 'But of course.'

When Grace had paid her little bill she put the receipt in her bag along with the prescription and the medicine. There in her bag also were the seeds and Billy's little sketchbook. Dr Mukerjee moved in his seat, expecting her to rise. But she remained where she was.

'Doctor,' she said, 'while I'm here there's just one other thing . . .'

'Yes, what is that?'

'You're from India, I believe.'

'That is correct.' He nodded. 'I'm from Calcutta. Though I have lived in England for a number of years.' He frowned slightly, showing his puzzlement at her question.

'It's just that –' Grace said, smiling, 'perhaps you can settle something – a little disagreement with my young brother.'

He smiled back. 'Well, if I can, certainly – anything that will help to pour oil on troubled waters.'

'You practised in India, did you?'

'Yes, but –'

She took the sketchbook from her bag, opened it at the drawing and laid it on the desk before him. 'I wondered,' she said, 'if you would be familiar with this plant. I'm given to understand that it grows commonly in India. It's found also in Brazil, I believe and in Africa and –'

He broke in, cutting her off: 'That's the castor oil plant. Oh, yes, that's well known in India.'

'The castor oil plant.'

459

'That's what it's commonly known as. Because we get castor oil from it.'

'And it grows in Brazil also . . .'

'Yes, Brazil, Siam – and many African countries. It needs a hot climate to really grow tall. Though it's not exactly a good plant to have growing around a house. Particularly where you might have small children.'

'Why is that?'

'Because of the poisonous nature of its seeds. They're deadly. Some people find the plants very attractive, and they're used in gardens for landscaping. Well, in the tropics they can grow so tall – very impressive plants indeed.'

'But you say they're poisonous.'

'The seeds are, yes.' He indicated the drawing with his fingertip, touching the part where the fruits were shown. 'The fruits are very attractive. They're bronze-to-red in colour, and some of them are spined – it depends on the variety. Though in India people often remove the fruits before they ripen, because of the poison concentrated in the seeds. As I say, it wouldn't do for children to get hold of them and start chewing them up.'

Grace gave a little nod. 'But I find that puzzling. You say the plant gives us castor oil – but at the same time it's said to be poisonous.'

'That's correct. The oil from it is used medicinally, but other parts of it are very deadly, oh yes.'

'I had some seeds . . .' she said, and dipping into her bag again brought out a little screw of paper. This she opened and spread, and revealed the seeds she had taken from Edward's drawer. 'These,' she said. 'Are these the seeds of the plant?'

The doctor bent closer and looked carefully at the mottled, bean-like seeds. 'May I ask, where did you get these?' he asked.

Grace was not sure how best to answer this, and went for

the truth. 'They came from a plant at the house,' she said after a moment.

'Growing in a greenhouse, yes?'

'Yes.'

'Yes, it would have to be.'

Smiling again, making light of the whole issue, she said, 'As I said, I was having an argument with my brother and –'

'Oh, there's no doubt about it,' he said, ' – these are from the castor oil all right. They're easily recognizable – very distinctive.' He gave an emphatic nod. Then, taking up his pen, he used the tip of it to move one of the seeds on the paper. 'In the wrong hands those could be very dangerous. Very dangerous indeed.'

Grace did not respond verbally, but merely looked at him questioningly.

'There have been many cases of poisoning with such seeds in India,' he said. 'Very often farmers have poisoned their neighbours' cattle with them.' With a slight, ironic smile, he added, 'And sometimes their mothers-in-law.'

Grace said, 'But I still don't understand how the plant can be beneficial and poisonous at the same time.'

'As you know, castor oil is commonly used – and its manufacture is quite an industry. But a part of the seed other than the oil is absolutely deadly.'

'What is that?'

'It comes from the heart of the seed, right inside the kernel – and just the tiniest portion of it is poisonous.'

'And if you swallowed one of the seeds you –'

'Oh, you'd need to have more than one. Probably nine or ten. A smaller number could still make you very ill. Three or four would probably kill a child. I must add that I'm not an expert on ricin – that's what the poison's known as.' He pointed to the written title on Billy's drawing. '*Ricinus communis*. Oh, ricin is one of the deadliest natural poisons known to man.'

'One of the deadliest, you say.'

'Absolutely.'

'And I'd never heard of it.'

'I doubt that you would. It doesn't grow naturally in England. It doesn't grow naturally in any of the chilly European countries. It needs a warm climate – or at least a temperate one. Of course countries like India and Brazil and Africa are perfect. I doubt very much that England has ever had a case of ricin poisoning. I've certainly never heard of such a thing.' He shook his head. 'And something else,' he added, '– you spoke just now about swallowing the seeds. Well, it wouldn't do any harm to swallow them. They would just go straight through, and be passed in the normal way.'

'So you'd need to chew them.'

'Oh, indeed. There's a story of Greece from ancient times that suspects were given these seeds, and told to eat them, to chew them up. If the suspect died, that was a sign that he was guilty; if he lived, then he was innocent. But what happened is that sometimes the suspects would be given the tip: "Don't chew the beans. Pretend to chew them, but swallow them whole." And they did, and they lived.'

A little pause, then Grace said, 'And if a number of seeds were ground up, and fed to someone, what would happen?'

'Well, with enough seeds it would be fatal. Though probably you wouldn't need to grind up the whole bean – that would be rather gritty to eat. Probably it would be better to crush the bean and take out the centre. Do this with several beans and mix the stuff with food, and this would be deadly. Quite deadly.'

'What kind of form does it take – the illness after swallowing the poison?'

'Well, I never actually had a proven case in India. Mind you, I left the country soon after I qualified, so I wasn't practising there for very long. But such cases were well known to the medical profession. And as for proving a case – this isn't so easy. The thing is, the poison doesn't leave any residue in the body. It's all excreted in the normal way – so all you're left with is the effect – the devastation. Which, of course, along with the symptoms, can be pretty conclusive anyway.'

Grace paused a moment before her next question, then said, 'What are the symptoms, can you tell me?'

He pondered this question for only a moment before answering, 'It takes two to three days to die – and there's a gradual weakening, loss of appetite, sickness, diarrhoea, fever. Heavy perspiration – and towards the end the patient is generally rambling and raving. I think the suffering must be very bad. Sometimes the illness is misdiagnosed – it's been put down to septicaemia – blood poisoning of unknown origin. It has certain things in common with such an illness.'

Grace said, 'Do you know how soon after the poison is taken the symptoms begin to show?'

'They wouldn't show up immediately. Certain poisons are instantaneous in causing responses, but not ricin. It takes some time for the symptoms to manifest – sometimes up to ten hours – then there's no going back. I know these things because it's one of the things we were taught to look out for as medical students. Such a poison being available to just about anybody. And there's no antidote, as far as is known.'

A little silence fell, then Dr Mukerjee said, 'I don't know what else I can tell you, Mrs Spencer.'

'Oh, you've been so helpful. It's been fascinating. And I've taken up so much of your time.'

'Not at all. I'm happy to help out if I can.' He smiled. 'It certainly isn't something I ever expected to get asked about in a place like this.'

*

Back at Liddiston station Grace caught the train for the one-stop journey to Berron Wick from where she set out to walk to Asterleigh.

As she walked she thought of what the doctor had told her: outward manifestations of the poison usually started several hours after it was ingested. She thought of the symptoms that the doctor had described, and saw Mrs Spencer once again lying in her bed, tossing and turning in her fever, her voice coming in broken fragments of nonsensical speech.

And she saw again the scene earlier in the bedroom as Mrs Spencer had lain in bed, recovering so well from her bout of pneumonia; and she heard again her words saying that at Mr Spencer's insistence she had drunk some broth before he had left, before he had gone off to make his journey for his business abroad. And hours later Mrs Spencer had been taken so ill, and her illness all in tune with the symptoms so recently described by Dr Mukerjee. But no, surely not, a voice in her head protested. Surely such a thing could not have happened. But how else to explain Mrs Spencer's sudden deterioration when she had all but recovered from her common illness? And how else to explain the seeds in Edward's drawer? They had been put there by him and no one else. And surely there could be no innocent explanation for such an act. Another question came into her mind: what were the seeds doing still in his drawer? If he had made use of them, then why was he keeping them still?

The deepening conviction seemed so overwhelming that it filled her thoughts and blotted out everything in her sight. She was aware of nothing of her surroundings as she passed along, her feet taking her automatically in the right direction. And so at last she came to Asterleigh.

Back in the house she went to the conservatory again, and looked once more at the spot where the plant had stood growing in its large pot. Of course it was not there. Did she,

she asked herself, think earlier that perhaps she had imagined its absence?

After changing out of her outdoor clothes she went into her sewing room and there sat by the window.

Edward got back to the house just after 6.30. Grace was still in her sewing room when she heard the sound of the carriage on the gravel. Billy was with her, having come to her after having his high tea in the kitchen. 'That's Mr Edward coming in,' Billy had said, moving to the window and looking down. Then, turning to Grace:

'What's the matter? Is something wrong?'

'The matter?' Grace had said. 'Nothing's the matter.'

'You're so – quiet and – strange. Has something happened?'

'No, nothing,' she had said, forcing a smile at him which, she could see, he was doing his best to take at face value. 'You're imagining things again.'

Soon afterwards Billy had gone to his room. He was never known these days to hang about in the presence of Edward Spencer.

A minute after she heard Billy's receding footsteps on the stairs she heard the approaching steps of Edward.

He came into the room and looked at her with a smile. 'I can always find you in here,' he said. He had shed his coat and hat and now undid the top button of his waistcoat as he stood there. He held a glass of whisky in his hand.

'Yes, well, it's my special room,' she said, flicking a glance at him.

'Your special room?' He gave a chuckle.

'I like to have a little place I can think of as my own.' She could feel her smile false on her mouth.

He nodded. 'Quite right too. Everybody needs some little place that has a degree of privacy.'

She half-hoped that he would be in no mood to dine with

her tonight – though she knew she was only putting off the inevitable – and would instead choose to have a tray sent up to his study. But this evening he seemed to be in a better mood and no mention was made of his eating alone.

Somehow Grace found herself getting through the meal, though at times she wondered how she managed it. The conversation between herself and Edward was a little stilted and desultory, but it was not infrequently like that of late. Besides, Edward himself did not seem so forthcoming as usual, notwithstanding that he had been drinking whisky quite steadily before they sat down at table, and partook liberally of the wine throughout the meal. When at last they got up from the table he told the maid that she could bring the coffee as soon as it was ready, and he and Grace went into the drawing room.

A bright fire was burning in the grate with the logs crackling and hissing. As Grace sat down, Edward moved to the drinks tray and poured himself whisky from the decanter. Grace did not so much as acknowledge the action with a glance but fixed her eye on the flames of the fire, longing for the time to pass.

'Would you like something?' Edward asked, his free hand touching the top of the sherry decanter.

'No, thank you,' Grace replied.

'Are you sure? It's going to be a cold night.'

'No, really, thank you.'

Edward nodded, and with whisky glass in hand, moved to stand with his back to the fire. A wind had sprung up also, Grace could hear; it was moving around the house and now starting to rattle the windows. Listening to it, she thought of that evening long ago when she had sat here with the first Mrs Spencer and the wind had howled about them. What changes had been seen in the intervening time. Then, on that occasion, she had been a paid companion,

Mrs Spencer her mistress. Now the title of Mrs Spencer was hers, she was mistress of the house – for what it was worth – and the first Mrs Spencer was in her grave.

The maid, Effie, brought the coffee in on a tray and placed it on the coffee table before Grace where she sat on the sofa. Grace thanked her, and silently the maid departed. The girl's appearance, Grace thought, could be seen as her cue: she must at some time, and soon, bring up the matter of the maid's reference.

'Are you ready for your coffee now?' Grace asked, and Edward gave a brief, irritable shake of his head. 'I don't want any coffee. I've got enough trouble sleeping as it is.'

'One small cup?'

'I told you, I don't want any.'

Grace gave a small nod of acknowledgement, then took up the coffee pot and poured a small cup for herself. She did not want any coffee either, but it was a small ritual that helped pass another minute. 'Oh, I have to tell you,' she said, as if the thought had only just that moment occurred to her, ' – I had occasion to go into your study yesterday.' And then added before Edward could leap in: 'I had to get Effie's reference.'

'How did you get into my study?' he said at once. 'The door's locked. I always keep it locked.'

'Mrs Sandiston unlocked it for me.' She paused, added, 'I asked her to.' She flicked a glance at him and then looked away again. He was gazing at her with a dark expression, his hand with his whisky glass half-raised.

'It's just that – there was some little panic over getting Effie's reference,' Grace said. 'You said you'd write it and leave it out in the hall.'

'I forgot,' he said, his eyes never leaving her face for a moment, as if afraid of missing something that was not in her words. 'I've got a lot on my mind.'

'I know that, Edward. Anyway, as I say, Mrs Sandiston opened your study door and I went in and found the reference at once. There in the middle drawer where you'd left it.'

The briefest pause before he said, 'And what else did you find?'

'What?'

'I said, what else did you find?'

She forced herself to look directly at him now, her unflinching gaze meeting his own. 'What else did I find? I didn't find anything else. I wasn't looking for anything else. I opened the middle drawer of your desk and there was the maid's reference. I saw what it was at once, so I didn't need to go rummaging around.'

Silence between them, a silence that hung in the air like a fog untouched by the sound of the wind that buffeted the house. It was a silence that Grace knew she must break in order to save the situation.

'Anyway, that was it,' she said, almost breezily. 'I gave Effie her reference and she's sent it off to whoever is wanting to see it.' Then she added, equally lightly, but with just the right touch of concern for the maid, 'I hope she gets a decent post. I don't mind telling you, I shall be sorry to see her go. She's a very obliging girl.'

'So you told me.'

Grace took up her cup and sipped her coffee.

Edward took another swallow from his whisky glass then said, 'So how was your shopping expedition?'

Grace gave a little laugh. 'My shopping expedition? Hardly that. Hardly an expedition. Just a little trip. I only wanted a few colours of silk and some odds and ends.'

'Is that all.' He paused. 'And what did the doctor have to say?'

The question took her completely by surprise. How could he know that she had paid a visit to Dr Mukerjee? It was not possible. How could it be?

'The doctor?' she said.

'Dr Mukerjee. You went to see him after your shopping trip.'

It took all her control to say calmly, 'Oh, that was nothing important. I wanted to see him about – well, I haven't been sleeping so well lately, so I thought I'd call and get him to let me have some medicine or make me up a prescription for something.'

'And did he?'

'Yes, he gave me a little hydrate of chloral and a prescription for more if I need it.'

'I didn't know you were having trouble sleeping.'

'Yes, for some little while now.'

'Why didn't you tell me?'

'You're so busy, Edward. You have enough to deal with – all the demands on your time.'

'You should have told me.'

'It's not that important.'

'I'll be the judge of that.'

She said nothing.

'I thought it might be to do with something – something more important,' he said.

And hearing his words she realized that he was referring to her having possibly conceived. Something more important.

'It was just sleeplessness,' she said. She hesitated, and added, 'How do you know that I went to see Dr Mukerjee?'

And now the silence was back. But this time Grace was not aware of the sound of the wind. Only of the beating of her heart and the dampness of her palms.

'How do I know?'

'Yes, how do you know?'

He lifted his glass, threw back the whisky into his mouth, swallowed, then said, 'Because it's my business to know.'

'Your business?'

'You're my wife.' He crossed over to the side table and sharply put down his glass on the tray. 'I have a right to know what my wife does when I'm not around to keep an eye on her.'

'You've been spying on me.'

He turned and looked at her, saying nothing. Giving a little gasp, Grace put down her cup and raised her hands to her mouth. After a moment, she said, 'Tell me, please, how you knew.'

'I have my ways.'

'Yes!' she cried. 'Yes, you have your ways. You have Rhind. You have that monster Rhind. You've sent him following me, haven't you?'

Still Edward said nothing.

'He's a monster,' Grace said. 'That man hates me. He wants me gone from here, you know that, don't you?'

'That's a bit strong, my dear, isn't it?' said Edward. 'After all, he's only doing what he's told.' Lifting the decanter, he poured more whisky into his glass and added a dash of soda water.

'Only doing what he's told,' Grace said with contempt in her voice. 'Yes, and he will do anything you ask him to do. And also he'll do things you don't ask him to do. Whatever he thinks suits you he will do. Anything to please you.'

Edward said, 'Well, I hardly think I have any reason to complain about that, do you?'

'He's a dangerous man, Edward. More dangerous that you think. He – he's unbalanced. You must know that yourself.'

'He's a faithful servant, that's what he is. And so long as he stays that way I shall have no complaints.'

'So you admit it – you set him to spy on me.'

'Could anyone blame me?'

'What!'

'I'm only looking after my interests.' He took a swallow from his glass. 'Protecting my possessions.'

'I am not one of your possessions.'

'You're my wife.'

'Edward –' As Grace spoke his name a little sob rose up in her throat. She set down her coffee cup and hung her head.

And then she was aware that Edward was there, sitting at her side on the sofa, his arm reaching out to draw her to him.

'You mustn't disappoint me,' he said. 'Oh, Grace, you must not. I only want you to love me and be a good wife to me. That's all I've ever asked, you know that.'

And she could not protest. She could not make herself say, I have been a good wife to you, for she knew she had not been. She had made love to another man, she had loved another man. Loved him still. At the same time, she had neither loved Edward, nor made love to him; she had submitted, that was all.

Now, feeling his arm drawing her to him, she tried a little to resist. 'Edward, I can't believe you've done such a thing – to set Rhind on my trail like that. In God's name, how could you?'

'I just told you.' As he spoke she could smell the whisky on his breath, and the smell made her catch her own breath. He drew back his arm, stretched out his legs before him on the carpet, then went on:

'Don't forget I have my reasons to be suspicious.'

'What reason have I ever given you?'

'You were seen with your old lover – isn't that reason enough?'

'I was – ?'

'You know what I'm talking about. When you were on the platform at Redbury. Rhind saw you then, the two of you. You already know that. Granted, his train pulled out

471

before he could see anything else, but he certainly saw the two of you together. And you've admitted to that.'

'So I have – but I told you there was nothing to it.' Her lies did not come any easier; there was just less shame following them. She said, partly to gain time and composure: 'And speaking of Mr Fairman like that. He was your good friend. Once.'

'Once, yes. And there's no limit to the things a good friend will do to you, nor how many times he'll stab you in the back.' He paused. 'I wouldn't ever tolerate you going off with another man,' he added quietly.

Grace said nothing.

'I told you this before.'

'I'm aware of that . . .'

'So take note of it. And remember that what is mine I keep.' He paused then repeated the words, 'What is mine I keep.'

'I heard you the first time.'

'You have to love me. You're my wife. You have to love me.'

Grace did not answer, but waited a moment, then said, 'I shan't finish my coffee. I shall go to bed. And I'll take a little of the medicine the doctor gave me.'

'Yes, that's it,' Edward said belligerently, 'take some of your medicine so that you can make sure you're asleep when I come to bed.'

Grace rose and started across the room. 'Goodnight, Edward,' she said.

Upstairs she undressed and got into bed. She was bone tired, and felt that she barely had the strength to hang up her clothes.

Once in bed she turned on her side and closed her eyes. And please, Edward, the words went through her mind, leave me in peace tonight. Sometimes of late, when he had

472

been drinking, he had taken to sleeping alone in the second bedroom. She hoped fervently that he would do so tonight.

She tried her best to relax, but sleep would not come. She did not want to be awake when he came to bed. If she could be asleep when he came in perhaps he would not disturb her, but her rest remained uneasy and she lay looking wakeful into the room, now lit only by the light of a single lamp.

But then at last she fell into an uneasy sleep.

Grace was awakened to the knowledge of his presence with the sound of the bedroom door closing. She had no idea what time it was, or how long she had been sleeping; it seemed like only moments. With the realization of his being in the room she kept closed her eyes and did not move, hoping he would believe her to be still asleep, and listened to the movements as he went to and came from his dressing room. And then, after some time, there was silence. But he was not in bed. Judging by the sounds she had heard of the last moves he had made, he was somewhere in the middle of the room. She thought she could hear the sound of his breathing.

After some hesitation she flicked open her eyes a crack and ventured a swift glance into the shadows.

He was there, just standing there in his shirt and trousers, his head turned towards the bed. At once she closed her eyes again. And the silence crept on, and still there was nothing but the sound of his breathing and the gentle ticking of the clock on the mantelpiece. He had not seen her open her eyes, had not realized that she was looking at him. Then, moments later, she felt the mattress bend under his weight as he sat on its edge. 'Are you awake?' he whispered sharply near her ear.

She opened her eyes. 'Edward . . .' The note of sleepiness in her voice was real, but if he heard it he did not heed it.

'Listen to me,' he said. 'Don't sleep – listen to me.'

She could smell so strongly the whisky on his breath as he leaned close to her, and hear too the slurring of his words.

'What – what is it?' she said. 'I'm so tired.'

'Listen to me.'

'What? What?'

There was a sudden little flurry of movement, and she realized that in bending over her he had overbalanced and almost fallen across her. But he recovered himself, putting out an arm to support himself, his hand pressing just beside her pillow. He must have been drinking quite heavily, she thought. 'What – what time is it?' she asked.

'Time? I don't know. Who gives a damn what time it is. I'm trying to talk to you. Listen to me. And turn round.'

She did as she was bidden, turning in the bed so that she now lay on her back.

Seeing her like this in the soft light of the lamp he leaned down to her. And she felt the pressure of his moist lips on her cheek, and then, as if he had just missed his mark, on her mouth. She kept her own mouth closed and made no sign of returning his kiss. Her eyes were open now.

Then his head moved again, this time bringing his mouth closer to her ear. Not to kiss her, though, but to whisper to her in a slurred, drunken hiss:

'I did it – did it for you.'

She said nothing.

'Did you hear what I said?' he murmured after a moment, drawing his head back slightly, 'I said I did it – for you.'

'Yes,' she breathed, nodding her head slightly on the pillow. She had no idea what he was talking about.

He straightened then a little, and sat looking down at her, frowning, his mouth pressed shut. She could see in his jaw a little muscle working away.

'You don't know what I'm saying, do you?' he said.

'What? No. No, I don't.' She did not want to hear. 'Edward, I'm so tired.'

'Yes, I know all about that. Listen to me – I might never feel like saying this again.' There was a little pause in the quiet of the room. Then he said: 'She was not well, anyway.'

'Who? What are you talking about?'

'Eleanor. She was not a well woman. She never had been. She was always somewhat – somewhat weakly and frail.'

'Eleanor? Why are you talking about her?'

He went on as if she had not spoken: 'And you know she was quite a lot older than I.'

'Edward . . .' His words were taking on something that was alarming. A part of her was able to see the direction in which they were leading, and at the same time she instinctively shrank from it.

He gave a groan and shook his head. 'I never wanted her to suffer. Believe me. But I had to do it. Our marriage was going nowhere. I had no more life with her. Anybody with any sense could see that. I could never have a child with her. She had no interest in the house. The only reason she lived here was because I insisted on it when we were married. She'd have been content to live with me in some small cottage somewhere, I swear to God.' He fell silent for a moment, looking off into the shadows of the room, as if reading his past.

'And there's another thing – the life she had with me was better than the life she used to have. She'd have been the first to tell you that. So at least I gave her something real, something positive for some years of her life. That's something I can be glad of. But she couldn't give me what I wanted, could she?'

Silence. Grace realized that it was a question addressed to her.

'Couldn't she?' she said.

'No, of course she couldn't. Oh, at first, yes. She had the

house and the business. And that's what I wanted. This house particularly. It should have come to me anyway. Everything should have been mine when Gresham died. So I was only getting what was my due, wasn't I?' He sighed. 'But it wasn't enough. Having the house wasn't enough, was it?' He paused and said again, 'Was it?'

'I don't know, Edward. Tell me.'

'Well, of course it wasn't. I saw you, Grace. That day in your father's yard. And I had to have you as well.'

Chapter Twenty-Two

Grace got little sleep that night, and when she did manage to doze off she dreamed, and her dreams were touched by Edward's revelations. In her nightmare she saw again the first Mrs Spencer lying in her bed, first tossing and turning, and then her body wrenching and writhing in convulsions. And then the woman was pushing her sheets aside and getting up from her bed, and moving towards Grace, her dead eyes raised to the ceiling. Grace had silently shrieked and, turning, tried to escape. Her legs were like lead, however, and would carry her no more than inches.

In the morning she had lain there with a heavy head, her eyes still closed, feigning sleep, while Edward rose and dressed and left the room.

She followed very soon afterwards, and to her surprise found him in the breakfast room, drinking coffee and smoking a cigarette, that morning's *Times* open beside him. By this time he was usually on his way, and she wondered at the deviation from his usual routine.

As if answering her unspoken question, he said, 'I've had my breakfast. I merely wanted to see you for a minute before I set out.'

'Oh?' she said, prompting him, but he said nothing more. She poured herself a cup of coffee, took some toast and sat down at the table. She had no appetite.

'Is that all you're going to have?' he said.

'I'm not that hungry.'

'It's not enough to keep a sparrow alive. I hope you're not

sickening for something.' He drank from his coffee cup and took a drag from his cigarette, then added, 'I didn't have much appetite myself this morning. That's what comes of having that extra whisky.' He smiled, but it was an awkward smile, without any real humour. 'That extra one will always do it, you can be sure.' He got up and poured himself more coffee. 'It certainly gives a chap a devil of a thirst.'

His tone was light, and intentionally so, Grace thought. He was trying to go on as if nothing had happened between them, as if the dreadful things had not been said; trying to put on an appearance of normality. He did not even comment on her own taciturnity, which he could not but be aware of. She would not, could not join him in the charade and be party to the deception. She concentrated on her coffee.

'I don't think I told you,' he said, folding the newspaper and setting it aside, 'but I shall be off to Italy again in a few days. And soon I shall be going there for the last time. Now I've made my decision to sell up I want to get it done. And thank God – I shan't have that damned business hanging round my neck for too much longer.'

'It'll be a weight off your mind, then, if you find it so onerous,' Grace said stiffly.

She wondered if this – his intention to sell the soap factory – was what he had meant by having something to talk to her about. She could not think that it was.

'And perhaps when that's gone,' he said, 'and there's a few less calls on my time – maybe we can have a little more time for ourselves.'

Grace said nothing.

'That would be nice, wouldn't it?' he said. 'We could go to Italy purely for pleasure. Wouldn't you like that? I could take you to France. I'll take you to Paris. And Brazil. Have you ever thought you might like to see Brazil? We'll go to Rio. I know it well. You'll find it's like a different world.'

It was all empty talk, she knew. They would go nowhere. Perhaps Corster, perhaps Redbury or Bath. But as for those other places, no. She would never see them. All his money, all his dreams, were set in this house. To perfect his possession – that was his one driving thought. He would never be satisfied with it until it was finished. Perhaps only then would he feel it was completely his own.

And how did he feel about her? He loved her, she thought, but he had also made it clear that, in his eyes, she was another of his possessions.

She nibbled at the toast and sipped the coffee. She could not bring herself to look at him across the table, though she could often feel his burning glance upon her bent head. After a time, when at last she found it unbearable to sit there with him, she murmured an excuse, got up from the table and left the room.

In her sewing room she slowly paced to and fro, from the fireplace to the window and back again. She could not relax over the breakfast table with Edward. She doubted that she could ever relax with him again. As she arrived at the window for the second time she glanced down and saw Rhind enter the yard, leading the horse and carriage, ready to take his master to the station. Quickly she averted her glance and turned back to pace again. Then, moments later she heard approaching footsteps on the landing and the door opened and Edward appeared in the doorway.

'I thought I'd find you here,' he said, and came into the room and closed the door behind him.

He moved across the carpet and came to halt in front of Grace where she had stopped beside her sewing table.

'Why did you leave?' he said.

'Edward, please – I didn't feel well.'

'You didn't feel well – you've only just got up.'

'I'm not sleeping. I told you that.'

He stood in silence, as if weighing the situation, or thinking of words to say. Then he said, 'Listen – about last night . . .'

Grace said nothing, but hearing the words looked down at her hand at it lighted on the tabletop, her finger moving to skim its polished surface.

'I was drunk,' he said. 'There, I've admitted it.' A smile again, like the one he had given downstairs. 'And how often will you find a husband admit to such a thing? Not in a month of Sundays, I should think. But it's true. I had too much whisky, and it's the devil's own brew, it is. You wouldn't know it, but it makes a man say all kinds of crazy things. Things that are just made up out of the air, for no reason at all that anyone could fathom.'

Grace remained looking down, watching as her finger traced a slow little circular pattern on the oak. She could not look him in the face. At some other time were she to avoid his glance like this, she could well imagine him saying, *Look at me. Please look at me when I'm speaking to you.* But at this moment she believed that he as well as she preferred to avoid direct eye contact.

'Yes, people say insane things when they have the drink in them,' Edward said. 'Like me last night. And I wanted to tell you – I said some crazy things, didn't I? I can hardly believe some of the things I said to you. Well, it's not so much what I said, but more what you might have inferred from what I said. That you might have gone off with the wrong idea or something. I think perhaps you did – which is why this morning you won't say boo to a goose.'

Flicking a glance at him, she saw that he spoke with a faint earnest smile on his face, a smile that begged for belief and understanding. She had never seen him look like this before.

'Did you hear what I said?' he said after a moment.

'Yes.'

'And have you nothing to say?'

'I don't know what you want me to say.'

He seemed momentarily at a loss at this. 'I'm not asking you to say anything.'

Her sewing basket was on the table, and beside it a little flannel shirt that she had been making. She picked up the shirt and said, 'I'm making this for Mrs Castle's little boy. I should have had it done by now. I said it would be. Poor things, they have so little.'

'Damn the shirt,' he hissed, and wrenched it from her hands and threw it down on the table. 'Look at me when I'm speaking to you.'

She raised her glance, and he looked directly into her eyes. Putting his hands flat upon the table he leaned towards her, putting his face close to her own. 'I'm through with playing these blasted games with you, madam,' he said. 'I've tried to meet you halfway, but you'll have none of it. So, you can think what the bloody hell you like, and the devil with you. There's no way you can hurt me, anyway. You're my wife, and you'll stay my wife.' He was shaking in his fury, she could see, his lips were pale, drawn back over his teeth. She found herself shrinking from him, drawing back slightly, her heart pounding against her ribs.

'Yes, you're going to stay my wife,' he said. 'What is mine I keep. I've told you that. There's no man who will divide me from what's mine. D'you hear? What's mine is mine – to keep. Until such time as I have no use for it.' He paused, licked his dry lips. 'Just remember that. You're my wife – and in case you choose to believe in some half-cocked story you've dreamed up, remind yourself that wives can't speak out against their husbands. And in case you're in any doubt there, I'm talking specifically about a court of law. And let me tell you something else: If you were foolish enough to speak out against me, there's nothing anyone could prove. Nothing. Do I make myself clear? I'm not an idiot, so don't underestimate me. You hear me? So I suggest you make the best of what you've got. Yes! Make the best of what you've got and stop hankering after your fine Mr Fairman. Just count yourself lucky.'

'Lucky!' she murmured on a little sob, unable to stop herself.

'Yes, lucky!' he said bitterly. 'You *had* nothing, and you *were* nothing, and I took you and gave you everything. Your brother too. Where would he be if it were not for me? I gave the two of you a fine house to live in – how else would you ever get to be mistress of a place like this? – and you had a husband who loved you. And who still would love you if only he could see a glimmer of hope. But there's not, is there? I can see you'll never change.'

He straightened. 'I'm leaving now for the mill. When I come back this evening I want to see some changes around here. For I'll tell you something, I'm not prepared for things to go on as they are.'

When Edward had left, leaving the door open behind him, Grace got up and closed it, then moved back into the room and sank into a chair. And there she sat while the minutes ticked by, and ticked by into an hour, and still she did not move.

She remained there in the silence of the room; there was no sound at all coming to her from the house, no sound coming up from the stable yard. Billy would have gone to school ages ago. She missed him. At times such as this she would have liked to have him close by, comforted by his common sense and his optimistic outlook. This, though, she had to handle on her own. This was not something she could bring Billy into.

At one point she picked up the little shirt that Edward had so angrily dashed down, and thought for a moment that she might work on it, and try to finish it for the Castle boy, but she could not bring herself to so much as thread a needle, and she set it down. It could wait for another time.

She must do something, however, and at last, without purpose, she got up and left the room.

Still without purpose, she moved along the landing and there opened the door to the studio. Mrs Spencer's studio. For she could never see it as anything other. Now in the open doorway she stood and looked into the room. It had hardly changed since the last time Mrs Spencer had worked in it. And Grace's portrait was still there. She picked it up and placed it on the easel and stood back and looked at it. It was very lifelike, she thought, and what a pity it was that Mrs Spencer had never got around to finishing it.

She wandered around the room while the memories came back. She saw herself again as she had stood there on that day over three years ago, when she and Billy had come to deliver the framed canvases. She could see herself in her linen dress with the flowers on it; see Billy once again, rushing towards the panic-stricken bird. That was such a happier time, a time before the world had changed for them both.

She turned, made her way to the door and back out onto the landing.

She was halfway down the stairs leading to the hall when there came a ring at the doorbell. She got to the hall just as Effie came from the rear of the house and moved towards the door. Out of curiosity, Grace lingered while the maid opened the door and spoke to the man who stood on the front step. She heard the stranger ask whether Mr Spencer was in, and the maid replied that he was not. At this Grace stepped forward.

'I'm Mrs Spencer,' she told the man. 'Can I help you at all?' She turned then and nodded to the maid, saying, 'It's all right, Effie,' and the maid went away.

Tipping his bowler hat to her, the caller told Grace that his name was Connors, that he was from the Apex Insurance Company, and that he was there to see Mr Spencer on the matter of a policy he was taking out. 'I could have written to him on the matter,' the man said, 'but I found myself in the area, so decided to call in person.' He was a tall man, with a thin face, and dressed against the cold day in a dark brown wool coat with an astrakhan collar. He carried a briefcase which he held up as he spoke, and tapped it, adding, 'It's a document I've brought that needs his attention. But if he's not here I'll make an appointment and come back another day. I'm sorry to have troubled you.'

'No, wait, please,' Grace said. 'If you tell me what it is you want, I might be able to save you another journey. You say it's about a particular policy.'

'Yes, a life insurance policy.'

'And what about it?'

The man hesitated as if uncertain whether to continue, to divulge information. Grace said, 'I'm Mrs Spencer; I'm sure I can help you.'

'Yes, perhaps you can, ma'am.' The man nodded, resigned. 'As I'm sure you're aware, Mr Spencer's very recently started to take out a life insurance policy on a member of his family. You do know about it, ma'am?' The latter was half-question, half-statement.

'Yes, of course,' Grace heard herself say, '– he's mentioned it,' and then, 'But please, come into the hall.'

The man entered, taking off his hat as he came.

'That's it,' Grace said as she closed the front door, 'come in out of that cold wind.' She turned and gestured to the sofa. 'Please, sit down.'

'Now,' Grace said, sitting beside the man, 'you said my husband has started to take out a life insurance policy. What do you mean, he's *started* to take it out?'

'Only that it can't go through just yet, ma'am, as there's a little information required about the insured.'

'Oh, I see, then tell me what you want to know and I'll be happy to help you, if I can.'

'I'm sure you can, ma'am. It's just the matter of the date of birth of the insured.'

'What date did he give you?'

'He gave the day and the month, but no year.'

Throughout the brief exchange Grace had felt her heartbeat increasing. Thoughts were flying through her brain with such swiftness that she could scarcely examine them. Edward had insured her life. But of course. Of course. It made sense. And he would have insured the first Mrs Spencer too.

'The year,' she heard herself saying, 'well, I was born in 1867.'

'No, ma'am, not you,' he said. 'It's Master William Barratt Harper.'

When the man had gone, back out into the chill November day, Grace had stayed trembling in the hall. She had not given him the information he required. On hearing that it was Billy who was the subject of the policy, she had said to the man, 'Oh, but you must come back and see my husband. He will deal with it himself.' And the man had looked at her bewildered, puzzled at her behaviour after her former cooperation. But still he had gone, putting his hat back on his head, giving it a pat and stepping out again into the wind. Very well, he had said, he would write and make an appointment with her husband.

With the door closed behind the man, Grace had stood there, unable to think of what to do. It was Billy's life that was at risk. As she raised her fingers to her cheek she saw that her hand was shaking.

Eventually she left the hall and moved back to the sewing room. She went there in the lack of having any other place she could think of going to. Just as she had before she began

485

slowly to pace, ending up at the window where she looked down on the stable yard. And there she saw Rhind moving about in the course of his business. Almost as if he could sense her eyes upon him, he suddenly raised his head. And for a brief moment their eyes met. Quickly she turned away and moved to her sewing table, where she sat down in her little chair, the Castle boy's shirt beside her next to her sewing basket.

She had to get away, she knew, and she had to take Billy with her. Without the shadow of a doubt she knew that as long as he stayed at Asterleigh his life would be in danger.

But what could she do? Her instinct was to run at once to Kester. He would know what to do. But she could not, must not do that. For one thing she must not involve him in the situation in a way that could put him or Sophie in any danger. The thought briefly flashed through her mind that she and Billy could go to Aunt Edie's but she knew that that would be no good. For one thing, Aunt Edie was too set in her ways to suddenly agree to share her home indefinitely with relatives, no matter how fond of them she might be. In addition to which she had not space to accommodate both herself and Billy. And besides, Edward would find her in no time, and he would not be content to allow her to remain away from him if he could prevent it.

The answer, the only answer, she thought, was for her and Billy to get right away, somewhere Edward could not find them, and ideally somewhere he wouldn't think of looking. They could go abroad perhaps, to America or Australia, or New Zealand. Many young people were emigrating to the colonies and building new and successful lives for themselves, so why not she? And in an English-speaking country her abilities as a teacher might be sought after; with good fortune there was no reason why she and Billy should not make good lives for themselves.

But travel cost money. And that was one thing she did

not have. With Edward always keeping the purse strings so tight, and letting her have just enough for her essentials, there had never been the opportunity to put anything by.

But that, she eventually decided, was where Kester could help. If he could lend her enough money to be able to get away and make a new start . . . It would be one act of assistance and then he would no longer be involved.

She remained sitting there for some time, and then, on a decision, got up and went into the library.

At the writing table she sat and took from a drawer an envelope and paper. Then, dipping her pen into the inkwell, she wrote:

Asterleigh

Dear Kester,

    Billy and I are in need of your help. I cannot go into the reasons now, but I beg you to believe me when I say that our situation is desperate, and that we must get away from here without delay.

    Will you meet Billy and me tomorrow at twelve o'clock by the church in Corster, in King's Square? I shall keep Billy home from school, and we shall be ready and waiting for you.

    Another thing. I have to ask you this now, so that you can be prepared, is it possible that you can lend me some money? It goes without saying that I shall pay you back. But I am desperately in need of financial help; indeed, without it I cannot see that we shall get anywhere.

    I am sending this with one of the maids. Please send back a brief word confirming that we can meet. I feel sure you will not let me down, and I shall wait to hear from you.

    Grace

On an envelope Grace wrote Kester's name and address, and then, having blotted the ink, sealed the letter inside.

And now what to do about it? Certainly she could not send Rhind; he was the last person she could ask. Nor could she go herself, for Rhind would almost certainly be watching her movements. After her observed visit to the doctor, Grace had no doubt that Edward was having her movements observed.

After a little further thought she went to Mrs Sandiston, to ask if she could spare one of the maids to go on an errand into Corster. The housekeeper replied that Effie, the maid who was due to leave for other employment, could go in for her. 'I'll tell her to put on her hat and coat and come to see you, ma'am,' she said.

'Thank you. Tell her I shall be in the sewing room.'

Twenty minutes later Effie came up to the sewing room where Grace was waiting for her. She was a tallish girl, dark and attractive, and wearing a mauve hat and grey cape.

Grace had made a list of three items she wanted the maid to get for her from the art supplies shop in Corster centre. She had listed two oil colours: viridian and cerulean blue, and a small bottle of linseed oil. It was such a small requisition, but there simply was not the money to spare for a lot more. She would like to have dispensed with the visit to the art shop altogether, but some purchases were necessary if there was to be a perceived genuine reason for the girl's going.

Grace handed the small list to the girl, along with sufficient money for the purchase, and her train fares. And as the girl looked at the list Grace was conscious of how trivial the errand's purpose sounded. Effie, however, accepted it without a flicker of a question in her expression.

The maid had put the list into her bag and was turning away, when Grace said, 'Oh, Effie – one other thing . . .' And when the girl turned back, Grace was holding the envelope addressed to Kester. 'Would you take this also?' Grace said.

'It's to go to Mr Fairman in Crescent Gardens. Do you know it? You're from Corster, aren't you?'

'Yes, ma'am.'

'And do you know Crescent Gardens? I believe it's on the south side of the town, near to the canal.'

'I know it, ma'am.'

'His house in Crescent Gardens is called the White House. It's all written on the envelope. Can you get there all right? Will you need to take a cab?'

'No, ma'am, I can walk.'

Grace put the envelope into the girl's hand. 'You won't lose it, will you?'

'No, ma'am.'

'And make sure you go to deliver the letter before you go to buy the oil paints. All right?'

'Yes, ma'am.'

'I mean the paints are not nearly so important. So if you don't have time to buy them it won't matter. We can get them another day.'

The girl nodded.

'Yes, and when you give the letter over to Mr Fairman, you wait for a reply, all right? He'll give you an answer.'

'Yes. But ma'am – what if the gentleman's not there?'

Grace put a hand to her head. This was a question she had not wished to deal with. 'Then you must wait for him.'

'Yes, ma'am.'

'Wait for him. If he's expected back, then wait for him. However long it takes.'

'Yes, ma'am.'

'And, Effie –'

'Ma'am?'

'Not a word to anyone else about it – do you understand? Don't mention it to anyone – Mrs Sandiston or anyone, all right?'

'Yes, ma'am.'

'Can I trust you? I can, can't I?' Grace's heart was thudding violently, while at the same time she was trying desperately to sound calm.

'Of course, ma'am.'

'You bring the answer back to me – but no one is to see you do it, all right?'

'Yes.'

'You'll remember that, won't you?'

'I will.'

'Right, then, thank you. If you leave now you'll be in time for the train at twenty past. Off you go, then.'

She stood watching as the girl moved to the door and let herself out onto the landing.

Later that afternoon, after Billy had got in from school and had had his tea, Grace went to his room. She knocked at the door, called out, 'It's me – Grace,' and he called out, 'Come in,' and she went inside and closed the door behind her.

'I was coming to see you in a few minutes,' he said. In the pale light of the lamp and the last of the daylight he was sitting on the floor making a kite. The diamond-shaped body of the kite had already been made and now he was attaching its tail, a long string with paper bows attached at intervals.

'You'll strain your eyes,' Grace said. 'This light isn't good enough for such close work.'

'I'm all right,' he said. He looked down at his handiwork for a moment, then turned to Grace. 'I want to get this done for Saturday. Roland and I are going onto the heath. I'd like to take it into school tomorrow and show him if it's ready.'

'I wanted to see you about school,' Grace said. 'You won't be going in tomorrow.'

He gave her all his attention now. 'What d'you mean, I won't be going into school?'

'You mustn't mention anything to anyone, but something's come up, and I want you to stay at home.'

'What for? What d'you mean? What's come up?'

'I can't tell you right now. But I'll tell you in due course. This is why I came to see you now – while there's no one else about. Please – trust me.'

'Of course.' He frowned. 'But I just don't know what's going on.'

'I told you – I'll let you know later on. I can't tell you yet.'

'All right.' He nodded. 'So what d'you want me to do? Just stay here in my room in the morning?'

'Yes. After breakfast just come back to your room and stay here. I'll come and get you.' She backed to the door. 'I shall be in the drawing room for a while now if you need me. But don't mention anything about what I said in front of anyone else.'

'Not even Mr Edward?'

'No, not even Mr Edward. No one at all.'

'All right. Is Mr Edward going to be there in the drawing room?'

'Well, not yet awhile. He's not due back from the mill yet.'

'He's back. He's been back ages.'

'Surely not. I haven't seen him.'

'I have. When I came in from school I saw him coming out of the stable and crossing the yard.'

On leaving Billy's room, Grace went to the drawing room, and forty minutes later Billy joined her there. He had washed his hands and combed his hair. 'Did you finish the kite?' she asked him, looking up from her book.

'Almost.' He took a seat near the fire and opened the book he had brought with him. He was reading *Gulliver's Travels*. Although he sat reading in the room, and Grace was reading also, it was sufficient comfort for each of

491

them to have the other's company, silent though it might be.

A sound came at the door, and then Edward came into the room. He looked at Grace and said, 'Why that sideways glance? Am I not allowed to take time off from my work now and again?' He crossed to the fire, picked up the tongs and adjusted one of the burning logs. 'Yes, I've been in the house some time.' He turned and looked at Billy. 'And how are you, young William? Are you well?' Their paths did not often cross during these winter evenings.

'Yes, thank you, sir.'

'And you're keeping out of mischief?'

'Yes, sir.'

Edward put back the tongs, stretched his hands out to the flames for a moment then straightened. 'I think I shall eat in my study tonight,' he said to Grace without turning. 'If you'd be so kind as to ask Mrs Sandiston to send up a tray.'

'Very well.'

He gave a little nod, then walked across the room and out of the door.

'Is there something wrong?' Billy asked, looking in the direction taken by his brother-in-law.

'Why do you say that?'

'I don't know; he looked – strange.'

'He's all right.' Grace could not pursue the subject. She was wondering now whether Effie was back from Corster, and if so, whether she had managed to see Kester and bring a message from him. Perhaps, the thought went through her mind, she had not seen him. Perhaps she was still waiting for him to return to his home. Perhaps he had gone away. In which case Effie would already have returned, empty-handed.

Grace rang for the maid and the young girl Annie answered. Grace instructed her to tell Mrs Sandiston that Mr Spencer would eat in his study, and she herself would eat from a tray in the drawing room. Then as the maid moved back to the door, Grace said, 'Tell me, Annie, is Effie back from Corster? She was going to get me some items from the art supply shop.'

'No, ma'am, she's not back so far. We expected her a while ago.'

Grace thanked her, and the girl left.

An hour later, Billy said he would leave and go to his bed. Grace, much preoccupied, did nothing to dissuade him.

She ate alone in the drawing room, and close on 9.30 went upstairs to her bed. She had given up hope of hearing from Effie tonight. She could not imagine what had happened to her. The girl would surely have been back by this time.

There had been no further word from Edward, or any sight of him, and, lying in the bed, she hoped that he would choose to sleep in the spare room and leave her in peace.

She lay awake for a long time, through her mind darting myriad thoughts, thoughts of Edward, her meeting with the insurance agent, and pondering on why the maid had not returned.

Without any word from Kester, what was she to do?

Hours passed before she slept.

She awoke to find herself alone in the bed. So, Edward had slept in the second bedroom.

In her peignoir she went to the breakfast room where breakfast had been set out. Edward was already there, eating eggs and kidneys. He looked up as she entered the room and gazed closely at her, eyes slightly narrowed, as if he was studying her expression.

He said, 'Good morning,' to her, still watching her as he ate, but she did not reply. She helped herself to some scrambled eggs and toast, and a cup of coffee, and sat at the table sipping from the cup.

'I said, "Good morning," to you,' he said after a few moments.

She inclined her head a little and murmured a good morning in return. Edward said, his face grave, 'Did you sleep all right?'

She gave a little shrug. 'I slept eventually.' The toast was like cardboard in her mouth. She ate because it gave her something to do, gave her some way of occupying her hands, and to a degree diminished the need for conversation.

'I slept eventually also,' he said, nodding, his mouth full. 'I had a lot of things on my mind. I still do have, for that matter.' He paused. 'Aren't you going to ask what it is that's on my mind? What are my preoccupations? A dutiful wife would surely do so.' He smiled with this last, and she looked up and caught the smile and saw that he was toying with her. She lowered her head again and concentrated on the food on her plate.

Taking up his coffee cup, Edward took a sip from it and shook his head in distaste. 'Coffee's cold,' he said. 'How's yours?' Without waiting for Grace to make any response – which she did not attempt to do – he rang the bell for the maid. Very soon Effie was there, slipping into the room and facing him as he turned towards her.

'You rang, sir.' She did not turn in Grace's direction, though Grace kept her eyes fixed upon her. Grace wondered when she had got back; it must have been late last night after she, Grace, had gone to bed, or this morning before she had risen. Obviously it had not been possible for Effie to get word to her. Had her message been delivered to Kester? If so, what message had he sent back? And where was it? But perhaps it was only a verbal message . . . The questions went through Grace's mind, and still she kept her eyes on the girl, willing her to turn to her and give some sign – a direct glance would suffice – but there was nothing;

494

Effie kept her gaze intent upon her master. For a few moments Grace hovered on the brink of asking the girl whether she had bought for her the oil paint and linseed oil – something was needed; anything to get an acknowledgement of the errand – but she held back, afraid. And then Edward was speaking. The coffee was cold, he said, could she bring some fresh? And the girl nodded yes and withdrew. When she had gone, Edward looked closely at Grace, and said with a lingering frown:

'Is anything wrong?'

She looked at him sharply. Why had he asked such a question? Had she given herself away in some manner?

'It's just that you looked a little – a little tense when Effie came in,' he said. 'I wondered why you should look at her like that.' He pushed his coffee cup away from him. 'I shan't want any more coffee, mind you,' he said. 'I haven't got time for it.'

'Then you needn't have bothered to get more on my account,' Grace said. 'I shan't want more either.'

'Oh, you can speak,' he said. 'I thought for a minute there you'd lost your tongue.' He studied her and she felt herself colouring under his gaze. 'Tell me,' he said after a moment, 'what will you be doing with yourself today?'

Her glance was cold as she lifted her face to him. 'Are you remotely interested, Edward, in what I do?'

'What? Of course I'm interested. You're my wife, aren't you?' He put down his knife and fork, took a last drink of his coffee and wiped his mouth with his napkin. As he tossed the napkin down, he added, 'I hope when this is all over we can get something – recapture something – of what we once had.'

Grace thought, of what we once had? What did we have? We never had anything.

Edward stood up. 'I must get going. A very important meeting in Redbury. I can't afford to be late. Rhind will

495

have got the carriage ready.' He stood in silence for a few moments then said with a faint smile, 'I won't give you a husbandly kiss, my dear. I somehow have the feeling it wouldn't be welcomed.' He put his head a little on one side. 'And to tell you the truth, I don't think I'm really so eager to start giving you demonstrations of a spouse's affection. If you see what I mean. I've no doubt that that'll change in time, but for the moment . . .'

He let the unfinished sentence hang in the air. Grace looked down at her plate. She just wanted him to leave. As soon as he had gone she would call Effie to her and hear what the girl had to say. Then, if Kester was able to meet her – and she had no doubt at all that he would – she would get dressed and pack a few things for Billy and herself, and then they would get away. She would never have to breakfast with Edward again. She would never sit at this table again. She would never again set foot in this house.

And now Grace could see on the rim of her peripheral vision that Edward had crossed to the door. She gritted her teeth, waiting. In just a few moments he would be gone.

But no, still he hovered there, and then the next moment he was coming to her side. His hand came out towards her, and she flinched.

'Don't,' he said. 'Don't do that. You moved as if I were about to strike you. Why should you do that? I merely wanted to give you this.'

And a movement in front of her face drew her gaze to the envelope that he laid down beside her breakfast plate. It was the envelope addressed to Kester, the one she had given to Effie.

She felt her heart lurch; it was as if her blood were stilled, cold, in her veins. She stared at the envelope with its gaping flap.

'Yes,' Edward said, 'it's come as a bit of a shock to you, I can see. I thought it might.' He put out his hand, took up the envelope and withdrew the letter. Grace heard the rustle of the paper as he opened it up. Then she heard him say, 'Quite touching, really, I suppose – for someone who is not me, of course.' He began to read the words that Grace had written: '"*Dear Kester, Billy and I are in need of your help. I cannot go into the reasons now, but I beg you to believe me when I say that our situation is desperate, and that we must get away from here without delay . . .*"' He paused, then said, 'This is quite dramatic, you know. Anybody must agree with that. And quite heart-wrenching too. Unfortunately, it's not going to happen. Your Mr Fairman isn't going to be there under the church tower, is he?' He paused. 'Is he? No, he's not. I can tell you that now. But there, now that you've seen this,' he dropped the letter, letting it fall beside her plate – 'you won't be expecting him to be there, will you?'

She could do nothing but sit there, listening, while her heart pounded in her breast and her pulse beat in her ears so loudly that she thought it must drown out all other sound. She could hear the faint smile in his voice as he continued:

'So there won't be any rush for you to go and get into your travelling clothes or start packing your bags. Do you understand that, Grace?' And now he leaned over her. 'You're not going anywhere. Unless you go with me, or you go with my permission. How do you think I got where I am today? I got here in the house because I set my mind on certain things. And as I told you, I usually get what I want, and what I get I keep.'

Her heart would not stop pounding in her breast. And through it all the questions poured through her brain. How? How had he got the letter?

And then the answer came, as if she had spoken her thoughts aloud.

'And don't be cross with young Effie,' he said. 'It wasn't

her fault. I saw her as she was leaving. I was just coming in as she came out of the drive, and I stopped the carriage and asked her where she was going with such purpose.' He paused. 'Aren't you curious to know what was said? Well, anyway, she said she was to go into Corster and buy you some oil paint. I couldn't believe it. I have to admit that it sounded very strange. I mean you haven't touched your painting in ages. So, I thought, how did it come about, this sudden desire to immerse yourself in your painting again? And when Effie told me of the few little items you wanted, I was even more puzzled. For so few things you were sending the girl all that way. Surprising? Yes, I found it somewhat surprising, I have to admit. But then, after more questioning of the girl it came out that there was more than one goal to her errand. And eventually I got hold of the letter. You mustn't blame her, you understand? Once I'd read the letter I told her she was to come back *late* last night, to get the last train back. I've no idea what she spent her time doing. She probably went to see her family; she said she comes from Corster.' He paused. 'I hope you're taking all this in, are you?'

Grace did not answer. She was looking down now at the open letter lying before her.

Edward said, 'I told her she was not to tell you that she'd given me the letter. I told her on pain of my taking away her reference. So you can't blame her. You don't, do you?'

Grace drew in her breath and tried to speak, but could not make a sound. Her lips moved, but no sound came.

'No,' Edward said. 'She's a poor simple girl who was only doing what her master instructed.' Now he turned and started away back towards the door. 'Oh, and by the way,' he came to a brief halt and turned back to her, ' – I saw Billy this morning coming from the kitchen after his breakfast. I spoke about your keeping him back from school. He seemed rather surprised that I should know about it, and was a little reluctant to speak of it. I soon persuaded him to, though.'

Now Grace found her voice: 'What have you done?' she burst out, raising her head to him.

'Now, now, there's no need for panic.' He smiled. 'He just realized that I knew more about it than he'd imagined. Anyway, I told him he should go to school after all. So he went off. We can't have his education suffer because of your foolishness.'

He opened the door, then turned back once more.

'By the way,' he said, 'I've had second thoughts, and I'm going to have Johnson drive me about today. I'll leave Rhind here – just to make sure you're well looked after.' Then he raised his hand in a sardonic farewell, turned away and was gone.

Chapter Twenty-Three

Grace remained sitting at the table long after the door had closed behind Edward, long after his footsteps had faded in the hall. Before her the coffee in her cup grew cold, congealing with a faint cloudy skin on its surface. Near it lay the letter and the envelope.

What could she do? she silently asked. She was lost. Her cause was lost. There was nothing she could think of that would help her situation.

But the fact remained that she had to get away, and she had to take Billy with her.

Somehow she would see Kester and get him to help them. For the time being Billy was safe in his classroom. Her first task was to see Kester.

She sat there for another minute and then purposefully stood up and pushed back her chair. In one movement her hand swept up the letter and the envelope and then she was turning, moving away and out of the room.

In her dressing room she changed into her outdoor clothes and boots and then took her purse and emptied it onto her dressing table. She had so little – just a few shillings and some coppers. It would suffice to take her into Corster. Scooping up the coins, she tipped them back into the purse.

She then set about packing up some of her things into a bag. She could not risk going to Billy's room and getting his belongings; they would have to wait. The next step would be to get Rhind out of the house, for she had no doubt that he had been instructed to keep a watchful eye on her.

She stood there in the middle of the room for some moments, then took off her blouse again and put it aside. That done she put on her bed jacket and got into bed. Heart thumping she reached out and rang the bell for the maid.

With the neck of the bed jacket pulled up high around her throat she lay waiting to hear the approaching footsteps. And then there they were, and moments later Effie was knocking at the door and entering the room.

'You rang, ma'am,' Effie said, looking with some surprise at Grace lying back with her head on the pillow, and quickly added, 'Oh, ma'am, are you ill?' Her voice and face were all concern.

'I'm afraid I am, Effie,' Grace said. 'Thank God you're here.' She clapped a hand to her mouth as if retching. 'I feel dreadful. My heart is pounding and I feel terribly sick. Bring me a bowl, will you?'

Effie stepped smartly into the dressing room and then emerged carrying a wide, shallow basin. As she put it into Grace's hands she said, 'What can I do for you, ma'am?'

'I need the doctor,' Grace said. 'Go and ask Mr Rhind to fetch Dr Ellish for me, will you? Be as quick as you can. And then come back and tell me if he's going.'

'Yes, ma'm.' At once Effie moved back to the door. As she reached it, she turned and said with consternation in her voice, 'Oh, ma'am, I'm so sorry about that letter. I didn't want to let –'

'It's all right.' Grace cut off the girl's words. 'Don't give it another thought. Just hurry and send off Rhind for the doctor for me.'

The door closed behind the maid and Grace lay with her hearing focused on the sound of the girl's footsteps fading away. Her heart was hammering. Would Rhind be taken in? The minutes seemed to be dragging by.

And then at last there were approaching footsteps again and a tap on the door and Effie was entering the room.

'How are you feeling, ma'am?' Effie said. 'Are you any better?'

'I'm afraid not, Effie. Did you tell Rhind?'

'Yes, ma'am, he's saddling up the mare right now.'

'Thank you. I can't imagine what it is that's come over me. It's all very strange.'

Effie hovered at the bedside for a moment, then moved to the window and looked down onto the carriage drive. Two or three minutes went by then she gave a little nod and said, 'There he goes now, ma'am. Mr Rhind, off down the drive.'

'Thank you.' Grace could hear, very faintly, the sound of the mare's hoofs on the gravel.

'I'll rest now, Effie,' Grace said. 'Please show the doctor up when he arrives. In the meantime I'll ring for you if I need anything.'

'Yes, ma'am.' With a nod, Effie left the room and Grace waited once again as the girl's footsteps retreated on the landing.

She moved then with great swiftness. In moments she had thrown off the bed jacket and pulled on her blouse, outdoor jacket and cloak. Then in seconds the cloak was fastened at her throat, her bags were in her hands, and she was at the door.

Carefully, silently, she opened it a crack and stood listening. There was no sound. Silently she crept from the room, along the landing and down the stairs. Praying that she would get out before one of the maids saw her, she at last reached the front door.

She found the wind surprisingly cold and strong as she let herself out into the air, and she tucked her chin more deeply down into the collar of her cape. Keeping as close as possible to the side of the house, she hurried to the left, ignoring the drive, and ran across the hard lawn towards the paddock. Without hesitation she pushed the bags under the fence and ducked through after them. Heedless of her boots and the hem of her dress on the rough turf, she hurried on. Keeping under the cover of a fringe of trees of ash and silver birch, she took a route that ran parallel with the road. And now as she paused and looked back, she found the house was almost hidden from her sight by the trees. She sighed with relief at this; there was little chance now that anyone from the house would see her.

She pressed on, and eventually came to a spot where the edge of the paddock diverged from its parallel route, the way ahead being lost in a thicket of small trees and shrubs. It was time to move out onto the road. She found a suitable spot in a gap in the hedge, and by crossing a narrow water-filled ditch, got through to the other side, with relief feeling her boots striking the firm soil of the road.

Eventually she reached the outskirts of the village, where she turned into the yard of Mr Renshaw, the fly proprietor. To her great relief she found that he was at home and available for hire, and in minutes she was in his carriage – 'You're in an 'urry, ma'am,' he said as she climbed aboard – and being driven off to Berron Wick station.

At the station she got the train for Corster, and in her seat sat watching the familiar scenery go by, mentally checking off the landmarks. She would never, she said to herself, come this way again. Liddiston . . . Upper Callow, and at last, Corster.

There was no free cab waiting when she got out of Corster station, and it was too far to walk with her bags. She must wait, then, for one to come along. But eventually a cab was there, and she was getting in and giving the driver Kester's address.

At her destination she paid off the driver and as the carriage drove off she stood on the pavement before the house, a Georgian building with tall, elegant windows and cream-painted facing. Pushing open the gate, she walked up the path to the front door and rang the bell.

It was answered by Kester's cook-general, Mrs Love-grove, who said at once: 'Why, Miss Har— Mrs Spencer – what a surprise to see you here.'

'Hello, Mrs Lovegrove,' Grace blurted out. 'I've come to see Mr Fairman. Is he at home?'

'I'm sorry, ma'am, but he's out.'

At these words Grace felt that she could weep. 'Do you know when he'll be back?' she asked.

'No, I don't – though I think it won't be for some little while yet.'

Grace gave a little groan. It was worse still. 'Can you tell me where he's gone?' she said.

'He mentioned something about going to Marshton, though exactly where, I couldn't say.'

'Oh, dear,' Grace said, 'it's imperative that I see him as soon as possible.'

'Well, ma'am, I don't know what to suggest. But you look very – well, rather distraught, if I might say so. Would you care to come in and wait for him, ma'am?'

With some relief Grace thanked her, followed her in and deposited the bag in the hall. Her reticule she kept with her as Mrs Lovegrove led the way into the sitting room. 'Perhaps you'd care to take off your cloak, ma'am,' she said. 'I'll get the girl to bank up the fire a bit and make you a cup of tea.'

Grace said she was most grateful, and moved to a chair near the fireplace where the fire was burning low in the grate. She would keep her cape on for a little while, she said.

As Mrs Lovegrove went away, Grace stretched out her hands to the embers.

A young maid came in after a minute and banked up the fire and stoked it, and then with a little bob went away again. Grace sat as if mesmerized, watching as the lengthening flames licked at the wood. Mrs Lovegrove came in with a tray set with teapot and china, and put it down on a small table at Grace's side. Was there anything else she could get for her? the woman asked, and Grace thanked her and said there was not. Mrs Lovegrove withdrew.

Grace took off her cape, laid it on the sofa nearby and then poured herself some tea. She sat sipping its welcome warmth, though barely aware of its taste. Where was Kester? He must come soon; she could not wait for ever. But the time went by and still he did not come.

An hour after the maid had taken away the tray, Mrs Lovegrove came into the room and asked if Grace would like some more tea, and perhaps also a sandwich. Surely, she ventured, Grace must be hungry. Grace assured her that she was fine, and needed nothing more. And she waited.

It was after two when at last Grace heard footsteps in the hall and then the door opened and Kester was coming into the room.

'Grace,' he said, stepping urgently towards her. 'I could scarcely believe it when Mrs Lovegrove told me you were here.'

'Oh, Kester –' Grace got up as he approached and stepped towards him.

He held her, his arms around her. 'What is it?' he said anxiously. 'What brings you here like this?'

Urging her to the sofa, he sat beside her and, as quickly as she could, she told him of what had taken place, seeing his eyes widen and his frown deepen as she revealed the scope of Edward's suspected treachery in his first wife's death, and of her fears for Billy.

'We must go to the police,' Kester said.

'There's no time for that,' Grace said. 'And in any case,

what could I prove? Nothing. I could prove nothing. They'd say it's all in my head.'

'Then what do you want me to do? I'll do whatever I can, you must know that.'

'I'd like you to lend me a little money, Kester. If you will – enough for Billy and me to get away somewhere – some place where Edward won't find us, won't think of looking for us. Will you do that?'

'Of course, yes, but I can do more. I can –'

'No, please, I don't want you to do any more than that. That's all I need. I don't want you to become involved in any way.'

'But, Grace –'

'No. You have a life here with Sophie and nothing must be allowed to jeopardize that. You don't know him as I do. He hates you already, suspecting how I felt for you, guessing what you are to me in my life.'

'I'll let you have some money, of course I will,' he said, 'but where will you go?'

'I don't know yet. I've packed a bag – it's out in the hall – and now I must get to Billy's school. He's safe there for the moment, but if I'm not there to meet him he'll head on back to Asterleigh. I must get there before school comes out, and then the two of us must get away. I don't know where yet; I haven't decided. But I can work that out on the way to Culvercombe.'

'I don't have that much money in the house. I would need to go to the bank. I can go there now and –'

'Kester, there isn't time. I must get to Culvercombe.'

'Well, then, I'll get funds for you first thing in the morning. Then I'll help you get away somewhere. And when this is all over we'll be together. You understand?'

'Yes. Yes.'

'But for the time being you and Billy can stay here overnight.'

'No, Kester, that won't do. This is the first place he'll come looking for me. We'll have to go somewhere else. A hotel or somewhere – but not one around here. Believe me, he won't be content simply for me to walk out of his life. He's made that very clear.'

'All right, then, I'll get together what money I have to hand – there's a reasonable sum – and then we'll go and get Billy.'

'It's not necessary for you to come with me. I told you: I don't want you to become any more involved than is absolutely necessary. With a little money I can find a hotel for us tonight. Then we can make final arrangements tomorrow.'

She clasped her hands together and got up. Glancing at the clock on the mantelpiece, she said, 'I can't stay any longer; I have to go. His school comes out at four. I have to get there before then. I can't take the chance of him going back to Asterleigh.'

'Right, I'll get my coat and then we'll go. We'll leave your bag here for the time being and pick it up later, when we get back.'

She opened her mouth to protest, but he held up a hand, palm out. 'It's no good your protesting, Grace, I'm coming with you and that's that.'

He went out of the room and returned a minute later wearing his coat, his grey ulster, and even through her fears one part of her mind recognized it, the coat they had lain on together when they had made love . . .

'Come,' he said, 'we're ready.'

Together they left the house.

They must get a cab for the station, Kester said as they started off, and they looked anxiously up and down the street as they walked. There was none immediately available, however, and they had to walk half a mile before one pulled up at Kester's signal.

Grace sat back sighing with relief as the cab set off for the station. At last they were really on the move.

They had to wait over half an hour for the train, but eventually it drew in and they climbed aboard. In the carriage they entered sat a woman whom Grace knew vaguely by sight, and for a moment she felt a stab of self-consciousness at being seen with Kester. But she thrust the feeling aside; what did it matter what anyone thought? Let them think what they wanted; it was only important that she did what she had to do.

Culvercombe had no railway station, so it would be necessary to travel on to the one beyond: Coller Down, from where they could travel back to Culvercombe by cab. At last, after what seemed an eternity, the train pulled in to Coller Down and they got out.

Fate seemed to be against them here again, for there was no fly available immediately, and they had to wait ten minutes or so before one came into the station yard. As Grace climbed aboard, Kester gave the driver their destination. Moments later they were setting off.

Culvercombe was a picturesque but simple place with the school situated in a turning off the high street. It was ten minutes to four when the cab pulled up outside the school gate and Kester asked the driver if he would wait; they would be wanting, he said, to go on back to the station.

Grace felt a great sense of relief that they had got there in time. Had they arrived after school had come out, she thought, she could see them walking in Billy's footsteps, hurrying to catch him up before he arrived at Asterleigh. But they were in good time, and just for a few moments she could afford to relax.

Not long afterwards, a minute after four o'clock, the main door of the school opened and the children began to

508

come out. At once Grace leaned forward, her gaze skimming the heads of the children. The boys and girls straggled out into the winter afternoon, wrapped against the cold, some singly, others in pairs, and Grace watched, waiting for Billy to appear among them.

Within five minutes most of the children had gone by, chattering among themselves, happy to be out of school again for the day. But Billy's face had not been among them. Grace waited. And now the surge of children had diminished and only two single children emerged, a boy and a girl, both hurrying away to join their friends.

'Where's Billy?' Grace murmured.

'Is there another door?' said Kester.

'No,' she said, 'they all have to come out by the main gate. I'll go in and see where he is. He's probably stayed behind to help his teacher.'

With her words she drew her cape about her, opened the door of the cab and stepped down.

Entering the school gate, she crossed the yard and went into the building, finding herself in the hall that she had first seen when accompanying Billy on his first day at the school. There was a cloakroom on the left and a classroom opening off to the right. The door to the classroom was open, and she could see the rows of desks and benches. As she looked in, a woman appeared in the doorway on her left. Well over thirty years old, she had a plain face with her hair pulled back in a bun. Grace recognized her at once as Billy's teacher, Miss Merlin. Dressed now in her coat and hat, the teacher carried a bunch of keys in her hand. As she locked the door she turned and smiled at Grace: 'Good afternoon, can I help you?'

'I'm sorry to trouble you,' Grace said, moving to her. 'I'm Mrs Spencer, and I'm looking for my young brother, Billy Harper.'

'Billy?' The woman looked Grace up and down. 'Oh, he's

gone. He left about two hours ago.' She frowned slightly, obviously somewhat puzzled.

'Gone?' Grace said. 'Gone where?'

Miss Merlin's frown deepened. 'Well, I was told he went to you.'

'By whom? I don't understand. What's happened?'

'Just about two o'clock,' the teacher said, 'Billy was in class when a man came for him. He said he came with a message from you, that Billy was wanted at home, urgently.'

Grace felt a chill run through her, and the raising again of the beating of her heart. 'I sent no message,' she said. 'Who was it came for him?'

'He didn't give a name, I'm afraid. The man who came for him was short, dark-haired, rather wiry in build. About forty-five or fifty. They drove off together.'

'Thank you.' Grace knew all she needed to know.

Grace thanked her again, and leaving the older woman standing there, a frown of perplexity on her brow, went back out to where the cab was waiting.

The driver, seeing her approach, got down and helped her up into the carriage, and closed the door behind her. Kester looked at her anxiously as she sat down beside him.

'Well?' he said.

Grace found that she was trembling. 'Rhind,' she said. 'Edward's man, Rhind. He's been to the school and taken Billy away. It happened about two o'clock this afternoon. Billy's teacher just told me. Apparently Rhind told her that he was wanted at home by me.'

'And he's taken him away.'

'Yes, they went off in the carriage. To Asterleigh, without doubt.' She pressed a hand to her breast. 'Edward must have come back home sooner than he anticipated.' She gave a little nod. 'I must go to Asterleigh. Now. I must go now.'

'Of course.'

As he moved to speak to the driver, Grace put a hand on his arm. 'Kester, you can get the train back to Corster. I told you, I don't want you to be involved in this. Please.'

'It's no good your protesting,' he said. 'You can't go there alone. I wouldn't consider it.' Turning from her, he spoke up to the driver. 'Take us to Asterleigh House, on the Berron road, if you will.'

'Very good, sir.' The driver touched his hat, flicked at the reins, and they were starting off again.

Dr Ellish had come to the house only to find that his supposed patient was not in residence, and had departed in high dudgeon. Edward, on his return not too long afterwards, had found that Grace was missing and had flown into a rage. How, he asked Rhind, could he have been so idiotic as to go rushing off for a doctor when that had been such an obvious ploy to get him out of the house. And now his wife had gone away, and there was no telling how he was to get her back. Rhind had seen his master angry before, but it had been nothing to the fury that he now found turned upon him. It had occurred then to Edward that perhaps there was a way. Perhaps, he thought, the boy was still in school.

'Do you know which direction Mrs Spencer took when she left the house?' he had asked.

'The maid said she saw her going east, towards Corster.'

'Then perhaps she didn't go to the boy's school first.'

Rhind then had been ordered to get the carriage and drive to Culvercombe and see if Billy was still there. As it turned out he had been, and it was no difficult business to get him out of his class and into the carriage. Now the boy was safely in the house, shut in his room.

Getting hold of Billy and bringing him back had done nothing, however, to diminish Spencer's anger towards Rhind. Leaning across the desk, he had said to him, 'Now get out, but stay handy in case I need you. And let me tell you one thing: if ever you let me down again like this you'll be out of my employ.'

Rhind could scarcely believe that he was hearing such words, and had left the study with his humiliation burning and his resentment building. His own anger was not directed at Mr Spencer, however, but at his master's wife – who had spelt trouble from the very first day.

As he walked along the passage he glanced to his left where a maid had left the door open and he found himself looking in at the first Mrs Spencer's studio. He pushed the door wider and stood for some moments in the open doorway, gazing in. Then, after glancing swiftly around him to see that he was not observed, he went inside.

The portrait was the thing that had attracted him. The first Mrs Spencer's portrait, unfinished, of the companion.

He stood before it for some minutes and then stepped closer. Nearby, on the painting table was a candlestick and a box of Lucifers. He took up the small box, opened it and took out a match. He held the match in his fingers for several seconds and then struck it.

He put the match's flame to an old rag that had been left near Mrs Spencer's palette. The rag flared and, using a paintbrush, he pushed the burning rag acrosss the table so that its burgeoning flames licked at the corner of the painted canvas.

The journey, just over three miles, seemed to Grace so very long. She reminded herself that Billy walked it both ways on every one of his school days, but on the other hand his route would not have been the same. He would not have kept to the roads but would have taken shortcuts on footpaths across the fields. Further to Grace's increasing desperation, the pair of cobs that drew the cab were old and made their way slowly, one of them occasionally wheezing in a disturbing way. Just after the crossroads near Coleshill they came to a long, very steep hill, and looking at the climb before them the driver pulled the cab to a halt, then turned and apologetically asked Grace and Kester if they would mind getting out and walking. Otherwise it would be too much of a strain on his animals, he added. At once the pair agreed to his request, and Kester helped Grace down and began to walk up the hill beside the horse-drawn cab. Walking behind Kester, up the long, steep incline, Grace sometimes felt that the journey seemed unending. But then at last they reached the top and the carriage came to a halt and Grace and Kester got back into their seats. Moments later they were off again.

In the studio Rhind watched rapt as the portrait was consumed. But the flames did not stop with the picture. In a very short time they had spread, first igniting the easel on which the canvas had rested, and then taking in the table on which was held the array of painting materials. So quickly the fire was getting out of hand, and all at once Rhind's gleeful fascination was gone and he was trying to put it out. He took cushions from chairs and tried to beat out the flames, but it was not now possible, the flames had taken hold and would not readily relinquish their grip. And already now the flames had spread and were rushing up the curtains at the nearby window.

And now Rhind could see the futility of his efforts and, after turning helplessly on the spot for a moment, he dashed from the room, terrified of being observed near the scene of the growing disaster.

It was several minutes before one of the maids ran to find Edward and told him that there was a fire.

The light was beginning to fail as they neared their destination, and then, turning a bend in the road, Grace saw the dark shape of Asterleigh on the side of the hill. At the sight she gave a little cry, her hand flying to her mouth, while Kester gasped. 'Dear God!' Grace cried, 'the house – it's on fire!'

The servants were out on the forecourt as the cab stopped and Grace and Kester scrambled out. The smell of burning was almost overpowering, and the roar of the flames was a constant terrifying sound. Grace looked quickly around her, and then dashed over to Mrs Sandiston's side. 'Where's Billy?' she asked her, raising her voice to be heard above the noise of the flames. 'Have you seen Billy?'

'No, I haven't, ma'am. Not lately, anyway.' Mrs Sandiston, usually so in control, wrung her hands, while tears streamed down her cheeks. 'I saw him come in earlier and go upstairs with Mr Rhind.'

Grace looked around for Rhind, but he was not to be seen. 'What about Mr Spencer?' she asked. 'Have you seen him anywhere?'

'I think he must be still in the house, ma'am. Mr Rhind too. I think they're trying to save whatever they can.'

Kester said, 'Has anyone gone for the fire brigade?'

'Mr Johnson rode off,' Mrs Sandiston said. 'But it'll take ages for them to get here.' She waved a hand at the burning building. 'And then what will they be able to do? It's spreading so fast.'

As Mrs Sandiston spoke the last words Grace turned and ran towards the house. She was joined immediately by Kester.

It was the left, western part of the house that was burning, great flames belching out of the broken windows all along its lower face, the smoke, dark and thick, coming out in great clouds. The front door had been left open by the servants, and Grace and Kester ran up to it, quickly looked inside and then dashed into the hall. On entering they saw at once that the fire had spread along the ground floor passage and was licking at the left flank of the stairs, threatening to spread up to the first floor.

The air was full of smoke, and it burned the backs of their throats and stung their eyes. Kester, followed by Grace, ran towards the right flanking stairs and bounded up, a hand covering his mouth. Reaching the first-floor landing, he turned and said to Grace who came hurrying after, snatching for breath after the dash up the stairs, 'You look in the rooms here, and I'll go on up to the floor above.'

She nodded at him, her eyes smarting, and turned and dashed away. In the same moment Kester swung about and continued on up the stairs.

Grace's first destination must be Billy's room, and she hurried towards it. The fire had not reached this part of the building yet and she was able to make good progress. She had to be quick, however, for she feared that the fire would catch up at any time.

Reaching Billy's room, she flung open the door. It was empty. His unfinished kite lay on his dresser as he had left it. There was nowhere he could be hiding. She turned and ran on to the next one. She flung this door open too, and found it empty also. On the landing she turned in a circle, for a moment at a loss as to which way to turn. Then, with direction once more, she set out to look in every room in the eastern wing.

Kester, reaching the floor above, had immediately run around the gallery, dashing past the two figures in their niches. They, fixed, unmoved by the scene of the disaster, stood looking out over the hall, their gazes focused on infinity, untouched, unaffected by the smoke that drifted over them. In between them the empty niche stood thrown in deeper shadow.

Kester finished his dash around the gallery and ran on towards the western wing. He was growing more desperate now, as the flames here were terrifyingly threatening, and he knew there must be so little time. With the crackle and roar of the flames and smoke coming up through the well of the wide hall, he turned from the gallery and dashed along the landing, calling out as he went: 'Billy! Billy!'

One who heard the call of Kester crying out was Rhind, who arrived at the other end of the gallery just as Kester ran from it onto the landing of the west wing.

So, Rhind thought, the man Fairman had come into the house looking for the boy . . .

Kester called again, and had got almost to the end of the landing when he heard a voice cry out from behind a door, 'I'm here!' and he turned at the sound and found the door with a key turned in the lock. In seconds the door was open and he was going in. Billy came towards him with eyes wide with fear.

'It's all right,' Kester said as the boy wrapped arms around him. 'It's all right.' He held him tightly, reassuringly, just for the briefest moment, then said, 'We'll get out of here now. Come on.'

Holding Billy by the hand, he hurried to the open door and looked out along the landing. He could see that smoke was now pouring onto the landing, while he could feel the heat growing by the second.

Opposite the room in which they stood was another room, with its door open. Kester could see that it was a bathroom. At once he took off his coat and, snatching at Billy again, ran across the landing. Inside the bathroom he wasted no time but at once bent over the tub and turned the taps on, so that the water came gushing and splashing into the tub. Without hesitating, Kester threw in his overcoat, saturating it in seconds. Then, lifting the heavy coat out, he called to Billy, 'Come here. We must keep you safe from the heat and the flames . . .'

Billy immediately stepped to Kester's side and Kester knelt down and lifted the wet, heavy coat to wrap it around the boy's body.

And then suddenly the room was filled with a greater movement, and Kester and the boy turned and saw that Mr Spencer was there, terrifyingly close, his eyes the eyes of madness, rushing in with hands outstretched and screaming Kester's name in fury. Kester had no chance at all. Before he had time to react, Mr Spencer was upon him, all his weight behind the attack and, seizing Kester by the shoulders, was slamming him back against the bathtub. With a crack that rang in the room, Kester's head struck the tub and he fell, toppling sideways onto the floor.

Mr Spencer, barely spending the time to observe the result of his attack, looked back over his shoulder onto the landing and saw the smoke hanging in the air, felt the great heat from the nearing flames. Then, looking back from Kester to the boy, he snatched up the wet coat and wrapped himself in it, the cloak section up over his head like a hood.

Grace, having looked in every room in the eastern wing of the house, came running from the landing back towards the stairs. Her heart was thumping in her breast, and her breath came in gasps. As she reached the stairs she looked out into the well of the hall and saw that the fire was consuming the tapestries and the curtains. The flames seemed to be strengthening by the second and were now right up the western staircase, past the first-floor landing, and halfway up the next flight.

Where was Billy? And where was Kester?

High above in the cupola the brilliant windows cracked

517

and shattered in the heat and now came crashing down onto the marble tiles below. Grace turned; she must go up to the third floor. As she put her foot on the first step to start up, she glanced upwards at the gallery on the floor above, high above which the cupola filled with the billowing smoke. And in spite of her panic and terror a part of her mind registered that the dark figure was back in his niche: Rigoletto, crouching there, partly hidden behind the shifting veil of smoke that passed before it. But for some reason, perhaps due to the smoke, or the heat haze, it looked somehow unfamiliar. It was larger now, and its stance was slightly different.

And then a movement beyond the figure caught her attention and she saw the figure in the familiar grey ulster come out of the landing entrance onto the gallery, and she called out, 'Kester! Kester!'

The man turned at the sound of her voice and looked towards her and at the same time the statue in the niche moved.

It moved. She could see it move. And seeing it her heart lurched and she screamed out. Before her eyes it seemed to straighten a little, and as she watched it balanced itself and then leapt.

'Kester!' she shrieked again. 'Look out! Look out!'

But as the figure in the coat took the warning and spun, Rhind was already upon him, leaping across the small width of the gallery and catching him even as he himself was seen.

And in that same moment Rhind saw his mistake. But it was too late, and as he clasped his master's body to his own they fell against the rim of the railing. Grace heard Edward cry out, 'Christ! Oh, Christ!' and watched as for a moment they hovered there like dancers executing a delicate manoeuvre. For a moment it appeared that they might yet gain safety, but it was not to be, their imbalance had gone beyond saving. Another second, and with their actions appearing almost in a motion that was slower than in reality, they teetered against the rail and then toppled over.

Grace, her hands to her mouth, saw them fall with a thud onto the marble floor below.

She heard then a cry that brought her gaze upwards again, and now she saw Kester coming staggering through the smoke, pulling Billy by the hand. She could hardly believe what she was seeing. But the next moment they were through, and dashing round the gallery to Grace's side. She saw at once that Kester was bleeding from his head, but she made no mention of it; there would be time later.

'Quick,' she sobbed as they reached her, gasping from the smoke and the heat, 'we can get out the back way.'

And the three turned from the burning hall and gallery and dashed back along the landing. Here the air was relatively clear, and was so much easier to breathe. Moments later they had reached the top of the servants' stairway, and with Grace ensuring that Billy was all right, they hurried down.

Reaching the ground floor, they dashed through the passage near the kitchen and out into the air.

There, outside, moving away from the house, well away from any perceived danger, they came to a stop and huddled together, their arms around each other.

Now, now at last, they were safe.

Epilogue

A gypsy has called at Birchwood House, selling paper flowers, clothes pegs and little sprays of heather for good luck. She has come to the rear door, and by chance has caught the master of the house as he goes towards the garden, a tray in his hands. He looks at the basket holding the caller's goods and shakes his head. 'I'm afraid I can't be any help to you at all,' he says. 'You'll need to speak to my wife.' And Grace comes immediately behind him, and he says, 'Please, ma'am, talk to my wife,' and, freed of responsibility, murmurs a 'Good day,' and moves on towards the garden.

On the grass of the green lawn Billy and Sophie are lounging on rugs, taking in the sun of a glorious September. They are dressed in their oldest clothes, clothes suitable for lounging in the garden without having to heed the risk of grass stains. There is a tray nearby, bearing glasses and a pitcher that has recently held lemonade. And there are tea plates too, now holding only crumbs. In a few days the two children will be starting back to school.

Kester appears, sets down the tray of tea things and takes his seat in a garden chair.

'Where's Mama?' Sophie says.

Kester replies: 'She's talking to a visitor, a caller.'

'Who?' asks Billy.

Kester lowers his voice to answer, 'A gypsy lady – selling things.'

'What is she selling?'

'Oh, all kinds of things. She has a basket full. Clothes pegs and paper flowers and things. I'm a coward, so I left your sister to deal with her.'

After a couple of minutes Grace comes from the house and takes the vacant chair facing Kester's.

'Did you buy anything, Mama?' Sophie asks.

Grace nods. 'A few pegs, that's all. Mrs Lovegrove said we could do with them.' She looks at Kester and says, lowering her voice, 'She said we're going to have a boy.' As she speaks she lays her right hand on the swell of her belly. 'She said she can tell.'

Kester chuckles. 'And did that bit of information cost you?'

'No, no.'

'Was she talking about the baby, Grace?' Billy says.

'Of course. What else.'

'I hope it *is* a boy,' he says.

'Yes,' says Sophie, 'so do I.'

As Grace pours tea for herself and Kester, Sophie says, 'Was it the same gypsy woman who had the birds?'

'No, I don't think so,' Grace says.

'What birds?' asks Billy.

With contributions from Sophie, Grace tells of buying the birds, the golden oriole, the thrush and the skylark, and letting them go. 'You remember,' Grace says. 'I told you about it.'

'Yes,' Billy says. 'I wish I'd been there.'

A minute passes, and Sophie says, 'I can't wait for the baby. Oh, it'll be so exciting.' She looks over at her father. 'Won't that be exciting, Papa?'

'It will indeed,' he says.

'What will he be when he grows up?' Sophie asks. 'Will he be an architect like you, Papa?'

Kester laughs. 'Oh, not necessarily. He can be anything he wants to be.'

'Anything?' says Billy.

'Anything,' says Kester. He pauses, then adds, 'As with you two. If I had my way you would be whatever you want to be in life.'

'I could be a nurse like Miss Nightingale,' Sophie says.

And from Billy: 'Could I be a painter?'

'If you want to be,' Kester says. He leans across and takes Grace's free hand in his. 'You're free in this world. Like the skylark, the oriole and the thrush, you're absolutely free.'